Doctor Watson's Trunk

The
Continuing Adventures
of Sherlock Holmes

ROBERT DOUGLASS ARMISTEAD III

outskirts
press

Doctor Watson's Trunk
The Continuing Adventures of Sherlock Holmes
All Rights Reserved.
Copyright © 2017 Robert Douglass Armistead III
v3.0

Outskirts Press, Inc.
http://www.outskirtspress.com

ISBN: 978-1-4787-7934-6

Outskirts Press and the "OP" logo are trademarks belonging to Outskirts Press, Inc.

PRINTED IN THE UNITED STATES OF AMERICA

ACKNOWLEDGEMENTS

For being supportive in this effort, I thank my brother, the criminologist and private investigator, Dr. Timothy Armistead, without whose help this book would never have come to fruition and my friend Col. Bob Cleaves (ret.). My rescue cats, ever patient, watched over my primitive typing and didn't chide me when I made the many mistakes I had to delete and re-type. Sitting on my printer, CPU, desk and table, they kept their real thoughts to themselves.

Contents

INTRODUCTION

After Sherlock Holmes retired to the South Downs to raise bees - and of course, study and document their habits with his usual care and precision - Dr. John Hamish Watson reopened a medical practice and continued to live at 221B Baker Street for several years. Finally however, the absence of the excitement of sharing adventures with the great detective and acting as his biographer wore down the good Doctor's *joie de vivre*, and he decided to close his medical practice and retire as Holmes had done. He wrote his intentions to his cousin in Scotland, Ainsley Douglass, and received an enthusiastic response with an invitation to come and live with Ainsley and his wife Bonnie. "Our children have families of their own now, and as Bonnie and I are getting on, we find that rattling around in our big house just increases our feeling of loneliness. We would love to have you here, both for your company and, of course, your fascinating recollections of your adventures with Mr. Holmes. We still regale our friends with our own story of how Holmes brought justice to our little village. Please consider retiring with us."

Watson was so taken with the offer that he immediately sold his practice, packed up his belongings, said a tearful farewell to Mrs. Hudson and her son Billy (now a family man himself), and moved in with Ainsley and Bonnie, enjoying their company and completing a task he had put off - writing the true story of the struggle between Holmes and the criminal mastermind, Professor James Moriarty. Possibly he never considered the time to be right for publication, because he never submitted his manuscripts to the Strand, the magazine which had printed most of Watson's accounts of Sherlock Holmes's exploits, but filed them away in an old leather portmanteau he stored in a trunk in the attic.

Years later, when Ainsley, Bonnie and Watson passed on, the property was left to the Douglass brothers, Ian and Conan, who moved to the large house with their families and proceeded to upgrade the old place with extensive modifications. Later, Conan was offered an excellent job in Edinburgh and moved his family there. When Ian and his wife, Ellen died, the house was left to Ian's son, Aiden, who renovated the house, and in so doing, found the old trunk while cleaning out the attic. He discovered Watson's Indian Army uniform and many other keepsakes, among them the portmanteau with several handwritten manuscripts. Not being very familiar with the history of Doctor Watson and his association with Holmes, nor with document restoration, he wrote to the Baker Street Irregulars, a group keeping the Holmes story alive, about his find, asking what his course should be. A member of the Irregulars and I had previously been in contact about some discrepancies in the Canon and he suggested to Aiden that he send the manuscripts to me, a rather distant relative of the Douglass clan, but very conversant with Holmesiana and document restoration.

Thus, after struggling with the good Doctor's handwriting for some time, seven of the previously unknown adventures are before you in this book. The main interest, I think, is the true recounting of the Holmes/Moran/Moriarty quiet but deadly battle of wits, and the real reason Watson wrote the "Final Problem", a narrative long considered to be somewhat out of character for the confident, skilled, Sherlock Holmes. We now know the real story - along with other hitherto unpublished entries in the remarkable history of two old friends and compatriots.

I hope you enjoy these, the further exploits of Sherlock Holmes and Dr. Watson.

Robert Douglass Armistead III

THE SHAKESPEARE AFFAIR

IT WAS CLOSE to midnight; the dimly lit hallway illuminated only the one a man walking quietly to the door of a suite in the elegant hotel. He knelt on the thick carpet, pulled two slim metal rods out of a leather pouch, and with a small scratching sound, inserted them into the lock. Only a tiny metallic clicking sound broke the silence and a moment later the man slowly opened the door just enough so the hall light could allow him to inspect the parlor of the suite. No lights were on and the suite was silent as he opened the door wider, slipped into the room, crossed to the door to the bedroom and put an ear on the door panel. No light could be seen from under the bottom of the door and no sounds could be heard. Using the feeble light from the hall, the man went quickly to the small writing desk provided for the guests and turned on a small reading lamp. The light shown on a man of average build wearing a cap with gold thread stitching proclaiming "The Windsor Hotel". He began to gently pull out the drawers of the desk. The first two were empty so he pushed them back carefully. In the third and last drawer was an old and very ornate box measuring about ten by twelve inches. He lifted it out, opened the box and yes!; it was there. In his haste to leave with it, he reached out to extinguish the lamp but bumped it – over it went with a crash. He glanced at the door to the bedroom, heard a noise, and ran out, closing the door behind him. Maybe the two Italian men wouldn't come out – but he was ready if they did. Valentine sat up straight in bed; "Proteus, Hai sente un rumore."

---— 1 —---

His brother woke up, startled by Valentine's urgent tone. They threw off their bedcovers and rushed into the parlor. Valentine turned on the main light and they could see the broken lamp on the desk. "Il quarto!" Proteus shouted and ran to the desk, pulled out the third drawer and screamed, "Il quarto e andato!" They ran out of the room looking both ways frantically. And there at the far end they saw the thief. He turned toward them for a moment, tucked the box into his shirt and sprinted around the corner. They ran after him shouting "Fermate il ladro!, Polizia di chiamata!" but when they reached the far end of the hall and turned the corner where the thief disappeared, he was nowhere in sight. The only thing they found was a cap with "The Windsor Hotel" in gold stitching in the entrance to a hallway that led off in both directions. They quickly got their robes and hurried down to the night manager's office to report the theft. Soon, several police constables arrived and began to search the hotel. A worker was stopped on his way out of the hotel and the two Italians identified him as the thief. No quarto was found and the worker was arrested and taken to Scotland yard.

It had been an unusually warm summer in England and I remember it was the twelfth night in August of that year that I needed only a sheet on my bed to sleep comfortably. I was so comfortable in fact, that I overslept; at least until I heard a sharp rapping at my door.

"Watson, you layabed," the amused voice of Sherlock Holmes came through loud and clear, "come to breakfast before it gets cold."

Wiping the sleep out of my eyes, I called out, "I'll be right there; you can eat my porridge but don't touch the ham!"

I heard a chuckle from the other side of the door as I got up and threw on my robe. Entering our sitting room, I saw Mrs. Hudson, our estimable landlady, finish emptying the serving tray and place a shiny coffeepot in the center of our worn but serviceable dining table. She turned to us and in her slightly countrified accent said, "There you are gentlemen, porridge, shirred eggs, biscuits and gravy and a nice cut of ham, just as you like it."

We thanked her, poured our coffee and dug in to our breakfast with enthusiasm. "You know, Holmes, when you woke me I was dreaming I was in a lovely forest glade with odd looking people and white-clad fairies dancing all around." Holmes looked up from his coffee; "Must be the warm weather affecting your romantic faculties Watson. This winter you'll probably dream of exploring the arctic with an Eskimo maiden!"

As we were idly chatting while finishing our meal, Holmes cocked an ear towards our door. "I think I heard the outer door, and now I believe that's someone on our stairs."

"Holmes, who could that be at this hour?" But at that moment came a knock at our door and a voice announced, "Message for Mr. Sherlock Holmes."

Holmes got up, took a coin out of our 'change mug' on a small table by the door and opened it up to a smartly clad young lad holding out a half-sheet of message paper. Handing the coin to the messenger, Holmes asked him to wait in case there would be a response. After glancing at the note, Holmes said, "It's from Inspector Lestrade." and taking the message to our shared desk, he quickly scribbled an answer on the back, handed it back to the messenger and gave him another coin.

"Please deliver this to Inspector Lestrade at Scotland Yard." Our messenger smiled, tucked away the coin, saluted, and hurried down the stairs.

Holmes sat down and poured another cup of coffee. He had a slightly puzzled look on his face. "Watson, he wants me to listen to a man who has been arrested for the theft of a particularly valuable item. He wants me to hear this man, Winters, out. Strange. I haven't read the early paper yet, perhaps there's a clue to this."

Holmes picked up the morning edition of our paper, took his coffee cup and settled down in his armchair. After opening it up to the front page, he let out a loud "Ah ha! Indeed; here it is Doctor, 'Robbery at Windsor Hotel. Valuable Shakespeare Item Stolen. Suspect in custody.'

According to this, two Italian gentlemen from Verona, came here for an annual charity auction at the Windsor and had a quarto of Taming of the Shrew stolen from their room last night. They intended to offer it at the auction. Well then, we must get dressed and go and hear what this Winters has to say. It's been a bit dull around here lately and I'd welcome a new case - if that's what develops anyway!"

We dressed quickly and soon went downstairs where Billy, Mrs. Hudson's boy, had summoned a Hansom. Holmes tossed a coin to the driver and called out "To Scotland Yard please." Our driver snapped his whip in the air and we clattered off. I sat back to

enjoy the fine morning but I noticed Holmes had a look of concentration so I didn't say anything that might disturb his thoughts. After a few minutes, he smiled and said, "It's bad to read too much from insufficient data. We must wait for more clay before we can make any logic bricks." With that, he relaxed and we rode in silence the rest of the way to Scotland Yard and whatever it was that made Lestrade call for Sherlock Holmes.

When we pulled up at Scotland Yard and went inside, Lestrade was waiting for us. The small but energetic inspector greeted us and said. "Thanks for coming Holmes. There may be nothing in this, but Mr. Winters is so insistent on his innocence and pleads his case so vigorously, I thought you might like to listen to him." Lestrade escorted us through the lobby and down a corridor, unlocking two doors as we went, to a holding cell. "Winters is an attendant at the Windsor Hotel."

When Lestrade unlocked the door and we went in, I saw a man probably in his mid-forties sitting dejectedly on a bench. He still had on his Windsor uniform and a cap with "Windsor Hotel" in gold embroidery lay on the bench beside him. He was clean shaven except for a bit of stubble. He had blue eyes and short trimmed, pale tan hair. When he saw us he jumped up, stretched out his arms and in a most pitiful voice, exclaimed. "I did not steal anything, I swear I would never do such a thing. Please help me!"

Holmes put his hands on the pleading man's shoulders and gently sat him back down on the bench. Winters was of average height and physique. "Now Mr. Winters, relax and tell me your side of the story. Remember, I know only what I read in this morning's paper."

"I'm sorry sir, this affair has shattered my nerves. I can hardly think straight but I'll do my best." Winters put his hands on his knees and looked up at Holmes. "I work for the concierge at the hotel. I run errands, deliver notes to and from guests, arrange cab service, and even help out by serving drinks at the annual ball and charity auction put on by the Merry Wives group. They raise money for a widows and orphans fund. This event is very important to them. I was in the hotel late last night taking inventory and locating things that will be needed. I was just finishing when two constables stopped me and started asking questions. The next thing I knew I was hustled upstairs to a guest room where two extremely excited foreign men identified me as the person who stole a valuable Shakespeare item from their room. They say they saw me running down the hall after hearing a disturbance in the main area of their suite. As it was late, they had retired, but ran out after hearing a noise. Mr. Holmes, I swear I was never in that hallway at any time last night, never! That's the whole truth, sir."

Holmes nodded his head and I could see that familiar abstracted look that meant he was evaluating what he heard and examining possibilities. He had picked up Winters's cap and was slowly turning it over and over. He set it back down, turned to Lestrade and said, "Inspector, I'm going to see what I can discover about this matter. Mr. Winters, I can't promise anything at this juncture, but I will try to help you."

Our new client practically collapsed back on the bench and thanked Holmes profusely but I noticed a disapproving look on Lestrade's narrow face. We left Mr. Winters and as we made our way out, Lestrade, unable to maintain his composure any longer, barked at Holmes. "I must say I can't believe you gave such hope to a clearly guilty man! He's been identified by two eye witnesses - what more can you ask? As he was fleeing down the hall he turned his head toward his pursuers and he had the Shakespeare book in his hand. They could see his face, Holmes! After turning a corner the Italians lost track of him but they found his cap in one of the side halls."

Holmes looked at Lestrade with that sardonic expression he gets when he thinks an important point has been missed.

"But Lestrade", I interjected, he has his cap. It's on the bench bedside him." Lestrade persisted, "Of course he has a cap, he could easily have picked up a new one from the storeroom. He has a key."

Holmes glanced at Lestrade and asked in a condescending tone. "Two telling clues, eh, Inspector?"

As we arrived at the main door of the Yard, Lestrade pulled Holmes aside and said very softly, "Could I have a moment of your time, Holmes? I would appreciate your advice on a different case that has me baffled."

Holmes smiled, I could tell that he was thinking that bafflement was Lestrade's normal condition. "Certainly Inspector, how can I help?"

"Well," Lestrade whispered, "we thought we had nabbed a foreign agent who was spying on our military facilities. We watched him for several months and tracked him to an old stone house just outside London. We were absolutely certain he had incriminating documents so we stationed men to watch the house while we organized a search party. The men watching the house swear he arrived and went into the house so we swarmed the place....." Holmes broke in, "And you found nothing."

"Yes, we couldn't find the agent or the papers. We searched everywhere in the house and outbuildings with no result - no agent and no papers! The servants were tight-lipped and we got nothing from them. Holmes, the men we had watch the house are very reliable and we had the whole property covered. We have identified the man as a Frederick Duke. He has the reputation of being a professional, 'for hire', spy. We are frankly stumped, sir. Is there anything you can suggest I do now?"

Holmes paused, ran a hand through his hair, thought for a minute and asked the inspector, "You say the house is old - do you know how old?"

"I don't know but it seems quite old - at least two or three hundred years - maybe more. Why?"

"Inspector, have you ever heard of Nicholas Owen?"

"No I haven't. What's he got to do with this."

"Nicholas Owen was a clever man and builder. He designed many priest holes in the days when the word 'mass' could get you a date with the executioner. He came up with many very clever hiding places for priests who would sneak into England to say mass to secretive Catholic families. These Jesuit priests knew they were done for if they were caught - tortured and then killed. In fact, that fate happened to the unfortunate Mr. Owen. I suggest you carefully measure the outside and inside of the house and then you can compare measure for measure and possibly find a discrepancy between them. It may give you a clue to a missing secret space. I suspect that the servants have been well paid to provide him with food and water and to keep quiet. That's assuming he's there of course. You can also enlist the help of an historian who is familiar with that dangerous period. That's all I can offer at the moment. Good luck with your search, Inspector."

Lestrade brightened, thanked Holmes, and as we were leaving, Holmes leaned out of our Hansom and said,"By the way Lestrade, that remark I made about the 'telling clues' - concerns the two most favorable points in Mr. Winter's favor."

As we drove off I could see Lestrade raise his eyebrows and the look of perplexity returned. I have to admit, I was puzzled also.

"Watson, I think we owe ourselves a stop for lunch at Simpsons and then off to the Windsor Hotel." I agreed heartily; especially about the lunch!

After our light lunch we hailed a cab and soon arrived at the opulent Windsor Hotel.

Holmes asked to see the day manager and we were directed to an office off the main lobby where we met with Mr. Hugh Evans. After explaining our visit - that we were asked by Inspector Lestrade to look into the theft, he welcomed us and escorted us upstairs to the aggrieved Italian's room. Signori Valentine and Proteus, two young men whose anguish over their loss of a significant Shakespeare quarto was evident in their gesticulations, wringing of hands and rapid and loud Italian. They tried at first to tell their story simultaneously until Holmes held up his hand, shook his head, and stopped their stream of mixed Italian and English wailings.

"Please signori, please just one at a time. Whichever of you speaks the best English will please start from the beginning of this robbery." Signor Valentine gently put his hand over his brother's mouth and volunteered to relate their troubles to us.

"I talk best English I think, so I tell you all what happened. We bring book of great value to auction - book in family for many years - is Shakespeare quarto which our great-grandfather accepted as payment for debt many years ago. We are printers, Signor Holmes.

We are here to sell book because family business is bad now because family not keep up with times. We are now too slow for customers; we need newer presses but do not have money for them. Is why we at last have family's say so to sell book. It is only thing can save business, Signore Holmes. We came here yesterday evening, got room and Signor Evans take us to room of auctioneer to register our treasure for auction. Was some others there also doing the same. We meant to put book in safe of hotel today." He sat down in a chair, put his head in his hands and rocked back and forth. "Now is too late! We have disgraced our family and failed our job. What can we do Signor Holmes?"

Holmes had been pacing the room while Valentine was speaking and stopped in front of the Italian, asking, "Has the room been cleaned today?" After receiving a "si" from Valentine, Holmes shook his head in disgust. "I'll bet all the clues went out the door with the chambermaid, Watson." He made a slow tour of the room and ended up examining the door lock with his folding magnifying glass he always carried. "Well Watson, at least we have a tiny bit of evidence here." Putting the glass back in his pocket, we said goodbye to the brothers and headed for the main ballroom where we hoped to find the lady in charge of the coming extravaganza.

Lady Portia Wedgewood-Benn was a small, voluble, ball of fire. As she was the organizer, planner and spirit behind the charity auction and dinner dance, she was, as one of her helpers told us, "Everywhere at once!" We found her at a table, making a map of where she wanted the tables and the stage set up. She was dressed in what I presumed was the latest style, and wore a bright purple scarf around her neck. We sat down at the table and introduced ourselves. She brushed a stray strand of hair out of her face, and said, without pause, "Oh Mr. Holmes I've heard of you and you must be Doctor Watson can you help me? This theft is just awful!"

I admit I almost took a step back under this verbal onslaught. Holmes had a slightly amused expression on his face. "Lady Portia, I will do everything I can to retrieve the quarto. Anything you can tell me about the coming festivities may help my investigation."

Lady Portia looked quite pleased to be asked about her event. She shoved aside the map she was marking and brightened somewhat. "Mr. Holmes, I sponsor this gala every year for the benefit of a widow and orphan's fund. All the proceeds from the auction and the dance go to the fund. We pay the hotel for the orchestra and the ballroom and give the auctioneer a percentage so it encourages him to get as much as he can for the auction items. They all have a declared minimum price for the owner and the fund gets anything over that price."

Holmes nodded and asked, "You mentioned the dance also. How does that contribute to the fund?" Lady Portia actually beamed at us.

"Oh, that's the most fun of all. Many of the ladies volunteer to be dance partners. They all go to one side of the room and the men then choose a partner for one dance.

They pay 10 pounds and the husband of the lady chosen also pays 10 pounds. No husband may choose his own wife and the dance goes on until everyone wears out!" We call the volunteer ladies "The Merry Wives" and myself and a few other ladies go around with decorated baskets to collect the money. Then we serve the dinner and hold the auction. Mr. Holmes and Doctor Watson; we have a wonderful time and we also welcome single men." And with that she speared us with a meaningful look!

Holmes gave me a quick, wary glance and asked Lady Portia, "If I may ask your Ladyship, how much do you usually make from all this?" She smiled widely and told us they could make as much as five thousand pounds. Holmes gave a startled whistle; "I had no idea you could do so well."

Lady Portia suddenly slumped back in her chair and with a wistful look, brushed another stray wisp of hair from her face and looked at us with a beseeching expression. "That is why the Shakespeare quarto is so important. It is.....was.....the key auction item for us. The Italian gentlemen from the printing business in Verona put a very reasonable price on the piece so I think we could have made a very large profit from it. Mr. Holmes, it could have brought as much as practically all the other auction items combined."

"Do you run the auction too?"

"Oh, Heavens no; we hire a professional auctioneer. We will have a new man this year, our regular auctioneer moved away so we put an ad in the paper. Three men applied but one, a Mr. Angelo Bernardino, was so energetic and seemed to know all about auctioneering, that we hired him. He also said he needed the money and was willing to take less percentage than we usually offer. He said he would work hard to get the best prices possible for the auction items."

We got up from the table and Holmes put a hand gently on Lady Portia's shoulder; "I promise I will do everything I can to solve this crime."

As we took our leave Holmes looked pensive and deep in thought. I well knew that countenance, accordingly I didn't bother him for any conversation on our ride back to Baker Street.

When we were settled in our rooms, Holmes went to the mantle, gathered up a few dottles and leftovers from previous smokes, stoked his old briar pipe, lit it, and began to pace up and down. I expected a long and smoke filled hour but he stopped suddenly and turned to me. "Well, my friend, let us now review the salient facts as we have them."

I was delighted and surprised by this as he often didn't discuss a case this soon.

"I'm all ears Holmes, what are your thoughts?" He resumed his pacing but slower.

"The way I see it, Doctor, the first question to answer is; how did the thief know about the extremely valuable quarto, and, where it likely was."

I was happy that I might be able to contribute. "Well, the Italians seemed very talkative, possibly they were overheard talking about the quarto. Then there is the thought that they were followed from Italy by someone who knew about the treasure."

"Well summarized. But if that is the case, then the thief and the quarto are probably gone and out of our reach. Remember too, that they had just arrived - not much time for news of the prize to spread. " Holmes stopped pacing, sat down in his armchair and sent a few wisps of smoke ceilingward. "Ah! Watson there is another way someone could have become aware of the book. Recall that Valentine told us that Evans took them to the auctioneer's room to register their auction item? The register book is not secret - anyone may have seen the entry. Valentine told us some others were in the room to do the same. We know that whoever found out about the quarto acted very quickly and with daring to steal it."

"Of course, Holmes! You may have hit upon it. But before we go on, you told Lestrade he had pointed out two clues that actually favored Winters. What were they?"

"Very well; the first is the cap. You know my methods, Watson. I examined that cap as Winters was bewailing his fate and it was somewhat scuffed and the headband was stained with perspiration. I'm certain it was his cap. That blows Lestrade's version away, and the cap that was found was not cast off by Winters in a desperate escape. The second clue is, I admit, a stretch; but you remember that Valentine said the thief turned and faced the Italians before sprinting away in the labyrinth of corridors? Why did he expose his face like that?"

I thought about that for a moment. "Lestrade said the thief clearly wanted to see how close his pursuers were."

"Yes, Lestrade may be correct..........but does no alternative explanation occur to you? Well, we will have to put that aside for now. I must visit the manager again to determine whether Winters had a passkey to the rooms. If so, the shiny small scratches I saw around the keyhole - fresh ones - will also tend to eliminate Winters as a suspect. I will also contact a few collectors here in London who I know could afford to buy the quarto. I must warn them about anyone trying to sell such an item. I doubt the thief would be that brazen, though. I feel he's more likely to take it to Europe."

The following day I did not accompany Holmes on his visits to the collectors he mentioned, to Lady Portia or the hotel manager, since the activity of the previous day caused my gamey leg to ache quite painfully from the damage done by a jezail bullet I received at the battle of Maiwand. I tried to read but our case kept intruding into my thoughts so much that I decided Henry Murger's "La Vie de Boheme" would have to wait.

It had been a bright sunny summer day, but the shadows were beginning to lengthen by the time Holmes returned, picked out his cherry wood pipe and had to pinch out some fresh tobacco from the Persian slipper because he had smoked all the dottles and awful leftovers already. Not that the fresh tobacco was much better! He relaxed in his well-worn but comfortable padded armchair and neither of us spoke for a while although I was itching to hear about his day and what he found out.

"Not much, Doctor."

I was startled out of my thoughts but got over it quickly because Holmes, with his reasoning and observational skills often seemed to be reading one's mind. Lestrade was so used to it by now that he usually just eyed Holmes, shook his head slightly, and went on with the conversation.

"That was the easiest deduction you've made in a long time, Holmes."

"Yes, Watson, that was indeed a simple one. Unfortunately, my answer was accurate. I did find out that Winters carries no passkey. It's locked up in the manager's office and must be signed out. The auctioneer had been at the hotel for over a week to log in and register a description of each auction item. So Winters could still be the thief if he picked the lock - but where did he learn that skill? I favor my original conclusion that Winters is not the thief. I think we must seek our villain elsewhere. By the way, Doctor, Lady Portia batted her big blue eyes at me, patted my arm, and said that you and I would be 'more than welcome' at the dance."

"I fear that she'll never give up on us, Holmes." He chuckled and settled back in his chair. After a silent minute or two, Holmes got up, put his pipe back on the mantle and said the words that I dreaded but was not surprised to hear.

"I think we actually should go. We haven't seen all the players in this drama yet - including Signor Bernardino, the auctioneer, and just perhaps, our presence might induce the thief, assuming he's still here, into some ill-considered action. Watson, I have a hunch that he has not made his escape yet. A sudden disappearance might cause some unwanted attention. I must admit, I'm frustrated with this situation."

The next two days brought no news from any of Holmes sources. Each tine there was a knock at our door, Holmes would almost leap out of his chair, hurry to answer the knock but the first three trips brought nothing of value to the case. Finally, a messenger brought a note from Lestrade which Holmes almost tore in his haste to read it. After examining it, he disgustedly threw it down on our table. "Lestrade writes, 'Nothing new', not that I expected much from the official inquiry. Bah! This is getting us nowhere."

He strode to our front window, a spot at which he often paused to weigh a situation and consider actions. "One more day to the Gala and we are no closer to netting the thief. Watson, we must visit the hotel again. Lady Portia's arrangements for the festivities should be complete and I want another meet with our gale-force hostess. I haven't yet spoken to the auctioneer. He should be setting up for the auction by now. I want a word with the night manager also."

After a quick, light, supper, we took a cab to the hotel and had no trouble locating Lady Portia, who was dashing about with a coterie of helpers in her wake, trying to keep up. They were placing cloths and center pieces on the tables and locating potted plants around the room according to her Ladyship's directions. Holmes finally caught her eye and she rushed over to us; a most hopeful look on her face. Holmes held up a hand;

"I'm sorry Lady Portia, but I have not as yet recovered the quarto." Obviously quite disappointed, she nodded sadly, "I know in my heart that it's probably useless, but we had such high hopes for its return. And those poor young men here from Italy; I know they feel awful. Just think, such a small delay in securing their treasure in the hotel safe and their world suddenly collapses."

Holmes took Lady Portia's hand and gently patted it. "Don't lose hope yet. Believe me, I have not given up on this case. Now, if you'll excuse us, I need to have a word with Mr. Goodfellow, the night manager. Watson, I'll be just a moment and I'll meet you at the stage - I see it's been set up."

I made my way through the tables and across the dance floor to the stage area where several musicians were arranging their stands. A lectern and a small table sat at the back of the stage; likely for the use of the auctioneer. Just then, from the far side of the stage, a man popped out and hurried to the table. He had a bushy moustache and a shock of dark brown hair which matched a dark complexion, bespeaking a sunnier clime than England! He placed a ledger, a gavel, and a water glass on the small table and then quickly vanished behind the side curtain. Lady Portia was accurate about his energy. I was sure he would extract as much as possible from the crowd. The musicians were just finishing their pre-dance set up when Holmes arrived by my side.

"Mr. Goodfellow verified everything we have heard. He was just about to relieve Evans when Evans came back to the office and related the events after the arrival of the Italians. Evans explained that both men looked extremely tired and begged off putting the quarto in the safe until morning. Goodfellow says he and Evans were a bit upset by the Italian's decision, but then again, not everyone consigned their goods to the hotel safe. They debated an attempt to talk the Italians into letting them put the quarto in the safe but Valentine had been very adamant and insisted they were exhausted and would bring the book to the hotel office first thing in the morning, so the managers gave up. Evans went home and Goodfellow got busy with his duties."

"Holmes," I cried, "What a fiasco! It would be a comedy of errors if the result were not so serious." As we were talking, the auctioneer hustled out on the stage again, this time depositing a notebook on the lectern. As he turned to go, he paused briefly and he and Holmes stared at each other for a moment. Holmes started to raise his hand but the auctioneer disappeared through the curtain. Holmes had a most curious expression on his face - brows drawn and eyes almost shut; as if he was trying to remember something just out of reach. Answering my unspoken question, as he often did, he said, "Something just tickled my memory, but I can't believe what just flashed by. I'll have to put it down to accidental similarities from past encounters. Watson, I suggest we head back to Baker Street. I think I have a three-pipe problem to work on."

True to his word, after we arrived the room filled with smoke from his potent shag. I endeavored to remove some by opening our front window and fanning the smoke with a folded newspaper but it did little good so I retired to my bedroom. I read for a while but I was tired from the day's activities so I went to bed. I could hear Holmes pacing for a bit and then some plaintive strains on his violin. Listening to them, I soon fell asleep.

The next morning, as we were working on one of Mrs. Hudson's country breakfasts, Holmes announced, "Well Doctor, lay out your seldom used formal wear - we will emulate Terpsichore tonight, continue our investigations, and, in no small measure, make Lady Portia pleased that we accepted her entreaties to attend the Gala."

I admit I didn't consider this idea as a delight, but I knew Holmes had a purpose in mind. "Holmes, of course I will go with you, but with my dicky leg, I'm not sure how much tripping of the light fantastic I'll be doing. Tripping maybe, but not lightly!"

Since we had plenty of time before the dancing began, Holmes spent the next three hours contacting some of the collectors he had warned about the theft. However, on his return, he said dejectedly, "No luck; no one has tried to sell the quarto to the most obvious collectors. I had not considered it a likely event, but all the same, we have to follow every path we can since we have so little to go on."

The festivities were due to start at three so we had a light lunch and soon I was somewhat hopefully unpacking my formal attire - I wasn't sure I could still get into it. I managed, but it was apparent from the effort it took, that Mrs. Hudson's cooking, delicious as it was, had taken a toll. When I went into the parlor, Holmes commented with a grin, "I see your suit shrunk a bit - must be the climate."

We arrived at the Windsor and were soon making our way through the crowd of bejeweled ladies escorted by their elegantly attired husbands. We came across Lady Portia as we entered the ballroom. She was obviously in her element, greeting guests right and left, rushing about with last minute instructions to her helpers, and brushing flying wisps of hair out of her face. I think she was a little surprised to see that we actually took her up on her rather coy invitation. She greeted us enthusiastically but I noticed a small questioning look. Holmes told her he was still working on the case and that we weren't staying for dinner but would be back for the auction. He added, "I would like to talk to your auctioneer; do you know where he might be?"

"I'm sorry Mr. Holmes, but he told me he had a few errands he had to do and would be back soon." She waved a finger at us and twittered, "As long as you dance, dear boys, I'm happy.

We located two chairs at one side of the room and while we waited for Lady Portia to open the dancing, I asked Holmes why we were not staying for dinner. "Doctor, we could eat at good restaurants for a month for what these guests are paying for one meal! Besides, we didn't sign up for dinner and it's too late now."

We didn't have long to wait as Lady Portia mounted the stage, profusely welcomed the guests, explained the rules and finally, with a great flourish, waved the musicians to begin the dance music. She then joined four volunteer ladies and, with their decorated baskets, circulated among the guests collecting the dance fees. Holmes gave me a rather pained glance and said, "Well Doctor, just keep thinking about what a good cause this is!" Then he got up to pick out a partner and I, resigned to my fate, followed.

Since my pocketbook and my gimpy leg could take only so much, I danced with but two ladies, a Baroness bedecked with enough glitter to stock a jewelry store and a small, demure lady exquisitely gowned and coifed. As soon as our dance started she asked me what I did. Unaware of the consequences, I told her I was a doctor. During the entire dance, which seemed to last forever, she riddled me with questions about what her many symptoms meant. Finally, the ordeal ended and, with great relief, I limped off the dance floor and resettled in my chair. Although Holmes was an excellent athlete and danced very well, he soon joined me.

"Watson, that is the limit of what I can bear for now. That French Countess actually invited me to visit her at her Chateau in

Bordeaux, 'when my husband is busy with his precious wine business.' Let us quickly be off to Baker Street and the rest of that roast Mrs. Hudson made today. We have a good three hours before the auction and I am very curious to see Mr. Bernardino again."

As we walked out of the ballroom, I looked up at Holmes, and as mischievously as I could, said, "A French Countess, eh?" I got a withering glance, but I noticed a small grin as he turned away that I think he didn't want me to see.

Back at Baker Street, we both shed our formal outfits and donned more comfortable clothes. Mrs. Hudson and Billy brought our suppers, which we dispatched with gusto, took our coffee to our favorite comfortable chairs and relaxed for a while, Holmes with his briar and me with a cigarette. The calm atmosphere was shattered when Holmes got up quickly from his chair, strode to the mantle and slammed down his pipe.

"Watson, I have it! Oh, what a blind mole I've been. It was right in front of us! Quickly, load your Webley; we must get to the Windsor before our quarry has escaped."

While I loaded my pistol, Holmes sent Billy out to get us a Hansom. I grabbed a jacket and slipped the gun in a pocket. We hurried downstairs and out to Baker Street just as Billy had whistled a cab for us. Holmes tossed a coin to the driver and yelled, "To the Windsor Hotel as fast as you can!" The driver looked at the large coin, stuffed it in his pocket and said. "Yes sir," cracked his whip in the air and shouted to his horse. "Dul, dul!" and off we went at a great rate.

Holmes leaned over and said, "Doctor, you have been a very patient ally. Let me explain my haste. Through my thoughts on this case, the nagging question was, Why did the thief turn around? I know Lestrade thinks it was to see where his pursuers were but that bothered me. Why bother to look when he knew that two very loud

Italians were running after him? Watson, the only conclusion that seemed to me to fit was this; he turned so they could see his face!"

"But Holmes," I protested, "The Italians could identify him later in case they had a chance if they saw his face." Holmes held up his right index finger and smiled.

"Just so, Watson. I believe he wanted to be seen. Now close your eyes and picture the auctioneer, Mr. Bernardino. You saw him twice, briefly I know, but can you see his face?" I did as Holmes said and told Holmes I thought I had a reasonably good remembrance of his looks.

"Excellent; now remove the glasses and the beard. Still good?"

"Yes, I think I have it, Holmes."

"Good, now remove the moustache and mop of hair, lighten his skin color, focus on his narrow face and piercing eyes. All right? Now, Watson, put a Windsor Hotel cap on him and who do you see?"

I jerked up abruptly in my seat, opened my eyes wide and answered, "Holmes, it's Winters! But it can't be, I know he's in a Scotland Yard cell." Holmes raised his eyebrows in a questioning expression and waited for my brain to catch on. "Holmes! The auctioneer is in disguise. He removed it to impersonate Winters because he realized he resembled him. It was to pin the theft on Winters!"

"Bravo, Doctor. That's precisely what I think took place."

"But Holmes, to succeed with an elaborate disguise like that - the beard, hair, moustache, and the complexion - he'd have to be as skillful in disguises as.....as..."

"Thank you, Doctor; I do pride myself in that area. But Watson, make no mistake; we are up against a formidable foe - clever and quick." Holmes paused and ran his hand through his hair. "It still nips at my mind, Doctor; I can't get over the feeling that I've run across him before."

When our cab pulled up at the Windsor, Holmes and I quickly jumped out of the Hansom and dashed through the lobby and into the ballroom. What a shock we got when we saw that the guests were dancing!

"Quick Watson, something is wrong - we must find Lady Portia at once!"

Holmes pointed across the dance floor. "Look, the auctioneer is not here. I think we indeed crossed paths previously and he identified me."

I spotted Lady Portia by the stage, pointed her out to Holmes and we hurried over towards her. We threaded our way through the dancing couples and as soon as we reached her, Holmes asked urgently' "Lady Portia, what has happened here?

"Oh, Mr. Holmes, I'm sorry you missed the auction, but Mr. Bernardino came to me in a panic and said he had just received word that a close relative has been seriously hurt in an accident and he must leave as soon as possible. We had just finished the dance so I asked the management to delay the dinner so we could have the auction immediately. I must say, Mr. Holmes, Signor Bernardino raced through the auction like the Devil was after him. It was done in half the usual time. We then had dinner served and now we are just enjoying the end-of-evening dances."

Holmes gave Lady Portia a most serious look; "Lady Portia, did you put the dance and auction checks in the hotel safe? This is of the utmost importance!"

"No. When the auction was finished, Signor Bernardino very kindly offered to take the dance money and auction proceeds to the night manager and have them put in the safe. We can count it all out tomorrow morning, settle up what we owe him. and take the balance to the bank."

Holmes looked stricken by this news, shook his head, and spoke to her Ladyship in the most serious of tones; "My dear Lady Portia,

I'm very much afraid we have all been taken in by this Bernardino fellow. I can't take the time now to explain; I need to see the manager as soon as possible, but if I'm correct, the money and the Shakespeare quarto have been stolen."

Lady Portia clapped a hand to her forehead and collapsed into the nearest chair, all her usual energy and drive drained away. She seemed to be trying to talk but couldn't manage it. Holmes put a hand on her shoulder gently. "Do not despair yet. How long ago did you give the money to Bernardino?"

With teary eyes, she answered; "Maybe about twenty minutes ago - possibly a little more. Oh, Mr. Holmes, this charity affair has been a labor of love for me for years. To think tonight may be a horrible disaster is unbearable!"

"I must go now and check out his room. If he's gone, as I fear, we know with certainty who the thief is and I'll do everything I can to retrieve the money and the quarto. Come Watson, we must find Mr. Goodfellow and have him open Bernardino's room."

Holmes raced off towards to manager's office, but I knew I couldn't keep up. "I'll meet you by the stairs", I called to him. He nodded briefly as he hurried off. When I reached the stairs nearest the manager's office Holmes and Goodfellow were already halfway up to the first floor, taking the steps two at a time. When I gained the top of the stairs, I saw Holmes and the manager a few doors down the hall. Goodfellow used his passkey and they both disappeared into the room. As I reached the door, Holmes shouted, "Check the wardrobe."

When I entered the room, Goodfellow was standing by the now empty wardrobe shaking his head. Holmes pointed to a small dressing table. "Well, there's no doubt now. There's the proof." On the table was a makeup kit, a fake beard, moustache, a dark brown wig and a pair of eyeglasses. Holmes held the glasses up; "Notice Doctor, they are just plain glass. More fakery. Nothing more here gentlemen.

Let us hurry down and talk to the doorman." As we were leaving the room, I noticed Holmes quickly check a bottle of brown face make-up and a comb. He threw them back down on the table, put a bottle of some liquid and a cloth into his jacket pocket and we headed out to question the doorman.

By the time I managed the stairs and hurried out through the ornate main door, Holmes was talking to the doorman, a tall, thin, middle-aged man who looked pleased to be the center of attention. "Yes sir, the man you described caught a cab not more than ten minutes or so. He seemed to be in a great hurry, throwing his suitcase into the cab and shouting to the driver that he had to catch the next train to Scotland. He had a big hat pulled down over his face but I recognized the voice. It was Mr. Bernardino for sure sir."

Holmes gave the man a coin and said, "Good work my man; now please get us a cab at once." I saw Mr. Goodfellow come through the door and Holmes had a brief word with him. The doorman had gotten us a cab; there were usually several waiting at the street for customers so we climbed in and Holmes tossed the driver a large coin and yelled, "To Victoria Station - as fast as you can!"

As we settled in the cab, Holmes turned to me and answered my unspoken question; "I had Mr. Goodfellow contact the Yard immediately and ask that an inspector and a constable meet us at the station as soon as possible. I told him to tell the Yard that Sherlock Holmes says it's extremely important. A major crime is in progress. I hope that will do the job."

Since Victoria Station was the closest terminal with lines to most parts of England, I understood Holmes's instructions. The thief would likely head there. I turned to Holmes; "I don't have my Bradshaw, I suppose we'll have to check the train schedule to Scotland when we get to Victoria."

"My dear Doctor, you should be able to deduce why we won't need to check any schedule to Scotland." He gave me a slight smile.

I mulled that over in my mind for several minutes and finally, exasperated, I asked Holmes why we weren't interested in the Scottish trains.

"Think back to what the doorman told us - Bernardino shouted his desires to the coach driver so anyone near could hear. Why would he do that?" Suddenly, it made sense. "Of course, Holmes, he wanted to mislead any pursuers. It's simple."

Holmes gave a small shake of his head. "Yes, everything is simple once it has been explained."

Victoria Station was busy as usual with cabs lined up letting passengers off and picking up new ones. As soon as our Hansom stopped we climbed out, Holmes tossed the driver a coin and we made our way through the bustling crowd. As we got to the entrance, Holmes put a restraining hand on my shoulder; "Doctor, please wait here and watch for Scotland yard while I check the train schedules."

"But Holmes, how do we know which train he will take?"

For just a fleeting second, I saw a flash of doubt flick across his normally alert, composed features; then, "Watson, we can only guess at this point; but considering the well planned scheme he hatched and the speed he reacted after, I'm sure now, he caught a glimpse of me when he was setting up for the auction. He will probably realize that soon the police throughout the country will be looking for him. I think he will therefore try to get as far away as quickly as possible. I imagine, noting his cleverness and haste, he saw us leave during the dancing and grabbed a chance to increase his 'take' by convincing Lady Portia to change the schedule so he could get away with not only the quarto, but the dance and auction money as well. We know that Lady Portia fell in with his request, not only to accelerate the auction but give him the dance money.

He then, as we discovered, packed up and left immediately, removing the more obvious parts of his disguise. I'm also guessing that he had already concealed the quarto so all he had to do was dump the money in his suitcase and 'fly the coop' as they say."

Leaving me to watch for the Yard, he hurried off to examine the big schedule board posted by the ticket windows. In what seemed like an hour but was probably only fifteen minutes or so, I saw inspector Peter Jones and a very large constable pushing through the crowd. I waved and shouted and Jones, whom Holmes described as not very bright but tenacious as a bulldog, came over to me with the PC in tow.

"Doctor Watson, I was looking for Holmes. What's going on? I know it must be important or he wouldn't have asked for our help."

"Inspector, we are trying to catch a thief who has stolen thousands of pounds that should go to a widow and orphan's fund. We need to quickly find Holmes - I'll fill in the details while we look for him."

With the large constable plowing through the crowd ahead of us, we arrived in the main station area and as we approached the ticketing windows I saw Holmes striding towards us. He reached out and shook hands with Jones and turned to the big PC. "John Rance, is it not? I believe you were involved in the case Doctor Watson has dubbed 'A Study in Scarlet'. I'm happy to have you with us now."

"Aye sir, and quite an affair it was too. Where are we headed?"

"We must go two platforms over. The train for Plymouth is due to leave in twenty minutes."

This announcement startled me but I didn't have time to ask any questions as Holmes hurried off, the inspector and Rance in tow. I tried to keep up but my game leg was beginning to throb and I fell behind the fast-paced trio. As I reached the platform Holmes mentioned, I saw the three of them in a tight group just behind the last car of the six-car train. Holmes waved me over and begin to lay out his plan. "Gentlemen, we are looking for a man of average height and weight, brown complexion, narrow face with small, piercing eyes and thin lips. He will probably be wearing a large hat pulled down over his face. He has, I believe, light brown hair, cut short. He is agile and quick and may be armed so we need to subdue him quickly. I must keep out of sight as we search for him because I'm sure he recognized me at the hotel and I don't want to warn him of our presence. Watson, you and inspector Jones lead the way. I doubt he remembers you, Doctor, he was quite focused on me in the hotel. These last two cars are coach and the next three compartments. I fully believe he will engage a compartment but we have to eliminate the coaches first. Rance and I will wait at the head of the car - out of sight if possible - and Watson. you and Jones walk the car. If you see him, give Rance and me a call. Inspector, don't be fooled; he is dangerous. All right, let's get to it."

Jones and I waited for Holmes and Rance to enter the car by the forward door and then the inspector and I entered by the rear door and walked the car, but we didn't see the auctioneer. We repeated the search in the next car, but again, no thief.

We gathered just outside the first of the compartment cars and Holmes gave us his plan for searching them. "I was sure he would take a compartment for better concealment. He will have drawn the curtains so we need a strategy to make him open them. John, you and the inspector will follow Watson. He will check the compartments with the curtains open and signal if he sees our quarry. When you come to a compartment with drawn curtains, knock and loudly say there has been a mix up and you need to check the occupant's ticket. Your uniform looks enough like a conductor's so I think the passenger will open the door after a peek through the curtain. If you encounter a stubborn refusal, knock and demand to see a ticket! We will be right behind you. Doctor, you walk on the opposite side and if you spot the auctioneer, tell Constable Rance at once. We don't have much time so let's get started."

Rance moved aside and I went from the rear of the car to the front but didn't see Bernardino. Rance, Jones, and Holmes then followed but there was only one curtained compartment and an elderly lady opened the door. Rance went through the routine of checking her ticket and we moved on to the next car. There were three curtained compartments and we had no trouble having the occupants open the door for Rance to go through his routine. When we met with Holmes before checking the third and last car, Holmes had a very concerned and drawn look. He whispered to me, "I know you're wondering why we are inspecting this particular train. If my assumptions are correct, he would want to leave England fast and quietly. This train goes to Plymouth, where he could easily get a fisherman to take him across the channel. He has a lot of money to buy passage to France where he could then disappear into Europe."

"But Holmes, wouldn't it be easier to take a train to Dover and be ferried across?"

"No train to Dover for another two hours, Doctor. I feel quire intensely about this case. If he escapes, he wins, and I'll never forgive myself for not recognizing the clues sooner. I believe I know who he is; as unbelievable as it seems to me. Rance is ready, if he's not in this car I swear I'll retire!"

We entered the last car as quietly as we could and Rance and I began our slow walk down the center aisle, Rance on one side and me on the other. I admit I was not optimistic about our chances. Holmes had put his skills on the line and I could imagine him slipping back onto cocaine use if this effort failed. I had fallen a little behind Rance -we were now almost to the end of the car and my worry was intensified almost to desperation, but then I saw Rance stop two compartments ahead and knock on the door. No elderly lady this time. I heard an unpleasant voice call out loudly. "What the devil do you want? I'm busy!" I saw Holmes's attitude suddenly change from a slightly forlorn look to one of excitement. He nudged inspector Jones forward, closer to the door. Rance gave his speech about needing to see the man's ticket; only this time it was in a loud, stern voice any real railway porter would be proud of. This time the occupant apparently realized he had to comply and opened the door just enough to poke his hand out to show Rance his ticket. He had seen enough of Rance's uniform through the opening however, to see it was police and not a real porter. With a screamed curse, he tried to slam the door shut but the big constable wasn't having any of it and pushed the door open and shoved the man back into the compartment. Rance shouted, "It's him!" Jones and Holmes rushed in right behind Rance. Jones had his pistol drawn but it was unnecessary, Rance had the man securely pinned on the compartment's seat. Holmes and the inspector said simultaneously, "Well done, Constable!"

Not content to submit quietly, the man let out a tirade, "What's the meaning of this outrage? I have done nothing - I'm just a businessman on my way back to Venice after selling antiques from Italy." He put on a look of affronted innocence but Holmes wasn't buying it.

"So, how did the auction go?"

"I know nothing about auction. I finish here and go back home."

I noticed that as he was saying this, his eyes flicked over quickly to a suitcase in the corner and then back to Holmes. Inspector Jones looked confused and unsure of what to do. Holmes, who had apparently caught the quick glance to the suitcase, said in a firm voice, "Inspector, please have Signor Bernardino - or whomever he may be - open his suitcase."

I smiled inwardly as I thought we might actually save Lady Portia's fun and recover the quarto for the two devastated Italians, but Inspector Jones spoke up and my heart sank.

"Mr. Holmes, we have been following your instructions because of your past successes, but I don't know that we can force this man to show us his private property without something besides your suspicions."

"What?" I exclaimed loudly. I expected Holmes to react similarly, but he replied to Jones in a calm voice; "Inspector, if you would please grant me just a minute, I think I will be able to provide a reason to continue this investigation." Holmes then took out the cloth I saw him put in his pocket from the table in the auctioneer's room along with a bottle of some lotion. Seeing this, our captive jerked his head back and forth vigorously but Rance held him firmly.

"You can't do this" he screamed, "I'll have you all in court - I'll have your badges! And you, Sherlock Holmes, will pay dearly for this . . . this tempest; this illegal restraint of an honest merchant! This is much ado about nothing, I am innocent!"

Holmes gave him a smile, a thin, sardonic smile. "Why. my goodness, whatever happened to your Italian accent?"

Inspector Jones narrowed his eyes and also addressed the man; "And how did you know this is Sherlock Holmes? No one mentioned his name. Well, speak up!"

Since our prisoner had nothing to say and cast a look of pure hatred at Holmes, Jones waved a hand towards him, as if to say "Go ahead." Holmes then put a generous dollop of the lotion on the cloth and asked Rance to hold the man's head firmly.

Holmes turned to us and explained his deductions. "When I saw the tan makeup on the table with the false beard and wig, I examined the comb and noted short, light brown hairs. I was certain our auctioneer didn't come by his tan complexion from the sunny climes of Italy."

Our captive hissed at us and squirmed but the big constable's grip was too much to overcome. Holmes reached over and wiped the cloth vigorously over the man's face, stepped back and so we could see the now pale complexion grimacing at us. I thought Jones's eyes would pop out of his head; "Good Lord! It's John Clay. Holmes, this is almost beyond belief! How did you know it was him?"

I was as startled as the inspector; "It's the man we caught trying to rob the City and Suburban bank, Holmes."

Jones threw his arms in the air. "Why didn't you tell me we were hunting Clay?"

Holmes turned to Jones and gave him a look with which a schoolmaster might skewer a naughty student. "Because, my dear Inspector, I was never told that John Clay was no longer serving time as a guest of the Queen. He should have been yet in prison. To be frank, I'm not pleased." Jones looked at the ground as the school-boy might have done.

"Mr. Holmes, I apologize most sincerely. Clay faked a sickness and when a guard took him to the infirmary, he grabbed a heavy glass container, knocked the guard on the head and took his night-stick, then used it to knock the doctor to the ground before he could raise the alarm. He then took a large surgical instrument to pry open the window, which was in the outer wall, and escape while the guard and doctor were unconscious."

Holmes slowly shook his head. "And the prison officials and the Ministry were so embarrassed they didn't want any outsiders or the press to get wind of it. Right?"

Jones nodded. "No one had ever escaped from there Mr. Holmes. The Yard was called in and we went through his cell thoroughly and questioned his cellmate at length. He told us Clay had bragged that he had criminal friends in Edinburgh who would hide him so we concentrated our search there. Mr. Holmes, we were completely fooled. I admit it. I would have told you but the whole thing was under tight secrecy."

"Officialdom strikes again, eh inspector? Well, at least we nabbed him. I think this train is about to depart. Let's have a look into that suitcase and then we need to depart also!" Suiting the action to the word, Holmes placed the suitcase on the seat but it wouldn't open. "Watson, while our quarry is well under the control of PC Rance, check Clay's pockets for a small key. Try his watch pocket first, it's perfect for a small key and the way Mr. Clay just now glared at me, I think we're on the right track - if you'll forgive the railroad pun."

Holmes was right; there was a small key in Clay's watch pocket. Holmes tried it and the suitcase opened to reveal a pile of money and checks, obviously thrown in hurriedly. Holmes riffled through the few clothes and the scattered money but then slammed down the suitcase lid and announced, "No quarto. Where is it Clay?"

Clay glared at Holmes; "Go to blazes Sherlock Holmes, I don't know anything about a Shakespeare piece." Holmes smiled and picked up the suitcase. Turning to Clay he said, "My, my, Mr. Clay; another slip. I never said it was a Shakespeare item."

As we filed out of the car, Clay resumed his belligerence; "Well, Holmes, if you're so bloody smart, you go find it yourself. You just inspected my suitcase with what result, no quarto eh.?" Rance stood Clay up and we headed for the car's door. We quickly got off the train and we could see the last-minute passengers scrambling to board. Holmes had ignored Clay's last outburst and spoke to Jones; "We didn't have time to search Mr. Clay on the train. Is there an office or some private place we can use for the purpose?" The inspector thought briefly and pointed to the ticket windows.

"There's bound to be offices behind the counters; I'll talk to one of the clerks."

Jones went to the nearest window, showed his identification and waved us over. "He is going to open the door to a scheduler's office. It's empty now so that should do." We followed Inspector Jones around the corner of the ticket counter area to a door about ten feet down a narrow hallway where the clerk was just opening a door. Holmes thanked the ticket agent and we entered a somewhat untidy room equipped with a table, two chairs and a desk lamp. Train scheduling charts and papers were scattered over every inch of the table. Holmes shoved aside enough to create a clear space, put down the suitcase and turned to constable Rance; "Please restrain our voluble friend here while I search him."

I expected Clay to resume his diatribe, but he just stood there with a nasty grin on his face while Holmes searched him quite thoroughly. After a minute or two, Holmes stood back, put his hands on his hips and shook his head, visibly disappointed. "Well," sneered Clay, "I guess the vaunted Sherlock Holmes wasn't so bloody smart after all. No quarto, Mr. Detective?"

I felt as let down as Holmes. "Do you think he may have hidden it in the hotel? I was so sure that you had lifted the dark cloud hanging over the case; but now it seems there is no silver lining to it." To my surprise, Holmes whirled around and smiled; "Thank you Doctor! In our haste to leave the train I totally neglected an important detail. I did not inspect the lining of the suitcase. I will remedy that now, thanks to your observation."

Hearing that, Clay, with a frantic effort, twisted away from Rance and dashed toward the door. The constable was having none of it however. Two big steps and he had Clay by the collar. Yanking him around, Rance actually lifted Clay by shirt collar, stuck his face close to Clay's and said, quite menacingly; "Try that again and I'll tie your feet together and carry you to the lockup!" Rance set Clay down and shoved him into one of the chairs. As Clay saw Holmes open the case, all the steam seemed to leave him and he slumped forward on the chair.

With Clay under control once more, Holmes turned his attention to the suitcase. He lifted out the rumpled clothes, tossed them on the desk and carefully stacked the bank notes and checks beside the case. He shook the case, turned it around and finally asked me; "Doctor, check this lining please. What's your observation about it?"

I felt the lining; it seemed out of place in the rather average looking suitcase. "Holmes, isn't this lining too plush to be in such an ordinary suitcase?"

"You've hit it right, Watson. My folding knife is at home. I left it there because it badly needs sharpening. Please loan me yours." I handed my knife to him and he started to run the blade around the edge of the lining but stopped, and with a satisfied grin, pulled out the lining completely and held the case so we could see the inside. "You see, gentlemen, the lining was not sewn in at all, but merely pushed down."

Nestled in the cut out section of what looked like a blanket that had been placed under the lining was a yellowed book, doubtless quite old. Holmes held the case out to me and with a big smile, said, "Do the honors, Doctor."

With somewhat trembling hands, I carefully took the book from its nest. There, in faded printing ink was 'A Wittie and Pleasant Comedie Called The Taming of the Shrew'.

"Holmes, this is it - what a treasure, to be sure." I turned the cover page and a small piece of paper fell out. Reading it, I turned to our little group; "Listen to this, 'only quarto of the taming of the shrew pub. 1631 stansby'."

Inspector Jones shook his head slowly; "Wonderful work Mr. Holmes. Constable Rance and I are proud to be of service. I apologize again for not telling you about our sullen captive's escape. I swear it will not happen another time."

Holmes and I replaced everything back in the suitcase and let the clerk know we were leaving so he could lock the door. As we emerged from the station to the cab pickup area we shook hands with Jones and Rance - who, I noticed, kept one big hand firmly clamped on Clay's shoulder. Holmes addressed the two 'yarders'; "Thank you for showing us the best of the Yard tonight, gentlemen. Inspector, when can I retrieve the case? I should do all I can to return the prizes to their rightful owners as soon as possible."

Jones gazed off into space for a minute and then said, "Holmes, I don't feel we need to keep the suitcase; we have so much on Mr. Clay, we really don't have to produce the case for trial. Our unhappy prisoner will receive more time for his escape, by far, than for this robbery. I doubt he'll be getting out for a very long time, if ever! Take the case and thrill Lady Portia and the two Italians!"

"Thank you Inspector. Come Watson, we must see if Lady Portia had the stamina to await our return. As for you, John Clay, you are not a merchant, you are a fraud and a criminal. Valentine and Proteus are honest, hardworking merchants. If you were really selling antiquities from Venice, I'm sure they would have been stolen!"

Inspector Jones and Constable Rance escorted Clay to their police cab and headed off to Scotland Yard - probably to a raucous welcome. We caught a cab and rattled off to the Windsor; doubtless to a deliriously happy Lady Portia and a noisy celebration from the Italians! Holmes put the suitcase on the floor of the cab and I gratefully rested my bad leg on it as I was beginning to feel the effects of our adventure and even a brief respite was welcome.

When we reached the hotel and exited our cab, the doorman rushed over and greeted us enthusiastically; "Did you get him? Did you get him? I heard about the thefts. Lady Portia is still here. Is the money in the suitcase? I'm sure that's the one the auctioneer had."

Holmes laughed and put out a restraining hand on the doorman's shoulder. "Please my good man, one thing at a time. Yes the money has been recovered, the thief is headed to Scotland Yard, and the Shakespeare prize is safely in the suitcase. Now where is her Ladyship?"

"I think she has established a sentry post in the lobby. You had better tell her while she's sitting down - she may faint!" He rushed over to the ornate door, opened it with a flourish and waved us in.

As we crossed the lobby on our way to the night manager's office, a loud, joyous shriek stopped us in our tracks. Lady Portia, who had indeed set up a sentry post, rushed over to us and threw her arms around Holmes. Her face was streaked with tears and smeared makeup, her once elegant gown rumpled. She was shedding makeup and tears of joy on his jacket. I had to turn away because the startled, surprised and embarrassed look on his face was so comical I was about to burst out laughing! I swear he even blushed!

Lady Portia, a foot shorter than Holmes, tilted her head back and in her usual non-stop way, said; "Oh Mr. Holmes is that his suitcase did you catch him? I was so worried I didn't know what to do did you get the money back?"

Holmes gently extricated himself from the excited lady's determined grasp and turned his head towards me and gave me a look that clearly meant "Don't you dare laugh!" Nodding his head at her he spoke calmly about our success in nabbing John Clay, alias Bernardino, the auctioneer. "Yes, dear Lady, we are bringing back not only the money from the auction but the Italians Shakespeare piece as well. I think it wise now to find Mr. Goodfellow and secure the recovered booty in the hotel safe - and do it without delay."

We didn't have to look for Goodfellow as he had heard the noise and came running toward us from his office. His face plainly shown with excitement and anticipation.

"You did it didn't you - I can tell from Lady Portia's face you got the money back. Did you catch the thief also?" Holmes smiled and assured the manager that we did indeed.

"England will the better when this dangerous and clever criminal returns to the iron bars and stone walls of his previous quarters. We now need your good offices to put away the money - and the quarto, in your safe."

We followed Goodfellow into his office and Holmes put the suitcase on the manager's desk and the safe was opened by the very relieved and happy manager. He brought out several boxes and Holmes unloaded the case. When all the money had been put away Holmes carefully placed the quarto in a box and Goodfellow added it to the stack in the safe and locked it. I think we all heaved a sigh of relief. Holmes shook hands with Mr. Goodfellow and gave Lady Portia's hand a gentle squeeze; "Watson and I will go now and tell the Italians the good news. It's been a harrowing experience for all us, but it's over now except for the anticipated loud celebration we will be soon receiving from our foreign visitors."

Lady Portia was not through however. She grabbed Holmes head, pulled it down and planted a big kiss on his cheek! With an astonished look, he said a quick "Thanks" to her, gathered himself and strode rapidly around the corner to the stairs. As we climbed, he gave me another "Don't say anything" look, as he could hear me try to stiffle a laugh.

I kept climbing the stairs, looking straight ahead all the way.

We arrived at the Italian's door and Holmes knocked. As we got no response, he knocked harder and soon a sleepy and dispirited Valentine opened the door. When he realized we were both exhibiting happy smiles his eyes opened wide. "You....you.."

"Yes", Holmes replied, "we got the quarto back and it's in the safe where it should have been before." Valentine never heard the last part as he dashed away calling loudly for his brother Proteus. Holmes glanced at me and made the understatement of the night; "Watson, I think they're quite pleased about this."

"Pleased" was hardly the word for the celebration that ensued. The brothers actually danced around the room, stopping repeatedly, hugging us and shaking our hands until Holmes wished them well and promised to provide a list of Shakespeare collectors in London so they could still sell their precious treasure and save their printing business.

As we started to leave, Valentine stopped us and, with a penetrating look at Holmes, said to his brother, "Proteus, bring the lamp closer, Mr. Holmes has been injured!"

I looked at Holmes and quickly announced, "No, it's nothing; I'm a doctor, I'll take care of it."

With that we left the still celebrating Italians and as we descended the stairs Holmes said, somewhat testily; "What the devil was that all about? I'm not injured."

Barely keeping a straight face, I said. "I didn't notice before in the dim light on these stairs but you have a red smear on your cheek thanks to the enthusiastic Lady Portia."

Holmes' look of perplexed annoyance was suddenly replaced with the same startled embarrassment as before and he quickly reached into his jacket pocket, pulled out the lotion bottle and the cloth he used to expose John Clay's disguise and vigorously scrubbed his cheek.

"Watson, let us depart swiftly - I've had enough thanks for one night."

As we hustled across the lobby we could see Lady Portia and Mr. Goodfellow in conversation. The manager saw us and Holmes put a finger to his lips. Goodfellow winked at us as we increased our escape speed toward the door. As we made it, we saw the doorman was already getting a cab for us. He turned and with a sweeping gesture, waved us through the big door and actually saluted us, which amused us no end. We didn't have long to wait for a cab as one was already stopping at the entrance. Holmes pulled out a coin and tossed it to the driver, a big man with a ruddy complexion, a shock of black hair and a long, curling moustache. To complete the picture, he was wearing an opera cape, fastened at the neck with a bright red cord.

We paused at this unexpected sight, glanced briefly at each other, and then climbed into the Hansom and settled into the seat. His voice, almost as big as he was, greeted us, "Buonasera Gentlemen; you are pleased to have the best driver in all of London at your service." Holmes and I exchanged smiles and Holmes called up to the driver, "And we are pleased to be in your cab. We would be very happy if you would take us to 221 Baker Street."

"Very soon you will be there." And with a great "Whoop" we were off and rattling towards home. None too soon for me as my gimpy leg was beginning to throb painfully.

I was about to ask Holmes several questions I had about the case when our voluble coachman suddenly broke out with:

"Jamme, jamme, 'ncoppa ja'
finiculi, finicula,
'ncoppa, jamme ja',
finiculi, finicula."

Holmes and looked over at me with a wide grin and I realized that no conversation was possible so we both simply sat back in our seats and for most of the drive home were treated to a medley of Italian folk songs interspersed with an operatic aria or two.

When our musical Hansom stopped at our door, Holmes took out another coin - a bigger one this time, tossed it to our enthusiastic vocalist, and said, "Thank you for a most entertaining ride!" He tipped his cap and announced, "I am at your command anytime. You ask for Georgio Bernardino and I drive for you."

As Georgio "Whooped" his horse and sped off, we stood absolutely speechless for a minute and then looked at each other and both burst out laughing.

"Well, Doctor, we now know there is at least one real Bernardino in London!"

As we were both tired from the day's excitement, I decided not to press Holmes about the case, but when we had settled down in our parlor, he brought it up himself. "Watson, I know you are curious about my actions today so I suggest we relax with a couple of fingers of our single malt with a spritz of soda and I'll explain how the events played out in my mind."

I reacted immediately, got the glasses and the gasogene while Holmes retrieved the Scotch from the liquor cabinet. Holmes got a pipe from the mantle, I found a pack of Bradley's cigarettes and we settled into our favorite chairs. Holmes began without preamble. "As you know, my first clue that there was more to this case than at first glance was Winter's cap. It did not fit Lestrade's theory of the theft and Winters's guilt. Next was the curious chase as the Italians ran after the thief. When the thief - whom we know now was John Clay - turned and gave his pursuers a good look at his face I thought there was something suspicious about it. Lestrade, and you, Doctor, wrote it off to seeing how close the Italians were behind him. I put that thought aside for the time being. Then the intense scrutiny of me by the so-called auctioneer was peculiar it seemed. I thought I recognized something familiar about him, but, as I had not been informed of Clay's escape, I dismissed the feeling. Then, after our supper I realized that, with a few minor cosmetic changes, the auctioneer resembled Mr. Winters. That's why I was in such a rush to return to the Windsor. Alas, we were not in time to thwart the plans of Clay, who certainly did remember me and acted with audaciousness and haste. His plans then changed when he saw I was not present. He saw an opportunity to escape with not only the quarto, but also the auction and dance money. Whe we heard of the events from Lady Portia followed by our inspection of Clay's room, my suspicions were confirmed."

"Holmes, you take my breath away. But how did you know he would take the train south instead of to Scotland as he had announced to the cabby?"

"Ah, there he slipped up. That loud call to the driver was meant to deceive us - at least that's what I deduced. I thought that since he would know certainly that his plan would be discovered, he knew he would be a target for law enforcement throughout the country quickly. What to do then? Take the next train to a south port city and pay a fisherman to take him to France when he could then disappear and be out of our reach.

"Of course, Holmes. I see your reasoning. But if you were wrong. . ."

"You just hit on my worst fear, Watson. If I thought wrong or if Clay deduced what I deduced and actually took a north train, we lost and the money and quarto were gone. I can't adequately describe how devastated I was beginning to feel as coach after coach failed to contain Clay as we inspected the south train!"

"It was greed, Holmes, greed did him in. If he hadn't tried to take all the money along with the quarto, he would have been long away when we returned to the hotel. Not to mention the prospect of beating Sherlock Holmes!" Holmes gave me a wry look.

"Yes my friend, I admit my self esteem would have suffered greatly, but fortunately he didn't pull it off. He came too close Watson, too damnably close however. He may be the cleverest and quickest crook I have come across yet. I think we had better retire to our respective bed chambers, Doctor. It's been a day I would not care to repeat."

I was in total agreement and was getting out of my chair when we heard the outer door close and steps on our stairs. We traded puzzled looks. Holmes opened our dooe and revealed a young messenger with an envelope in his outstretched hand. "Mr. Holmes? Here's a message from Mr. Goodfellow at the Windsor hotel, sir. He said to wait if there's a return message, sir."

Holmes opened the envelope, removed a small notepaper. "It says, 'After you left I talked - well actually, mostly listened, to Lady Portia. She wonders, seeing as how the auctioneer is no longer in the picture, if it would be all right if she added what would have been his cut to the money for the charity. Even though he offered to do the auction at half the usual rate, it would still add a nice bonus to the fund.' I see no problem with that, do you, Doctor?"

"I see no problem at all. Young man, please tell Mr. Goodfellow we think it's a splendid idea." After the messenger left, something popped up in my mind. "Holmes, didn't Clay offer to work for Jabez Wilson at half wage to get the job?" Holmes turned to me and pointed a finger. "Indeed he did. Excellent Watson, excellent!"

After I awoke the next morning, I donned my robe and went into the parlor. Holmes, as was usual for him, was reading the morning paper. "Come Doctor, have a cup of fresh coffee Billy just brought up, sit down and listen to this report in the paper." I complied readily and pulled up a chair to the table. "Listen to this interesting piece; 'Dangerous Spy Captured. Inspector G. Lestrade of Scotland Yard received a commendation from the head office of the Yard for his cleverness in apprehending a notorious international spy. Mr. Frederick Duke, caught with important papers of a military nature, was arrested in his hiding place by the actions of Inspector Lestrade who very astutely measured the house inside and out and found a discrepancy which led the Inspector to a secret chamber where the spy was.

"'This successful pursuit should serve notice to criminals everywhere that they have little chance against the astute Metropolitan Police inspectors.' Well Doctor, what do you think of that?" And with a rueful smile, folded the paper and tossed it onto the table.

I couldn't hold back; "Astute? Lestrade couldn't find a big fish in a little bucket! Well, Holmes, someday people will find out the real story." Holmes yawned and poured another cup of coffee.

"Oh well, old friend, look at the whole picture; two dangerous criminals were caught, the widows and orphan's fund will get more than expected, the sellers will get their money and two Italian gentlemen will return to Verona heroes. Watson, I call that a good week's work and all's well that ends well, eh, Doctor?"

"Amen to that Holmes, amen to that!"

END

THE SCOTTISH HEIRS

IT WAS SUNDAY, the ninth of September,1888. I had taken a quick walk to enjoy the first of the brisk fall weather because soon the leaves would begin to fall, winter would move in and the trees would stand as naked sentinels against the leaden sky. As I turned into Baker street and headed to 221, I saw Inspector Lestrade ahead of me just now knocking at the street door. I called out to him, "Lestrade, wait a moment and we'll go up together". The inspector glanced back at me and in a serious tone said, "Doctor Watson; I'm glad you're here. I need both your and Holmes' opinions on a very disturbing matter."

I opened the door and we started up the stairs. We hadn't quite made it to the top when the door to our rooms opened and Sherlock greeted us and waved us in.

"Well, well; it's a rare Sunday we see you, Inspector; to what do we owe the pleasure of your company?"

Holmes then saw the worried look on Lestrade's face and quickly moved a chair from our dining table for him. "Here Inspector, let me take your coat. Pray have a seat and tell us about your concerns. Would you like a drink? You look like you could use one."

Holmes handed me Lestrade's coat and I hung it on the coat rack along with my jacket. Lestrade actually slumped a little in the chair, the first time I ever saw him less than energetic and active. Sherlock poured small whiskies with a spritz of soda in each.

"Holmes, did you hear about the Bucks Row murder? It happened in Whitechapel nine days ago. She was a prostitute, name of Mary Nichols."

"I did, Inspector. Her throat was cut was it not?"

"Yes Holmes, it was in fact, slashed to the bone! Her skirt was pushed up to her waist but no other injuries were found at the autopsy. The two men who first saw her, carters on the way to work, thought she was either drunk or dead and went on. What they had not seen was the cut on her neck and the blood. No wonder they didn't notice any, because much had soaked into her clothes, and it was still just barely light.

"Very clearly outlined, Inspector. Now what can I do to help?"

Lestrade drained his drink in one swallow, leaned forward in his chair and announced,

"Mr. Holmes, there has been another murder! One so much worse it makes my skin crawl. I've seen a lot in my years on the force that I would rather not remember, but this one will haunt me for a long time. Mr. Holmes and Doctor Watson, her womb was cut out and the monster apparently took it with him and her intestines were pulled out and thrown over her shoulder!"

Even being an army doctor in a war had not prepared me for news of such an horrendous picture as Lestrade had just presented. Holmes sat bolt upright in his armchair, "When was this, Lestrade? I must examine the crime scene as soon as possible!"

Lestrade looked more downcast than ever. He shook his head sadly, stared at the carpet, and finally, looking at Holmes; "Holmes, I can't tell you how unhappy it makes me, but right now no one can examine the scene of this awful crime except inspector Abberline and the police doctor. I had to pull rank just to get past the constable on duty at the autopsy to verify what I had heard about the condition of the victim. Her name is Annie Chapman, another prostitute, murdered at 29 Hanbury street around five thirty Saturday morning.

Macnaughton and Warren and the Home Office have put a tight lid on this, Holmes. I have applied to be on the case but no word yet. Just one more thing, Holmes. I'm sure you have read about the big fuss over the paper printing that article about the "Leather Apron" found near Chapman's body. It turns out it had nothing to do with the murder but, as many Jewish slaughtermen wear leather aprons, it has created an anti-Jewish near riot. The inspector has been told that no more information is to be given to the press."

Holmes groaned, got up out of his chair and strode to the window. He stood there for a minute or so. "What a fiasco, Lestrade. The press can be a valuable resource if you just use it properly. I can understand their reluctance after this unfortunate mishandling though. Anything else, Lestrade?"

"Yes, I have heard that there is a nasty squabble going on between the Home Secretary, Warren and others in the command ranks. Anderson, the new C.I.D. chief, is, I hear, at his wits end over the low morale in the department due to these battles. I expect more shake-ups soon. It is of course, making it more difficult for me to get assigned to the case, but I'm still trying. Rest assured Holmes, if I get what I want, you will be given the chance to help."

"Thank you Lestrade, I understand your position, but can you get to me at least a list of the prime suspects – that is if there are any?! This last was said in a most ironic way.

"I am so sorry sir, I will do the best I can but I really don't think there is anyone except the mystery man called "Leather Apron". Even after the one found was proved to be not connected to the case, the story, as printed, has aroused tempers to a fever pitch. I don't know how much you know about Whitechapel sir, but I was posted there for a few weeks to help when several constables and two inspectors fell ill, and it's an experience I never want to repeat. Due mostly to lack of regular jobs, the place is full of the most destitute of people. Many are on the edge of starvation. So many women resort to prostitution that one constable told me that he counted more than 60 brothels in the small area of Whitechapel. Filth and decay are everywhere. Doctor, I once accompanied a House Inspector on his rounds and among the awful conditions we found was one room I'll never forget. Seven people lived in that one room and a dead child lay in one corner."

As I listened to Lestrade, I could hardly grasp the degradation these poor people lived with every day. "Disease must be rampant with conditions like you describe."

"Yes, doctor, in fact, many people have tuberculosis; Annie Chapman did, according to the autopsy doctor; an advanced case, which probably would have killed her in a year or so. The doctor told me that most of the prostitutes have it too; often along with other diseases."

Lestrade put his glass down and slowly got up to leave. I had never seen him so dispirited. I handed him his coat and he turned to Holmes, "I will do what I can, Holmes, but I can't promise anything with the conditions at the Yard the way they are."

Holmes put a hand on Lestrade's shoulder and escorted him to the door. "Understood. Thank you for doing everything you can. Please let me know if you hear anything else that might have a bearing on this terrible crime."

After Lestrade left, Holmes and I sat silent for some time trying to digest what the inspector had said. Finally, Sherlock got up and stood looking out the window as he often did. He then picked up a pipe, stoked it with fresh tobacco from the slipper and settled into his armchair. "Well, Watson, I fear things do not bode well for an outside detective in this horrific matter. I have practically nothing to go on. I feel the 'Leather Apron' fuss is a dead end and since I cannot examine anything connected to the case, I remain in the dark until Lestrade can get himself involved. If he indeed can, that is. I'm not bursting with optimism, as you probably have noticed!"

Just as I feared and, I think Holmes expected, no word came either on Monday or on Tuesday. By Wednesday, I was again fearing how this lull in activity might lead him back to the cocaine he had once conquered with the help of Dr. Freud. When I returned from billiards with my friend Thurston on Thursday late afternoon, the thirteenth, there was a letter addressed to me on the hall table by the stairs. I took it upstairs to our rooms and noticed that Holmes was pacing up and down the room with a small piece of notepaper in his hand. When he saw me enter, he walked to our dining table and tossed it down with evident disdain. "Read that, doctor!"

I picked up the paper which turned out to be a handwritten message. It said, with frustrating finality;

"Sorry Holmes, no chance for me to join Abberline
In investigation. Will send what information I can
squeeze out of other men involved. Not hopeful.

G. Lestrade"

I was quite irritated by that. I told Holmes I thought the officials were idiots. The best chance of catching this homicidal maniac and they don't ask for Sherlock Holmes! I also expressed the thought that jealousy played a part in this. The case could make a career for the man who solves it and they probably want to keep it in their tight little group.

"You may have a point Watson. By the way, I see some residents have formed 'The Mile End Vigilance Committee' so this case is becoming a 'cause celebre.' I hope it has some beneficial effect, but I have serious doubts. If the killer is as insane as I think, or at least has recurring spells of insanity, the watchful Committee may not deter him. The hope then is that they spot him in time to nab him before he makes his escape. Now doctor, I hope you have some news more pleasant than that from Lestrade."

Holmes pointed to the letter I had placed on the table while I read the disappointing note from the inspector. I picked it up and my mood brightened immediately. It was from my cousin Ainsley in Scotland. We stayed with him and his family for a few days a year or so a year ago. I opened it and read it out loud. "Dear Hamish," it began, but Holmes stopped me with a laugh and said, "Watson, your Scottish heritage is showing. I hope the letter is not in Scottish Gaelic!" I knew Holmes was having me on so I smiled and continued reading. "We miss you and your good friend Sherlock Holmes. I remember that he took to fly fishing so quickly we were amazed. I urge you to join us again. The fishing is excellent and we have two spare rooms now that the boys are both off at school. The weather is refreshingly brisk but it won't be long before the 'brisk' gives way to 'cold' so please consider spending a few days with us. Your favorite cousin, Ainsley Douglass."

Holmes got up from his armchair and began pacing with a most thoughtful look on his face. After some time, he stopped at his usual 'decision' spot, the window, turned to me and said, with determination, "Send Ainsley a message immediately, Doctor. Ask him to meet us at the nearest station – as I recall there is one not far from his house. Check your Bradshaw for the station and the train's arrival. Oh, and be packed and ready to depart Saturday morning!"

I almost leaped out of my chair I was so surprised and thrilled by his words. I couldn't have been more pleased. I asked why the sudden change. "Watson, as much I want this maniac to be stopped, it's obvious that I will get no help except what little Lestrade may pry out of the inspectors, which, I'm sure, will be of minimal importance in solving these murders. So, my dear doctor, please give me your cousin's address and I will let Lestrade know how to contact me with any little scraps of information he may come across. Meanwhile, we will take our leave of this frustrating situation and immerse ourselves in the clear, crisp air of Scotland and enjoy the gracious hospitality offered by your cousin."

I handed Holmes the envelope from Ainsley so he could get the address to Lestrade and happily hurried to my room and begin sorting through my wardrobe for the clothes I would need to take. After packing a suitcase I returned to our sitting room and got our Bradshaw from the desk we shared and wrote a response to Ainsley. I put on my jacket and called out to Holmes, who was in his bedroom packing, that I was going to post a note to Ainsley and pick up some cigarettes from Bradley's. I asked him if he wanted me to pick up a package of those floor sweepings he calls pipe tobacco to take with us. I could hear Sherlock chuckle. "No, I have enough of the evil leaves. Besides, I think I'll buy a new pipe while we're there and try a Scottish tobacco mixture. I think my clay pipe has about run its course."

I thought, thank goodness for that. I checked my Bradshaw. "If we catch the pre-dawn train we will arrive at Stirling, the nearest station to the Douglass home, by 4PM Saturday. I put that information in a note to Ainsley." Friday was spent finishing our packing, telling Mrs. Hudson our plans, scheduling a 3:30AM pickup with our local cab service and running a few errands. Holmes contacted Lestrade but the inspector had no news for us. To be honest, I was glad there was nothing from Lestrade. We had no vacation time away from London in over a year and I didn't want any scrap of tantalizing information to cause Holmes to call it off.

I had never finished Henry Murger's *"La Vie de Boheme"* so I packed that along with a slim volume for Holmes titled *"Fishing in Scotland"* which I bought at Hatchards Friday afternoon. Friday night, Mrs. Hudson promised she would pack a lunch for us and have hot porridge and coffee ready at three AM Saturday morning. We thanked her profusely, and I have no doubt that Holmes will put a little extra in with our next rent.

Even after turning in very early, 3 AM seems to come too soon, but we had everything ready to go and Mrs. Hudson was right on time with our porridge and coffee. At three-thirty our cab pulled up, the horse snorting in the chill morning air. We loaded our suitcases and lunch basket and got settled. Holmes tossed a coin to our driver and we clattered off.

The station was not very crowded at that early hour and we quickly got our tickets and, since we had only two suitcases and our lunch basket, we took it all to our compartment. Soon, the porter came by for our tickets and told us that we would have a fifteen-minute stop at nine and another at noon. With our breakfast of Mrs. Hudson's hearty porridge and the steady motion and click-click-click of our train we both found a comfortable position and dozed off. I awoke when we made our first, brief stop. I saw Holmes was awake and reading a newspaper he picked up from a stand before we got on the train. I must have gotten a wary expression on my face because Sherlock read it as he often did and said with a smile, "No, Watson, nothing in here that makes me want to jump off at the next stop and return to London."

We were now clear of Greater London and it seemed our train had picked up speed. Soon we made our nine o'clock stop and since we had our own food we had no need of the vendors at the station. I pulled out my book and read for a while and then dozed off again.

We made our noon stop and we got out and stretched our legs with a brisk walk. A few steps and I hurried back to our compartment and got my jacket for the balance of our walk.

We soon crossed the border to Scotland and then it was a mostly straight run to Stirling. We rocketed along at a great rate and I, finished with my book, dozed off again. When I awoke I saw Holmes put away *"Fishing in Scotland"* in his suitcase and tidy up some wrappings from our lunch. "Thank you for that informative guide, Watson, I shall endeavor to put some of its advice into practice. The trout may not appreciate your thoughtfulness, but I do. Put away your jacket and don your coat; we are almost at the Stirling station."

Stirling station is set in the Valley of Forth and when we stepped onto the platform from our train, the view of the valley and the distant hills was almost worth the trip, regardless of the fishing. This was 'Robert The Bruce' country, rich with Scottish history. But we didn't have much time to think about that because we heard a voice call "Hamish! Over here!" Ainsley was waving at us from the end of the platform. He was driving a four-wheel trap pulled by two fine looking stallions. He jumped down from the driver's seat to meet us as we brought our luggage over. Ainsley is strongly built, of medium height with light brown hair and a ruddy complexion. He greeted us warmly. A quick glance tells you he works the land.

"Welcome, welcome! I haven't seen you since a year or more. Put your things in the back and climb in. We have a ways to go and it'll darken in a bit so we better be goin.'"

We headed toward the hills beyond the station and after about half an hour, we turned off the paved road onto a country lane. Soon we crossed a bridge over a beautiful, clear stream where Ainsley stopped the trap and pointed down at the water, "They've been waitin' for you gentlemen! Tomorrow you can find out if they're hungry."

We soon pulled up in front of an old house that obviously had been mostly stone at one time but renovations had been made and much of the house was now of more modern construction. As we took our luggage out of the trap, Bonnie Douglass came rushing out and gave me and Sherlock big hugs. "Come in, come in and I'll show you your rooms; they're both upstairs. Ian and Conan will be sorry to have missed you. Unpack and freshen up and soon we'll have supper and you can tell us all about your latest adventures. Hamish has sent us fascinating letters about you, Mr. Holmes, and your exploits. Now follow me to your rooms and I'll go back and fix our food."

Our rooms were comfortable and each had a stone fireplace; a holdover from the original building. It was getting quite dark so

I lit a lantern on the bedside table and sorted out my clothes and toiletries. There was a bowl of fresh water in the old fashioned, but spotless, bathroom between our bedrooms. As I came out of the bathroom I was hit by a wonderful aroma drifting up from the kitchen. We had only a light lunch and I suddenly felt as though as I was starving. Holmes came out of his room, inhaled the delightful smell and said, "Watson, I'll be down in a moment. I wouldn't miss this meal even if Lestrade showed up at the door with an invitation from Sir Charles Warren himself!"

Our dinner of a lamb roast, potatoes and gravy, fresh baked biscuits and home grown vegetables was wonderful. Holmes looked at Bonnie and said, "My dear Mrs. Douglass, that was better than the finest restaurant in London could produce."

"Thank you so much Mr. Holmes; but it's Bonnie, please. Now you three boys retire to the sitting room while I clean up and make some fresh coffee and a few scones for dessert. I think Ainsley has some excellent Port that will complement everything quite well."

When we were through relaxing with our coffee and port, Ainsley got out the gear we would need in the morning; waders, creels, poles and an assortment of flies. He explained that you never know what the fish will fancy. "If they don't bite on one type of bug, switch to another," he said. After that we thanked Ainsley and Bonnie for the hospitality and went off to bed. As we were going up the stairs, Ainsley let us know he would be rousing us at 4:30. "Bonnie will have some porridge and kippers for you and then off you go. Bring back a couple of fat ones and we'll have stuffed trout or salmon for supper. Or maybe both!"

I was so comfortable after our marvelous dinner I think I fell asleep before I even thought about it. Four-thirty comes up quickly, but with such a good night's sleep, Holmes and I were ready to give the local fish a bad time. We all ate together and then Ainsley gave us our gear and went out to work his family farm and Holmes and I headed for the stream.

By the time we found a likely looking pool, dawn was just beginning to cast a pale light. We donned our waders, tied what we hoped was an enticing fly on our lines and waded into the chilly water. Holmes took little time to regain his form but I struggled for quite a while to get the proper wrist action to flip the bait out to just the right distance above the water to coax a fish to go after it. Just a bare flicker of a thought of London crossed my mind and I hoped no more than that came to Holmes. After a couple of hours and only two landed fish we moved on upstream to another pool where we had some good action right away. We fished for another two hours and then headed back. I asked Holmes if we perhaps caught too many fish. "No Watson, I think not. Did you not notice that small shed by the barn with the vent pipe? It must be a smokehouse. Some of our catch are sure to be headed there."

Bonnie greeted us and led us around to the back of the house where an old wooden table sat next to a big tub of water. She brushed some stray reddish-tan hairs out of her eyes, pushed the sleeves of her blouse up to her elbows and said to us "Now you just leave your gear inside the back door there. That's the mud room in winter but it's clean and dry now. I'll take care of these fish and then we'll have some lunch. Ainsley is out behind the barn feeding the sheep and Chloe, our cow."

We put our gear away as directed except for our fish knives and then returned to the table where Bonnie was going to work on our catch. We positioned ourselves on the far side of table and I reminded Bonnie that I was a doctor, and would help operate on the patients while Sherlock took care of the scales. We finished in good time and Bonnie put all but one large trout in a basket and, as Holmes had thought, headed for the shed with the vent pipe. Ainsley came around the corner of the barn and saw us washing our knives and hands and smiled at the bucket of entrails "Ah, good day at the stream I see! Nice work. We'll have a lot of smoked fish for winter and I have a bucket of fertilizer for the garden."

Bonnie had returned and went in to fix our lunches. Ainsley pointed out some of the features of the place. "I have a small greenhouse on the south side of the barn. We can grow some vegetables for harvest as late as November, so long as it doesn't cloud over too much. I buy a quarter pig so we have some bacon and ham and the chickens are in a wire-mesh fenced and covered yard back of the barn. Hawks like chicken as much as we do!"

Bonnie called us from the back door so we settled at the dining table. "Sliced lamb from the roast, bread baked fresh this morning, butter courtesy of Chloe and a few vegetables. I hope that satisfies." We both assured her that it more than satisfied. The rest of the day was spent in walking around the grounds and exploring the surrounding area a bit. That evening we had the best stuffed trout either one of us had ever eaten, After dinner Bonnie invited us to go with them to the local chapel for what she called "a very short service and then meet some local people."

Since we had no other plans, we cleaned up and dressed a little more presentably and went with them. The quaint little church was about 15 minutes away on a back road we had glimpsed on our walk but didn't follow. There were probably 30 people there and as Bonnie had said, it was a short service. I admit I didn't understand much of it, as the parson spoke with such a dense Scottish accent that I just followed what the others did. After the service there were some scones and tea served by church ladies, including Bonnie. Holmes and I were introduced to too many people to remember, but several had heard of Holmes through Ainsley and Bonnie. We then made our way home in the moonlight and after securing the horses in the barn, Ainsley joined us in a nightcap and we called it a day.

We hadn't planned any further fishing until Wednesday because Ainsley worked as a bookkeeper for a small manufacturing company in Stirling on Wednesdays and Fridays. However, our plans to spend a leisurely day with Ainsley and Bonnie went awry by ten in the morning when a firm knock at the door came and Bonnie announced, "Mr. Holmes, a friend of ours, inspector Boyd McDonald, would like to speak to you."

I was not pleased with this but I saw a brief smile cross Holmes's face. Bonnie brought the inspector in and he immediately greeted us warmly and shook our hands with a firm grip. "Mr. Holmes, what a treat this is to meet you; and you too, Doctor Watson. I have heard much about your remarkable exploits from the Douglasses. But, sir, I didn't come here just to meet you, although it is certainly a pleasure; no, I would like to solicit your opinion about an incident last evening that may have been an attempt at murder."

Ainsley showed his surprise by staring intently at the inspector and I thought Bonnie could not possibly have opened her blue eyes any wider. Holmes put down his coffee and gestured to McDonald, "Please, Inspector, take a seat and let me have the details."

"Thank you sir, here's what I know so far. Last night at Forth House, Elspeth McCallum, the heiress, who just returned from serving for several years in Africa for a ministry based in London, stepped out on the front porch for a bit of fresh air. The porch was very dark as something was wrong with the normal illumination. As she was standing there, she was suddenly grasped from behind and a hand clamped over her face. Before her attacker could do anything else, the cook came out of the door with a lantern. He was going to join her because the kitchen was quite stuffy and he knew she had gone out to get some air. As he turned the lantern her way, her assailant saw the light, let her go, jumped over the balustrade and ran off. The cook tried to follow but the man sped around the corner of the house and disappeared in the darkness. It was a moonless night,

Mr. Holmes, so it's no wonder he couldn't follow the man. Now here's why I thought you might be interested, Mr. Holmes; the cook swears he saw a knife in the man's hand flash in the light. As he let her go, he must have raked his hand over her face because she has a nasty abrasion on her nose and cheek. What he may have had in that offhand we can't tell for sure of course. We can think of no reason for someone to try to kill her. Mr. Holmes, will you accompany me to Forth House and talk to her?"

I knew what Holmes' answer would be before he said, "Of course, Inspector. There might be little to go on but I'll do my best to help. Watson, I trust you will go with us. The poor lady may need your medical expertise." I said I'd be happy to go but I had not brought my medical bag. Ainsley offered to let me take whatever I felt I might need from the house for medical supplies so I gathered up a few things and we followed Inspector McDonald to his hansom, the door adorned with a crest and "Stirling Constabulary" below. McDonald snapped the reins and off we went.

We soon arrived at Forth House, a place of more modern design than the Douglass home, but I noticed that the grounds were not very well tended and the gravel drive to the main steps had more ruts than proper maintenance would have allowed. The windows were dirty looking and the house had an air of neglect. Inspector McDonald saw my look of surprise at the conditions and offered, "The original owner, Angus McCallum, was a wealthy builder and shipping magnate. He built this about 90 years ago. He had a son, Alasdair but no daughters. Alasdair lived here after Angus died. Alasdair had a daughter and then, three years later, in 1860, a son. Unfortunately, Alasdair's wife died soon after. The daughter, Elspeth, went into ministry work and left for Africa eight years ago. The family heard very little from her because communications from Africa are sketchy at best. When Alasdair died, the effort was made to get in touch with her since she was the primary heir. The ministry she joined, Ministry of the Cross, based in London, said that they had heard she was going to return to England and Scotland and they would contact the estate when she arrived but she had set no date for her return. James McCallum, the youngest offspring, was then named temporary Regent of the estate until such time as Elspeth returns to claim the estate."

As we exited the Hansom, Holmes turned to the inspector, "It doesn't appear that James has done much to keep the place in good order, does it?"

"Mr. Holmes, that's not the half of it. I'll give you some more information after our visit but now we had better announce ourselves."

We mounted the steps and while the inspector knocked, Holmes went to each side of the large porch and peered over the balustrades into the flower beds flanking the porch. I knew he was looking for footprints of the assailant, but when he joined us at the door, he had a curious look on his face and gave me a brief, almost imperceptible shake of his head. "The ground isn't hard, but no prints, Watson." I didn't have time to quiz him as the large door was opened by a rather gaunt, stern faced woman probably in her fifties. She was not very hospitable.

"What do you want here? Who are you?" she asked, as if we had just ruined her day.

"I am Inspector Boyd McDonald with the Stirling District Constabulary. We are here to interview Elspeth McCallum."

Grudgingly, she stepped aside and we entered the reception hall-way that obviously had once been very elegant but was now dingy from lack of upkeep. The hallway led in to a spacious room which was apparently now used as a sitting room. The woman didn't bid us be seated; she simply said gruffly, "I'm Mrs. Grimesby; I'll get Elspeth," and turned on her heel and left.

While we waited, Holmes walked slowly around the room, stopping occasionally to give some object a closer look. There were several paintings on the walls and Sherlock looked closely at them during his tour of the room. We heard voices coming from the hall-way leading to the other parts of the house and in a moment the dour woman came in with a lady of medium height with a very tan complexion. There was a narrow bandage around her head and some gauze across her nose. The sour faced woman announced "This is Elspeth; Mr. McCallum will be here in a moment. He wishes to be present when you talk to her. He is very protective of her." She said this in a most commanding way; turned and left the room. Holmes went over to her and said quietly, "I know you've had a terrible ex-perience, please sit down and tell us about it. My name is Sherlock Holmes, this gentleman is Doctor Watson, and the other, the impos-ing fellow over there, is Inspector Boyd McDonald of the Stirling Constabulary. Are you up to recounting the events of last night?" She was about to reply when a smallish man entered the room from the main hall. He was probably about five foot six, lean, with a very dark reddish complexion. He was dressed in casual clothes with a silk scarf wrapped around his neck like someone who wants you to think he's and actor or an artist. A large, ornate ring looked out of place on his small left hand. He spoke in a reedy voice with an un-dertone of hoarseness,

"I am James McCallum, owner of this house; and who are you? Mrs. Grimesby said one of you is an inspector. Why are you bothering Elspeth?" McDonald responded immediately. "Yes, I am Inspector McDonald and these men are Sherlock Holmes and Doctor Watson. We are here to investigate the incident involving Miss McCallum late Sunday night. If it was an attempt on her life, I think that's cause enough for us to be here."

McDonald spoke with what could be called "official firmness" and the look on his face brooked no argument. "Doctor, will you please examine her injuries and give us your conclusions." I went over to the chair she was in, lifted the gauze covering and announced that I saw a crescent shaped abrasion on the right side of her nose and several scratches on the right cheek. The scratches were scabbed over but I detected some infection underneath. I said I would need to apply some antiseptic to them and also to her nose and will put a bandage on because the abrasion is fairly deep. I said I would check later to see if there is any infection there also. I hadn't examined her head injury so I removed the cloth wrap and asked her what had happened.

"I had just arrived in London and was on my way to check in at Ministry of the Cross, the people who run the hospital and church in The South African Republic. I was almost to their location, but when I stepped into the street to cross to the block they're on I was run over by a cab that must have gotten out of the driver's control. The next thing I knew I was in the office of a local doctor. He fixed me up and told me to keep the wound covered for a few days. He told me the wound looked like a part of a horse's hoof. After I rested for a bit, I went on to the ministry. They told me they had let James know of my arrival in London and that I would be at their office that day. He had not been by yet and they very kindly put me up in a nearby hotel because my head was pounding and I was very sore all over. They said they would tell James where I was when he arrived to pick me up the following day as I clearly needed rest. I cleaned up as best I could, Doctor, but I had so many scratches and bruises to tend to that I finally gave up and went to bed. When James came to take me home the next day I was so sore I could hardly make it to the cab."

Inspector McDonald had been listening attentively and now addressed James, "I'm taking her into protective custody until we decide the seriousness of this incident. Doctor Watson; that will also give you a chance to more closely examine and treat Miss McCallum. Mrs. Grimesby, please prepare an overnight bag for Elspeth."

Mrs. Grimesby gave the inspector a withering look but turned and stomped off down the hall. James followed her out of the room.

Holmes leaned over to Elspeth and asked in a quiet voice, "Where is James's study?" She looked quite surprised but answered, "Down the hall, second left Mr. Holmes." He then whispered to us, "If anyone should ask, I'm looking for the lieu d'aisance." He strode quickly down the hall and disappeared into the room Elspeth had indicated. Inspector McDonald was talking to her about taking her to a safe place so I took the opportunity to look around the room, especially at the portraits on the wall next to a large bookcase. There was one of a man who looked to be around fifty years old, in clothes that were probably turn-of-the-century style. Inspector McDonald saw me looking at the painting and said, "I think that's Angus McCallum himself and the one next to Angus is young Alasdair I'm sure."

I heard footsteps coming swiftly down the hall. It was Holmes returning from his foray into McCallum's study. "An interesting tid-bit, doctor. Looking at the paintings? The two portraits are by a John Hunter; also the one of Elspeth and James on the far wall."

Mrs. Grimesby came in with a small traveling bag, dumped it unceremoniously at Inspector McDonald's feet. He picked it up and we made our exit and piled into Inspector McDonald's hansom. He turned to Holmes and asked, "Mr. Holmes, do you think I did right to remove Miss McCallum from the house for her own protection?"

"Absolutely, Inspector. Please take us all to the Douglass home; I'm sure Elspeth will be safe there while we work on this problem."

When we pulled up in front, I went quickly to the door while Holmes was helping Elspeth out of the cab. Bonnie had already opened the door. She probably had heard our approach and I knew she was anxious for news of our investigation. I explained briefly why we brought a passenger with us. She was her usual hospitable self and actually went out, took Elspeth by the hand, and escorted her into the house. Ainsley had come in by that time and he and McDonald took the police cab around to the animals' water trough.

When we all were together in the sitting room, the inspector recounted our experiences for Ainsley and Bonnie. Holmes asked for some note paper and a pen. "I'm going to write out some questions that can be answered only in London. Inspector, I assume you can contact Scotland Yard faster and with less curious eyes on the message than we can. I have some work for Inspector Lestrade to do for us that should clear up a few points for our investigation. If he is not involved in a case I'm sure he will respond to our request. It will probably take him all day tomorrow to answer. Ainsley works Wednesdays in Stirling so Watson and I will ride in with him and call on you. Does that sound acceptable?"

"Absolutely, Mr. Holmes; I'll send it off as soon as I return to the station."

Ainsley and the inspector went out back to hitch up McDonald's horse while Holmes was writing his message to Lestrade. I asked Bonnie if it would all right if Elspeth stayed overnight as we were concerned for her safety. "Why of course, Hamish, this house has a maid's quarters which we never use. There's a single bed, a stand and a small dresser. I know she'll be comfortable."

I had Elspeth lean back in her chair while I removed the field dressing I had hastily applied, but before I could clean her wounds, Holmes stepped over to the chair. "Let me take a quick look, doctor, before you re-bandage." I moved out of the way so Holmes could see. "Yes, a crescent shaped wound. About an inch outside dimension and perhaps three quarters inside. It wasn't a sharp edge or it would have cut much deeper. Thank you Watson. Don't worry Elspeth, Doctor Watson will take good care of you. Your head wound doesn't look too bad. You were extremely lucky; one inch lower and you could have been killed."

When I finished, Elspeth thanked me and then turned to Sherlock, who was just completing has message, "Mr. Holmes, so you really think all this is necessary? In your opinion, am I in actual danger?"

"I am convinced that the flash the cook saw was indeed a knife. Why someone would want to kill you is the key to this affair. It is what I am working on now. By the way, I do not think it was some deranged person. I think it was someone who knew exactly what he was doing."

Inspector McDonald and Ainsley had come in from taking care of the horse and Holmes handed the message for Lestrade to McDonald. "I have suggested other inspectors to Lestrade in case he is too busy."

"I will dispatch it as soon as I get to the station. Ainsley very kindly fed and watered my horse, so I'll be on my way. Miss McCallum, you're safe here, but no one else is to know where you are."

After Inspector McDonald left, Bonnie took Elspeth and her bag to her new room. As soon as they left the sitting room, Ainsley addressed both of us; "Gentlemen, it's rumored that James McCallum is not only a drunkard, but he may have gone through a sizable inheritance without regard to his sister, the primary heir. We know he closed up the house, let the staff go and hired a management firm to watch the place. Then he went off to London to, as he mentioned to a neighbor,'live the high life'. That was over a year ago and we heard nothing about him except a few ugly rumors concerning his excesses. Remember, Elspeth was still in Africa and James was granted regent status in Elspeth's absence so he could 'maintain the estate'. I'm sure you saw how well he did at that, doctor!"

I said that I was not surprised about the drinking because of his deep red complexion with obvious broken veins. I also expressed the thought that he must have been a heavy drinker even before his escapades in London. Holmes glanced over at me and gave me a little smile. "As Watson knows, I came across a couple of interesting facts during our visit to Forth House. James McCallum's finances are at low water. He also has a bill from the Albemarle Club – it's marked 'Urgent.' I rather imagine it's for overdue fees. It's fitting that it's from them; the most Bohemian club in London!" With that, we had a quick supper, said our "goodnights" and went to bed.

The next day, Tuesday, Holmes and I got in some more fishing as there was nothing more we could do except to keep Elspeth safe and wait for word from Lestrade. We helped clean the fish and were pleased that Elspeth, looking more alert and cheerful than the day before, joined in. The rest of the day passed quietly. Sherlock and I helped Ainsley with some farm chores and Elspeth helped Bonnie with cleaning and kitchen work. When we sat down for supper Bonnie and Elspeth brought out two platters, one with a grilled trout and the other with a salmon covered with a superb herb sauce. Elspeth told us proudly, "Bonnie told me how to make the sauce – I even picked and chopped the herbs from her garden!' Holmes smiled and said, "I'm glad to hear that, I meant to ask you before; what staff does James have? We have had the distinct displeasure of meeting Mrs. Grimesby and we know there's a cook, but are there any others?"

"No sir, just the four of us, although there is a gardener who comes occasionally. I don't think James pays him much because he isn't there very long when he does come. I am trying to take a bigger part in running things but James says I should go easy until my head and face heal." Holmes said firmly, "The sooner you can take over the inheritance the better! You apparently are not aware of just how carelessly James was spending the estate money while you were in Africa. He closed the house, let the staff go and installed himself in the most Bohemian club in London and proceeded to, as he remarked to a neighbor, 'live the high life'. I think as Watson said, he must have been a heavy drinker before, but probably hid it from his father, Alasdair. Without any restraints, he could indulge in any of the unsavory pursuits London has to offer. I'm afraid he may have gone through a lot of your money." Elspeth looked shocked but determined. "Then I shall redouble my efforts. I wasn't aware of my brother's escapades. I will schedule a financial audit from our banker right away."

We finished our dinner and since Holmes and I were traveling with Ainsley in the morning, we retired early. Bonnie and Elspeth had breakfast ready and we were on our way before the sun rose. The weather was still clear but fall was sending chilly harbingers of its arrival. When we arrived in Stirling, Ainsley drove the trap about a block past his work to the stables. "I leave the trap here and the stableman feeds my horse and stores the trap until I'm through working. I'll drop you at Inspector McDonald's station first. Mr. Holmes, I can leave at two o'clock if you need me to."

"If Lestrade finds what I suspect he will, it would be of great use if you can be ready by two. I expect we will all need to get together later today for what I think the American Indians call a 'Pow-Wow'."

Ainsley drove off to work and Holmes and I entered the Stirling police station where Inspector McDonald was headquartered. When we asked the duty officer for the inspector, he nodded and told us he had been informed we would be calling. "I'll fetch him for you gentlemen."

Holmes looked around the entry room; "Clean and neat Watson, if a bit stark. Ah!, look at that portrait on the far wall, Hamish." Holmes said it with a smile. I went over, knowing who it was.

Under the portrait was a small bronze plate, engraved in medieval Gaelic, "Roibert a Briuis;1274 -1329". I didn't have time to look at the portrait of the 'King of Scots' for long, as Inspector McDonald came out of the main office to greet us. He was holding a piece of paper in his hand.

"Mr Holmes, I have a brief note from Lestrade. He promises a full report later today. Do you wish to wait here?"

"Thank you, Inspector, but I think Watson and I will take a walking visit around this bustling city and be back later. If things develop as I think, we will need your good offices to form a plan to snare this villain."

As we left I turned back to McDonald and asked him where we could find a good tobacconist. Holmes muttered, "Floor sweepings indeed; humbug!" but I noticed he said it with a smile. As we strolled along the busy streets I simply walked along, enjoying the sights and feel of the place while Sherlock, as usual, noted every shop, and every street and its cross street. I have no doubt that if we ever again find ourselves in Stirling, Holmes will know exactly where "McDuff' – Greengrocer" and "The Book Nook" are. After several hours, we felt as if lunch was called for and we stopped at a small restaurant for a light lunch, after which we continued our walk. Soon we turned into the street that leads back to Inspector McDonald's station. Two blocks down toward the station we saw a window full of paintings. Holmes said, "I'm curious about the man who painted those portraits at Forth House. Let's go in and ask about Mr. Hunter."

Inside were many paintings arrayed around the room and on all the walls, but few portraits. The proprietor, a Mister Darrow, asked if he could help. Holmes asked about John Hunter and Darrow said, "Oh, you mean John Kelso Hunter, sir? He was a painter who did portraits in addition to other works. I believe the McCallums sat for family portraits. Hunter was related to the McCallums of Troon so possibly there is a family connection. He is represented with four works in the Royal Scottish Academy, sir. He died in 1873, I believe. Are you looking for a Hunter, sir?"

"No, not at present thank you; just getting some information." I reminded Holmes that we were on the street that Inspector McDonald said the tobacconist was located. Sherlock gave me a wry smile. "You aren't going to forget, are you doctor?"

In fact, the next block brought us to "Abbot Macnab; tobacconist". We entered and a marvelous aroma filled our nostrils; raw tobacco of many lands all waiting for the expert to mix the almost endless variety of smokes. A smallish man of about fifty greeted us.

"My friend Doctor Watson claims I need to improve on my

choice of tobacco and perhaps invest in a new pipe. I brought a small sample of my present blend. What do you think?" Holmes handed Mr. Macnab a little package of his tobacco and the tobacconist, after opening it and sniffing it, put it quickly down on the counter. "Kind of harsh, isn't it sir? I hope you're not a heavy smoker of this . . . uh, stuff." With an immense effort, I contained my laughter but I couldn't help a snicker or two escaping.

"I'd like you to try 'Macnab number 3' sir, Latakia, Turkish, a bit of Deer's Tongue leaves for aroma, all in a medium base. It's my best selling blend sir." Holmes glanced at me with an "All right, you win" look and said he'd try a half ounce. Mr. Macnab put some of his mix on a scale, weighed out half an ounce and put it in a folding pouch.

"Anything else, sir?" I didn't wait for Holmes; I pointed to a rack of pipes on the side wall.

"I have just the thing. It's a gourd fitted with a meerschaum bowl and an amber tip. I tell you honestly sir, it's the coolest, driest, most comfortable smoke there is. My customers have switched to this pipe and thrown their old clay pipes away! It's called a Calabash." Holmes glanced at us both, "All right, it's two against one. I'll take a pipe."

After that little victory, I felt the day was going quite well and even though my leg was beginning to hurt due to all the walking we had done, I was in high spirits. Now, if only Holmes could solve the problem of the Forth House, it would make this vacation a great success.

We soon arrived at Inspector McDonald's station. It was near two, so we were close to ending our day in Stirling. As soon as we opened the outer door, the duty constable recognized us and went in back to let McDonald know we were there. After a minute or two, the inspector came out waving a message form.

"Mr. Holmes, I just got the report you were expecting from Inspector Lestrade. I hope you don't mind, but I read it; he got all the information you had asked for sir." Holmes took the message, read it carefully, folded it and handed it to me. "Well, I think that settles it. Inspector, can you leave now? We need to go to Ainsley's work and tell him to meet us at his place as soon as he can. Tonight we may be able to create a fitting end to this affair." McDonald got his jacket from the coat stand and said to Holmes, "You mean you think we can solve it?"

"Inspector, it's already solved; now what we have to do is prove it." We waited outside while McDonald got a police cab. We piled in and headed for Ainsley's work, just adjacent to the large Almond Iron Works area. When we arrived, Ainsley was already waiting for us in his trap. After a shout from Holmes, we both rattled off to the Douglass home.

Bonnie was surprised to see us, since we were an hour earlier than Ainsley usually got home from work. Inspector McDonald and Ainsley drove their vehicles around the back to tend to the horses and Holmes and I went into the house. Holmes put a hand on Bonnie's shoulder;

"We need to have a strategy meeting, Bonnie. Where is Elspeth?"

"She's out in the yard picking herbs for dinner and checking for any late eggs. How does a roast chicken and Scotch Woodcock with herbs sound Mr. Holmes?"

"My mouth is watering just from hearing about it. As soon as Ainsley, Inspector McDonald and Elspeth come in we should gather in the sitting room and I'll explain what conclusion I have reached about this case and how I arrived at it."

"You and Hamish go ahead and I'll bring everyone in."

We went to the sitting room and Holmes arranged the chairs in a semicircle and put his facing it. It wasn't long until Bonnie gathered everyone and brought them into the room. As soon as we were all settled, Holmes began without preamble; "The first clue I had was the condition of the flower beds at the side of the porch. The man who attacked Elspeth jumped over the balustrade to escape and so must have left footprints. When I looked at the beds the next day however, there were no prints and the ground looked like it had been smoothed over. Who did that and why? That is why I asked you, Elspeth, about any staff, and learned that the gardener was not on staff but came only occasionally. So, if not him, who else? The cook I knew was out because he was the one who came out with the light and very likely saved your life! That suggested to me that the assailant had unusual footprints; either a telltale pattern or very large or very small feet and didn't want them seen. We then met with you Elspeth, and James McCallum. I withheld judgment until I heard about the exploits of how your brother handled your estate in your absence. Then I was quite sure why you were attacked and I also concluded that he was going to murder you and let the police think that a homicidal maniac was on the loose; he probably thought that the recent Whitechapel killings would influence the investigation."

Bonnie's face went pale and Elspeth murmured "My God!"

"I took advantage of the absence of James and Mrs. Grimesby to sneak a peek into James' study where I discovered his checkbook care-lessly open on the desk and also a notice from the club he joined in London, and yes, Inspector, that was probably illegal! Anyway, I found he was at low water financially; I also wondered as an afterthought, how did the man even see Elspeth in the dark? The porch was not il-luminated – by the way, Inspector, I would take a good look at that; I think the lack of light was not accidental. I then found out that James hired the help in London. Why not hire local people? Not a critical point but a bit strange. Lastly, why had the man run around toward the back of the house? A short sprint to the road and he would be impossible to find. More suspicion that James was the man."

"Now to the message from Inspector Lestrade of Scotland Yard in which he did some research in response to some requests I made.

First, I wanted to know if there were any eyewitnesses when Elspeth was run down by what was assumed to be an out-of-control cab. Lestrade says there was no one he could find, but when the people at the Ministry rushed out to see what the excitement was all about, they were told by several people that the driver was a small man wearing a black coat with a large hat with the brim turned down. He kept going after hitting Elspeth and wheeled around the corner and sped off, whipping up the horse as he went."

"Oh my gracious Mr. Holmes, do you think he ran over me on purpose?"

"Elspeth, I do indeed think it was a premeditated act. Inspector Lestrade couldn't find any stables nearby that rented a cab but he didn't have the time to check every one. He was told by the Ministry people that James had called on them the previous day and they told him that Elspeth was due to stop by to see them 'around noon' the next day. I think James rented a cab and waited for you to show up and then tried to run you down. In checking with the manager at the Albemarle Club, Lestrade found that McCallum had rung up a huge bill two months past and then abruptly left without, of course, paying it. Lestrade also discovered that Mrs. Grimesby and the cook, Arthur Burns, list themselves together at several placement agencies. Lestrade says that he found nothing substantial, but their pasts seem to be 'murky'; his word.

"Why James would want Elspeth dead is obvious: he can't run the house, the money is almost gone and he can't sell it now that Elspeth is here. With her out of the way he would be able to sell the house for a good price. It's a fine house, although neglected for several months and then he could continue his drunken, downward spiral. Oh, yes, and by the way, you can thank James for that damage to your nose. That big ring of his must have caught your nose when he ripped his hand away from your face as he made his escape. I would bet anything that the dimensions of your injury exactly match those of the ring. Now to sum up; as Inspector McCallum will tell us, we have nothing but circumstantial evidence so far and it is unlikely we will find anything more damning."

Elspeth sank back into her chair with despair. "Oh, Mr. Holmes, then we can do nothing to find justice?"

"I have a plan, but it's a risk and you are the key. It might be too dangerous for you but I can't think of anything else that will lead to James's undoing."

"I can't continue to live in fear Mr. Holmes. I'm willing to do whatever is necessary to expose James as the villain that he apparently is. Please, Mr. Holmes, what is your plan?"

Holmes explained what he had worked out. We all sat silent for some time; then, as if on cue, everyone started talking at once:

Bonnie: "It puts poor Elspeth in too much danger."

Ainsley: "I agree the danger is very real, but I don't see any other way to get him."

McDonald: "Ainsley's right; it may be the only way, and Elspeth said she wants to do it."

Elspeth: "No more talk about whether or no. I'm determined to go with the plan so let's get on with it!" Holmes looked at Elspeth and said, with great respect in his voice, "You are a brave woman Elspeth; now here's what we need to do……."

Bonnie fixed us a light supper while Inspector McDonald and Ainsley went out to get the horses fed and watered and Holmes rehearsed Elspeth in her part for the coming drama. I prepared a slide-equipped bullseye lantern so we could remain in the dark until we needed the illumination. Elspeth would have a lantern but we would have been remiss if not providing a second source. Ainsley and the inspector came in and we sat down and had supper. As soon as we finished, Holmes had a few words for Elspeth while Inspector McDonald fetched his police cab from the barn.

" Stay with the cook and Mrs. Grimesby until they are ready to retire. Light the lantern and give that little speech we rehearsed to James and hurry out to the barn. Don't worry if he reacts more swiftly then we anticipated; Ainsley will be in the shadows near the back door with his trusty Penang Lawyer! I do think James, if my assumption of his guilt is correct, will wait until you are in the barn to try anything. I hear the police cab, so stay calm."

"I will do my best. Thank you all for your wonderful support."

After Elspeth and the inspector left for Forth House, Ainsley and I nervously paced around the sitting room but Holmes, who contained his emotions well, sat in a comfortable chair, got out his new pipe, stoked it with Abbot Macnab Number 3, lit it, and began puffing away. The smoke had a pleasing aroma and I actually think it helped us relax a little.

"We must leave by seven, gentlemen," Holmes announced. I got my heavy coat ready and we had a cup of fresh coffee Bonnie brought to us. She looked more nervous than we were!

Even though Ainsley's trap had good lanterns and the crescent moon gave us some light, it was still a tense ride to Forth House. As we approached, we saw a lantern ahead by the roadside. It was McDonald who had just left the house and was tethering his horse to a tree. We pulled up and got out of the trap as quietly as possible. Ainsley also tied his horses to the tree. He whispered to us, "They have been fed and watered so I'm sure they'll be quiet. As it's late, they will probably go to sleep. Anyway, I think we are far enough from the house that no one will hear."

We extinguished all the lanterns and made our way to the entrance to the grounds. Thanks to the neglected condition the place was in, the gates were never closed. I was glad of that as I wouldn't have relished a climb over the old stone wall that surrounded the property. As quietly as possible, we walked to the back of the house. Ainsley hid in the shadows where he could watch the door and Holmes, Inspector McDonald and I went on to the barn. We opened the barn door just enough so we could get through with the least noise. Holmes lit one of the lanterns and led us to the back of the barn where there was a work table. Setting the lantern down he located two places among the feed sacks, straw bales and equipment where we were close enough to prevent any harm to Elspeth but out of the light so we could not be seen.

"This will do. When Elspeth comes in I will pull the slide over the lantern lens so it will be instantly available if needed. It's almost eight so be ready; Elspeth will be here soon."

I was thinking that our walk through the grounds was a lot less stressful than the one we had to make at Stoke Moran. Thank goodness James didn't keep wild animals! Now we had to wait, hoping that we hadn't put Elspeth in a desperate situation we couldn't control. I could smell the oil smoke from Holmes' lantern but since Elspeth would have one, the smell wouldn't give us away. The darkness seemed stifling, no sound but an occasional snort and scuffling from the McCallum horse in the only occupied stall. Waiting tensely in the pitch black, it seems time has stopped and you begin to think everyone can hear your breathing. Finally, we heard the barn door open wider and then, a lantern light and Elspeth came in. I could hear Holmes beside me breathe a deep sigh of relief. He whispered to me, "Now doctor, the game is well and truly afoot!"

Holmes briefly flashed his lantern so Elspeth would know we were here and ready. She walked to the table, put her lantern down and whispered, "Mr. Holmes, I did what you asked. I gave the little speech I rehearsed and James looked at me with pure hatred in his eyes."

The waiting now seemed almost too tense to bear but we didn't have long to agonize about it. Only a few minutes after Elspeth came in we saw a figure at the barn door silhouetted in the pale moonlight. Closer and closer it came until we could see, in the lantern light, James McCallum in a large black coat. He stopped and just stood there glaring at Elspeth.

Holmes tapped me on the shoulder and quietly handed me the bullseye lantern. No doubt he thought his help may be needed at any time now. Then, in a vicious tone, James spoke to Elspeth.

"So! You think you can get the best of me, do you. I will sell the house and go back to London and you will not stop me! You were lucky to escape in London and on the porch the other night, but you can't escape now." Elspeth spoke up bravely, "It was you then who tried to kill me, wasn't it? My own brother! Do you really think you won't get caught if you kill me here? You are the obvious murderer."

"Do you think I don't know that? I will find another woman after I kill you and kill her too. They will think there's another madman here like Whitechapel. I will rip both of you to pieces!"

James then threw off his coat and pulled a fish-gutting knife out of his belt but before he could do anything else both Holmes and McDonald stepped into the light. James froze for an instant when he saw the men but then whirled and slashed at the lantern on the table, knocking it over and extinguishing the light. I opened the slide on the bullseye Holmes gave me. The beam fell on James, running down the aisle toward the door. Suddenly he stopped. Ainsley had appeared in the doorway. James then dashed to the stall where the horse was, opened the gate and rushed in. Holmes and McDonald were getting close and Ainsley shouted, "He's going for the horse!"

We were about to race to the stall when we heard the horse snorting and stomping around and then a horrible scream. Elspeth was putting out a small fire the smashed lantern had caused and I rushed to the stall with the light. In the beam of the lantern was

James, on his back in the corner of the stall; the side of his head terribly broken in. The horse must have panicked and kicked him when he rushed into the stall in the dark.

"Well, Doctor?" Inspector McDonald asked me. I gave the lantern to Holmes and bent to examine the injury. "The skull is smashed; he's dead." Elspeth had put the fire out and joined us in the stall. She went to the horse, who was still snorting and bobbing and shaking his head, and managed to calm it down. We picked up the body and carried it out of the stall and secured the stall gate.

"My own brother, Mr. Holmes! How could these awful things have happened?"

"Alcohol, jealousy, and a weak personality. Something snapped in his brain. It's a family tragedy, but the best of the family survived and justice, in the form of a horse, prevailed."

We made sure the fire was out, secured the barn door and carried the body of James into the house. Elspeth roused the cook and Mrs. Grimesby and Inspector McDonald explained what happened.

"The medical examiner and two constables will be here in the morning to pick up the body. No need to get them here tonight as Doctor Watson has pronounced him dead and we all are witnesses. Please get a sheet or blanket and cover the corpse."

A sheet was brought in by Mrs. Grimesby and the body of James McCallum was duly covered. We were ready to leave when Elspeth, still a little shaky from the events of the night asked Ainsley, "Do you think it would be acceptable if I stayed another night at your house? I really don't think I can face sleeping here tonight after all that's happened."

"Don't even think about staying here tonight, Bonnie and I would be pleased to have you at our home."

We made sure the house was locked up and set out for the trap and McDonald's police cab. Holmes took the bullseye and lighted our way out the rutted drive and down the road. As Ainsley had predicted, all three horses were asleep. They awoke when they heard us approach and whinnied and snorted their greetings. We said goodnight to Inspector McDonald and it was a tired but happy foursome who arrived at the Douglass home. In her relief that we made it home safely, Bonnie was in tears, hugging us all but especially Elspeth. "You mean that speech Mr. Holmes gave you worked? Telling him that you had an appointment with your banker made him come after you?"

"It did indeed, Bonnie. It tipped scales, as they say. As much confidence I had in the men, I have to admit I was quaking in my shoes when James pulled out that horrible knife!"

Bonnie had us sit at the kitchen table and brought us sliced meat, bread and butter, and fresh coffee. Elspeth could manage only a bite or two and a cup of coffee but Ainsley, Holmes and I dug in with enthusiasm. Bonnie took Elspeth to her room and returned to clean up in the kitchen. Elspeth had offered to help but Bonnie wouldn't have it. We sat for a little while and Holmes, with a wry glance at me, got out his calabash and smoked some Macnab Number 3 for a bit. After we related the whole night to Bonnie, we all went to bed.

James McCallum was buried in the far corner of the family plot; Elspeth learned everything about the financial condition of the estate; and Sherlock and I stayed another week, fishing and touring the famous "Land of Robert the Bruce." Elspeth sent us a note saying that the headstone for James reads in part, "Death by misadventure." I remarked to Holmes that it seemed to me to be much too euphemistic but Holmes pointed out, "Perhaps; but it was her brother, after all."

We returned to Baker street on the 28th of September and found a note from Lestrade.

"I know you are on the way back so I won't send this to Inspector McDonald. Holmes, I have more information for you. Let me know when I can see you. G.L."

Holmes went out immediately and dispatched a message to Lestrade telling him to come at his earliest convenience. We didn't expect he would be around until the next day, but just before our supper time we heard footsteps on the stairs and Holmes opened the door, "Why, Lestrade; we didn't think you would be visiting us until Saturday. Please come in and tell us the latest in this Whitechapel business."

Lestrade came in, took off his coat, and took a seat facing us. "I have little in the way of anything but suspects Holmes. I have made a list of who Abberline feels are the prime suspects with what information about them I've been able to dig up."

"I thank you for that Lestrade. Let us see what the official thoughts are." Holmes took the list Lestrade handed him and studied it carefully, pausing occasionally to mutter something to himself. Finally, he put the paper down on our dining table and addressed the inspector. "I think two or three of these are the result of grasping at straws but there are a few that certainly grab one's attention. Druitt is of special interest, as is Thomas Cutbush, Aaron Kosminski, and the 'unnamed lodger'. Unfortunately, everything is suspicion and circumstantial. Watson and I had an experience just recently of that, and it took a dangerous stratagem to expose the villain. Anything else, Inspector?"

"Yes, Holmes, there is. I have a friend in the news business – I can't divulge his name you understand – who tells me that they received a letter that may be from the killer. They will make it public soon. Holmes, it is signed 'Jack the Ripper'! It also makes a promise to do a certain thing to the next victim. He couldn't tell me what the threat is because if it happens the way the letter writer says, it may mean the letter is from the real killer and that's important. As you can guess, the police and the papers have received many letters and postcards, almost all of them have been dubbed 'crank' by the inspectors. This letter may be the only genuine one."

"Well, Inspector, if it does prove out, the world will forever have a new name to add to the list of infamous monsters. Thank you, Inspector, for keeping me as close as I probably will ever get to this case."

Lestrade got his coat and was leaving when he turned to us and asked us to keep the source of the information he passes on to Holmes confidential. "I could lose my position if the chiefs knew. Doctor, please don't write about this until I retire."

We didn't have long to wait for the next visit from Lestrade. We had just finished breakfast Monday, the first of October, when the inspector once again knocked at our door. Even before he was completely in the room he blurted out, "Two more sir, two more horrible murders!" Holmes put down his morning paper and moved a chair out for Lestrade. The inspector was obviously very agitated and Holmes did his best to calm him down. I got a cup and poured him some coffee while Holmes took the inspector's coat and hung it on the rack.

"Now, please, Lestrade, tell us what happened."

"The letter I told you about – he did it, he did what he said he would do! He said he would 'clip the lady's ears off and send to the police officers', and one of his victims had an ear mutilated. I hear that the inspector thinks that after the first woman was killed, he was interrupted somehow and couldn't finish his gruesome work and hurried away to find another victim. And, Holmes, he found one; killed her and cut her up like a wretched animal in a slaughterhouse!"

Lestrade shook his head sadly, "And they still won't bring you in on it, Holmes. They put out a notice dated yesterday asking for the public's help. It was suggested they use bloodhounds but even that was a fiasco. They sent a note to Sir Charles Warren, who was negotiating with the owner of two bloodhounds to have them brought in, but they didn't know that Sir Charles had resigned! Nothing was done." Holmes shook his head sadly.

"Incredible incompetence! I advised the Yard years ago to develop a tracking dog capability. I know a dog I can count on in case the need comes up. Toby can track the slightest scent for miles. They should have been able to run the murderer down weeks ago. I know you're doing your best, Lestrade, and I appreciate it. After this latest outrage, the public will be screaming for vengeance, the press will be down on the police, the Whitehall department heads will be looking for scapegoats to blame, and poor Inspector Lestrade will feel like taking a long vacation!"

Lestrade gave us a thin, wry smile and a shake of his head. "Is there anything at all in the information I gave you about the main suspects that catches your eye?"

"Inspector, it is all thin as gruel in an orphanage, but if I had to focus on only one, my pick would be Druitt. I think he deserves more attention."

In the days that followed, every one of Holmes's predictions proved accurate. The public wanted just about everyone associated with the investigation sacked, the press was not much kinder, and the command structure was a shambles. The police and the papers received hundreds of letters and cards; some claiming to be from "Saucy Jack" himself, some accusing anyone they didn't like of being the Ripper. The two latest victims were also prostitutes, Elizabeth Stride and Catherine Eddowes. The rest of October held a few cases for Sherlock Holmes but most were what Holmes would call "trivial." The one that showed the real depth of Holmes's reasoning and deductive ability was the case involving the death of John Straker at King's Pyland, which I will relate one day.

When I came home from a bit of shopping early that November, Holmes was seated in his armchair with a letter in his hand. "A note from Elspeth, Watson. Hang up your coat, have some hot coffee to fight the London chill and I'll read it." I did as Holmes suggested and settled in my usual chair. Holmes unfolded the letter and read out loud;

> *"My dear Mr. Sherlock Holmes and Doctor Watson; well, my injuries seem to have all healed and I wanted you to know what my plans are. I found out what you had warned me about. James had wasted most of the money. I explained what I wanted to do with Forth House and my banker, Aiden MacLeod agreed. He has done business with the McCallums for forty years!*
>
> *"Just an aside: when the medical examiner and Inspector McDonald arrived to pick up the body of James, the chef and Mrs. Grimesby had packed up and left. The Medical Examiner, Doctor Brodie, said James showed early signs of syphilis. 'The High Life', Mr. Holmes, or the Low?*
>
> *"Now the best part: with the money Mr. MacLeod has advanced to me against the value of the house, I have scheduled a complete renovation, I'm taking cooking lessons from Bonnie, and with eight bedrooms, you will soon see an advertisement for 'The Forth House Fishing Resort'!*
>
> *"Thank you both for your wonderful help – you saved my life. I will never forget you!*
>
> *Elspeth McCallum"*

"A remarkable woman, Watson. What a spirit!"

I kept hoping that Sherlock would take a personal interest in the lady after such a praiseful remark, but apparently no woman can replace Irene Adler in his mind; at least not after only six months!

By the first week in November, some of the panic over the Ripper murders had subsided as no further horrors of the Ripper type had occurred. I took the opportunity to do a lot of reading I had put aside due to the flow of cases and Holmes worked at his laboratory table trying to find "a better test for blood, Watson. The old one is clumsy and, in my opinion, not reliable enough." As this endeavor had not, so far, produced some of the truly offensive odors that drove me to leave the room on occasion, I ignored the grunts and muttered comments that came from the corner. Holmes used his own blood in the effort to find a better test which was quite typical of his drive and determination.

Our quiet pursuits came to an abrupt halt, when, on Saturday, November tenth, Lestrade brought us news of the most horrifying Ripper murder yet; that of another prostitute, Mary Jane Kelly. "It was so ghastly, Mr. Holmes, that I know of one constable who rushed outside after seeing the body so as he wouldn't contaminate the murder scene with vomit! This woman had been renting a room for several months. The examiner feels that was the reason for the extensive mutilations; he had no interruptions and could do his insane work for possibly as long as two hours."

"And no dogs and no Sherlock Holmes!"

"Yes, you are unfortunately correct. Many people are being questioned and a reward will be offered. Mr. Holmes, do you think anything will come of it?"

"I'm not a betting man inspector, but I'd lay 100 to 1 against it producing anything of value. This monster has ducked into the shadows for months now; there's no reason to suspect any difference. The police have failed to use the tools most likely to track him down, bloodhounds, and, if used properly, the press."

I couldn't restrain myself; I blurted out "And mostly, Mr. Sherlock Holmes!"

"Doctor Watson, I couldn't agree more. Well gentlemen, I must be on my way. There's to be a meeting with Chief Inspector Swanson this afternoon. I may be able to bring you more details."

Nothing, as Holmes predicted, produced any positive results. The Ripper murders seemed to have stopped, and in support of Holmes' suspicions, the body of Montague John Druitt was found in the Thames, drowned; apparently by his own hand, on Monday, December 31st. Later information we received by way of an anonymous note, said that Druitt's own family had apparently believed for some time that he might be Jack.

After the Druitt drowning, some months passed with no more murders that could be obviously attributed to Jack. Lestrade kept us informed of the investigation but, as he said, "Only some suspects, Holmes. One after another has to be crossed off the list for lack of proof. Sorry I couldn't get you in on it."

Sherlock then summed up the whole Jack the Ripper case. "Doctor; some day, Judgment Day possibly, we will all watch as the real Jack the Ripper steps forward and announces his name as we turn to each other, perplexed, and say 'Who?'"

END

The Seaside Murders

THE CHILL GUSTS off the channel swept down the dock, parted at the two figures, and met again to continue their way. One of the men, heavy coat buttoned up to the throat, wool cap pulled down over his ears, gloves with the fingers cut out, mended his bait net with heavy thread, fingers stiff in the morning cold. His partner had joined him on the fog-wet, aging planks of the dock after stoking the engine and firing up the boiler. He turned away from the wind and lit an old briar pipe, puffing and wheezing to get it going, the smoke swirling away like wispy clouds on the wind. "Hear of the dyin?" he asked. "Aye, and it don't seem natchral, a big strong man like him. Doc says he had a fit an' his heart gave out." The net mender put away his tools and the two men swung their legs over the gunnel, cast off the lines and headed out into the channel. Removing his pipe from his lips the old fisherman said, "Do ye' reckon that's what done him in? Not I; methinks he was done a mischief."

October of 1888 was unseasonably warm in London and with the disappointment at the failure of Scotland Yard to stop the Ripper murders, I felt that Sherlock Holmes and I needed a change of scene. Holmes had resumed his search for a useful test for blood and the clinking of test tubes and the various smells that emanated from his corner worktable added to the depressing atmosphere of our sitting room. I was about to agitate for a respite from our stuffy surroundings when an unexpected letter arrived from Devonshire from a friend I met some years ago. I waited until Holmes was through with his current run of tests and had picked up his new calabash pipe and settled rather glumly in his armchair. "Holmes, I just received a letter from an old friend, Henry Smart, who lives in Budleigh Salterton, Devonshire. The town is near the outlet of the Otter River, I believe."

"Watson, you mean Henry Hawley Smart, the author? I'm familiar with some of his works. What does he have to say?" I opened the letter and read it aloud;

> "*To my battle weary friend Dr. John Watson; time goes much too fast. As I recall, we haven't seen each other for several years. You had just been home from Afghanistan and still recovering from a bullet wound as I remember.*
>
> *I have been writing, and now I see that you have also. I read your piece, 'A Study in Scarlet' in Beeton's. You have a most interesting roommate indeed! If I'm not being presumptuous, do you think Mr. Holmes would be interested in coming to Devon to look into a mystery that has the local police baffled? It's unexplained deaths that I believe are murders. John, I know you Londoners have your hands full with the terrible Jack the Ripper outrages, but I haven't seen Mr. Holmes mentioned in connection with that investigation. Please ask him for me if he would like to apply his talents to our problem. I can put both of you up here at my place, Laburnum Cottage, and I'd bet a tenner that the air is a lot nicer here than in London!*"
>
> *Best regards, Henry.*

Holmes smiled; "A 'tenner', Watson? I deduce that the author is also a horse race fan." I told Holmes that his deduction was indeed correct. His mother was the daughter of Sir Joseph Henry Hawley, a very wealthy racehorse owner and breeder. I suggested a little respite from London for a few days. We had never been ocean fishing and Sherlock would have a mystery to work on, not to mention the ocean breeze to wash London out of our lungs. I expected a lot of pacing and pipe smoking but I was wrong.

"Very well, doctor, I have had enough of this Ripper frustration and I have nothing except blood and chemicals to work on here, so check the southwest trains and let Mr. Smart know we'd be happy to visit him. I will inform Lestrade where to contact us, although I doubt anything of value will be forthcoming." Of course I was happy to oblige and after notifying everyone of our plans, we quickly packed and soon were on our way.

The train from Charing Cross station to Exeter was not the most luxurious ride but the line was rated one of the safest in England. Our train used the new air brakes and the latest in signaling devices and despite several stops, we made the trip in a little over five hours. The fresh ocean breeze hit us as soon as we stepped off the train and we both took a couple of deep breaths before leaving the platform. When we exited the small station we heard a voice hailing us from a trim, four wheel carriage.

"Over here gentlemen! Smart's cab company at your service! Welcome, John and Mr. Holmes to Devonshire; the most bracing air south of Scotland!"

Henry jumped down from his driver's seat and shook our hands warmly. "I hope, Mr. Holmes, that our mystery here will be worthy of your talents. And, there are some big fish out there just waiting for you two. I have a friend with a fishing boat and the salt water gear you'll need. None of that bait casting here!"

Budleigh Salterton was about fifteen miles from Exeter and Laburnum Cottage was set on a slight rise with a fine view of the coast and sweep of the channel. Looking at the cottage from the road, it didn't seem to be big enough for two visitors but as we rolled down the drive toward the back we could see that an addition had been attached to the house. Henry stopped at the small barn and we unloaded our bags while Henry put the horse and carriage inside. He led us through a neat garden to the rear door. Henry's wife, Alice Ellen, a trim, middle-aged lady with graying hair and a bright smile met us and waved us in.

"It's a pleasure to meet you both; Henry will tell you all about our puzzling deaths so I'll just show you to your rooms and fix supper. How does grilled stuffed cod, potato cakes and vegetables sound? Oh, and Devonshire cream and late harvest strawberries for dessert."

Dinner was as delicious as it sounded and when Alice brought the fresh coffee out she shooed us out to the parlour while she cleaned up. "Now you just relax and Henry will describe why we think something is wrong about the two deaths that have occurred recently." We found the parlour very cozy and comfortable. Henry and I lit cigarettes and Holmes pulled out his old briar and began stoking it with, I was happy to see, Macnab #3!

"This won't take long, Mr. Holmes. The two deaths were only a few days apart and both have stumped the medical examiner and the police inspector. The crux of the problem is that the condition of the bodies and their temperatures don't come close to normal limits. Watson, you know that the onset and release of rigor mortis is quite predictable."

"Yes, Henry, it's a good indication of time of death. I used it myself several times on the battlefield to determine when a soldier had died and I know Holmes is quite familiar with the phenomenon also. What was the discrepancy?"

"Doctor, both men exhibited the rigid muscles of rigor much sooner than normal and for a longer period of time. The first victim was a local fisherman; apparently on his way to do some night fishing. He staggered into a pub near the dock gasping for breath and holding his chest. He collapsed on the floor and while two men tried to help him, one patron ran for our doctor. About 20 minutes elapsed before Doctor Linacre arrived but he could do nothing to revive the man, who expired there on the floor. Mr. Holmes, all the muscles of his upper body were, as doctor Linacre put it, 'Hard as a river stone.' I don't know any more details but I'll take you to see him tomorrow. Obviously, rigor would not have set in nearly that fast normally."

Holmes had listened to Henry's story with interest. He put his pipe in an ashtray and leaned forward in his chair, "You said there were two; what about the second?"

"That happened just a week ago, in a small string of businesses opposite our beautiful stretch of beach. The local postman, a young man, very healthy seeming and athletic, suffered the same fate as the fisherman, but much more severe and faster. He had just delivered the post to Ellie Trent's antique and curio shop and would have stopped at Silas Moran's tackle shop but apparently never made it past a bench that's between Ellie's and Moran's. He collapsed just like the fisherman. He was noticed by Ellie Trent, the owner of the antique shop and Moran, owner of the last store, a tackle shop. Mr. Holmes, the witnesses say it was not more than 15 minutes before the doctor got there, but the poor man was already dead."

Holmes chimed in, "And with the same symptoms I fancy."

"Exactly, sir, exactly!"

"Poison, Holmes?"

"It seems likely. Henry, have any tests been run to detect poison?"

"Yes sir, but our facilities are quite limited. Our Inspector came down and took tissue and blood samples from both victims to Exeter, where more extensive tests can be run."

We sat quietly for a while, absorbing the information we just heard. Holmes broke the silence, "I hope we can have a word with the inspector. I would like to know what he has done to investigate this mystery. The doctor can wait. He will have written up his findings."

"Inspector Barrett seems to be rather close with any information, and a bit gruff, but you will meet him when he returns tomorrow evening from Exeter."

Nothing more could be done until Holmes had more information so we just reminisced for a while. Alice came in and urged me to recount some cases Holmes and I had been involved in, so I told her about the frustrations surrounding the Ripper horrors and our trip to Scotland and finally the recapture of John Clay and recovery of the Shakespeare quarto.

Henry then explained why he turned to writing; "The turf did me in gentlemen. I thought I knew enough from being so involved with the sport that I would have a lark but instead I ended up a 'dead duck'! I realized that I had better find a new career fast, so I used some of my war and my racing experiences and began to write. To my surprise and pleasure, my books have done comfortably well and Alice and I settled here in beautiful Devonshire. I think we had better turn in; we want to catch Inspector Barrett as soon as he arrives from Exeter."

Our rooms were small but comfortable and Alice had a light breakfast ready for us of shirred eggs, biscuits and gravy and a slice of ham. As soon as we finished our coffee, Henry asked me, "Well Watson, will your leg stand a walk? We're a small town and the police station is not far. By the time we get there Barrett should be back from Exeter with some news of the tests for poison."

"My leg is fine, Henry. Maybe it's the clean air, but I don't feel even a twinge this morning." With that we started off, glad to have brought along our heavy jackets; the breeze off the channel was crisp with a slightly salty smell. We walked for about fifteen minutes and found ourselves in the middle of Budleigh Salterton, a charming seaside town. Henry led us to the small but neatly kept police station and asked if inspector Barrett was back from Exeter. The duty constable nodded and went through the door to the back of the station. He returned with a tall middle aged man with a ruddy complexion, sandy hair, and a large bushy moustache. He did not seem overjoyed to see us.

"Hullo Henry; and who are these two gents? Not local folks I ken."

"Sherlock Holmes and Doctor Watson inspector. Doctor Watson is an old friend of mine; we were both in the India Army and Mr. Holmes is a consulting detective who has been of help to Scotland Yard on several occasions. We are here to inquire about the tests for poison in the two local unexplained deaths."

"Henry; this is a police matter and I'm na looking for outside help. What I have on this case is confidential police business."

I was about to protest but Holmes spoke up. "Inspector Barrett, I understand your reluctance to share with strangers, but I would ask you to please contact Inspector Lestrade at the Yard and ask him about Sherlock Holmes. I think you will find that my assistance has been of value and my involvement is usually anonymous. The official investigator gets the credit and my name seldom appears on any report. Doctor Watson has also been of help, especially on medical problems like the present situation."

Barrett gazed off into the distance, stroked his moustache a few times and finally agreed to contact Lestrade. He turned and headed back toward his desk, saying brusquely, "See me later today."

Since we were not going to get anything out of Inspector Barrett, Henry took us on a little tour of the town. We stopped at a small café and had coffee and rolls. When we were finished, Holmes asked if Henry would take us to the scenes of, as he called them, "...the probable crimes."

"I was going to suggest that myself, Mr. Holmes. The dock where Robert Quint, the fisherman, was stricken is closest; then we can look at the place by the beach where Nick Smith, the postman died."

A short walk took us to the fishing dock but Holmes was more interested in the pub where Quint died; "The Otter's End". We went in and sat at a battered table that looked as if it had been built about the same time as Stonehenge. The man behind the bar came over to get our orders and, as apparently everyone in town did, knew Henry. "Good morning Henry; and what will you and your friends have?"

"Three pints of the best, Richard, please. These are my friends from London, Sherlock Holmes and Doctor John Watson. Mr. Holmes would like, if you don't mind, to speak to you about the death of Robert Quint. Mr. Holmes, meet Richard Blaine, the owner of this estimable establishment."

"I'll bend your ears as soon as I bring you my best, gentlemen." And with that he hurried off and soon returned with three foaming mugs. After serving us, he pulled up another chair and said, "Quint staggered in lookin' in bad shape. We all thought he was drunk and started to laugh at him but in a second we saw that he was in trouble. He was flailin' his arms about and we could see he was trying to talk but couldn't get his breath. Then he clamped his arms to his chest and fell on the floor. I yelled for someone to get the doctor and two or three fellas tried to sit poor Quint up but he was rollin' around and the men couldn't get him up. Since it was late, doc Linacre had to throw on some clothes so it took more time than it would have daytime. By the time he got here Quint was blue in the face and wasn't breathin'. Doc tried everything he could but Quint died there on the floor without being able to tell us anything."

Holmes sat back in his chair. "An excellent account Mr. Blaine. Think back now; is there anything not directly connected with the excitement that you might have briefly noticed but dismissed because of the noise and confusion – which I presume was all around you at that time? Or anything that happened later, for that matter. Take your time."

Blaine put his elbows on the table and rested his head in his hands. We could see the wrinkles in his forehead as he concentrated. He thought for a minute more and then sat up straight.

"I have something Mr. Holmes but it might not be very important. Another man came in when we were carrying Quint to the doc's cart. He came over to me and told me he had seen two men on the dock and he was sure one of them was Quint. The other man wore a heavy coat and a large hat with the brim turned down. He walked briskly off the dock toward town. That's all the man could tell me because he walked along the dock for a few minutes and then came in to the pub. He didn't see anything else. I told inspector Barrett, Mr. Holmes."

"Thank you Mr. Blaine. Did you by any chance get this man's name?"

"The only thing I heard was that one of the men, I don't know who, called him 'Harrison'. I'm sorry Mr. Holmes, but things was a bit noisy and I was tryin' to settle down the place"

We left the "Otter's End" pub and walked toward the site of the second mysterious death. Just out of the main town, the road leads to a beautiful stretch of cobblestone beach in a crescent shape from headland to headland, washed by the sweep of the channel. Our road ran along the crescent, dividing the beach on the south from the businesses on the north. As we approached the beginning of the shops Henry told us about them.

"It's October now and you will see that several places are boarded up for the winter. The first one along here is Abbott's Rentals; during the summer he rents beach chairs and umbrellas. Next is Nathan's Cookery; he makes sandwiches and snacks for the beach crowd. As you can see, he has closed shop also. The next store is empty. It was a beachwear shop but the owner, Keith Martin, didn't do well enough so he moved to Torbay. Next to that is Trent's Antiques and Curios.

Ellie Trent is one of the last two people to see Nick Smith alive. The last shop is Moran's tackle shop. He's new here; bought the shop about four months ago. He also built an artificial tide pool which is very popular with the summer tourists and the children. He seems to have a good knowledge of saltwater animal life. The space between Ellie's and Moran's once had a shop but it burned down a few years ago and nobody has rebuilt. The town council put that bench you see in front of the open space as a resting spot for people taking in the ocean scenery. That's where Ellie and Moran found Nick dying."

Holmes suggested we start with the antique shop since it seemed to be the last shop at which Nick Smith delivered mail. We entered and as usual, the owner knew Henry by name. "Ellie, these are my friends Sherlock Holmes and Doctor John Watson from London. They are visiting with Alice and me and as Mr. Holmes is a detective, he is looking into the two mysterious deaths we have suffered."

Ellie Trent was quite a bit younger than I had anticipated. She looked small and delicate with light brown hair and blue eyes. The shop itself was so packed with goods there was little room to spare between the tables and shelves. She seemed pleased to see us and greeted us in a firm voice. "I am happy to meet you both. I would normally be closed but for these terrible events. Inspector Barrett asked me to stay while the investigation is continuing. Now, what can I do to help you, Mr. Holmes?"

"As I have heard only bits and pieces of it, I would appreciate it if you would tell me everything you remember, starting with the arrival at your shop of the postman."

"Nick came into my shop and handed me the mail – it was the fourth post of the day – and I fixed a cup of tea and a biscuit for him as I usually do. As it is generally tea time when he makes my afternoon stop, he takes the tea and biscuit and goes out and sits on that bench for a bit and then returns the cup and goes on to Moran's place. That completes his rounds and he returns to the post office.

We don't have as many posts here as in many cities because there is no train service yet and the mail has to come by trap from Exeter. We have only four posts a day. Anyway, after a few minutes I figured Nick would be about through with tea but as I opened the door, I heard a crash that could only be Nick's cup falling to the ground. I turned around and was on my way to get a dustpan and broom when I heard a terrible strangled cry. I rushed out to see what had happened and I saw Nick thrashing around and gasping for breath. Mr. Moran was standing near the bench with an envelope in his hand; evidently an outgoing letter for Nick. He rushed to Nick and began massaging his throat and yelling 'What is it Nick? What's wrong? Miss Trent, go for help quick!' There are several houses about fifty yards behind our row of stores and I ran as fast as I could to ask for someone to get doctor Linacre. It was probably at least twenty minutes before the doctor could get to us and by that time it was too late. Poor Nick had died several minutes before. I left the remains of the cup where they were in case the police needed to test the tea. Since I had a cup after I poured the one for Nick, I knew it was not the tea, but I know not to remove possible evidence."

Holmes looked surprised and pleased at the report we just heard. "Ellie Trent; that was one of the best recountings I have ever heard. You are obviously very observant. Thank you for your help, but I think we better move on and talk to Mr. Moran now before he closes."

We took our leave and walked toward the last shop in this little row of businesses. Holmes stopped by the bench where Nick Smith died and made a quick examination but turned away with a shake of his head. "Nothing much here; some tiny pieces of the cup Ellie told us about; no new marks on the bench itself; let us go on to Moran's."

A sign on the window of the shop said "Moran's Tackle Store and Tide Pool". In the shop, one side and part of the back wall contained fishing poles and nets and other angling needs. The store didn't seem as big as the others and by the west wall, built on a platform of bricks, was the tide pool. Henry showed it to Holmes and me. It was made of rocks of various sizes, all cemented together to form a wall about a foot or so high surrounding a sandy bottom. Little clumps of seaweed dotted the sand and several sea anemones clung to the inside of the stones. As we stood looking at the pool, a door opened in the plain side of the back wall and a small man with brown hair and a pale complexion stepped out and spoke to us in a rather impatient manner. "I was just closing. What is it you want? Oh, it's Mister Smart; need a pole or a new reel sir?"

"No thanks, not this trip. I want you to meet two friends of mine here from London. Doctor Watson and Sherlock Holmes. They are here looking into the two tragic deaths and thought you may be able to shed some light on the events. Mr. Holmes would appreciate it if you could simply tell us what you saw and did."

"I don't think I can be of much help sir. I know poor Nick always stops for tea at Trent's and rests for a bit on the bench. I heard a loud cry and ran out to see what was wrong. I could see that Nick was having some sort of a fit. Miss Trent came out and I called to her to get help and went to Nick. I could see he was trying to say something so I tried massaging his throat to help him speak. Ellie ran off to one of our neighbors to fetch Doctor Linacre and I continued trying to help Nick. I thought perhaps a piece of biscuit had caught in his throat so I leaned him forward and pounded on his back. It was then I felt him stiffen and grab at his chest.

I couldn't do anything else, Mr. Holmes. He was already dead when the doctor arrived."

Holmes nodded; "Thank you Mr. Moran, for that description. On a different note, can you tell us about your tide pool, I find it very unique and interesting."

"Yes sir! That's my pride and joy. I built it myself to study the creatures of the tide pools. It's a lot of work but it's worth the effort and it does attract the tourists."

We went over to the pool and Moran explained how it worked. "You see, gentlemen, under the sand I have some tubes with small holes. They are hooked up to an air pump with a wheel which I operate several times a day to keep the water aerated. I also get a fresh bucket of seawater every morning and drain out some of the old water. You can see some tiny fish, a few small crabs, snails and sea anemones. I keep the seaweed trimmed down so it doesn't take over the tank. The round snails you see eat the algae off the rocks and I feed the little fish a bit of commercial fish food from time to time."

Holmes had been following Moran's explanation closely and now he pointed to several small things, each about two to three inches in length, on the sandy bottom. "Those things with the cone shapes; what are they?" Moran seemed a bit put out by that.

"Oh, those are just another type of snail sir. You often see their empty shells wash up on the beach. If there's nothing else I need to close now. I live in the back and my supper is cooking."

Holmes had been glancing at a shelf next to the pool that held a number of small glass containers, one small one that seemed to be covered with a thin membrane of some kind, a pair of tongs, and other items apparently useful in maintaining the pool. Now he turned to Moran and said, "No, I won't keep you from your meal. I appreciate your help in clarifying some of the details of this unfortunate event." Holmes reached out his arm to shake Moran's hand and after a hesitation, Moran obliged. I had noticed a large ring on Moran's hand before and now I saw Sherlock pick up Moran's hand briefly. "That's quite a handsome ring Mr. Moran. Is it an heirloom? It looks rather like an antique." Moran seemed uncomfortable with Holmes's scrutiny.

"Yes, it's over two hundred years old. Now if you will excuse me I have to close up."

And with that, he went to the door and held it open, a gesture that clearly said "Good day!"

As we walked back toward town my leg was beginning to let me know it had had enough for the day. I told Henry that I had better end my day at his house and the two of them could then go on into town to see if Lestrade had softened up Inspector Barrett.

Much to our surprise, as we came to Henry's place, a police two-wheel trap was in the cobblestone drive that led to the back of the house. Holmes remarked. "It would seem that we have been spared a walk to town. I'm curious to hear what the inspector has for us." Alice must have heard us coming because the door opened and she announced, "Come on in, you have an official visitor."

As we went into the sitting room, the tall, lean figure of Inspector Barrett was standing in the middle of the room. His countenance was more relaxed than at our first meeting and he reached out to Holmes and they shook hands. "Mr. Holmes, I am sorry I treated you rather gruffly at our station. Inspector Lestrade answered the request for his opinion of you sir, and I am quite impressed with his response. Please understand that I had no idea you were more than just curiosity seekers."

Holmes gave the inspector a smile. "I certainly do understand, Inspector Barrett. Now I suggest we all get comfortable and share our findings."

There was a fire going and Alice said she would make fresh coffee so Henry, Holmes and I hung up our jackets and settled into our chairs. Inspector Barrett pulled out his case notebook but Holmes suggested that he first relate what information we gathered, "So you can check what we did against your notes and see if we agree on the main points." Barrett agreed, so Sherlock went through our day with his usual precise recall ability. Barrett nodded when Holmes was finished. "Excellent Mr. Holmes; we agree. We might have done this as a team. Now let me add a few details from my own work. First, the tests for poison were, to quote the official report, 'unavailing';

but strong consensus is that the deaths were from an 'unidentified poison that paralyzed the chest muscles which resulted in asphyxiation of the victim.' Second, I found the witness, a Harrison Book, and he related that who he saw on the dock was certainly Quint. He was with a smallish man who was wearing a heavy dark colored coat and a large hat with the brim turned down. He couldn't see the small man's face as he hurried by and off the dock. Book continued on and then went into the Otter's End pub. He remembers hearing a guttural noise but he thought it was just Quint clearing his throat. As to Nick Smith, it seems that Smith never got to Moran's shop but died on the bench. In his postal bag were several outbound letters he picked up on his round but no undelivered mail except a letter addressed to the tackle shop. We are not much farther along than when we started."

"To the contrary, Inspector. If I can verify two more ideas I have about this case, we may have our killer – because gentlemen, I am quite certain the deaths were murders!"

Inspector Barrett put down his coffee cup and stared; "I would'na be surprised if they were Mr. Holmes, but how done and by whom?" Sherlock sat back in his chair and asked the inspector; "One; can you exhume the body of Nick Smith, and two; is there a library in town?"

"Since this may be a murder case, I think I can get an exhumation order, Mr. Holmes; and no, we don't have much of a library yet but there is a good one in Exeter."

"Fine, Inspector, I shall need to get a ride to Exeter in the morning and I'll plan on meeting with you when I get back to see about the exhumation. Now, let me draw a sketch of what your doctor needs to look for if the body is disinterred." Alice went to a cabinet in one corner of the room and handed Sherlock a pad and a pencil. "Henry keeps these all over the house in case he has an idea he wants to jot down for a new story."

When the sketch was finished, inspector Barrett looked at

it carefully, folded it and said to Holmes, "There is a cab service in town; Ben Heston will be open by 7:30 and with luck I'll have an order and a digging crew by nine. But Mr. Holmes," Inspector Barrett said with a big smile, "you'd never a'got all this done except for Inspector Lestrade's good offices! By the way Mr. Holmes, Inspector Peter Jones also put in a good word. He said you were of great help in capturing a dangerous criminal."

I couldn't keep quiet. I humphed loudly and said that Jones never would have caught Clay without Sherlock Holmes. Nor would the treasure have been found!

We soon broke up our little meeting; Inspector Barrett set off for his house and Henry, Sherlock and I had a nightcap. Alice said she would have a quick breakfast ready at 6;30 so Holmes could get an early ride to Exeter. Henry suggested that he and I get in some fishing while Holmes was off to the library at Exeter. Holmes said he thought that was "A splendid idea, Henry. Doctor, I think you would enjoy that much more than a boring trip to Exeter and back." Henry looked pleased at that. "I have a friend with a fishing boat, an expatriate escaped from the turmoil in Spain. I'm sure he would be glad to take us out on the briny!"

After breakfast Holmes left for town and Henry and I set off to the fishing dock. The air was chilly with a light fog, but nothing like a London fog, thank goodness! There were four boats tied up and several men in heavy naval Pea coats readying their fishing gear. As we came to one trim boat, white with red stripes just above the waterline, a husky man with a seagoing, tanned leather look was just stoking his engine. He paused in his work to wave us aboard. The stern deck was clear with a rack of various sizes of poles attached to the rear wall of the cabin. This boat was more set up as a for-hire craft than for regular commercial fishing. After firing up the engine he came up the narrow steps from below decks to greet us. Behind him we could see the small steam engine, clean and shiny. Obviously, he was very proud of it.

Henry shook his hand and turned to me; "Doctor Watson, meet Martin Santiago, the best fish sleuth on the south coast." Mr. Santiago was "Happy, happy, happy" to meet me and shook hands with a grip that made me wonder if my hand would still function. Martin checked his engine, which by now had enough steam; Henry cast off the lines and used an oar to push us away from the dock, and we were on our way.

We were about fifteen minutes out when Henry gave me balance lessons. "Use your knees to keep your body upright and keep your feet flat on the deck. Martin has prepared some bait. I'll get a pole for you and show you how the drag works. I want to see you hook up with a big one today!" Henry detached a pole from the rack and handed me the biggest rod and reel I'd ever used. "This wheel on the side controls the drag – clockwise tightens the drag and counter-clockwise loosens it. I'll bait your line and we'll get started."

The line had a large hook and Henry took a cleaned mackerel out of a bait box, placed the hook inside and stitched the hook in with a curved needle and heavy thread. The point of the hook was protruding from the rear of the fish, pointing towards the head. "Now, John, when we troll, the bait will appear to swim normally. The hook point faces forward so a hungry fish who grabs the mackerel will likely get hooked and then the fun begins!"

I practiced balancing while we continued into the channel and soon Martin slowed the boat and Henry, who had also baited a pole, showed me how to drop the baited line over the stern and let the line run out about a hundred feet before stopping it. Martin yelled down "Some big cod here. We go slow, let bait sink, then we go faster – maybe big fish follow."

We put our poles in holders attached to the transom, sat down on a couple of folding chairs and relaxed. The water was beautiful and the sea air salty and fresh. Over all, a delight I had never experienced. I told Henry we had to get Sherlock out here before we returned to London.

The euphoria lasted about twenty minutes. I was gazing out over the water when I heard a loud singing noise and my pole bent over from almost straight up to straight out. Henry yelled "Grab the pole John, you've got one" Martin slowed the boat and I hung on to the pole for dear life! Finally, the pressure on the pole eased up and Henry told me to pull back and then reel in while lowering the pole. "It's called pumping, use both arms to pull back. Keep at it and soon you'll bring it up to the boat - I hope." I tried to do as Henry said and keep my balance on the rolling deck at the same time. In what felt like an hour but was probably only twenty minutes or so, my arms felt like they were on fire. Trout fishing was never like this!

"Here he comes John. Hang on, Martin's coming with the gaff. Keep the pressure on." I held on the best I could and soon the biggest fish I ever hooked broke the surface of the roiling water. "Back up now John" Henry yelled at just about the time I thought my arms would detach from my body, Martin leaned over the transom with his gaff and suddenly I felt the line slacken and Martin and Henry began to pull the fish aboard. I don't think I ever felt such physical relief in my life!

Henry and Martin pulled the fish in, laughing happily all the while; detached the hook and took the mangled mackerel from the fish. Martin held my catch up; "Is good cod 'eh, thirty – forty pounds 'eh! You good fisherman, Señor Doctor." I tried to get my breath as Martin put the cod into a holding tank below deck. Henry stepped over and slapped my shoulder,. "Well John, what do you think about deep sea fishing?" I handed Henry my pole, sat down in my chair, and asked him where the nearest trout stream was.

When we docked I asked Henry if I could help pay Martin for the trip. "No, John; but I appreciate the thought. If you have no big plans for the cod, why not give it to Martin? I have plenty of fish put away and he would be most happy to accept the cod for the trip. He will sell it to restaurants in town and in Exeter and keep some for his family." That was certainly a fine arrangement as far as I was concerned, so we informed Martin. He gave us both a big smile and we waved goodbye and left for Henry's place – a bit wobbly on my part I'm afraid!

When we arrived at Laburnum Cottage, the police trap was again parked in Henry's drive. We went inside and Inspector Barrett and Holmes were just finishing a light lunch. As soon as Alice saw us she brought two plates and coffee cups. Since our appetites had been whetted by our seagoing trip, we both dug in with abandon.

When we were finished, Henry related our channel adventure to the applause of Holmes, Alice and even the inspector. Holmes addressed us then; "Inspector Barrett says he has some very interesting news for us and I have the answers I was seeking in the Exeter library. Inspector, why don't you tell us what you found because if I was wrong, we are done and my news is superfluous."

"Mr. Holmes, you were not wrong. I got approval for the exhumation, organized a work crew and had the coffin out by ten. Doctor Linacre, who is our official medical examiner in addition to his normal practice, used your sketch to re-examine the body of Nicolas Smith and found just what you proposed – tiny puncture marks; one on his right arm just above the wrist and one very difficult to see just under his left ear. Doctor Linacre was embarrassed that he had missed these, but as he has never been involved with a case like Quint's and Nick's, I don't think it reflects badly on him."

"Absolutely correct inspector. Now if I add what I found in Exeter, I think we have a complete picture of two diabolical murders." Alice stared at Sherlock, wide eyed, with a shocked look on her face. "Oh, Mr. Holmes, such an awful thing to have happened in our lovely town! Please tell us how you figured all this out."

Holmes settled back in his chair. "Let me go over the points that caught my attention. First, there is the odd nature of the fatal symptoms; Watson and I both suspected some kind of poison but there was no proof of that being the murder weapon. Then there was the difference in the effects; remember, Quint had time to stagger to the pub and didn't die for another 20 minutes or more. This gives us a total time of about 30 minutes since our witness, Mr. Book, heard a throaty noise from Quint and the time he died. But with Nick Smith; he died with the same symptoms in half the time. I had to put the puzzle of that aside until I had more data. Two things bothered me with our interview in Moran's shop. One was the way he brushed aside my question about the cone-shaped shells in his tide pool. He was very forthcoming on everything in the pool until I asked him about the cones. Then, I had noticed the large ring on his left hand and when I got a closer look, I found it quite interesting. There is also the letter found in Nick Smith's postal bag. It has been assumed that it showed that he never got to Moran's, but it bothered me. Miss Trent said she saw a letter in Moran's hand and assumed it was for the post. Inspector Barrett just told us that Nick's bag held a few out-going letters and one undelivered to Moran. Inspector, were any of the outbound letters from Moran?"

"Mr. Holmes, I looked carefully at them all and none that I remember were from Moran. That does seem suspicious. I'm sorry I missed that before."

"At the library in Exeter, I looked up the cones and found a report from Professor Jason Gould of Victoria University. They are called 'cone shell snails' and here is the key; they produce one of the most concentrated and toxic venoms of any animal known. The end of their proboscis houses a tiny rack of almost microscopic harpoons that they fire into prospective prey. The harpoons carry this deadly toxin and the reaction is swift and paralyzing. The snail then sucks the prey in and digests it. Professor Gould notes one occasion when a lab assistant *with gloves on!*, accidentally brushed a snail and it fired one tiny harpoon through the glove. The man was in hospital for two weeks recovering. The question arises naturally, how could a person with a supply of the venom, attack with it?"

Alice stood up from her chair, put her hands on the table and announced, "This is too scary! I need a break. Who wants fresh coffee?" Everyone relaxed a little then and Henry went out to the kitchen to help Alice. Inspector Barrett leaned over and said in a low voice to Sherlock, "You know who the murderer is, don't you?"

"Yes, but it may be tough proving it." Henry brought a plate of cookies in and sat down. "Alice will be here with the coffee in a minute. By the way Mr. Holmes, it's your turn next out there where the real fish are. John can tell you how exhilarating it can be. A thirty pound cod can wear out an unsuspecting landlubber, believe me!" I heartily agreed and we all had a laugh. When Alice came in with the coffee we all looked toward Holmes again.

"The second thing I discovered at the library was this," He pulled out a folded notepaper from his vest pocket and unfolded it on the table so we could see it, "Does this look like something you've seen recently?"

We all studied it and Henry, Barrett and I all said at once, "Moran's ring!"

"Precisely, this is a sketch of an antique ring exactly like Moran wears. The important thing is what the ring really is. Look at the other side of my sketch." Holmes turned the paper over and the entire top section of the ring was now open, exposing a sharp spike. Henry stood up and said in a loud voice, "It's a poison ring! Holmes, do you think Moran's ring is like this one you drew?"

"I'm positive it is, see the tiny lever on one side; that releases the hinged top and exposes the spike. Some of these poison rings have a cavity for powdered poison. Some were not meant for murder but for suicide in case you were caught and destined to be tortured. Those were hard times, my friends! I remember Ellie Trent telling us she saw Moran massaging Nick Smith's throat. I think he did that to hit Nick with a second dose because he had made that cry Ellie heard and Moran couldn't risk Nick saying anything. That's when Nick got the puncture wound on his throat. I believe that Moran turned the ring inside his palm, opened it, and acted as though he overshot a bit when he reached for the letter; Nick would naturally have handed it to

Moran. No need to go the shop with Moran right there. He stabbed Nick's wrist and took the letter. I think he panicked when Ellie Trent came out so soon, so he put the letter back, hoping that everyone would think he had no contact with Nick until he faked helping him."

Inspector Barrett scratched his head and asked Holmes, "How did Moran get enough poison from those tiny snails to do all that devilment?"

"Ah, yes, Inspector, that's what I presume the little bottle with the thin membrane and the tongs were for that I saw on the shelf back of the pool. I didn't attach any importance to them at the time but when I read Gould's article it suddenly dawned on me. I believe Moran milks the snails the same way a researcher would milk a snake to study its venom and develop an antidote. The snail would be too dangerous to milk by hand so Moran used the tongs to hold the snail while he gets it to attack the membrane. A swipe of fish oil on it and the snail is quite likely to fire its harpoons. After some work using the six cone snails I counted, I'm sure he could collect enough to coat that spike in his ring. As far as motive goes, we're still in the dark. I would like to check his mail but I imagine he burns anything that might be incriminating. Inspector, can you ask the new postman to jot down any return and outgoing information on Moran's mail.?"

"You bet I can Mr. Holmes. I'll talk to him as soon as we're through here."

"Just one more thing Inspector; would you ask your night constable to keep an extra watch on Miss Trent's house? I consider her the only reliable witness to the events surrounding the death of Nick Smith – which I now am quite sure was a murder. Moran might think Ellie Trent knows too much. Maybe it might be a good idea to ask her to close now and not open until we think it's safe. I don't imagine she'll mind as she was ready to close for the season before the tragedy."

"Mr. Holmes, I'll go there now and then see the new postman. I believe we have enough evidence to take Moran in for questioning, but that would give away that we suspect him and if we can't make charges stick, he's alerted and would have time to cover his tracks."

"That is exactly right inspector. A very cogent analysis, indeed. We have to devise some way to trick him into exposing his guilt. I have some ideas along that line but we must weigh any scheme carefully or he might escape justice."

There was nothing more we could do that day, so the little meeting broke up and Inspector Barrett left to see Ellie and the new postman. Henry suggested that we all pile into his carriage and take a tour of the Devon countryside. Alice quickly prepared a lunch basket and Holmes and I helped Henry load a feedbag and a covered bucket of water for his horse. We all took our jackets; the brisk October air was soon to be chilly November air. We went along at a slow pace, enjoying the lovely Devonshire scenery while Alice made like a tour guide. After a bit we pulled off the country lane we were on and made a lunch stop. Henry fed and watered his horse and we sat and ate on a blanket that Alice brought. Henry suggested that Holmes and I come earlier in the year next time and we all take a holiday train trip from Exeter through to Penzance. Alice said with a big smile, "It should be safe; I think all the pirates are family men now!" We all had a good laugh. Holmes asked, "When did you see it? It was first performed near here, was it not?"

"Yes, Paignton. Alice and I saw it there at the Bijou Theatre in 1879, around Christmas I think. Then it opened in New York and finally in London."

We packed up then and finished our circular tour, arriving at Laburnum Cottage about 3;30. Henry put the carriage away and he and Sherlock gave Henry's horse a grooming while Alice began preparations for supper. I washed up, since parts of our ride were over some dusty country lanes. I was just about to go out and see how the grooming was going when I heard a trap pull into the drive. To my surprise, Inspector Barrett stepped out with a man, obviously a postman. I waved them around the back to the barn where Holmes and Henry were. They heard us coming and came to meet us.

"Mr. Holmes, this is Brian Tuke, the postman taking over Nick Smith's route. I had him note down any letters to or from Moran as you suggested and he has a bit of news from the last post." Holmes stepped forward and shook Brian's hand and introduced him to me and Henry. "We appreciate your help in this mystery, Brian. What have you found?"

Brian Tuke was probably middle aged, a bit paunchy, and when he doffed his hat to us, an unruly thatch of reddish hair sprang up almost comically. He reached in his vest pocket and handed Holmes a piece of notepaper. "This is what I copied from the last post, Mr. Holmes. I hope it helps you and the inspector."

Holmes spread the note out and after reading it, said, "This is the name and address of another Moran, a Col. S. Moran c/o The Rag, 36 Pall Mall, London. Brian, did you notice any reaction by our Moran?"

""Oh, yes sir. He told me to wait, he said he might have an urgent response. I noticed sir, that when he tore the envelope open and read the letter he turned sort of pale, you know, like it was bad news. He didn't write a response sir, he just waved me away. Mr. Holmes, can I ask you something? What in the world is 'The Rag?'"

Sherlock and I broke out with a laugh. Holmes explained the name. "The Rag is really the Army and Navy Club. It got its nick-name soon after it was founded when a character named Captain

'Billy' Duff complained that the food was 'Rag and Famish'. It was intended as an insult because the 'Rag and Famish' was a notorious, squalid, gambling house populated by down-and-out losers! The members of the club were amused rather than offended and nick-named the club 'The Rag' and it's been known as that ever since. The food is much better now, by the way. Inspector, I think, with this news, we had better act immediately. Obviously the letter had a serious effect on Moran. Do you agree, Inspector?"

"Mr. Holmes, I most certainly agree. Let's take my trap and get over to Moran's without delay. Brian, you have been of great help, thank you. Can we leave you here to walk back to town?" Brian nod-ded and we packed ourselves into the trap. It was somewhat crowded getting four people into a trap made for three but the ride was short and the excitement was high. We would have to, as the card players say, "run a bluff" with Moran. If it didn't work we would probably lose the chance to prove he was the killer.

Inspector Barrett pulled the trap into the empty lot between Ellie Trent's and Moran's. As we turned the corner of Moran's shop we saw his 'Closed' sign in the window. We could see he was doing something at the tide pool because he had the tongs in his hand and was moving from the pool to the equipment shelf and back again to the pool. The front door was locked and the inspector knocked very loudly. Moran jerked his head in the direction of the door, saw it was Barrett and scowled noticeably. In a very commanding voice Barrett called out "Open up, Mr. Moran, this is official business!"

After another scowl, Moran came and unlocked the door. He didn't open it, but instead, just turned his back and walked back to the tide pool. Inspector Barrett opened the door and we all trooped in. Moran's manner hadn't improved. "What's the meaning of this intrusion, can't you see I'm busy?"

Holmes went over to the pool, looked into it while Moran fussed with something on the shelf. "I see the six cone snails are missing.

Where might they be? In that bucket I see at the end of the pool perhaps?" Moran turned from the shelf and held up the tongs. In the end was a snail. He dropped it in the bucket Holmes had noticed. "Yes, I am returning them to the sea. You haven't told me why you have barged into my shop in such an overbearing manner." Inspector Barrett moved face-to-face with Moran. "You, Mr. Moran, are suspected of killing Robert Quint and Nicholas Smith with cone shell snail venom. By sending tissue and blood samples to Professor Gould at Victoria, the toxin that killed them has been positively identified. The body of Smith has been exhumed and tiny puncture marks found. If that ring of yours is what Mr. Holmes thinks it is, it will have traces of the venom still on it and Gould can match it with the poison that killed Quint and Smith." Inspector Barrett held out his hand and said in very commanding voice, "The ring please, Mr. Moran!"

Moran stared at the inspector for a long moment and then began working at the ring with his right hand. "It's very tight, Inspector, I will try to work it off." It seemed he was turning and pulling at the ring but with a sudden effort he reached down and grabbed the bucket with the deadly snails and threw the contents at us in an arc of water and snails. Holmes yelled "Don't touch them! Back away! Inspector, watch out for his ring!"

Barrett reacted immediately and grabbed Moran's ring hand and clamped it closed. With his other hand, the inspector pushed Moran into the shelf and pinned him there. Holmes rushed over to the shelf and picked up the tongs Moran had been using and the now empty bucket. "Don't move. I'll put the snails back in the bucket." Most of the snails had fortunately bounced off us and on to the floor. Holmes was picking them up when Moran screamed and had a look of pure terror on his face. He choked and began gasping for breath. Inspector Barrett looked at Holmes with a puzzled frown. "What's going on, Holmes?"

"Inspector Barrett, I think you'll find that Moran had managed to turn and open the ring exposing the poison spike as he pretended to have trouble getting it off. When you grabbed his hand, you closed his fist and the spike that was meant for you stabbed him in the palm."

Barrett let go of Moran, who sagged to the floor, now clutching his chest. I started to rush over to help but Holmes put out his arm. "No use Watson; he got a full dose. There's nothing you can do. We have no anti-venom or any way to save him. Inspector, look at his hand." Holmes was right, Moran had managed to turn the ring to his palm and push the little lever that opened the top and exposed the spike while he was pretending to get the ring off. Holmes bent over and inspected the ring. "Inspector, if you had grabbed his arm instead of his hand, he might have still been able to hit you with the spike. Instead, I think justice prevailed. Doctor, please see if you can find that letter that seemed to provoke all this. Possibly he was in such a panic that he didn't have time to burn it."

As Inspector Barrett and Holmes moved Moran to a dry area of the floor and Henry took the bucket with the cone shell snails out to throw them back into the ocean whence they came, I went to the back where Moran lived. The small room had a cot with a side table, a small stove and a hook from the ceiling for a lantern. A chamber pot was tucked under the cot and a water bucket was near the stove. I thought my search for the letter would be difficult, but there on the bedside table was a torn envelope and the letter. It looked to be rather short. I took it to Holmes who was now carefully removing Moran's ring while inspector Barrett made entries in his case notebook. Holmes scanned the letter and said, "Let us wait for Henry so I shan't have to read this twice. Moran is dead. Apparently he got a large dose when his ring was squeezed into his palm as he tried to stab inspector Barrett. We'll put a blanket over him and as soon as the inspector drops us off at Henry's he will get Doctor Linacre and they can transport the body to the morgue."

Henry came back a few minutes later with the bucket, now empty of its deadly cargo. Holmes waited until Inspector Barrett had finished his notes and then addressed us. "Well, gentlemen, we have the answer to one puzzle and a new one yet to pursue. Here's what this short letter from a Col. S. Moran to Silas Moran says:

> 'Silas; The Professor is quite upset about your latest test of the poison. He says you were stupidly careless in testing the new, higher concentration in the daylight with a potential witness only a few feet away. We knew the results had to be quicker so the victim wouldn't have time to talk but you acted rashly and stupidly. Now, it would be too suspicious to eliminate Trent. Also, that Holmes person you mentioned nosing around; he already has ruined a plan the Professor had worked out with a friend of ours who could have delivered several thousand quid. The professor was going to have you test to see if darts could be made so the venom could be delivered at a distance with an air rifle but that will now have to wait.
>
> He wants you to destroy any evidence of your work there and leave. Do it now! Burn the store down if you have to. Take the train from Exeter to London tonight if you can or tomorrow at the latest. I'll meet you at the Rag.' S.

I assume, Watson, that this professor, whoever he is, refers to our little skirmish with John Clay. I should like very much like to know who this 'eminence grise' is. I think we have done all we can here. Inspector?"

"I agree Mr. Holmes, I have Moran's key so let's lock the shop and I'll take you gentlemen home and go for the doctor."

Inspector Barrett drove us to Henry's, where an anxious Alice was waiting to hear what transpired. She listened wide-eyed while

Henry related our adventure. "My goodness, what an exciting time. You boys must be famished. I have a large goose roasting along with some herbed potatoes and vegetables. That should finish off your day in good fashion." We all enthusiastically agreed. After freshening up we met at the dinner table and since we were all quite hungry after our exertions at the tackle shop we made short work of the goose.

We were all in the parlour after dinner, relaxing with coffee and jam-filled tarts when Inspector Barrett arrived. Henry waved Barrett to a chair and Alice supplied him with coffee and a tart. The inspector announced, "Well, Doctor Linacre is going to rule it 'Accidental death while resisting arrest.' which I think is an appropriate call." We all agreed that was the best result. Barrett continued; "Mr. Holmes, what now? Moran was obviously being run by men above him who had criminal motives. Do you intend to go after them; and if so, how?"

Sherlock put down his cup of coffee and leaned back in his chair. "We have at least two paths to find and expose this criminal activity. One is to keep watch on Moran's shop for a while. When he doesn't show up at the Rag, this Colonel Sebastian Moran will get worried and want to find out what happened, and if the incriminating letter was found. I suspect that he will have someone else come here to poke around. I don't think he will personally appear and risk possible arrest. With a lot of shops closed for the winter, a new face would stand out and with everyone in town being intrigued by the double murder, it would be odd if he was not spotted. If Moran does come or sends someone else you can be sure they will be suitably disguised – perhaps as a farmer, come to town to shop or a tourist come for some fishing. It would be natural for a tourist to check the tackle shop. Another path is to investigate Moran at the Rag itself. I will do that whatever else we do here. Inspector, I think we can use both of these approaches, your people here and Watson and I in London."

"Mr. Holmes, I think that's the right way to handle this. I'll alert my folks right away tomorrow. When will you and Doctor Watson be returning to London?"

"It will take a couple of days for Moran to be really worried when Silas does not show and Henry and Watson have been doing their best to get me out on the saltwater, so I shall give in and tomorrow set out to best the doctor's big catch! Then Watson and I will return to the fogs and smells of London and see what we can discover about Colonel Moran and this shadow figure, the professor. You have been a pleasure to work with, Inspector Barrett."

"And I have found that the assessment Lestrade provided me was, if anything, understated. You know to reach me at the station and if you tell me where to send news to you I will keep you informed. Tomorrow my men and I are going to tear down the tide pool and return the rocks to the sea and clean out the backroom. Thank you all for your help; I'll be on my way."

The next day Holmes made good on part of his promise; he went fishing with Henry on Martin Santiago's boat while I packed our bags so we could leave right after lunch. I had everything ready when Henry and Sherlock returned and Alice was just setting out our lunch. Holmes had a wry look on his face when they came in and hung up their jackets and said, "All right Watson, you're still the saltwater champ! I caught two fish and together they wouldn't be as big as yours. Martin said he weighed yours at thirty-five and a half pounds."

We had a fine lunch and Henry and Alice drove us into Mr. Heston's cab stable for our trip to Exeter. They volunteered to take us clear to Exeter but we didn't want to be such a bother so we said our goodbyes, thanked them for their hospitality, promised we would visit them again, and headed off to the Exeter train station.

Later, as we boarded our train in Exeter, Holmes turned to me and remarked, "We seem to have had two skirmishes with this mysterious professor without being aware of it until now. Watson, I think the professor and I will tangle someday."

END

THE ABDUCTION
OF LADY "X"

SHERLOCK HOLMES HAD just finished his breakfast, stoked his old briar pipe, and settled down in his armchair when we heard footsteps on the stairs. He put the pipe aside in the chipped, stained pottery ashtray he prized for some unknown reason and said, "Watson, I do hope we don't have a client this early, I'm not sure I could take on another case right now."

We had just returned from the north after an exciting but exhausting case I will call "The Avenging Ghost of Ayrshire" when I can collect my thoughts and write it up. A knock at our door and a call of "messenger" put us at ease. I had finished my second coffee and biscuit with Mrs. Hudson's strawberry preserves so I answered the door. A young man we knew well handed me an envelope and saluted smartly. "A message for Mr. 'Olmes doctor." I took the envelope and handed him a coin from a jar we kept on a stand by the door just for that purpose. "Here Eddie, wait just a moment please. There may be an answer."

I gave the message to Holmes and after opening the envelope and glancing at the message, he said, "No answer, let Eddie go on about his errands." Eddie saluted again and sprinted down the stairs.

"Well, well, Watson, listen to this. 'Coming this noon. Must see you concerning highly important matter. Secrecy vital. F.O. in panic.

Mycroft.' Good gracious, Watson, what calamity is the Empire facing now? Of course, the Foreign Office is often having one fit or another!"

"But Holmes," I protested," your brother has never sounded so upset. It may be as he says, 'highly important' that he see you." Holmes retrieved his briar, knocked out the ashes, tamped down the tobacco and relit it. "I'll peruse the morning paper and see if there's any hint as to what Mycroft is so agitated about."

Nothing in the paper gave a clue so Holmes tossed it aside and began pacing the room, finally settling back in his armchair. He was acting calm and contemplative, but I knew he was quite anxious to hear what Mycroft had to say. He never paced like that unless something was piquing his curiosity.

Promptly at noon we heard a loud knock at the outer door and soon a heavy tread on our stairs. Holmes got up and opened our door and the large, commanding figure of Mycroft Holmes strode into the room and began to speak to us in a manner that bespoke urgency. "Sherlock, you must drop your little cases. The balance of power and the influence England has on the Continent is in danger and..." Holmes broke in before Mycroft could carry on, "Mycroft; please have a seat and start from the beginning."

Mycroft heaved a sigh, moved a chair to face us and with some effort, sat down. "I'm sorry, I'll start with the general situation. Countries have always tried to forge ties with other countries to create allies, build trade, and strengthen their militaries. The tradition that we usually follow is intermarriage. I know you're aware of that strategy. We have been working for a year on a particular effort involving the son of the present King of a certain European country and a young Englishwoman. The young woman's name is Ellen, but she comes from a very private family so I think we should refer to her as 'Lady X' and leave her surname unspoken."

I noticed Holmes gave a tight little smile at this, but nodded and said, "Yes, that will do fine, Mycroft."

"The situation in Europe is very volatile," Mycroft continued, "and our influence there is tenuous at best. If we can encourage a marriage between these two young people, our position in Europe would be improved to a great degree. I can't be more specific about the two right now but I'm sure you understand."

Holmes leaned back with another very slight smile, gave his brother a stern look, and said, "I understand everything except why you're here, Mycroft."

"I apologize Sherlock; the reason I'm here is that the lady has gone missing - perhaps even kidnapped!"

Holmes abruptly put his pipe down and sat up straight on the edge of his chair. Mycroft certainly had our attention now. Mycroft continued, "Scotland Yard has been unable to locate her. I'm asking you to try to find her, Sherlock. We're at our wit's end. The young heir to the throne is frantic, the whole government is on pins and needles. Sherlock, will you please do what you do best and help your country?"

Holmes shook his head slowly, "Mycroft, you must know that for me to aid you, I have to have more information. There is little you've said that does me much good. For example; when did she vanish, have the family received a ransom demand, and possibly most importantly, *cui bono?* Could a European country decide to quash this possible new alliance? Give me something to work with, Mycroft."

"Sherlock, I can give you little, I'm afraid. So far, no ransom has been demanded - which worries us the most. There are, as you surmised, several foreign countries that would be quite pleased if England could be denied any strong alliance with another European country, but we don't know of any with knowledge of our, shall I say, endeavors in the realm of romance."

"Come now, Mycroft, with every country having one or more spies here, do you really think none of them - some quite clever, by the way - have not had a clue to your fostering of this relationship, no matter how hush-hush you've tried to keep it? I'll do what I can but don't get your hopes up too high. We have to face the possibility that she may already be dead. That sounds dreadfully blunt, but with no ransom demand, what are we to think? Where did she go missing?"

"It appears that she was out for a gallop on her favorite horse and was taken somewhere along the trail she was following. The horse returned to the estate on its own, but without Ellen. Sherlock, I'll keep you informed immediately if I learn anything more."

After Holmes insisted, Mycroft gave us the general location of young Ellen's home, and then he heaved his large frame out of the chair, waved a weak goodbye to us and hurried out of the room. Holmes put down his pipe, took off his robe and headed for his room. "Watson, this afternoon will be very boring as I search for an opening to this mystery. As this is Thursday and as I believe this is your billiards day with your friend Thurston; why don't you go ahead and I'll meet you back here later. Don't fret, doctor, I promise I won't leave you out of any interesting activity that might come up."

As much as I enjoyed seeing Sherlock Holmes at work, I knew he was right. "Very well, I'll plan a regular Thursday and see you toward suppertime."

When I returned from billiards later that day Holmes was already back from his investigations. He was standing at the front window, arms akimbo, shifting from one foot to the other. I was immediately energized; he did that only when intensely excited by a case. As soon as I entered the room he spun around; "Watson, I'm glad you're back. We have much to do before night falls. Get your warm clothes out," he paused, "and your pistol!"

"Holmes! You found something important about this case, didn't you?"

"Indeed, at least I hope so, Watson. I've told Mrs. Hudson to make us an early supper - we may be out most of the night. Sit down for a moment and I'll fill you in about my activities today."

I brushed some chalk dust from my sleeve and sat on the edge of my chair, anxious to hear what Holmes had discovered. He tamped down some tobacco (McNab #3, I was glad to see) in his now oft-used calabash and, pulling a straight-back chair from our dining table, began. "Well Doctor, as I foretold, it was a boring quest until I reached Goldschmidt and Howland, a new house-agent firm. You see, Watson, I had so little to go on I settled on the idea that whoever it was who planned this kidnapping would need a secure place to keep his hostage. It was that or the other alternative; that she had already been killed. But if that was so, then there is nothing I or anyone could do. Naturally, I went with the one giving at least a thin chance of making some progress. My thinking was that the kidnappers would not want to be in crowded London. Somewhere isolated from prying eyes, but not too far away. I therefore, asked every agent if they had recently rented a house in a rural or semi-rural area near London. I had almost given up hope, as I had visited almost every agent in town when I arrived at Goldschmidt's. I can't tell you how much the news that they had rented an old manor house only ten miles from town just last month excited me. Even more so when the agent said, 'Mr. Holmes, I can't for the life of me think why he wanted to rent that relic. It's not been lived in for three years and it was near a derelict then. Blimey, I didn't believe him at first, but, Mr. Holmes, he handed me a large deposit and a month's rent in advance.'

"Naturally, I wanted to know the name of the renter so I made up a story about possibly sub-leasing it when he was through. The agent then let me see the rent agreement. The signature was just a scrawl but as you know, I made a study of how the script of various languages differs in character, and Watson, the handwriting was most probably of someone from Eastern Europe."

"Amazing Holmes. I'll get my things together and be ready right after supper."

After we ate, Holmes had Mrs. Hudson's son, Billy, get us a cab. As we put our heavy jackets on I noticed Holmes got out his "Penang Lawyer" and attached it by a strap to his side. He had shortened the weighted cane so it didn't drag on the ground and it made a very effective weapon, especially in the hands of a single-stick expert like Holmes. I put my Webley in the pocket of my jacket and we went downstairs and out to our cab. I noticed Holmes had stuffed a deer-stalker cap in his jacket pocket as I had also. He slipped a coin to Billy, as he always did, tossed another to our cabbie and we were off.

"I have rented a cab for us for the night, Watson. We will pick it up and proceed to the old manor house. I am struggling to retain the hope that this will not be, as Mercutio said, a wild goose chase."

When we got to the cab stables, Holmes dismissed ours. A stable boy came out to meet us leading a horse who looked fresh and ready to go. The boy hitched up the horse to a light Hansom cab and said to Holmes, "He's a good one sir; all fed and watered sir. I put a full bag and a covered water bucket in the cab as you ordered sir." Holmes gave the boy a large coin and climbed up on the driver's shelf as I seated myself and raised the mud guard. Holmes shouted down as we clattered off, "Relax if you can Doctor, it's going to be about an hour and a half's drive."

It was indeed an hour and a half. We kept to main roads most of the way but ended up on two rural lanes where the going was much slower due to a heavy ground fog that had settled in. Twice Holmes stopped to peer around but then continued on at a slow pace. Finally he stopped our cab and got down from the driver's platform and whispered to me, "See that crumbling stone wall, Watson? Our target is about fifty yards west. I'll tie our horse to that tree up ahead. We'll have to go on foot from here. I just hope the directions the house agent gave me were accurate."

"I'll bring the feed and water bucket Holmes." I got down from my perch and followed Holmes as he led the horse a few yards to the tree he had spotted, tied him to it and I set the feed and water down so he could reach it. He snorted a bit but Holmes whispered to him and he quieted down. Holmes turned to me, pointed to a low spot in the wall and we climbed over the pile of broken stones and set off toward what we did not know.

The light of the half-moon came through the fog faintly, robbing the color from the land, making spectral shadows of the trees and bushes. Dead leaves were thick on the damp ground, muffling our cautious footfalls as we inched forward. The large manor house was dark except for dim yellowish light in two curtained windows. The small spots of light in that great, dark expanse served only to give the building a gloomy, forbidding presence. We made our way to a place behind a large bush where we could see the old house and find a way in.

Suddenly I caught a fleeting glance of something or someone moving near a small copse of half-barren trees near one of the lighted windows. I parted the branches of the bush I was behind to get a better look when I felt a steely grip on my shoulder and a harsh, whispered, "Get down Watson! I think we have been seen."

I ducked down as Holmes pulled me firmly to my knees. Just then I heard a "twang" and something blew through the branches where my head had been only a brief moment ago and then a solid thump as whatever it was hit a tree a few yards behind us. Holmes said softly, "A crossbow Watson, a quiet and deadly weapon. He must have seen some movement through the brush even in this poor light. Didn't care what it was, obviously!"

"I have my Webley, Holmes."

"We can't see him clearly enough Watson, and it's too far away for a pistol shot. Not only that, we can't fire a shot unless it's absolutely necessary. A shot will alert anyone in the house and that would put Lady Ellen's life in more danger."

"Then what can we do? We must try to save her! I think that shot tells us you are correct about this being the right house."

"Remember that old stone wall we saw when we crept in? It's falling down in places but it should be enough cover for me to sneak around the back and subdue our touchy assailant. Fortunately, I have my old Penang Lawyer with me."

Holmes gestured to me to move back a few yards and settle behind the tree that was now sporting a nasty looking crossbow bolt.

"Give me five minutes to gain the wall. Then, every minute or so, keep our marksman occupied by tossing a stone or a mud ball into the bushes. Do not stand up or move from behind this tree for more than a brief second to do that! Every time you hear a muffled 'twang' you know another bolt is on the way!"

Holmes turned and quietly crept away toward the crumbling wall that was probably built in the time of Shakespeare. I settled myself behind the tree struck with the first bolt and felt around for a rock or dirt clod with which I could distract our watchful opponent.

Finally I felt a good sized stone under a covering of dead leaves, loosened it from the ground, and carefully crept out from behind the tree just enough to be able to throw it toward the bush from which we had been watching the old house. I was sure the search to find the rock had given Holmes enough time to gain the cover of the ancient wall. Bracing one hand on the tree, I pitched the rock as hard as I could into the bush and ducked back behind the tree. Only a few seconds later I heard a definite twanging noise just as Holmes had said, and another bolt shot through the bush and whistled away in the mist.

Cautioned by that quick reaction by the bowman, I hunkered down and felt around again for a suitable missile. I couldn't find another rock so I made a ball of leaves and damp earth and waited what I judged was about another five minutes and again threw towards the bushes, but this time a little farther to left, hoping to draw his attention again. Sure enough, another deadly shaft ripped through the bushes. I still could not find a rock so I made another mudball, waited a few minutes more and threw it even farther left. Again, a twang followed by a swishing noise as the bolt tore through the bushes. This time however, I heard a loud exclamation of "What the bloody hell......?" and some grunting and scuffling. Then, quiet. I could hardly breathe, waiting for the outcome of the struggle. Then a loud whisper in a familiar voice, "Watson, come quickly, we must hurry!"

I felt as though a weight had been suddenly lifted from my shoulders. I ran as fast as my gimpy leg would allow towards the copse from where Holmes had spotted the watchman, who was now sprawled on the ground while Holmes re-attached the weighted stick to a loop on his belt. He gestured to me to help him drag the unconscious man toward the back of the house. Holmes spoke quietly, "I saw a back entrance right around the corner of the house when I was stalking our friend here. It's probably a servant's door. Let's pull him inside and find a place to tie him up."

We found some steps leading to a small door. We carried our 'hors de combat' opponent up the creaking planks. Holmes tried the old latch; it squeaked noisily but as Holmes slowly pushed on the door, it opened, its hinges complaining mightily all the while.

The door opened on a narrow hallway lit only by a dim yellow light from an open door about fifteen feet ahead of us. Holmes said softly, "Probably a servant's room; let's take him there."

We tried our best to be as quiet as possible but the floorboards creaked and groaned. I heard a muffled chuckle from Holmes as we neared the doorway where the faint light was coming from. "Not the most stealthy approach, eh, Doctor. Have your pistol ready, please." We put our burden down and Holmes carefully peered around the jamb. "No one in, Watson; let us deposit our marksman and see about securing him."

The room was about eight feet by ten with a cot, a chair and a small table its only furniture. A lantern sat on the table, casting a light on the faded and torn wallpaper. We sat the watchman in the chair and Holmes used his pocket knife to cut some strips from a thin blanket on the bed and used them to tie up our slowly recovering guest. Holmes gave me a sly wink and said very sternly, "If he tries to yell, shoot him!" The fellow opened his eyes wide, looked at the Webley, grunted, and muttered, "Ain't a soul 'ere to yell it to nohow."

"Watch him Watson, while I find that other room with the light we saw; I think it must be either the next room or the next after."

Holmes started down the dingy hall while I kept my eye on our now fully conscious prisoner. In no more than one or two minutes, Holmes called loudly in a voice edged with urgency, "Doctor; tip the chair on its back and come quickly! I found Lady Ellen."

Since Holmes had tied each leg of our bowman to a chair leg, I knew he wouldn't be going anywhere. I tipped the chair on its back and hurried down the hall. About twenty feet away I could see Holmes silhouetted in the dim light, gesturing to me. "Come Watson, I fear she is not in very good shape."

I rushed down the dark hallway to the doorway where Holmes was and past him into the dingy room. A pale looking young woman was on a small cot, lying on her side, a tangle of blonde hair spread out on a dirty pillow. A lantern sat on a small table near the only window in the room; a cane chair leaned crookedly next to the table; the faded and torn wallpaper was in the same condition as in the first room.

The young woman didn't move or open her eyes as I leaned over her, so I gently shook her shoulder and put my other hand on her forehead as a rough check of her temperature. I pulled back a worn blanket that covered her. She was wearing a rumpled dress that looked expensive even in its wrinkled condition. She opened her eyes and tried to speak but seemed groggy and disoriented. I told Holmes I thought she might have been drugged but I saw he was already examining a glass he found.

"Quite so, Doctor, I smell the dregs of some narcotic in this glass; no question. Can you get her up and wrap her in that blanket while I go and bring the Hansom to the door? I think we had better remove her from this place as soon as possible."

I nodded, and Holmes sprinted back down the hall toward the door. As I endeavored to sit her up, she opened her eyes wider and seemed to be recovering somewhat from whatever drug they had given her. I noticed a pair of ragged slippers at the foot of the bed, and as she was now sitting on the edge of the cot, I put them on her feet, wrapped the blanket around her shoulders and asked her if she could stand.

"I'll..... try. Are you a ....a....doctor?"

Making an obviously difficult effort, she did manage to stand, so I finished winding the blanket around her. I told her my name and that Mr. Sherlock Holmes and I were here to rescue her. Her speech was very weak but as I helped her take a few steps she seemed to get a little stronger as we made our way out of that awful room. Down the creaking hall we slowly walked, each step an effort for her. As we came to the open door of our prisoner's room she glanced in and whispered, "Bad man!" She continued to mutter that all the way down the hall until we reached the back door and the steps. I supported her as we took the stairs one slow, careful step at a time.

We didn't have long to wait, for in no more than five minutes I heard the clatter of hooves on the cobblestone drive and Holmes pulled up in the Hansom cab. He jumped down and we lifted the young woman onto the seat, I got in and held her, put the mud guard up and Holmes climbed up to the driver's platform. He cracked the whip sharply in the air and we were off. Our horse had had a good rest and we fairly flew along at a great rate away from that depressing place.

After a few minutes Holmes shouted down, "Hospital, Watson?" But she heard, shook her head and said "No......need food, water; no hospital, not hurt." I yelled up to Holmes that we should just go to Baker Street - she didn't seem to have any injuries that would require hospital care. As the night air was damp and chilly, I took off my jacket and put it around her shoulders. After a harrowing ride we made it to town and headed for a cab stables where we could get a fresh horse for the rest of our journey.

When we pulled up at a stables, a young ostler came out to meet us and I saw Holmes hand him a large coin. "We need a fresh horse quickly my man." The ostler raised his eyebrows, took another look at the coin, stuffed it in his pocket, and proceeded to unhitch our horse, lead another out of the stable and soon we were on our way again. As Holmes climbed up to the driver's platform he called down to the young man, "I'll swap the horse for our other one in the morning."

About twenty minutes later we arrived at our digs and Holmes and I helped the young lady down from the cab. Holmes unlocked the outside door and asked, "Can you take it from here? I must go to the Yard and take a constable back to the house and nab our guest. He will do less damage in a cell without his bow. Besides, a police wagon will be faster than our horse." I nodded that I could take care of our passenger and Holmes jumped up to the driver's perch and headed off. "I'll notify Mycroft as soon as I can."

A pale, washed out dawn was just breaking; morning rays of the sun were doing their best to pierce through the mist and announce a new day. We went inside and I was happy to see that Mrs. Hudson was up already and came down the hall to meet us. "I heard the door, doctor, so I....Oh! My goodness, who is this young lady? I think she needs my attention."

I explained that she had been kidnapped and Holmes and I had rescued her. "And I think she needs some warm food and hot tea!" Putting her arm around the lady's waist, Mrs. Hudson led her away to the kitchen. "I see you could use some hot tea also, doctor Watson. I'll bring some up soon."

I thanked our peerless landlady and headed for the stairs to our rooms. Now that the excitement was over, I realized that my game leg was throbbing and I was exhausted by our adventure. I slowly mounted the stairs, entered our sitting room and collapsed in the nearest armchair. True to her word, Mrs. Hudson soon brought up a pot of hot tea and a couple of biscuits. "Where ever have you been, Doctor? The knees of your trousers are all muddy, your boots are too, and your hands look like you've been playing mudpies with the children!"

"Yes Mrs. Hudson, it's been a wet, muddy night. How is our guest doing?"

"She ate a biscuit and jam, drank two cups of tea, and she's now asleep on a cot in the maid's room. She'll be fine Doctor, don't worry. You better tend to yourself now." I took Mrs. Hudson's advice and cleaned up and changed into some fresh clothes. It was almost seven o'clock and I was beginning to feel a reaction to our adventure so I made myself comfortable in my armchair and closed my eyes.

I suddenly awoke to a loud noise on the stairs. The door opened and Holmes and Mycroft came in followed by a handsome young man with a strained, slightly puzzled look on his face. Holmes smiled and said," Watson, it's time you got up and faced the world; it's almost noon. I have been very busy indeed since I left you here at dawn."

"Good Heavens Holmes, I feel that I just dozed off a minute ago!" I started to ask how the lady was but Holmes quickly put a finger to his lips so I remained quiet.

"Doctor Watson, meet this anxious young man who is so curi-ous about why Mycroft and I hustled him to our digs this morning. Please excuse me for a moment and all will be revealed."

Holmes went out the door and I could hear him calling Mrs. Hudson. A couple of minutes later I heard steps on the stairs and into the room came Sherlock and Mrs. Hudson escorting the lady. The young man looked like he was going to faint! Ellen's eyes wid-ened and she rushed to the young man and threw her arms around him. All he could say was "My dear, you're safe, you're safe! But what happened?"

Holmes, who was now leaning against the mantle, stoking his calabash, smiled and said, "My brother will fill you in on your way to her home. I hope you forgive the little surprise Mycroft and I cooked up for you." Turning to Mycroft, Holmes said, pointing the stem of his pipe at the tearfully happy couple, "I dare think your alliance will be soon secure."

The young man, still holding her close, turned his head to Holmes; "How can I ever repay you for this, Mr. Holmes? It's incredible!"

"Just take good care of her and have a happy life; she's a brave young lady. Now you should go and inform the anxious family. Mycroft, thank you for bringing this case to me."

As they headed to the door I saw Mycroft do the most brotherly thing I had ever seen him do; he smiled and gave Holmes a firm pat on the shoulder. Coming from the stern and often imposing brother, it was a most pleasing revelation.

The next morning, as I was relaxing in my chair and Holmes was reading his paper, we heard our page open the street door and a mo-ment later Billy tapped on our door. I got up and got a coin from our 'messenger jar' and opened the door. "Message and an envelope for Mr. Holmes, Doctor Watson". I thanked Billy and closed the door.

I handed the note and envelope to Holmes, who set the envelope aside and opened the message.

"It's from inspector Gregson. He's the man I tipped off at the Yard about the house and the kidnapper and his helper. 'Surveillance successful. Man drove up at dawn, rushed into the house, and quickly ran out. Armed constables yelled at him to stop but he pulled out a revolver and began shooting at them. They returned fire and he was killed. Inspectors are examining the labels on his clothes to determine where he may be from. Mr. Holmes, he had a vial of what our expert says is cyanide! They also found a note which seems to indicate more people are involved than this one man. I know you are always interested in such mysteries so I am sending it to you. Please retain it carefully. I will be by later to get your opinion and retrieve the note before I get in trouble for showing it to you'.

"Well, well, Watson, what could this be." Holmes took the crumpled paper from the envelope, started to read it and sat bolt upright in his chair.

"Watson! Listen to this; 'C. Received your note. I am appalled at your intention to blackmail family. Do you realize what kind of attention and manpower that would stir up? If you proceed with that action I shall deal with you. Do you understand? You are to use the liquid you were given; on both the guard and your prisoner. Do not try to make more money out of this than the generous fee you were given or you will end up with nothing. Do your job now! You were to have dispatched her at once. You wasted too much time already. We have been paid handsomely by a foreign country and if you foul up this job you will regret it. I shall have to return the money and you shall never see another day.' P."

Holmes chuckled, "Well, it's no wonder he rushed into the house. This note crushed his plan most effectively indeed!"

I almost shouted, "Holmes! We were just in time. He was going to murder her. Another three or four hours and we would have been too late."

"Watson, the lady was saved by the delay due to the greed of her kidnapper. Apparently he was told to take her to that isolated house right off and dispose of her and the guard; thus removing the lady and the only witness. I assume the guard also aided in the kidnapping, and, as they say, knew too much. But the kidnapper couldn't resist the temptation to make a lot more money out of it."

"But Holmes, why didn't he kill her first and still demand a ransom? The family wouldn't know she was already dead."

"They might have demanded proof she was alive and he couldn't have provided it. Another horrible thought is that he might then have sent them a severed finger or something gruesome like that. Fortunately, we'll never know to what lengths this villain would go."

Holmes returned to his paper and I, still very tired, dozed off in my armchair. I awoke to Holmes calling to me, "Wake up, the inspector is here to collect the note found on the dead man." Holmes was at the door ushering in Inspector Tobias Gregson, the man Holmes had called "the smartest of the Scotland Yarders". The tall, fair-haired inspector had a most interesting expression; a little guilty with a sly grin.

"I really shouldn't have sent that, Mr. Holmes, but I knew you might make something of it. Frankly, it puzzles me. It seems there is another criminal we should be after. Do you know anything about this 'P'?"

"Inspector, I think I have run up against this man before and I am now sure he is at the center of a criminal organization. I believe the 'P.' stands for 'Professor'. Who he is I do not yet know, but I'm going to try my best to ferret him out. Thank you for thinking of me, Inspector; here is the note you thoughtfully sent to me."

"You are more than welcome Holmes. Please call on me if I can be of any help in finding this 'professor'. By the way Holmes, our foreign specialist identified the dead kidnapper as a Carlos Espinosa, wanted in Spain and France for murder and kidnapping. Do you think you might uncover another scheme of this 'P' in the future?" Holmes opened the door for the inspector and they shook hands. Gregson started down the stairs and Holmes called after him,

"Oh yes, Inspector, I think we will cross swords again someday!"

END

THE HUNT FOR PROFESSOR JAMES MORIARTY

I WRITE THIS piece, the real story of the silent struggle between my friend Sherlock Holmes and Professor James Moriarty, Sr., not knowing if it will ever see the light of day, because of its political and military implications. Nonetheless, I confess now that my earlier recounting of the deaths of Holmes and Moriarty in "The Final Problem" was almost entirely fictional, to allow Holmes to disappear for some time on a critical espionage mission into Europe. Our humble rooms at 221B were, one momentous evening, host to The Foreign Secretary, Under Secretary of State for War, and the brilliant brother of Holmes, Mycroft. The details of that meeting are part of the secret history that all countries go to great lengths to conceal.

There were several reasons why Sherlock Holmes was chosen for the job; his extraordinary observational ability, his acting and disguise talents, and his knowledge of more than one foreign language among them. I realize that this last skill was not revealed in the stories I have narrated, simply because they almost all occurred in England.

In reviewing the story I was asked to write at that time titled "The Final Problem", I was amazed that my readers did not point out the seriously weak plot. The evidence to convict the whole large Moriarty network of criminals was in a little bundle tied with a blue ribbon? And can any of us believe the rather impatient, easily bored Holmes going off on a leisurely trip through Europe? Even with Moriarty on his trail? Holmes was cautious concerning his enemies, but never afraid. To flee from a man he could easily defeat would be untenable.

Me saying, in the story, that "I never heard" of Moriarty after Holmes had spent months combating him? That he never mentioned him to me is ludicrous. Perhaps the most telling mis-directions of the "Final Problem" are these: Holmes said that he would be required in court to convict the gang – but he was not there and the gang was, except for Moran and the gang's gunman, convicted. Moriarty was described in rather complete detail to me early in the story. That the professor could have passed me closely on the trail to the Reichenbach Falls and I would just ignore him is unbelievable! Finally: Holmes described him as quite tall and thin with the stooped shoulders of a scholar. Holmes, an accomplished single stick man, boxer and swordsman was also familiar with "Baritsu" - (misspelled by me in the story. It is actually "bartitsu"), a hand-to-hand fighting technique. That Holmes would have had the least bit of trouble breaking Moriarty's grip without himself tumbling into the abyss is ludicrous.

The addition, to my story "The Empty House", of three more sworn enemies dead set on eliminating Holmes, was just for effect. The temporary escape from justice of Colonel Sebastian Moran is true however, but only until Holmes returned from his spy mission. Moran was caught by Holmes, as narrated in my story "The Empty House". The air rifle was not built by the blind German, Von Herder, but designed by him and assembled by assistants. It was ordered by Professor Moriarty with the intent to fire darts with deadly cone snail venom, but Holmes ruined that scheme in the events I chronicled in "Deaths by the Sea". The story of final justice for Moran is chronicled in my narrative, "Justice Delayed".

And last, the story of the capture of Moran would give the impression that I had never seen him. Of course I had seen him on many occasions, since I had been spying on him at the Rag. but I hardly recognized him *in the dim light of the room, as his face looked haggard and worn. No doubt the relentless pursuit by Sherlock Holmes had taken a heavy toll on him. With the arrest of Moran, the Moriarty criminal organization was completely broken except for the dangerous gunman, Pigot. The following is, finally, the true story of those events.*

I The Hunt Begins

I came back to Baker Street early that Thursday, my usual billiards afternoon with my friend Thurston, because my shoulder was hurting, as it did occasionally. I had sustained a wound at the battle of Maiwand when I was hit by a jezail bullet while kneeling over a soldier who had been struck by a shell fragment. I was attempting to bandage his leg when the bullet hit my shoulder, nicked the subclavian artery, and ricocheted into my leg. When my orderly, Murray, got me to the India Army hospital, I had lost a great deal of blood but the doctors there saved my life. After I was stable, they removed the bullet that had lodged in my leg, but it had hit a tendon, damaging it beyond complete repair. My leg actually bothers me much more than my shoulder, but on this day that particular joint decided the stretch to support my cue was more than it would bear without complaint!

As I entered our rooms at 221B, Holmes was seated at our dining table with papers spread out covering every inch of the table. "Police reports Doctor, reams of them. I am attempting to isolate cases that might reveal organization and planning. In other words, my dear Watson, the possible presence of our mysterious professor lurking behind the scenes, pulling the strings and collecting his 'cut' without soiling his hands. And, Doctor, I have found several cases that point to a scheming brain; backstage, so to speak."

"Holmes! How in the world did you come by all these reports? Aren't they supposed to be confidential?" He put down the sheet he had in his hand and replied, "There are, as you can imagine, several successful Scotland Yard detectives whose careers I helped advance. Lestrade for one. I called in a favor and these piles of reports are the result. I have until tomorrow when a nervous Lestrade will come to retrieve them."

"Nervous? He must be quaking in his boots for fear that he'll be caught removing case files! Can I help in some way?" Holmes gave me a mischievous grin and announced, "Why certainly; as an ex-army man, you can join the 'Rag'.

"The Army and Navy Club? Why, for goodness sake?" Holmes got up and went to the mantle where his pipes and tobacco were, selected his cherry wood and began stoking it.

"Do you remember when, in the case of the double murders at Budleigh-Salterton, we discovered that Silas Moran had a brother, a Colonel Sebastian Moran, who received his mail at the 'Rag'? In the letter you found, the Colonel referred to 'The Professor'; obviously the real boss. Then there was the note found on the kidnapper of the Lady whom Mycroft called 'Ellen', that directly implicated this Professor. The note was signed 'P.' but I think it's clear who that is. I'd like you to join the Rag and do a little spying on the Colonel. What do you say to some espionage?" My aching shoulder was forgotten in my excitement to be a part of a Holmes case. "I'll go tomorrow and get an application!"

I got all my army papers together and tried on my old uniform with the happy result that it fit; snugly, but it fit. When I reached the 'Rag', I felt a catch in the throat - the war came flooding back in my memory. The horror of it would never fade completely away. I shivered at the thought of how hideous war was. I admit I was a bit gloomy when I went inside but the big man at the reception desk had such a happy expression on his ruddy face that my mood improved at once. He wore his old uniform also, and it must have been one of the biggest in the service. His voice was as big as he was.

"Hello, Doctor, welcome to the Rag." I was startled at first but remembered that my uniform had the medical corps badge. "What can I do for you this fine day?"

I showed him my papers and said I would like to apply for membership. He pulled out a drawer, handed me an application form and waved me to a small desk in an alcove about twenty feet away. As I was walking toward it he asked, "Did you get that bit of a limp in Afghanistan, Doctor?" Surprised again, I stopped and turned around.

"I didn't know it was so obvious. Yes, I got hit during the battle at Maiwand. You have a sharp eye."

"Aye, Doctor; I've been here some years now and I've seen my share of battle scars. From your uniform and your age I guessed it was Afghanistan that did you in. Your limp is probably not noticed by most folks but I have an eye for wounded soldiers and seamen. Just bring the application and your papers back here and I'll see that the membership committee gets it right away. They'll let you know by next week. If you have any questions about the application, just ask me; Lieutenant Angus Campbell at your service."

When I returned to Baker Street, I glanced at our table which was now clear of the piles of casefiles. A relieved Lestrade must have picked them up earlier. Answering my thoughts before I spoke; as Holmes often did, he said. "Yes, Watson, Lestrade came to get his smuggled files. I have taken notes and I'm ready to hear how your day at the Rag went."

I recounted my visit but I must have seemed hesitant in speaking about it because Holmes looked at me intently and asked, "What is it Watson, you have something about your visit at the back of your mind don't you?"

"You have me, Holmes. Yes I am concerned with the fees. Fifty pounds to join and ten in advance for the year." Holmes laughed, leaned back in his chair and said, "My dear fellow, when you are admitted, I will have sixty pounds for you to deliver to the Rag. I don't expect you to have to pay for my nefarious scheme." I was quite relieved.

"Thank you. I admit it was bothering me - my wound pension is much too thin to cover a sixty-pound bill. The clerk said I should hear from them by next week."

I spent the next few days with my arm in a sling to rest my shoulder. Holmes was often in and out of our rooms, sometimes several times a day. I understood that he was using his notes garnered from the case files to talk to people involved in the cases which he considered showed some signs of behind-the-scenes manipulation. Every knock at our door brought me hurrying, just in case an answer from the Rag had arrived. Holmes tried to calm me down; "A battlefield doctor, wounded in the Second Afghan War? They will certainly approve your entry, Watson, don't fret!"

Sure enough, on the fifth day after my visit, a Wednesday, came the good news - I'd been approved for membership. I was instructed to see Lieutenant Angus Campbell at the reception desk and sign up. I told Holmes, and he went to our shared desk, pulled out a cash-box from a bottom drawer, and handed me sixty-five pounds. "Here you are Watson. Use the fiver to get a meal at the Rag's dining room - I hear the food is vastly improved since Captain Billy Duff's days!"

The next morning I took a cab to the Rag; taking a deep breath, I went in. I was heading toward the reception desk when I heard a familiar booming voice call, "Ah, welcome Doctor Watson. Congratulations on your membership. Come on over and I'll sign you up and give you a free tour!"

It was indeed the large, ruddy faced clerk I met the previous week. He was as voluble and outgoing as before. My nervousness vanished by the time I reached the desk. I handed the lieutenant sixty pounds of the money Holmes had given me and Lieutenant Campbell gave me a membership form to sign. He then put a sign on the counter "Back soon" and we were off on the tour.

Although not luxurious, the Rag was neatly laid out with an understated decor. Military items, photos, and paintings adorned the walls. The number of famous soldiers and navy officers who were members was breathtaking; The Duke of Wellington, Prince Adolphus, Duke of Cambridge, Admiral Sir Phillip Durham, Admiral of the Fleet Sir Algernon Lyons, Field Marshall Sir George Stuart White, and on and on. Here was I, just a field surgeon - it was humbling and I guess it showed because lieutenant Campbell tapped me on the shoulder, waggled a big forefinger at me and said in a stern voice, "Doctor, you bled for England on the battlefield tending wounded soldiers; you belong here too! Never forget that. Not everyone here can say that they spilled blood for their country. Now let me show you the card room, the lounge and the dining room."

The Card Room turned out to be unexpectedly of great interest - the lieutenant mentioned Colonel Sebastian Moran and his Friday night to Sunday morning poker games!

When I arrived back at our rooms it was afternoon and Holmes was buried in sheets of notes, maps, and drawings. The room was full of smoke, but thank goodness, it was Macnab #3 and not his old broom straw tobacco. He looked up as I hung my jacket on the coat rack, "Well Watson; how's the newest club man? Nothing interesting so soon I imagine."

"On the contrary, Holmes. I heard about Colonel Moran without having to ask. It seems he's an inveterate card player and practically runs a poker game and plays many partnership games, too. Lieutenant Campbell mentioned that when showing me the large card room. There were several games going on when we were there but the Colonel was not playing in any of them. I found out though, that the poker and other card games Moran plays in run on Friday and Saturday nights - sometimes all night according to Campbell." Holmes smiled. Pointing his pipe stem at me, he declared, "Excellent, my dear Doctor! I couldn't have done better myself. Now, is there some place in the card room where you can observe whatever game Colonel Moran is playing?"

"Absolutely. There are armchairs placed all around the room; both for men waiting for an opening at a card table and those who just enjoy the atmosphere and don't play. I will be one of those - I have no intention of tangling with the card sharks!" Holmes chuckled and went back to his notes.

My early enthusiasm faded by the second week of my surreptitious spying. I had really not turned up any information of value on Moran, so I took a step I hoped would help our efforts to identify the 'Professor'. I volunteered to help Lieutenant Campbell with the mail duties. When I told Holmes, his reaction buoyed me immensely; "Watson! What a fine idea. Normally, I would think the professor and Moran would meet face to face, but the professor is so secretive they may stay away from much personal contact. Take a small notepad and jot down any information that might help us. I doubt the professor would put a return address on any letter to Moran, but let us hope Moran mails letters to him. Note anything that comes to or from the Colonel. At least we may be able to take another step forward in our quest."

In the meantime, I kept up my watch in the card room. It didn't take long to identify Colonel Moran, a man of slight build, light brown hair which he had let grow quite long, a straggly moustache, sallow complexion, and piercing dark-brown eyes. The impression he gave was one of a suspicious nature. I almost never saw him talk or laugh with any of the other members. He was also a steady but not ostentatious winner at poker and, I noticed, in the partnership games as well.

Lieutenant Campbell welcomed my help with the mail duties and in a few days I found I was handling the entire job; sorting the incoming mail and posting outgoing mail - always with my notepad and pencil at the ready. Nothing of interest came through for two weeks and my early enthusiasm was beginning to wane again when suddenly, while sorting the mail on Tuesday of the third week, a letter addressed to "Col. S. Moran" came in with no return address, but the single letter "P." I was debating whether to tuck it away and bring it to Holmes - I knew he could carefully steam it open - but Moran appeared before I could take any action and gruffly announced that he was expecting a highly important letter. "I'm damned sure it must be here in this post," he announced, so I had to hand it over to him. All I could do now was to hope he would be sending out a letter in answer.

"Well, Watson, any news from your new job?" It was after supper that night and Holmes was lighting his 'contemplation' pipe, an ancient Churchwarden, while I was finishing my coffee and one of Bradley's excellent cigarettes. I related the experience of the day with the brusque Colonel and the letter.

"Keep your notepad handy, Doctor, I feel that we are getting closer. Perhaps you would care to hear what I've been doing to advance our investigation?" Startled, I put down my coffee, snubbed out my cigarette and sat up straight in my chair. "I would be most interested Holmes, as you might imagine, I've been wondering what paths you've gone down lately. I see you every night poring over books and notes with grim determination."

"Watson, I think I have narrowed our search down to three real professors. I have been pestering librarians, Dons, ex-schoolmates, and old newspaper files clerks for information on any professors that might have raised suspicions of not so academic pursuits either at college or after. After three weeks of scrutiny, I found four professors that I considered worthy of more study."

"But Holmes, I thought you said three?" Holmes put his pipe down, broke into a grin and explained; "Yes, I did say three; one of the original four I singled out was caught in *flagrante delicto* and fatally shot by the lady's husband some 5 years ago! Needless to say, I crossed him off the list. Now I have three, and I'm hoping that a trip to see our repeat offender John Clay might narrow that down." I was caught completely off guard by that announcement. "John Clay! Holmes, why do you think he will tell us anything at all?"

"Oh, he won't!" I was totally at sea after that answer. I know I must have looked blankly at Holmes. He smiled and continued, "Remember that letter we found at Silas Moran's shop? In it, if you recall, he mentions 'the professor' more than once; and most importantly, in connection with the Windsor Hotel theft attempt; I'm certain that's the spoiled plot he refers to."

"Holmes, I hope whatever you have planned for Clay bears fruit. Who are your suspects?" Holmes shuffled through his stack of notes, pulled one out, glanced at it and began. "Professor of history, Augustus Dumbarton; 60, expert in the evolution of governments; became an avid anarchist and wrote vicious screeds to members of Parliament, bankers, and police officials in which he vowed to 'use any means to upset the prevailing order, including criminal activity.' He is generally thought to be mentally unbalanced and has seemingly disappeared. At least no one has heard from him in about three years. Number two; Obadiah Zebulon Druitt, taught military strategy - and yes Watson, he is a relative of John Druitt, the man I think may have been Jack the Ripper. He left two teaching jobs under a cloud but I couldn't discover exactly what the reasons were for his hasty departures. The fact that he taught military strategy caught my eye. Such a man could presumably organize and plan schemes of a criminal nature. The last of the three is James Moriarty, known by several ex-academics I talked to as a brilliant mathematician and logician but a secretive and not very friendly fellow. He doesn't correspond with any of his former academics to whom I talked. He studied for a short period under Alexander Bain, the famous Scottish scholar. I have written to Bain care of the college but I haven't a reply as yet. Well, my friend, tomorrow we shall see if we can penetrate the fog of uncertainty surrounding our suspects. I ordered an early breakfast from Mrs. Hudson as we are to meet Inspector Peter Jones who will be bringing Mr. Clay for a ten o'clock *tete a tete* with us at Wormwood Scrubs."

The day was perfect for a visit to the place; gloomy and chilly with a threat of rain. As we pulled up to the newly rebuilt prison, Holmes gave our driver an extra coin and asked him to wait. As we walked to the main entrance, Holmes said, "It looks neat and clean now does it not, Watson? Just give it few years in our London air and it will probably take on an appropriately grim, gray cast. And there, by the main gate I see Inspector Jones waving to us." We hurried over to where Jones stood.

"Hullo Mr. Holmes. I have Clay in an interview room waiting for us. Let's get you and Doctor Watson signed in. I still don't know why this special visit but I know I owe it to you."

"Many thanks Inspector. We won't be long. I just have a simple question I need to ask Mr. Clay." He turned to me and said, "Watson, I will be giving a little speech to our friend Clay. I won't be looking at him and I want you to appear uninterested but surreptitiously watch him out of the corner of your eye and tell me later if you spot a reaction to any part of my little talk."

Inspector Jones signed us in and escorted us down a long hallway, through two gates opened for us by prison guards and into a cell-like room where John Clay was seated at a table (which, I noted, was bolted to the floor), shackled at the ankles and with Hyatt darby handcuffs on his wrists. Clay was sitting in a metal chair and three more were on the other side of the table. Holmes quietly asked Inspector Jones if he would mind waiting outside the door - he didn't want Clay to be intimidated by an official. Jones looked slightly puzzled by this request but he nodded and left.

Holmes and I seated ourselves while Clay glared at us with undisguised malice in his eyes. Holmes started off by addressing Clay in a pleasant voice with a touch of irony. "I wonder if you figured out how I guessed you were on the southbound train and not the northbound that you so helpfully shouted out to the cabbie? Had you just thought about it further, you might have deduced what I deduced and acted accordingly - by actually taking the northbound train! You could have had the last laugh on Sherlock Holmes!"

Clay muttered something I couldn't hear, and probably wouldn't have wanted to hear. Holmes got out of his chair and casually walked to the small, barred window, and looking out, started to speak, "I have come to the conclusion that there is a criminally scheming mind at work behind the scenes. I further believe that this person planned and financed your escapade at the Windsor Hotel. I also think you saw a chance to make a financial killing when you, posing as an auctioneer, registered the Shakespeare quarto; and decided right then that you had no intention of splitting your ill-gotten gains with the 'Boss'. That's why I assumed you would head for the south coast and a quick trip across the channel in a fishing boat to France and freedom with a great deal of money to enjoy.

"The real planner of the scheme didn't know about the immensely valuable quarto. Right so far?" Clay flashed a look of pure hatred at Holmes but said nothing.

Holmes glanced at Clay briefly and said, "Thanks, I'll take that as a 'yes'. Turning back to the window, he continued, " Pursuing the thought of a 'Mastermind', I came up with three men I think would be capable of planning lucrative crimes and stay, unseen, behind the curtain, so to speak. I would like to hear your thoughts, as I know you are intelligent and quite aware of the criminal activity in London." Clay continued to stare straight ahead and said nothing, but I saw a slight grin. Holmes was playing to Clay's considerable ego.

"The first suspect - if you want to call him that - is an ex-academic, Augustus Dumbarton, expert in government. An avid anarchist, he has disappeared, but could be operating under an alias and pursuing his criminal threats. At least it's a possibility. Number two is Obadiah Druitt, who once taught military strategy. He left two teaching jobs under mysterious and dark circumstances. Certainly a strategist could run such a criminal enterprise. He also has faded from view. The last man is Professor James Moriarty, a brilliant mathematician but a man that ex-students and faculty call 'clever and scheming'. Any comments, Mr. Clay?"

"I ain't never 'eard o' any of 'em." Clay answered, using a faked East London accent whose sarcastic tone was obvious. I was infuriated, but Holmes just shook his head, walked to the door and knocked for Inspector Jones. When we were outside the room, Jones asked Holmes, "Well sir, did you learn anything important?" Holmes turned to me and answered Jones, "Let's ask Doctor Watson." Jones looked very surprised and still puzzled by the whole thing.

I was hardly able to contain myself. "Yes Holmes, Clay kept the same bored expression during your speech - except when you mentioned Professor Moriarty. Clay's eyes widened and his head jerked toward you. He looked completely shocked but recovered his bored look very swiftly." Holmes clapped me on the shoulder and gave Inspector Jones a small smile. "Yes Inspector, I think we did learn something important from our little chat. Come, Watson, we have work to do. Thanks again Inspector Jones." Jones had a look of shock at the way Holmes had tricked Clay into revealing what he never would have admitted. He leaned toward Holmes and asked earnestly, "Mr. Holmes, does this mean that you suspect this professor person of being the brains behind criminal goings-on?"

"Indeed I do, Inspector. And I ask for just one more favor; will you see that Clay doesn't get to communicate with anyone for a while. I don't want him alerting the professor to our discovery."

"That presents no problem sir; he is still under close watch and hasn't been released into the yard yet, so he has no contact with other prisoners and is not allowed visitors, either. He won't escape again, Mr. Holmes!"

We retrieved our cab and as we clattered home, I noticed that Holmes had that familiar, determined countenance that meant trouble for someone - in this case Professor James Moriarty.

II "The best-laid schemes o' mice an' men..."

In the days that followed our prison visit, Holmes concentrated his energy on trying to get a lead where Professor Moriarty might be, but at the same time not doing anything that might alert his target. He advised me to keep up my watch on Colonel Moran and the mail at the Rag, but the only letter Moran received during the next two weeks was from the Army - nothing from 'P'. Meanwhile, Holmes continued his search for Professor Moriarty. Much to his annoyance however, Inspectors Lestrade and Altheny Jones prevailed upon him to help them with open cases.

One evening after we had eaten supper, Holmes summed up his experiences with the inspectors. "I told Lestrade that the nephew had stolen the pearl necklace, and so he had. Lestrade didn't believe it at first because the lad had tried to make it look like a burglar had broken in by breaking a window but he did a poor job of it and I found glass slivers in the soles of his boots, no bootprints but his outside the window, and two cuts on his hands. He admitted he wanted to get an expensive gift for a girl he wanted to impress but didn't have the money for it. Simple case."

"What about Altheny Jones? He seemed totally at sea. It was a kidnapping case wasn't it?"

"So it appeared, Doctor. The supposed 'victim' was the daughter of a wealthy family in Sussex who fell in love, unbeknownst to the family, with the son of the town's greengrocer. Knowing that the family would never accept the young man, the loving couple devised a plan which involved the faked kidnapping of the girl and a ransom demanded of her family. They thought that it would get them enough money to elope and start a life somewhere else. However, Watson, you know that I am quite skilled at identifying handwriting, and in comparing the ransom note with the writing on a couple of love notes from the girl's swain that I found in her dresser, it was obvious what was really taking place. The family didn't want the publicity so they refused to prosecute the young man and the daughter was forbidden to see him again."

Holmes smiled and picked up his calabash from the mantle, packed it, lit it, and settled himself in his somewhat worn but comfortable big armchair. As the first puffs swirled away toward the ceiling, Holmes remarked, "I had to read a bit of those letters as I compared handwriting with the ransom note, doctor , and I predict that, ransom money or not, they will find a way to be together in the near future. *'omnia vincit amor'*, Watson!"

I continued my spying at the Rag but nothing came through the post for the Colonel and he sent nothing out for another week. But one day, a letter for him arrived with that 'P' in the corner, same as the one I had tried to get to Holmes. Again I was foiled in letting Holmes examine a letter that might contain the clue he needed to find the professor, because Lieutenant Campbell, trying to be helpful, picked up the post and told me, "Go get some lunch Doctor; I'll pass these letters out for you."

Two days later, while I was at the reception desk going through the latest post, I noticed Colonel Moran coming toward the desk with an envelope in his hand. I was getting ready to add it to the outgoing pile when he looked at me and suddenly tucked it away in his jacket, turned away from the desk, and strode out the main entrance door.

That evening, I related to Holmes what happened. He got up from his chair, walked to the window, and stood there looking out, arms akimbo. Finally, he turned toward me and in a concerned voice, said, "I can't make it out, Doctor; but I don't like it. I feel that something's wrong. Watson, I want you to be very careful; Moran may suspect you. I think he was going to send that letter out, but when he saw you at the mail station, he put it in his jacket so you wouldn't be able to see how it was addressed and so posted it at a nearby box instead. He may have sent a spy to Budleigh-Salterton to see what he could find out. The double murder would certainly be on everyone's lips. Someone may have talked about a 'Sherlock Holmes and a Doctor Watson.' It would not be a difficult job to get a description of us."

"Holmes, do you think he was sending a letter directly to Professor Moriarty?"

"I don't know. I had thought he and Moran would be communicating through a third party - perhaps a rented place where one of Moriarty's henchmen would receive the letter and then pass it on to the professor, but perhaps I'm making too much of it. It may be straightforward after all. Still, use caution. I have made some progress in tracking down our elusive professor and I am investigating a couple of promising leads but I certainly would welcome a breakthrough. He may be living under an assumed name and that makes it harder to locate him."

The following week was again, uneventful, and I was losing hope that I could help Holmes in our quest. Then, like an electric spark through my body, I saw, in the outgoing morning post I had been thumbing through lazily, a letter addressed to "Col. S. Moran." I was suddenly alert - but confused. Why would an outgoing letter be addressed to the man who receives his mail here? In the upper corner was no return address except "CSM." Still, I knew my duty; I pulled out a pencil and my notepad and wrote down the address, '10 Rillington Place, Kensington.' Could that be where professor Moriarty lived? Or was it a 'convenience' address for Moriarty to receive mail without revealing his true location? After mulling it over for a hour or more while finishing my mail job, I decided to find out! I told Lieutenant Campbell I was leaving and took a cab home.

Having learned a little about disguises over the years from Holmes, I wanted to look as inconspicuous as possible. My army trousers and a plain work type shirt would make me look like a common tradesman or a City of London worker. I tossed my notepad on our desk and put my pencil in my shirt pocket to appear more workmanlike. I had a further thought, tore off the top page of my notepad and put it in my pocket also. If I was quizzed about my presence I could show the paper with the Rillington address and claim I was sent to inspect the drains or some such believable story. Holmes wasn't there, and I thought of leaving a message but I didn't expect to be gone long and I wanted to pursue this opportunity without delay. It might provide just what Homes needed, so I went out, hailed a Hansom cab, and set off to Kensington.

As we approached Rillington Place, I wondered what to do about the cab. I thought it might be suspicious to drive up in a cab and then claim to be a worker, but as we started up the road I noticed a mews on the other side of the street so I dismissed my cab and walked the short distance to where number 10 would be. I found it at the end of the street of average dwellings, not fancy but not shabby. Number 10 faced north, with a walled-in space at the rear.

Perhaps a garden, although I couldn't see in from the front. Taking a deep breath, I knocked on the door. A strong, gruff voice came through a small peephole, "Who'er you and what d'ya want?"

"I'm here to inspect the drains. Is a Colonel Moran in? I was told he lives here." I thought I might have made a fool's errand out of my suspicions but the door opened and a large, rough looking individual looked me over and waved me in. "This house belongs to Colonel Moran then?" I asked. He gestured to a straight-back chair next to a small table in a quite sparse living room. Practically no other furniture except an old sofa and a small lamp stand occupied the rather dingy room. The big man turned around and said, "Na, he rents this place. I works for him." I sat down facing the door, wondering if I had made a mistake in acting so boldly. This hunt for the professor had consumed me to possibly too great an extent. I was about to get up and leave when the big man said in a menacing tone, "If you's inspecting the drains, where's yer tools? An' you don't look like no workin' man to me." I turned my head to look, felt my shoulder gripped roughly, and saw the man who had let me in swing some object at my head with his free hand.

I don't know how long I was unconscious, but slowly I began to see my surroundings again. I tried to move and realized I was now tied to the chair. Still groggy, I could make out the figure of the man. I thought he was going to hit me again but instead, he threw a jug of water in my face.

"Well, Doctor Watson, I see y'er awake again. Now I ken y'll tell me why you and Sherlock 'olmes is poking y'er noses where they doesn't belong."

My head was starting to clear but all I could stammer was "I......I'm here.....to inspect....the drains."

"Nay, y'er Doctor Watson." Pulling a crumpled letter out of his pocket, he thrust it in my face. "See this 'ere!" he yelled, "It be from my boss an' it tells me what you look like an' what to do with ya'. The Boss is; smart 'e is. Smarter'n Doctor Watson, 'eh? Knew ye' might come 'ere when ye' saw 'at letter he wrote just so's I can make ye' talk. He trapped ya', he did!" He banged the letter down on the table and I realized that my right arm was tied to the chair so my hand extended on to the table. I struggled but I couldn't withdraw my hand. The man grinned a terrible smirk, reached into his back pocket and pulled out a pliers.

"Now y'll tell me that what I want to know." Clamping my hand down on the table with one huge hand, he used the pliers to grab my thumbnail and give a firm yank. The pain was fierce. I yelled out and twisted back and forth but he had one foot on a low rung of the chair and I couldn't move.

"Aye; ye' don't like that much do ya'. I'll give another pull......'haps it'll come off this time 'eh? If it do, I got four more to work on. 'Ows ye' like that, 'eh Doc? Or ye' can tell me what you an' that 'Olmes gent is doin' in our bissness. 'Ow about it, Doc? Or shall I do ye' in slow like?" He gave another yank, sending waves of pain through my body. I could see the nail now covered with blood. I didn't know how long I could hold out under this torture.

Suddenly there was a loud knock at the door. The man put down the pliers and stomped to the door and shouted, "Get ye' off. Go 'way!" But whoever it was was persistent and knocked again. "Package for Colonel Moran." But the man yelled, "Leave it on the stoop, I say. I'll have it later." But the delivery man was not to be put off; "It's marked 'Urgent' and has to be signed for." My captor let out a string of curses but finally said, "All right, but be quick about it." I heard the door open and then a loud crash. The man swore and yelled, "What's this then?" A scuffle and then a sound like a cricket bat hitting a melon. I heard the unmistakable sound of a body hitting the floor and the delivery man rushed into the room. "Watson, what have you gotten yourself into?"

"Holmes!" Indeed, it was Sherlock Holmes, still with his "Penang Lawyer" in his hand. He put his stick down, pulled out his clasp knife and begin to cut my bonds.

"Watson, you're bleeding. Here, wrap my handkerchief around your thumb."

"Holmes; how did you find me?"

"Later, Doctor." Glancing briefly over his shoulder, he asked in a low voice, "How's our large friend doing? Has he recovered yet? Yell if he looks like he's on his feet."

I didn't understand why Holmes was instructing me to yell but I kept my eye on the portion of the body I could see sprawled on the floor just inside the front door. Holmes was cutting the ropes binding my legs to the chair when I saw some movement; the man was trying to get up. "Holmes," I whispered, "he's almost up. Shall I yell yet?" Holmes put a finger to his lips, "Give it a moment more." I didn't understand what Holmes was up to but I just kept my eyes on the man while Holmes was cutting the last of my bonds. "Holmes; he's on his feet now." I said in a low voice. "He doesn't look very groggy." Holmes glanced up from pulling the final rope from my legs.

"Now Watson; give it all you've got."

"Holmes!" I shouted, "He's getting away. Stop him!."

The man didn't need any further encouragement; he lurched out the door and we could hear his feet pounding the pavestones as he ran. I didn't know what to expect from Holmes and he surprised me once again by casually picking up the crumpled letter from the table where my captor had thrown it. He straightened it out, read it briefly, and then folded it and stuck it in his pocket.

"Well Doctor, we have a few minutes, so let's see if there's anything of interest we can find here before we depart this depressing place."

"But Holmes, He'll get away!"

"Yes; but if I'm right, he'll run to the mews I noticed as I came up the street, grab a cab and, I hope, lead us to professor Moriarty or Moran. I think he'll want to alert them of what happened here as soon as possible. My Hansom is just up the street out of sight. The cabbie is just waiting for my signal."

Once again, I felt how far behind Holmes I was in reacting to a situation and planning ahead. "But won't he realize we're following him? I'm sure he'll be watching for us."

"That's why we'll nose around here for a few minutes, call our cab, go to the mews and wait until the driver of our fugitive's cab returns. For a half-crown, I think he'll be happy to tell us where he dropped off his anxious fare."

"But Holmes, suppose he doesn't know where Moriarty lives? Should not we have questioned him instead of letting him go." Holmes looked pensive, but shook his head.

"Can you imagine that moose of a man ever telling us anything? I'm sure he knew that if he told us anything useful, the professor would deal with him in a way that would be permanent. I had to decide on a strategy immediately and that seemed to be our best chance to at least get a lot closer to Moriarty than we are now."

Holmes then took a few minutes to search the house but found nothing that helped. A few personal items, some food, a cot and some utensils was the total. "I think, Watson, that this place is just a mail relay station. Let us summon our cab; I think we've given our big friend enough time to escape."

We shut the front door - which now showed a broken panel and a loosely hanging hinge. When we reached the street, Holmes gave loud whistle and our cab wheeled out from behind a house two doors away and we headed toward the mews.

III " ....gang aft agley"

Holmes introduced us and asked the owner of the mews if a large, scruffy looking man had hired a cab. The owner, a small, wiry looking man with a tanned leather complexion, said, "Aye, that he did, and in a big hurry he was too. One of me cabbies had just come back from a run and was hitchen' up a fresh horse so's he could look for more customers and so he took the big fella. By the by, I'm Lucas McIvey at your service sirs. A couple of me cabbies should be back soon if you gentlemen needs a cab."

"No, we'll wait for the return of your cabbie who took the large man. I notice your left leg seems somewhat stiff. Was that what ended your career as a jockey?" Mr. McIvey's eyes opened wide and he took a small step backward. "How did you know I was a jock? Did you see me race?" Holmes smiled and said, "No, I noted your bad leg when you walked out to meet us, your very outdoors tan, and your boots; they are not the boots of an ordinary mews worker. They are riding boots, not worker boots. Your height and strong looking forearms proclaim a horseman; I guessed a professional jockey."

"Ya' got a sharp eye sir, I give ya' that. I rode for almost 15 years afore me mount stumbled bad and pitched me into the rail. It were a shame too as I had a good horse. What wasn't well known was how good he really was so I had a double carpet and could'a made a bag full. He ran good in the wet too and it were a rainy day. The dogs was up and as we turned home he run too near 'em, an' one leg slipped out. He got all tripped up an' that was me last ride. The docs never could fix all the breaks so I quit racin' and bought this stable and cabs. I can't race no more but I keep good care of the horses and I watch careful like how the boys treats 'em."

A bell suddenly rang in my memory. "Now I know why Lucas McIvey sounded familiar; I saw you race several times."

"Ah, an' did you float a quid or so on me, sir?"

"I certainly may have! But that was a long time ago. I still love the races but my financial position curtails my betting limits now. And that's probably a good thing!" McIvey chuckled and offered us two chairs in his small office. He put a teapot on a spirit burner and handed us a plate piled up with biscuits. "The wife makes these biscuits; I bring 'em for the cabbies as they don't take much time for food, fearin' they might miss a customer. Tea an' biscuits is 'bout all they have 'till supper at home."

When the tea was hot, Holmes and I slowly munched our biscuits and sipped our tea. I was dying to ask how Holmes found me and was about to ask but he read my thoughts as he often did. "I tried to call on you at the Rag to lunch with you but the big lieutenant at the desk said you rushed off after finishing the mail. I went on home and found you weren't there, but Mrs. Hudson said she heard you come in and then leave a few minutes later so I looked around to see if I could find a clue to your unusual activity. I saw you had gotten out your old uniform but only the pants were missing. I was puzzling over that when I noticed you had left your 'Spy notepad' on the desk. The top sheet was gone but in holding the pad on an angle I could see the indents your pencil had made. The rest was simple - I took a pencil and rubbed the side of the lead lightly over the marks and so was able to see '10 Rillington Place' appear. The whole thing worried me, so I engaged a Hansom, paid the driver well, and apparently barged in just in time to save the set of fingernails on your right hand! My dear Doctor; if you had written that note in pen instead of pencil, I dare say it would have gone very badly indeed!"

"Holmes, I can't thank you enough or apologize enough for my rash and ill-considered actions."

"No apology needed; just promise you won't do it again. I don't think you realized what vicious men professor Moriarty employs. And I am absolutely convinced that we have the right man in our sights. This episode confirms it."

After our leisurely tea and biscuit lunch, we talked about our search for the professor. Mr. McIvey came in between taking care of the horses and dispatching his cabbies and we talked and laughed about our turf experiences. As time passed, however, Holmes looked more and more serious and kept checking his watch every few minutes. "Watson, I fear I may have made a mistake by letting one of McIvey's cabbies drive our dangerous friend. I'll never forgive myself if harm comes to him." Just then we heard the unmistakable sound of hoofs approaching, so we rushed out to see if it was the cab the big man had hired. McIvey heard them too and joined us waiting to receive the Hansom. But to our horror, when it turned into the short path to the mews, we couldn't see any driver. McIvey shouted, "The horse came back by hisself! Mr. Holmes. what's this? Where's Evan?"

We all rushed to the Hansom to see, but Holmes held up a hand and shouted for everyone to stop until he could inspect the cab. We halted our headlong pace and Holmes began to walk quickly around the Hansom. When he got to the far side I heard him yell, "Watson! Come quickly, he's not missing, he's collapsed on the driver's shelf and he's in bad shape."

McIvey and I raced around to where Holmes was and immediately saw the driver lying on the driver's platform, his body and the platform covered with large patches of blood. Holmes and I climbed up to the platform and I quickly put my hand on his throat and, with great relief, felt a pulse; weak, but there all the same. "He's still alive, Holmes, but we need to get a doctor or get him to hospital right away. I don't have my bag but I'll do what I can. Lucas, please get me some clean water and something with which I can bandage his wounds and stop the bleeding." Holmes and I carefully carried the driver to a narrow strip of turf at one side of the path into the mews and laid him down as gently as we could. McIvey had thought for a moment after my request and then, slapped his forehead and replied, "I have just the thing; a roll of wrap I use when a horse has a hurt leg. It's clean, doctor, and I'll get a basin of water."

As Holmes continued his examination of the cab, one of McIvey's cabbies arrived and as soon as he stabled his cab he came running out to see what the excitement was all about. He was almost comic in appearance - a shock of wild red hair sticking out from under an old, faded, tri-color jockey cap, long curling handlebar moustache, and bushy eyebrows. He looked to be late middle-aged and so tanned you had to look hard to see all the freckles. Holmes collared him immediately; "My good man, do you know where Pinchin Lane is? I need you to go there and ask for Toby. He's in number three. Tell the man who lives there, Sherman by name, that Sherlock Holmes needs Toby quickly. Here's a half-crown for you and one for Sherman."

The cabbie looked extremely puzzled but responded enthusiastically. "Sir, I knows where every bloody thing in London be; good or bad if ye' gits me drift. I been doin' this for onto 20 years an' I learned plenty doin' it, believe me, sir. Pinchin Lane is in Lambeth, down by the docks, right? I'm Riley sir, but who is Toby?"

"Toby is a mutt with an extraordinary nose. I need him back here as soon as you can fetch him. Please hurry before the trail goes cold." Holmes then turned to McIvey, "Should we have Riley take Evan to hospital first and then fetch Toby?" McIvey shook his head, "No, I hear another cab comin' up the street - an' we needs a trap for Evan. Send Riley as you said." Holmes waved Riley on and the cabbie charged back into the stables and soon emerged driving a fresh cab and horse. With a loud cry which sounded like it could be Irish Gaelic, and a wave of his whip, he thundered off down the road. I couldn't help smiling. McIvey came out of his office and handed me a roll of bandages and a basin of water with a cloth floating in what turned out to be warm water. "I put some hot water in with the cold, doctor. Will it do?"

"Just fine, Lucas, thanks. I saw some bleeding from his side; help me get his shirt off so I can see the wound." McIvey supported the man's torso while I removed his shirt. Much to my consternation, there was an obvious bullet wound in his side that was still oozing blood. Since I didn't have my bag, all I could do was stanch the bleeding and hope the bullet hadn't done serious damage. I wrapped a strip of the bandage roll around the man's body and used the wet cloth to wipe his face and clean a bloody gash in the side of his head. The bleeding from the gash had slowed so I wrapped a strip of material around his head and tied it off. We let him down again and I asked McIvey if he had some brandy or something which I could give a nip to our patient. "Come now, doctor, a horseman without a drop or two of the old spirits? Not a bit of it. I'll be right back. And here comes a cab now. I'll have him get the trap right away and we'll get Evan to hospital quick like." He waved wildly at the cab driver and I heard him yell that we needed the trap right away.

After giving our injured driver a swig of the rum McIvey brought out, we all relaxed a little. The driver, whose name I learned was Evan Postlewaite, was also an ex-jockey who knew McIvey when they both rode. I could have guessed that earlier, as Evan was of the same build as McIvey and wore the same riding boots. Holmes was apparently through with his examination of the cab and came over to join us. I was very curious about the request to bring Toby, and as he usually does, he answered my thoughts before I could ask.

"Let me tell you what I found. First, I noticed, when we lifted the driver off his platform where he had collapsed, the blood from his wound must have run onto one wheel of the cab. That meant that we might be able to backtrack, using Toby's sensitive nose, to where the cab had been. Every time that wheel turned, it left a bit of blood I'm hoping Toby can detect. After noting that, I found a spot on the edge of the driver's partition with a patch of skin, blood, and hair. I think that must be where Evan's head injury came from.

He probably sustained it when he collapsed from his bullet wound. I discovered the distinct shoe prints of two people in the cab. One set of large prints, likely of your kidnapper, and a set of smaller prints. Then, when I thought I had wrung out everything I could, I saw, buried in the wall in front of the driver's partition, a bullet. I'll need to verify my conclusions with the driver whenever he is able to talk to us but I think what happened is this; the kidnapper had the driver take him to either Moriarty's or Moran's home so he could tell what happened; namely, my interference and your escape. He probably told the driver to wait and then ran to the house. Then, when he came out, there was another man with him. I can only take a guess what happened then. I believe the man, who had a pistol, ordered our driver to head for some little traveled area and then he intended kill the driver because he could tell the police (or us, Watson) where he had delivered the big man. I suspect it was Colonel Moran's house because I don't think Moriarty would trust his location to a gang member. Moriarty is, I'm sure, smarter than that. Now all we can do is take care of the driver as best we can. Mr. McIvey, when do you think your driver will be ready to take Evan?"

"Mr. Holmes sir, he should be bringin' the trap around in a moment. Doctor, how's he doin'?"

I had just changed his bandages and he was starting to come around some. The head wound didn't concern me much but the bullet wound needed attention. I gave him another small sip of the rum and he actually tried to sit up. McIvey saw him and came hurrying over. "Evan, Evan, can you tell us what happened? We'll get you to hospital as soon as we can."

Evan was groggy but began to speak to us in a low voice that was obviously painful to him. "I.......... I...'ave I been........shot? Hurts."

Holmes sat down and leaned close to him. "Evan, I'm going to tell you what I think happened to you. If I'm right, just nod. If I'm wrong, please try to tell me. Can you do that?" Evan listened to Holmes intently and nodded a bit tentatively. Holmes then began speaking slowly; "You drove the big man to a house - he told you to wait, went into the house and came out with a smallish man who ordered you to drive toward a more secluded area. Is that right so far?" Evan broke out with the same awestruck expression I had seen on many people when it seems Holmes had actually been at the scene. He stammered, "... yes,.....but how..... did you....know?" Holmes smiled and said. "Don't concern yourself with that now. Then, and now I'm really guessing, he shot at you and . . . wait . . . did he shoot the big man before shooting you?" Evan struggled again to sit up as he nodded his head slowly; "Not sure, think so . . . can't . . . can't 'member much, head hurts." We carefully laid him back down. The bullet wound must have made it very painful because he cried out and then fainted.

We sat there for about another five minutes when we heard the clatter of an approaching horse. It was the trap. Holmes called to the driver, "We need for you to take Evan to hospital - he's been shot!"

McIvey came out to where Holmes and I were getting Evan up. "Tommy's brought our big trap with two; it'll be easier to lay Evan down in. Any more questions for poor Evan, Mr. Holmes?"

"Just one." Holmes and I had Evan on his feet, ready to lay him in the back of the trap McIvey was having brought out. We were supporting Evan on both sides with our arms around him and his arms on our shoulders. Holmes turned his head and asked softly, "Where, Evan? Can you tell us?" You could see the effort to speak on Evan's strained face. He managed to say, ". . . to . . .Westminster . . . Middlesex . . . two in," and gestured weakly with one hand, "then west." That's all he could muster, but Holmes nodded, "Thank you Evan; we'll get him, I promise."

McIvey's driver, Tommy, had thoughtfully spread out a horse blanket and we carefully put Evan on it in the trap. McIvey handed Tommy a wad of bank notes and waved him off. "Give that to 'em at the hospital - should be 'nuff to get him cared for."

As Tommy headed out with Evan, McIvey came over to us and said, in a firm voice, "He's one o' mine, gentlemen, and I'll do for him, never fear. Get the nasty barstid that did him!"

Holmes shook hands with Lucas, "I will do everything in my power to bring this vicious criminal to justice." McIvey said, with a grim look, "An' if that justice includes shootin' the rat, more power to ya'! How's about tea, a spot of rum and a biscuit? I think y'r Toby will be here soon." Holmes smiled as he answered, "That's a fine idea, I'm ready for tea and a biscuit, and a spot of rum with them sounds irresistible. Watson, are you up for another of Mrs. McIvey's fine biscuits?"

"Indeed I am, Holmes; and the spot of rum isn't a bad idea either!"

As we were enjoying our snack, Holmes cautioned McIvey about giving out any information to strangers about Evan. "Tell his family of course. They'll want to see him in hospital, but if anybody else asks, just say you're worried - he's missing. Please tell your cabbies to act dumb if they're asked about him also. The villain who shot Evan may want to know if he survived. We need to let him think Evan must have died from his wound."

"I understand Mr. Holmes. Nary a word to no one - I promises."

We didn't have long for our repast. Just as we were finishing our snack, we heard, not only a horse nearing the mews, but the bark of a dog. "Holmes! I think our tracker is here."

"Good. We don't have a lot of time before it's dark. If our marvelous host, Mr. McIvey will do us one more favor and hitch a fresh horse to the cab Evan drove, we'll be out of his hair. And Watson, bring a bandage you took off Evan before you put the last one on. That will give Toby a good sniff when he tracks the cab wheel." McIvey was already working to free the horse from Evan's cab. I'll bring us a fresh horse when I unhitch this'un."

Toby had jumped down from the cab and was rapidly inspecting the area with his nose to the ground. He saw Holmes and dashed over to him, his tail wagging like he had just found a long lost friend. Holmes scratched him behind his ears, patted his flank and lifted him into Evan's cab. This puzzled me; "Aren't you going to have him smell the blood on the wheel?

"Too soon. There is only one logical road to take from here to Westminster so we'll save the time Toby would be leading us. We'll put him in charge when we get close to two miles in - I believe that's what Evan was trying to tell us. After the stop at what I think was Colonel Moran's house, Evan was told to drive west, probably to a more deserted area."

"But why shoot my kidnapper? Shooting Evan I can understand."

"Ah, there we have to make an informed supposition; I think Moran asked him about the letter and what he may have said to you. Finding out that the whole plan had unraveled, Moran was probably enraged at the failure of his henchman and decided to get rid of him as well as Evan. Remember, Moran was not only trying to protect himself but also Moriarty. But I'm sure when he calms down he'll realize that I'll be after them both."

McIvey had hitched up a rested horse so we thanked him for his help, told him we would return the cab as soon as we could and set off for Middlesex/Westminster.

IV Toby Draws a Blank

Westminster is not far from where we were in Kensington and the going was easy as carriage traffic was light. As we crossed into Westminster, Holmes called down from his driver's shelf, "Another mile or so and we'll let Toby lead us."

The late afternoon was pleasant and our horse was trotting along at a good pace. Toby had settled down and was napping with his head resting on my feet. He looked so peaceful I decided not to nudge him off. When we had gone what I judged to be about a mile and a half, Holmes pulled the cab to a stop and got down from his perch to get Toby started on his part of the plan. Toby woke up when the Holmes stopped the cab and he was wagging his tail as if to say "Let's get this going!" He jumped down from the cab and I gave Toby a sniff of the bandage - it had a good deal of blood on it because it was the first one I applied when Evan arrived. Toby took a smell and cocked his head comically like a gourmet sampling a vintage. Holmes then attached a long leash to Toby's collar and led him to a spot just ahead of our horse and tossed the reins to me. I pulled up the slack in the reins and got ready to follow Holmes and Toby.

Toby lowered his head, padded to the left and then the right . . . and stopped. Holmes led him a little farther up the road; Toby stopped again and looked up at Holmes with what I swear was a quizzical expression! "Holmes, what's wrong with Toby? He can't seem to find the scent." Holmes had a most puzzled and at the same time, frustrated look. "I don't know. I can't imagine the cab going up the other side of the road; any traffic would be right in their face, but I'll take Toby over there." Holmes then led Toby to the other side, but still nothing. Perhaps to show us what he thought of the fiasco, Toby found a convenient fence post and relieved himself on it!

"Watson, Toby's never failed. I must rethink my whole line of reasoning." Holmes led Toby back to our cab, tied the leash to a wheel spoke and sat on the boarding step of the cab with his hands on his knees. Since it was obvious he was in deep thought, I didn't distract him with any further questions.

Holmes was sitting on the step, I was leaning against the side of the cab, our horse was snorting a bit and stomping a foreleg and Toby had curled up in the grass verge and had gone to sleep. We could have been posing for a painting. After several minutes, Holmes straightened up; "Watson, let us reenact, as best we can, the action when small-feet stopped the cab. You be big-feet. We have just stepped down from the cab. Big-feet must have known by then that he was in a perilous situation. Small-feet must have decided to get rid of big-feet and Evan by then so what does he do?"

"Wouldn't he have shot Evan first so he couldn't escape in the cab?"

"I thought so at first, but what if big-feet senses what's about to happen to him and starts running away before small-feet can shoot Evan? Let's try that scenario. Stand with me as if we had just stepped out of the cab."

We moved to the position Holmes had described. We were close together, almost even with the front of the cab. Holmes now took a couple of long steps straight ahead which brought him almost even with the horse's rear. He turned and mimicked pulling a gun out of his jacket and pointing it at me. I turned to run but got only one big step before Holmes yelled "Bam! All right, Watson, you're shot." He paused and then, with a whoop, cried out, "Oh, Watson, what a blind bat I've been! Look where you are."

"Holmes, I'm just by the wheel, what difference does that make?"

"The blood, Watson, the blood on the wheel! - it's not Evan's, it's big-feet's blood. He was shot, probably sagged into the wheel or grabbed it to stay upright and in doing so bled on the wheel. It's not Toby's fault he couldn't find a trail, it's Sherlock Holmes's fault!"

All the activity woke Toby up. He was standing there, looking back and forth from Holmes to me, probably wondering how he ended up with two crazy people. Holmes laughed, untied Toby's leash and had him get a good sniff of the wheel, and then led him a few paces ahead of our horse. This time, Toby's tail went up straight in the air, his head lowered to an inch or two off the ground and he started off up the road. Suddenly he stopped and began to weave back and forth across the path and then charged off again. He kept repeating this pattern for two or three minutes until Holmes waved me to stop and pulled Toby's leash taut so we all came to a halt.

I called out, "Holmes; what's wrong with Toby? Holmes stood there for a minute or so looking as puzzled as I was. Then he clapped a hand to his forehead. "It's the wheel, Watson, the cab wheel has blood on only about two feet of the road surface and that leaves about seven feet of clean surface between deposits that Toby can detect. No wonder he wanders around - he loses the scent for seven feet of every wheel turn. If I can keep him going in a straight line perhaps he'll stop weaving. I'll try keeping a tighter hold on his leash and walking straight ahead."

Sure enough, with Holmes guiding Toby, we made much faster progress. As Toby got used to Holmes tugging him into a straight line, he stopped trying to go from side to side in between deposits and Holmes was able to loosen his hold and give Toby more slack. We were moving at a good pace now and soon came to a crossing. Toby started across the road but stopped halfway and again started weaving back and forth trying to pick up the scent. I stopped the cab and asked Holmes, "What's wrong now? Has the trail gone cold?" Holmes paused for a moment and then answered, "Didn't Evan say 'then west'? Perhaps this road is the one and this corner is where he turned south to return home." Saying that, he led Toby around the corner heading west and sure enough, Toby began pulling on the leash and we started going west. We were making very good time now.

As we continued on, it seemed Toby pulled harder and harder. Before long, Holmes was leaning back, Toby's neck was thrust forward and he began to bark. Holmes turned back to me and shouted, "Look Watson, in the ditch up ahead! I think it's the body of your kidnapper. We've found the crime scene. Stop the horse! Let's not disturb the area until I can examine it." At that, I backed off and tugged the reins until our horse stopped. He began bobbing his head, pawing the ground, and trying to back up. "Holmes, I think I had better let him back up until he calms down! Maybe he smells blood."

"Yes, and let me give you Toby so he doesn't walk all over the spot. I can see already where the grass verge has been trampled." Holmes slowly walked around the disturbed turf area, stopped several times and once knelt down and used his glass to examine a spot. He then went over to the body in the ditch beside the road and turned it halfway over. Finally, he got to his feet and came over to me, took Toby's leash and led him to the cab, lifted him up and took the reins from me.

"Yes, Doctor, the whole story is written here in the grass. The cab stopped, both men got out, small-feet walked three paces, turned facing big-feet, who had not yet moved. Big-feet then, I think, saw the pistol, tried to turn and run, but took only one big step before he was shot. As our little demonstration showed, he was even with the wheel at that moment. Small-feet then shot him again and he collapsed on the wheel. I found two bullet wounds on his body, Watson, and what was a pool of blood just by where the cab wheel would have been. The shot must have panicked the horse; I saw deep marks where the cab spun around. If the horse had not panicked and yanked the cab around, Evan would probably have been killed also, but since small-feet was right beside the horse, I think he was knocked off balance when the horse bolted and couldn't get a clean shot at Evan. I think he regained his balance when the cab was halfway turned, shot, and hit Evan in the side. Either that or his first shot was the one I found embedded in the cab wall and the next shot hit Evan. I can't be sure. In any case, if he shot again, it missed altogether as the cab wildly sped off."

"Holmes! It's just as you surmised earlier. What do we do now?"

"I'm going to take the cab to the other side of the road and see if I can determine what small-feet did after Evan got away. The verge grass shows foot prints easily. Without a cab, small-feet must have walked. I hope Toby can follow them as well as he did the cab."

Holmes took the reins again, turned the cab, and led the horse to the other side of the narrow lane. He handed the reins to me and got Toby out again."I must be careful that Toby sniffs only the footprints, otherwise, he'll follow the blood trail back the way we came!"

"What then? Shouldn't we notify the local police about the body?"

"In time Doctor, we can't waste the opportunity now when the footprints are fresh. Besides, Watson, your tormentor isn't going anywhere. We will see what we can do now and then we'll tell the police, return Toby, and, as the saying goes, 'head for the barn', how does that sound?"

"Wonderful. I've had enough excitement for one day!"

V. The Battle is Rejoined

As it turned out, Toby couldn't follow the footprints very far. He got us past the crossing heading east on the road but it soon widened and was covered with hoof prints and cab and wagon wheel ruts. It was obviously well traveled. I put Toby back into the cab with me and we continued east for about two furlongs when we could see we were coming up on a village. That explained the traffic that stopped our tracking; the road was the link to the Kensington road and thence to central London. Holmes called to me, "Let us find a police station and report our finding of big-feet and then head back."

We quickly located the local police station and Holmes very briefly told the P/C that we had merely spotted a body in the ditch west of the main road. He didn't give out any further details so we wouldn't be slowed answering questions. Holmes left our address and we wheeled around and soon were on our way to McIvey's mews. Since Lambeth was too far out of our way and as it was rapidly getting dark, Holmes decided we would leave Toby with McIvey and return him to Sherman the next day.

McIvey was happy to see us but we couldn't give him news that we caught Evan's assailant. Holmes did tell him that we have identified him and would continue trying to run him to ground. "Aye, that's all I can ask. Don't worry 'bout Toby, he'll be fine. Now, can I give ya' a ride home? It'll be a pleasure."

Holmes smiled and replied to Lucas, "Thank you Mr. McIvey, but we will engage one of your cabbies and pay the usual fare. We appreciate your help and hospitality; and, not least, your wife's biscuits." McIvey called a cabbie who was just leaving with a fresh horse to take us home and we bid "good evening" to him as we left for Baker Street.

Mrs. Hudson fixed us a quick supper and a large pot of coffee. "My, you boys look all ragged out. I'll have some fresh tarts for your dessert in a few minutes." We thanked her and didn't waste any time cleaning our plates of roast chicken, potatoes and peas.

"Holmes, I don't think I can stay awake for dessert; that was quite a day we had." Holmes had packed his calabash and settled back in his big chair. He turned to me and said with determination, "I think our colonel will be on his best guard now. Since his trap failed, he'll be looking for ways to minimize the damage. I imagine that will include removing Sherlock Holmes and John H. Watson from contention. If he doesn't, Moriarty, the math professor, might decide the colonel is a liability now rather than a right hand man and remove him from the equation, if you'll pardon the pun. I have read the letter your kidnapper left behind and indeed, Moran set a trap for you. He described you and said his information came from an agent 'the professor' sent to Budleigh-Salterton to find out what happened to Silas Moran. That's how the big man knew our names and recognized you."

"Holmes, I've been a dunce! I'll never go off on my own again."

Holmes warned Mrs. Hudson about strangers at the door and to check with us before letting in anyone she or Billy didn't know. She nodded, "My door's a strong one, Mr. Holmes, and I'll keep it locked from now on, believe me."

We both retired as soon as we finished the warm elderberry tarts Mrs. Hudson brought up to us after supper. We were both yawning profusely after our hectic day.

I awoke the next morning to bright sunlight streaming in my east window. It startled me so much I sat up straight in bed and checked my clock. It was nine o'clock! I threw on my robe and hurried out to our sitting room where Holmes was sitting calmly at our table reading the early edition of the paper. The remains of his breakfast showed how tardy I had been.

"Ah, Watson, I see you have recovered from our busy day yesterday. I'll ring for your breakfast. I told Mrs. Hudson to delay it until further notice as I heard the unmistakable sounds of heavy sleep emanating from your room. I didn't have the heart to wake you."

"Thank you, it was an exhausting day. It was such a disappointment not to have found Moran's house that it left me quite discouraged." Holmes folded his paper, smacked it firmly on the table, "Yes, and I'm going to try to rectify that today." And with that, he got up and headed for his room. A few minutes later, Billy delivered my breakfast – fresh biscuits, eggs, sausages, and a pot of coffee. I wasted no time reducing it to empty plates! I was just spreading jam on the last biscuit and about to pour another cup of coffee when Holmes appeared from his room. I know I stared at his outfit. "Holmes, what in the world? You look like a city worker."

"Right you are, Watson. Your posing as a drain inspector, even though it didn't work as you planned, gave me an idea." He strode to the desk and picked up a sheaf of official looking papers, tucked them in his shirt pocket and walked briskly to our door.

"Holmes, are you sure Moran won't recognize you?"

"Oh, I'm not trying to fool Moran!" And with that parting shot he left.

It's a comfortable and sometimes exciting life I lead and I wouldn't trade it for anything, but it can be awfully frustrating too. Not having the razor sharp skills of my friend often results in leaving me in a state of complete puzzlement. I don't have the grasp of a situation and the alternatives that Sherlock seems to immediately see and be ready to act upon. All the while I'm still struggling to get a handle on things. I understood that the struggle to find Moran and deal with both him and professor Moriarty was still very much alive. I figured Holmes would probably be gone for most of the day and as my shoulder was feeling normal again, and it was a Thursday, I would knock up Thurston and spend the afternoon at billiards. Maybe that would take my mind off our failed efforts to locate Colonel Moran. Unfortunately for my game, I found my concentration wandering, and Thurston gave me a good thrashing. As I made my way home I stopped at Bradley's for some cigarettes and at a small used-book store to get something to read. It turned out to be a good idea because Holmes didn't return until just before supper and the book helped keep my mind off our problem. It was a slim volume of Scottish history with a section on Scottish surnames. I found out mine was the eighteenth most common in Scotland.

When Holmes arrived, I rang for Billy to let him know we were ready for dinner. Holmes went to his room, changed out of his simple disguise and went directly to the mantle and his old briar pipe as soon as he came into the sitting room. I was dying to find out about his day but I knew he would come around to it in his own time. He lit his pipe and settled in his armchair.

"Watson, I actually made some good progress today. First I took a cab to McIvey's stable and retrieved Toby, took him back to

Sherman and paid him. Then I had my cabbie take me to the little village we saw before we lost Moran's trail and had to turn back. I had the cabbie wait down the road a bit. I then became an inspector from the City of London proper. I visited several shops, asking innocent sounding questions and shuffling through my papers as if I was lost. The papers, by the way, were ones I forged this morning while you were quite peacefully in the arms of Morpheus. The key paper is this one. Have a look."

It was a note sized piece of common grade paper with parallel lines drawn across the page. On the first line was "Colonel Sebastian Moran". The second and third lines were labeled "Address" but the writing was illegible. "Holmes, I can't read the address." Holmes smiled, "I know, I smeared it. Since I didn't know where Moran lived, I printed 221B, Baker Street and then made it unreadable. I showed it to the lady at the little general goods shop and told her I was here to inspect the chimneys and vents for fire safety and somehow the address got all smeared. I had made the other papers look like orders for inspections and flipped through them quickly for her benefit. When I got to Moran's sheet she shook her head and commiserated with me . . . and then, Watson, pointed out Moran's house! It was only two doors east of her shop."

"Holmes; what a coup! What then?"

"I took a chance that Moran wouldn't recognize me so I knocked on the door. I waited, but no answer, so I looked around the grounds. It's a house, not a cottage; newer than most of the other dwellings in town. From the looks of the village, the place is going through a gentrification process. People with means are moving there to get away from the ills of the City and enjoy clean air and country surroundings. With the steady card winnings you witnessed, I have no doubt Moran also has rooms in London proper to be close to the Rag and probably, his gang underlings. He can more easily pass on instructions from Moriarty that way."

"But Holmes, won't Moran hear about the 'safety inspector' from the local gossip?"

"I expect he will hear about my visit, yes. But as soon as my cabbie dropped me off I applied a stage moustache, a neat little goatee and slouched just enough to take off a couple of inches of height. I presumed that Moran received, through Moriarty, at least a passing description of me from his Budleigh-Salterton spy. For you of course, he saw you often at the Rag. He could describe you in detail to big-feet, whose name, by the way, according to the salutation on the letter from Moran, was Ambrose; a particularly inapt name for your deceased kidnapper!"

Billy and Mrs. Hudson came in with our dinners and we wasted no time digging in to Mrs. Hudson's country style cooking; roast duck, potatoes, beans and biscuits. When Billy came up, he brought fresh coffee and scones with strawberry jam and took our now empty dishes away. Holmes was going to the mantle to get a pipe when he remembered, "Watson, I have neglected checking my mail. Let us see if there's anything of interest in today's post." He opened our door and brought in a few letters from the small table outside the door on which Billy deposits our mail. "Ah, Watson, I've gotten a reply from Alexander Bain. Let's see what the great mathematician has to say about Moriarty." Holmes got his carved ivory letter opener - a gift from Lady Portia - from our desk and extracted a single sheet from the envelope. A look of disappointment crossed his face. "Bad luck, Doctor, this note is from Bain's solicitor; Bain died in 1877. I didn't know that when I wrote my request for information on Moriarty." Holmes continued reading and suddenly brightened. "Listen to this; his solicitor adds, 'I'm sorry that Professor Bain is not alive to answer your letter but I can tell you this; Professor Bain ended his relationship with professor Moriarty abruptly and informed me he had severed all connections with him.' Quite revealing I think, eh Watson?"

"It certainly coincides with your findings so far. What now, Holmes?"

"It's Friday evening. Doesn't Colonel Moran start his marathon poker game tonight?"

"Yes, he does; but do you think after all that's happened, he will still show up at the Rag?"

"Oh, I think so, Doctor. Why shouldn't he behave outwardly as if nothing was amiss? The letter to Ambrose was typewritten and Moran didn't sign it. The envelope was missing; I didn't find it when I inspected the Rillington house so Ambrose must have disposed of it. I'm sure it was Moran who shot both Ambrose and Evan. He knows Ambrose is dead and he probably thinks Evan is also. And even though he knows we are on to him, he probably thinks we have nothing we can take to the police. Of course he will be on his guard, and now that the Rillington mail relay station is compromised he and Moriarty must find some other way to communicate. That's our key, Watson. If he wrote to Moriarty from his home, there would be no need to use Rillington. He would probably use the direct method only in an emergency. He wouldn't want the local post people to see regular letters to Moriarty; they might notice and remember. After all, they sort the mail every day for each posting. In such a small village, the postman knows who sends to whom and who receives from whom!"

"Then how are we going to find Moriarty's address?"

"Because, Watson, I intend to break in to Moran's house tonight while he is at the Rag playing cards!"

VI In a Just Cause

My breath caught in my throat and I think my heart skipped several beats. "Holmes! If you're caught you'll be the criminal and Moran will be the victim! It could put you in prison." Holmes put down his pipe and gave me a grim smile. "Yes, but I'm convinced it's worth the risk. After all, I've done this before; and, as I recall, you were there to assist me."

"Milverton! Yes, I certainly remember since it was just in January. I haven't written it up of course, due to the famous people involved, but someday the story of how the sword of justice found a proper target will be told. So I'm going with you again, and don't even consider saying 'No'. As I recall we wore soft-soled shoes, dark clothes, masks, and took a dark lantern. Oh, and your very complete burgling kit. If that's all, I'll change and be ready in about fifteen minutes."

At first, Holmes looked quite grim, but then I saw him relax and give me a wry smile. "Very well, old friend, I won't argue, as I see you will not be deterred by any arguments I could advance. Just one addition if you please; I noticed a small kennel as I peeped over the side wall of Moran's place. I assume he has at least one dog, so obtain a bag of meat scraps from Mrs. Hudson while I change into some inconspicuous clothes. Tonight, the game is truly afoot!"

Mrs. Hudson was clearly puzzled by my request for meat scraps, but after several years of our sometimes strange doings, she just shook her head, smiled, and filled a small bag with leftover duck scraps and handed it to me. I hurried upstairs and changed into the darkest clothes I had, donned my soft-soled shoes and found the masks I had made for our Milverton adventure in the back of a dresser drawer. As I rushed into our sitting room Holmes was just putting his burgling kit in his jacket and I saw the dark lantern on our dining table. He addressed me then in a grim, determined voice. "Watson, please bring your Webley. I hope we won't need it, but we must be prepared." Hearing those chilling words, I went back into my room and tucked the pistol into the inside pocket of my jacket.

Holmes had already told Billy to summon a cab so when we exited 221, there was one just pulling up. We climbed in and Holmes gave the driver a coin and, to my surprise, told the driver, "The Rag, please." Then, to me, "I want you to quietly check so we can be certain Moran is at his usual Friday game. Just a quick glance will be enough. If anyone asks, you're just looking for a friend who's going to meet you for dinner."

When we arrived at the Rag, Holmes said, "I'll have our driver park across the road and wait for you." I hurried into the club, and as inconspicuously as possible, peeked around the corner of the entrance to the card room. Sure enough, Moran was at his usual poker table, so I went back outside and across the street where Holmes and the cab were waiting.

"It's all right Holmes, Moran is there." Holmes nodded and called up to our driver, "McIvey's stables on Rillington, in Kensington, please." As usual with Holmes, I was surprised and puzzled. "Holmes, why McIvey?"

"I don't want to let anyone we don't know and trust in on our late night escapade. We may be gone until near dawn. McIvey we know, will go along with anything that has to do with catching Evan's attacker. I will tell him as little as possible about our main objective, finding the professor, but anything we find to implicate Moran will be an added plus."

When we pulled up at McIvey's, Holmes dismissed our driver with another coin. We were happy to see that Lucas was still at work. He rushed over to us as soon as he saw us exit the cab. "Mr. Holmes, I saw Evan in hospital today. They've removed the bullet an' told me he should be all right. Seems it didn't hit nothin' vital. He's still groggy an' not sure what happened. His memory is still a mite hazy, ya' know. What brings you two here? What can I do for you? By the way, Mr. Holmes, there was a man here today askin' for Evan but I told him Evan was missin' an so was his cab an' I feared for his life. Was that all right?"

Holmes clapped Lucas on the back, "You couldn't have done it better. Now Doctor Watson and I have a very secret job to do that might take quite a while, but it has to do with nabbing the villain who shot Evan. We'll need a cabbie whom you trust to keep a tight lip. The pay will make up for any London customers he may miss."

"Mr. Holmes, I have just the man an' he's due back in a few minutes. Remember Riley?" Holmes broke out into a big smile, "Of course, he fetched Toby for us. Toby is how we found where Evan was shot and I'm sure I know who did it. That's what Watson and I want to verify tonight." McIvey grinned. "He's a bit of a show but he's been with me for years and I trust the big oaf completely. Now come inside and we'll wait for him. I'm real sorry, the biscuits is gone but the rum ain't. How about a wee drop?"

We gladly acquiesced and were soon presented two glasses with about two fingers of rum in each. McIvey sat down and fixed us intently. "It be a serious thing, right? I don't see two gents with a dark lantern, an' dark clothes everday; 'specially when one of 'ems got a bulge in his jacket what looks a lot like a pistol!" Holmes had his drink in his hand and stopped midway to his mouth. "Mr. McIvey, you should have been a detective. You are correct in assuming that Watson and I are on what could be a dangerous mission and we may need the support a Webley can offer. We are out to 'get the goods' as they say, on not only Evan's assailant but another criminal; a worse one in fact. I'm telling you this so you won't have any suspicions about our motives and actions. Fair enough?"

"More than fair Mr. Holmes; and more power to the both o' ya. I think I hear Alroy comin' up the road. I'll have him get a fresh horse. He'll be ready in ten minutes. I'll be lettin' him know we got a special job goin' tonight that'll pay him good and maybe nab the rat who shot poor Evan."

True to his word, McIvey and Alroy Riley had us on our way in ten minutes. Holmes gave pound notes to both McIvey and Riley for the night's work, causing the big Irishman to give out a loud 'whoosh'; particularly when Lucas gave the note Holmes had given him to Riley and said to us, "I feel I'm part o' this, Mr. Holmes, no need to pay me. God bless an' good luck."

Holmes told Riley to take the direct road to Middlesex/

Westminster and he would tell him when to stop the cab. Riley nodded, let out a whooping "dean deifir!" and we settled back, put up the mud board and hardly spoke until we were almost at the village road. Holmes called out to Riley, "Take the road to the village, it's about a quarter of a mile." Soon, the cab slowed and we turned east onto the well-used road. Just on the edge of the village, Riley stopped the cab, dismounted and leaned into the passenger space. "I didna' think you wished me to be yellin', so where do I drop you two?" Holmes looked slightly surprised and said quietly,

"You are a jewel Alroy; any time I have a clandestine job to do and need a ride, I'll ask for you. Take us slowly through the village, I want to check a house as we go by. When we get about a hundred yards past the center of the place, we'll get out and walk. Watson and I will probably need an hour. When we finish, we'll walk to where you dropped us off. Is there anything you can do to pass the time without disturbing any of the local people?"

"Aye, Mr. Holmes, about a mile from here is another little town - but that one has Ryan McDuffy's pub. He's me brother-in-law and I'll have no trouble doin' a pint and having a blarney with him. Don't worry, sir, I'll be ready to pick you up in an hour."

Riley climbed up to the driver's shelf and gave the horse a little flip of the reins. We proceeded quietly toward the little clump of houses. As we neared the store, Holmes nudged me and whispered, "Second house, Watson. See any lights?" I peered at the house Holmes indicated but all was dark. "I don't see a light anywhere, Holmes." He nodded, "Nor do I. Let us hope he doesn't leave a sentry. I doubt he knows we have any idea where he lives but we still have to be cautious." A few moments later Riley brought the cab to a stop and we got out as quietly as we could. Riley drove on slowly and we made our way back to Moran's house, went down a path at the side of the house to a wall that enclosed the rear yard. Holmes whispered, "Have the duck scraps ready, I didn't see a dog when I did my reconnaissance but there's a small kennel in the far corner. There is a gate here where the wall meets the house. It has a simple latch. We'll enter the house at the rear door - it's probably the door from the kitchen and pantry."

Holmes gently lifted the latch and slowly opened the gate but it made a creaking noise; not loud, but enough that we must have disturbed a dog. Fortunately, it didn't bark, but came toward us from the kennel Holmes had spotted, issuing a low growl.

I quickly pulled a scrap out of the bag Mrs. Hudson gave me and held it out as the dog came closer, still growling. I held the scrap out as far as I could reach and the dog must have gotten a sniff because it stopped growling. Now it was close enough to grab the piece of duck and that's just what it did. I tossed another piece on the ground in front of its nose and it seemed quite happy. Holmes leaned over and whispered, "While you keep it occupied, I'll go and open that rear door. When you've thoroughly domesticated our canine friend, follow me in."

Holmes had fired up his dark lantern when we got out of the cab and I could smell the oil fumes. He would need it to pick the rear door lock. He walked away toward the door slowly, checking back to see how I was doing with the dog, but it was enthusiastically chewing the meat I was feeding it and paid no attention to Holmes. In no more than two or three minutes Holmes briefly flashed the lantern light my way. I didn't know if I could join him or not - it depended on the behavior of the dog. I threw another scrap and, with great relief, saw the dog pick it up and trot back toward his kennel. I hurried to the door and as soon as I was in, Holmes closed it. We were now, in the eyes of the law, burglars.

"Watson", Holmes whispered, "I'm going to check out the house. Wait here." As I stood in that dark hallway, I couldn't help thinking of how vulnerable we were. I saw a couple of flashes from the dark lantern, briefly illuminating a room and then darkness again. I was feeling more and more apprehensive when I heard soft footfalls coming down the hall. I was relieved when I smelled the fumes from the lantern and Holmes said, in a normal voice, "Just us burglars. Come, I located Moran's study, Let us see what we can find." He led the way down the hall, through what must have been the kitchen, through another hall and into a room. "This is his study. Please check the curtains on the window. Make sure they're tight shut. I need to use that desk lamp." Saying that, he briefly flashed the light on a wall where I could see the outline of a window. I went over and found out they were not curtains but heavy, thick drapes. I gave them a good pull together so no gap would betray the light. "It's good, Holmes; the drapes are tight. Go ahead and try the desk lamp."

I heard a click and the light illuminated the room with a yellow glow. It was a small study with the desk the lamp was on, three chairs in addition to the desk chair, plain paneling on the walls, a bookcase and cabinet. I could dimly make out several pictures; they seemed to be of a military nature. Holmes immediately began to search the desk, pulling out one drawer after another and shuffling through the contents. He got to the last drawer, a large one which was locked. Holmes took his 'burgling' kit out of his jacket, opened it on the desk and selected two slim instruments. It took but a few moments of work and with a click, Holmes put the tools back in the case and pulled the drawer open. He moved the lamp closer and I could see a neat stack of folders. Holmes picked up a small handful, placed it on the desk and began looking through the folders accompanied by little low whistles and grunts. "Watson! What a treasure trove these are - each folder is a record of a crime, with details, names of participants, how much their 'cut' was and the amount the scheme produced. Moran must be Moriarty's accountant and main accomplice. Do you remember that gold bullion shipment that was hijacked from a guarded train car by some very slick robbers? Here is the whole scheme in detail in this folder - and I see that the guard from the bank was in on it. He was never suspected but I think the

Yard will be quite interested in this file. And this one shows how a relative of the Royal Family was defrauded of five thousand pounds in a land scheme. Ah, ha! And here, Watson, is the Windsor Hotel scheme, I'm happy to see it is marked 'Failed'. It was written with such pressure that the nib pierced the paper in two places! I don't like to gloat, but I think I'll have this sheet framed."

Holmes continued to quickly skim through the papers, removing each sheet and placing the empty folders back in the drawer. But after a few minutes, when he had gone through the whole drawer, he slapped the papers down, put his elbows on the desk and put his head in his hands.

"Holmes, what's wrong?"

"Watson, not one of these has Moran's signature; they're all typewritten. Worse yet, no mention of Moriarty in any of them. Clever devil; he's covered his tracks well."

"But Holmes, we can testify we.................oh, I see, we can't say in court how we got them. But there must be some way to connect these crimes to Moriarty." Holmes sat there dejectedly at Moran's desk. I went over in my mind, all the trouble we had gone to, to break the Moriarty gang, and here we were, stymied. Then, after several minutes, Holmes suddenly sat up straight. "I think you're right Watson, I can't think that the Colonel, as neat and military as he is, would not keep some correspondence, if only to protect himself from the professor should it come to a falling out. But where would he keep such potentially valuable letters? Watson, have you seen anywhere in this room where a safe could be secreted?" I looked around the room but nothing looked promising.

"No, I'm sorry Holmes, I haven't. Wait! Let me check behind the pictures - maybe Moran has a wall safe."

"Splendid Watson; and while you do that I'll see if I can spot any other likely hiding place."

As I started to lift the pictures, Holmes went to the bookcase and began pulling out a few books at a time so he could see the wall behind and then putting the books back and pulling out others. "Nothing here Watson. Anything behind the pictures?"

"No luck I'm afraid. Maybe there is no safe here."

"Last chance Doctor, please shine the lamp on the carpet in front of this cabinet; I thought I noticed a slight wear pattern when I went over to the bookcase."

I moved the lamp so more light fell on the area Holmes indicated. He got down on hands and knees and inspected the carpet. He straightened up with a satisfied smile on his face. "Watson, help me move this cabinet - I may have found Moran's safe. The carpet just in front looks disturbed." I hurried over and started to help Holmes move the cabinet and we quickly discovered that it was fairly light and easy to move. When we pushed it away from the wall Holmes' guess was proved right; a wall safe had been concealed behind it.

"Watson, please hand me my kit, I need the stethoscope. I've practiced on combination locks and now we'll see if I can crack a real safe!"

The safe was about a foot and a half square, inset in the wall so it was even with the surface. Since the safe was about eighteen inches deep, it must extend into a closet or pantry where it couldn't be seen. The cabinet could be shoved back flat against the wall. If Holmes had not noticed the slight marks on the carpet, we may have never found it. He crouched in front of the safe, put the scope by the dial, and began slowly turning it. As he turned the dial back and forth I could hear him mutter,"hummm, eighteen; uh.....three, yes, three; could be nine? Yes, by George! it's 18-3-9."

"Holmes; that's the first year of the first Afghan war! Moran picked an easy combination number to remember."

Holmes swung the safe door open and we could see a pile of bank notes and a few loose papers. "Money to pay off his henchmen, Watson, and some payment records. Not what I was hoping to find

. . . wait, what's this behind the packets of notes?" He reached in the very back of the safe, behind the stacks of money and pulled out a large, bulging envelope. He opened it and pulled out a thick pack of regular sized mailing envelopes. Holding one up to the light he almost shouted in his excitement, "Watson! These are letters from Moriarty! Quick, let's put everything back the way we found the room. Except for these, of course." He tucked the packet into the inside pocket of his jacket, folded the papers he found in the desk and gave them to me to put in my pocket. He put the stethoscope in his burglar kit and we shoved the cabinet back against the wall, put the desk lamp back where it had been, relocked the desk drawer and turned the lamp off after he relit his dark lantern. "Our hour is about up Watson; we need to quietly exit and hope that Mr. Riley didn't have too many pints with his brother-in-law."

We hurried back the way we came and when we reached the outer door Holmes put a finger to his lips as we tiptoed out and Holmes then relocked the door. He leaned close and whispered, "Do you have any scraps left?"

"Oh, my God, Holmes! I emptied out the bag to quiet the dog. I didn't think about our exit at all. Sorry."

"Then let us be as quiet as possible and make haste for the gate!"

We crouched down and rushed toward the gate. Fortunately, the only noise we heard from the dog was an inquiring growl and then nothing. Holmes managed to close the gate without much sound by reaching over the top and lowering the latch very slowly.

We walked down the path to the front of Moran's house where Holmes flashed his lantern to the spot where we had asked Riley to wait. Immediately, we heard the clip-clop of hooves and in a moment, Riley pulled up and in a low voice, he said "Ya' gents wouldn't need a ride home now would'ya?" I could see Holmes smile as he extinguished the dark lantern and we piled into the cab. Riley flipped the reins and we set off for McIvey's stables.

We weren't surprised that Lucas was still at his place since he was intensely interested in bringing Evan's attacker to justice. He hurried out to meet us as soon as Riley pulled in. Holmes forestalled any questions. "No, Lucas, the villain is still, I regret to say, among the living, but Doctor Watson and I uncovered some very incriminating documents tonight. With these and Evan's testimony, we should be able to put him away for a long time, and possibly even send him up those thirteen steps!" I thought McIvey would be pleased, but he beckoned us inside his office while Riley hitched up a fresh horse for our trip back to baker Street. He faced us with a very serious look.

"Mr. Holmes and Doctor Watson, I visited Evan after ya' left with Alroy this evenin' and the news is awful bad. Evan can't re-member a bloody thing about the shootin'. He don't even know for sure that the big man was shot or how he got that bullet in his own side. The docs tell me he must'a got this problem when he fell and gashed his head an' they don't know how long it'll last. Maybe he won't never remember. What now Mr. Holmes?"

"I must tell you, his word may be the key to putting this criminal away. I will do all I can, but we'll have to hope Evan recovers his memory soon. Watson, are you familiar with this problem?" Holmes and McIvey looked at me hopefully but I couldn't offer much.

"I am. I heard of this condition from an army doctor friend of mine. He told me that he had treated a few men, wounded in battle, who could not recall many, and sometimes, any details of the event. He followed one case for several years and found that the man's memory of the battle gradually returned, but it took a long time. Of course I don't know if that will happen to Evan. He may regain his memory soon. Medical science simply doesn't know much about the problem. I'm sorry that I can't be more positive."

"Mr. Holmes, I'll just hope Evan gets better. I'll let ya' both know if Evan remembers. Here's Alroy, ready to take ya' home. An' God bless ya' for tryin'."

Holmes tried to pay Riley for our trip home but he wouldn't hear of it. "Bless me soul gents, but two quid is more than enough for this night's work. If I got two quid every day I'd own me a cab business meself by now!" In a moment we were off to Baker Street, thankfully!

We bid our voluble driver "Good night" and went inside. As soon as we closed and locked the door behind us, Mrs. Hudson came out of her rooms wrapped in a shawl and with a night cap on her head. "My gracious; you boys must have been very busy tonight. Have you had any supper?" Holmes put down his dark lantern and patted our peerless landlady on the shoulder. "Not a bite, but I wouldn't dream of putting you out at this late hour." But Mrs. Hudson was already on her way to the kitchen. "Nonsense, it'll just be a minute and you'll have a nice plate of cold cuts and some fresh coffee."

When we got to our rooms, Holmes put away the lantern and put the pack of envelopes on our table. I put the papers I had with his and put the Webley away, hung up my jacket and just about fell into a chair at the table. Holmes came out of his bedroom looking fresh as he did this morning. Probably the excitement of the night energized him.

"Well, Doctor, do you want to delay our investigation of this treasure until we've had a good night's sleep?"

"Absolutely not! I may be worn down from our adventure, but my nerves are tingling so, I'm not sure I could sleep anyway, let's take a look. Moriarty must be lurking in those letters and maybe we'll get lucky and find his lair." Holmes smiled and I could see he felt the same as I. He spread out our "loot" and gave me half the papers he found in Moran's desk. "Go through those and see if the Colonel slipped up somewhere. I'll search this half. Then we'll tackle the envelopes."

We had only just finished when Mrs. Hudson came in with a plate of sliced meat, biscuits and a fresh pot of coffee. Holmes took the platter from her and said. "Mrs. Hudson, you are a jewel beyond price." She blushed a rosy red and said, "Oh Mr. Holmes, you are the flatterer, you are," and hurried out of the room chuckling.

When we had finished and poured our second cup of coffee, Holmes put the desk papers aside and spread out the envelopes, giving me some. "Examine them carefully, Doctor, we are looking for anything, even a hint, at Moriarty's location. And of course any other information that might be probative."

We sat there for quite a while. The only noise was the crackle of paper as we searched the envelopes and an occasional exclamation from Holmes as he came across an interesting tidbit of information. Finally, as I was just about through the stack Holmes had given me, an intense thrill went through my body; "Holmes! look at this, scribbled in the margin of this paper is an address and the single letter 'P'!" Holmes was galvanized into action. Springing out of his chair, he came around the table and peered over my shoulder at the paper. "Watson, I think you just solved the mystery! We must now see for ourselves if our quarry truly lives there. Are you up for a trip to Dover tomorrow?"

"Of course! But only after a solid night's sleep. I suddenly feel as if I'd been laying track all day." Holmes then clapped me so vigorously on my shoulder I was quite happy it was not my injured one.

"Then we will journey into the unknown early tomorrow. First, though, I need to dispatch a note to Inspector Gregson at the Yard."

VII End Game

After a good sleep, I felt rejuvenated and eager to join Holmes on his quest to find the criminal genius we knew as "The Professor"— James Moriarty, math expert and the organizer of a gang and planner of crimes ranging from kidnapping to fraud, robberies, and even murder. The only lead we had was a scribbled address on a sheet that I came across when examining the papers we found. When I came into our sitting room, Holmes was already at our table. He was stuffing the papers from the desk and the envelopes from Moran's safe into a small portmanteau, the papers in one compartment and the envelopes in the other.

"Ah, Watson; I assume from your bright-eyed countenance that you slept well and therefore are ready for our trip."

"Indeed I am; but are you taking the documents with us? It seems rather dangerous since we don't know what we will encounter if we do find Moriarty." Holmes finished putting the papers away, closed the case, and replied, "No Watson, this highly incriminating batch of pilfered documents is meant for Inspector Gregson, who is due here in an hour. Meantime, Mrs. Hudson will be bringing our breakfast in momentarily. I suggest we do a thorough job on it. We may not be eating again until supper."

We had finished eating and were having a second cup of coffee when we heard a knock at the front door. A few moments later Holmes opened our door and ushered Inspector Tobias Gregson in. "Have a seat my dear Gregson and allow me to explain what is so important about this hastily arranged meeting."

"Thank you Holmes; I've seen you do some amazing work, so I'm anxious to hear what you have for me this time."

Holmes sat down opposite Gregson and pushed the portmanteau over. "Please listen carefully, Inspector. This case contains an incredible store of information on the criminal activities of a gang run by unique individuals; an ex-professor of mathematics and an ex-army officer. They have turned their talents to crime - well planned; carried out by their henchmen - usually well paid, so they keep their mouths shut. You will find, in the loose sheets in this case, a particularly complete record of each crime, including the names of the perpetrators, the amount paid each and the total haul."

Gregson's jaw dropped visibly. "Good God Holmes, how did you come by such a thing?" Holmes relaxed in his chair and gave Gregson a wry smile. "Better you don't know the details, Inspector. Suffice it to say you can use the information to pursue the gang members but cannot present the papers in court. I have no doubt that some of the miscreants are already well known to the Yard. You can probably pressure them by describing their deeds and how much they were paid. If you can offer them a reduced sentence for their cooperation, I have a feeling they will sing like budgies! You can stick the paper in their faces, proving that you know all about their misdeeds, but remember; the only thing you need to present in court is their confessions"

Holmes then had Gregson open the case and extract a single sheet. The inspector's eyes opened wider and wider as he read. "Holmes; who wrote this? It's incredible!"

"Inspector, the author is the accountant, pay-master, and right-hand man of the spider at the center of this evil web. On one of the envelope sheets Doctor Watson found an address and a telltale initial. The accountant has very cleverly covered his tracks and will be, I predict, very hard to indict. The other compartment contains letters to this cohort from the leader of the gang. Don't open them just yet. Watson and I are going to investigate the address today." Gregson gripped the portmanteau tightly and leaned over the table with serious concern on his face.

"But Holmes, how will I know the names of these two you describe? What if, by some unfortunate happening, you don't, Heaven help us, make it back safely?"

"Inspector, I appreciate your obvious concern. You will find, in with the other envelopes, a small gray one, sealed. In it you will find a complete description of my findings - with names of our opponents. You will please promise to leave the envelope unopened unless Watson and I don't return. If you don't hear from us in three days, open the envelopes. That's all I can say now. Will you follow those instructions?"

"On my honor as a police officer, I will."

"Thank you, Inspector. Watson and I will be going in a few minutes. Please guard the case carefully. And thank you for working with me on this.' Gregson took the portmanteau and as soon as he had gone, Holmes turned to me and said with a rueful smile, "Well, my friend, let us pack a travel bag, head for Charing Cross station and the London, Dover and Chatham train. Oh, and by the way, pack the Webley and take a heavy jacket, Dover will be chilly."

We gathered our things for the trip and I noticed Holmes packed his burgling kit and the beautiful small spyglass given to him by a grateful client who cannot be named at this time. The outer case was about eight inches long, covered with tooled leather and trimmed in silver with an S.H. monogram. The scope had two inner lengths which gave it a very good sight range. I had seen it on only two previous occasions and I'm sure it was a prized possession. When we were ready to leave, we let Mrs. Hudson know we wouldn't be returning until late. We waved down a cab, arrived at Charing Cross just in time to catch the next train, and soon were on our way to Dover and what could be "the lair of the beast".

Dover was a bit cold, as Holmes had guessed so our heavy jackets were quite welcome. As we emerged from the Dover station, Holmes pointed south. "We take London Road toward the harbor. We must stop at the local post office and ask for directions to 'Harbor Cottage'."

That was the name I found in the margin on one of Moran's carefully detailed papers. Just two lines; Harbor Cottage, and Dover, with the initial 'P'. As we walked south on London Road, we came to the post office. As we were about to leave after getting directions, we saw a cab rushing down the street at top speed. I laughed and turned to Holmes;

"Holmes, someone is in a great hurry. I'm glad we weren't trying to cross the road!"

"Watson, the road we want is quite close. In fact, it's where that high speed cab is just now turning. Doctor, I have a nagging suspicion about this. Let's hurry to the corner and see if we can spot where Ben Hur is going."

We hurried to the corner and saw the cab just as it pulled up in front of a house about a hundred yards away. Holmes immediately dug into our travel bag, took out the spyglass, pulled it open, and pointed it at the house where the cab had stopped. He handed it to me.

"Quick Watson, I saw a smallish man with long hair jump out of the carriage and run to the door. Do you recognize him?" I took the scope and focused on the door of the house.

My heart seemed to freeze; "Holmes, it's Moran!"

"Yes, that's what I thought when that cab turned up the road the postal clerk told us was the way to Harbor Cottage. Moran has probably discovered his loss and felt he had to report to Moriarty at once. I imagine he engaged a special from Victoria station and arrived here shortly after we did. He's gone inside now and has the cab waiting, so I think he plans a brief meeting. I see a large hedge about fifty yards up the road. Let's hurry and use it for cover. As soon as Moran leaves we must confront Moriarty before he has a chance to work out a defensive plan."   Holmes quickly closed the glass, put it back in our bag, and we hurried to the hedge he had spotted. We crouched behind the thick branches and watched the door of the cottage. We only just made it in time as no sooner than we had hidden ourselves when the door opened and Moran emerged followed by a tall, slightly stooped man with a head of unruly gray hair. He was close behind Moran and was visibly upset, waving his arms and obviously berating Moran as they went. Moran jumped in the cab and we saw him gesture wildly to the driver to leave without delay. The cab wheeled around and set off down the road. The man stood there for a moment and then turned and hurried into the house.

Holmes tapped me on the shoulder and said, "I'm certain that's him!" We went quickly across the road and covered the few yards to the cottage in a minute or less. Holmes whispered in my ear as we went up the walk to the door, "We don't know what he might do; I suggest you have the Webley handy."

Holmes knocked on the weathered door and we stood there; not knowing how our boldness might be met by a possibly desperate man whose carefully built criminal network was falling apart around him. My hand was on my pistol in my jacket pocket.

After a few tense moments, the door opened and Moriarty peered out at us. I was astounded as he opened the door wide and waved us in. "Well, I see you have taken advantage of my colleague's rash behavior and followed him to my humble home. Please come in, Mr. Holmes, and you too, Doctor Watson. Oh, and you can relax your death grip on that gun in your pocket. I'm not armed. Follow me and we'll talk in my study."

This was said in such a calm off-hand way I couldn't conceal my surprise. Holmes responded with a thin smile and said to Moriarty, "As you doubtless have surmised, we have come to have what they call a 'heart-to-heart' talk about your activities." Moriarty turned to face Holmes and said grimly, "Or is it 'mano a mano' as the Spanish put it, eh, Holmes?"

Moriarty's study had obviously been rebuilt and recently furnished. Drapes of a thick, red material framed a large French style window padded leather armchairs sat opposite a medium sized desk of polished mahogany. Wood paneling covered all four walls, and a thick carpet with an oriental design made the room look like a royal duke's study. Several pictures and paintings were spaced around the room. The only piece that seemed out of place was a schoolroom chalkboard against one wall covered with mathematical calculations. Next to the board was a large bookcase with many impressive volumes. Holmes went over to the board and turned to Moriarty, who just then was seating himself behind his gleaming desk. Gesturing toward the chalkboard, Holmes said, "Math is not my *metier*, but may I ask, are you pursuing the so-called Fermat's Last Theorem? These equations seem to me to indicate that." Moriarty looked up in surprise.

"Yes, a good catch Holmes, as the fisherfolk here would say. You don't have some insight into the problem do you? There is a sizable prize for its rigorous proof. But I believe you are here on much more serious business."

Holmes crossed the room and stood in front of Moriarty's desk and, fixing the professor with an unblinking stare, said, "You know quite well why I'm here. I am aware of the extent of the criminal activities of your gang and what function you serve. Much damning information is now in the hands of Scotland Yard. Your lucrative schemes are about to collapse and you and your thugs will be bound for prison. Oh, and by the way, we didn't follow Moran, he got here later; we just waited until he left. He's too prone to shoot people and we aren't interested in a fire fight."

Moriarty sat up straight in his desk chair and glared at Holmes. "Then how did you find me. I've taken precautions to conceal my headquarters." Holmes relaxed his stance; "I assume the Colonel told you about his missing papers. One of them had a note in the margin - 'Harbor Cottage, Dover, P.' One could hardly mistake that clue."

"Idiot!" Moriarty hissed, his face turning red. "I trusted his word never to reveal any connection to me and he does this." He sat and pounded his fist on the desk. Holmes smiled a very wry smile. "I think he may have done other things he neglected to report. I noticed you were glancing quizzically at Watson earlier. Was that because your instructions to trap him and torture information out of him didn't meet with success? Didn't Moran tell you I intervened and how he took his defeat out on your 'heavy', Ambrose, by killing him because he didn't succeed? Or that he also shot the cabbie who brought Ambrose to his house? Thank you, your face tells me it's true. He withheld embarrassing information from you."

Moriarty had calmed down some from his previous tantrum. He took a deep breath and said coyly, "Well Holmes, even though that may be all true, there is no provable connection to me in those papers as Moran described them to me. Nothing but a note in a margin that could mean anything. Not only that, I know you stole them - they will never appear in court - they're inadmissible." Moriarty gave Holmes a smug look.

"Oh, I agree, professor; but that is not how the Yard will use them. They will round up the gang and let them know that the first one to talk will get a greatly reduced sentence. Do you really think there's no 'weak link' who will spill? And finally, just for your further concern; did Moran also happen to mention he kept many of your letters - envelopes and all, in his safe? The papers were in his desk but the letters will be opened by Scotland Yard inspectors when they clean out his safe."

I knew this was a lie but I also knew Holmes wanted to shake Moriarty enough to admit something actionable and, with me as a witness, present in court, so I kept quiet. I expected Moriarty to try and counter Holmes but he said, with pure hatred on his face, "Very well Sherlock Holmes, I may go down, but I'll take you with me!"

He yanked open a drawer and pulled out a pistol. The action caught me by such surprise that I felt frozen and couldn't move but Holmes reacted immediately and reached across the desk and slapped the gun out of Moriarty's hand. It fell to the floor behind the desk and Moriarty dove for it. Holmes sprinted around the desk to fight for the gun but Moriarty managed to shove his chair at Holmes which stopped him momentarily. Moriarty was able to pick the gun up and point it at Holmes.

I have to admit that in that moment my military training left me and even though I had a pistol in my jacket pocket, I reacted by leaping at Moriarty and throwing myself on the desk with my arms outstretched, managing to knock him back against the wall. Holmes had shoved aside the chair, grabbed Moriarty, and fell to the floor with him in a firm enough grip so Moriarty couldn't get his pistol leveled. Finally, I recovered my senses and pulled out my Webley. Holmes and Moriarty were locked in a life or death struggle for the gun so I couldn't get a clear shot. I stood there, pistol cocked and ready with no way to help Holmes. I felt as helpless as I ever had felt in my life. All I could do was wait.

With renewed resolve, I leveled the Webley just above the desk, determined to shoot Moriarty if he was successful in killing Holmes. I had taken an oath that states, "First, do no harm", but I could not let this criminal go free. Suddenly a shot rang out and then, silence. I could barely breathe but I managed to hold steady. Then, in what seemed like forever but was probably only a few seconds I heard a familiar voice from behind the desk. "Watson! Please don't shoot, It's me!" I lowered my gun and collapsed into a chair. Holmes stood up behind Moriarty's desk with his arms raised in comic surrender. "I knew you would be ready in case the professor won our little skirmish. I'm glad you didn't have to go against Hippocrates. Would you please check Moriarty's condition? I think he's dead because as we fought for his gun, I twisted his hand away from me and it fired in the brief moment that it was pointed at his chest."

I pulled myself out of the chair and went around the desk feeling a bit wobbly in the knees. I knelt by Moriarty's body but here was no pulse or breathing. "He's dead. No doubt." Holmes extended a hand and helped me to my feet. "Then let us put this room back in order so our involvement is erased. I'm going to place the desk chair facing open to his body so it will look like he shot himself and fell out on the carpet. Also, Watson, use your handkerchief to wipe everything down."

I had recovered my mental and physical equilibrium by that time but I didn't understand why Holmes wanted me to clean everything off. Reading my thoughts as he often did, he answered my unspoken question. "Mr. Francis Galton's research on fingerprints has finally piqued the interest of Scotland Yard. About time, in my mind. We don't want to leave any evidence of our involvement here in case some inspector shares my opinion of the importance of fingerprints"

Suddenly it made sense so I got out my handkerchief and began to wipe down the desk and visitor chairs while Holmes cleaned the desk chair and the back panels of the desk. "Watson, don't forget the doorknobs when we leave." He finished wiping down the wall paneling back of the desk, put away his handkerchief, and looked inquiringly around the room. "Watson, I'm sure Moriarty's safe must be in this room. Let us see if we can locate it. I think we have some time; the shot was muffled by our two bodies and this house is fairly isolated. I don't think anyone heard."

After looking behind all the pictures and removing enough books to see behind the bookcase, we came to what we thought was our last chance to find a safe - the chalkboard. We moved it and discovered a framed tapestry hanging on the wall that had been completely hidden by the board. We lifted it off its hanger and there the safe was; inset into the wall. I had set our travel bag down by my chair and Holmes now brought it over to the safe, opened it, and used his stethoscope from his burgling kit to listen for the 'click' of tumblers. After several minutes though, he took the scope off and shook his head; "This is a very late model safe and I can't get a good reading on the combination."

Holmes began to pace around the room, a look of intense concentration on his face. I spoke up after a couple of minutes. "But Holmes, even if you can open it and it contains incriminating documents, we can't take them or they become inadmissible. Moriarty is dead but his gang might escape justice that way." He stopped pacing and gave a little laugh.

"Ah, Watson, I had no intention of removing anything, I just wanted to verify the importance of the contents and leave the safe open to insure some intrepid Yarder didn't overlook it! Besides, I want it to seem as though Moriarty was sure he was about to be exposed and committed suicide rather than face prison - or the gallows."

"Shouldn't we leave now, since you can't open the safe?"

Holmes looked extremely frustrated and again seemed lost in thought. "Very well Doctor, one last try. Let's see if we can deduce the combination from what we know about Moriarty. We found out that Moran used a date as a memory aid; perhaps Moriarty has done the same." Holmes resumed his pacing. Suddenly he stopped and mused, "Moriarty was seriously into trying to solve Fermat's theory.................I wonder.........Watson, please see if there's anything in the bookcase on Pierre de Fermat - date of birth or death - whatever you can find."

I thought Holmes' request would take an inordinate amount of time and I was about to complain but as I examined the bookcase shelves I saw there were labels under some areas of books such as "Quadratics", "Algebras", "Calculus", and so on. Encouraged by this, I quickly scanned the shelves. "Holmes! Here's an entire shelf labeled 'Fermat'. I think I found what you wanted. The first book on this shelf is 'Ball, W. W. R., A Short Account of the History of Mathematics'." I pulled the book, out - it looked new - and opened to the table of contents. "Here it is Holmes, a whole chapter on Fermat. Born 17 August, 1601 or 1607, died January, 1665." Holmes turned again to the safe and began turning the dial once more.

"Watson, I'm trying combinations based on those dates. August is the 8th month so I'm trying 8-16-1." But after a few moments Holmes shook his head. "Now 8-16-7.....no....Watson, I don't think his date of death will work either, there's no '65' on this dial." Holmes thought for a minute and then, "What a dunce! I didn't try 17-8-1 or 17-8-7. If this doesn't work we'll take our leave."

Holmes busied himself again with the lock dial and suddenly he whipped out his handkerchief, wrapped it around the handle and pulled the door open. The safe was full of folders and loose papers which Holmes quickly thumbed through. "Watson! This is it. Scotland Yard will have all they need to sweep up Moriarty's entire gang and have admissible evidence to convict them! Now I'll leave the door ajar, and we, my dear Doctor will vanish. Don't forget to wipe the doorknobs as we go."

Our journey home was thankfully uneventful. Holmes stopped at the local police station on our way to the Dover to London train and, posing as a tourist, reported he had heard what he thought was a gunshot while passing "...that house up that little road overlooking the harbor." The duty P/C thanked him and said they would check it out.

When we arrived back at Charing Cross, we hailed a cab and went to Scotland Yard where Holmes left a message for inspector Gregson. When we finally made it to Baker Street, the day's excitement hit me and all I wanted to do was eat dinner and retire forthwith to bed. Holmes, however, was bright and cheerful; even after I pointed out a few bruises and scrapes he had gotten in his struggle with Moriarty. "I'll wash up, rub some alcohol on my wounds and be good as new. Let us enjoy a Mrs. Hudson repast and schedule an early breakfast because I feel Gregson will be here before the morning fog clears."

VIII The Missing Link

True to Holmes' prediction, we had just finished an early breakfast when Billy ushered in Inspector Gregson. "Have a seat, Inspector. Billy, you can take the dishes now and thank your mother for an excellent breakfast. Oh, and please bring a plate and a cup for our guest. We still have a few scones and a pot of jam and some coffee." Billy collected our empty plates and Holmes settled in his chair, smiled at Gregson, and said, "Well Inspector, what's the latest?"

"Some interesting happenings. We collared the bank guard who was listed on the paper you gave me. The crook was living the gentry life on a small estate in Cornwall! He put on a show of innocent huffiness, but he caved in when confronted with that paper showing him as the inside man in the robbery. We are now after the other three and what remains of the gold. I showed the papers to a small group of my close inspector friends and cautioned them as you explained the situation to me. Lestrade, Peter Jones and Anthony Hopkins are the only ones who have access to the papers. I'm keeping them very close to the vest buttons, as the card players say."

Holmes nodded his approval. "Excellent, Inspector. I knew you would use the information quickly, but I never suspected you would have such swift results! With all four of you working on this, I imagine that soon, the entire gang will meet at Wormwood Scrubs!"

Billy came in with a cup and a plate of fresh-baked scones. After a few minutes of suspended talk and the disappearance of scones, Holmes turned to Gregson and asked, "Any other interesting bits to share, inspector?"

"Yes, Mr. Holmes, there certainly are. We got a call from the Dover Constabulary late afternoon about a suicide. It seems a reclusive ex-professor of mathematics shot himself. We have dispatched an inspector to Dover because a safe was found in the study where the body was discovered. It contained what Dover said were highly incriminating documents; apparently relating to a criminal organization run by this professor, James Moriarty. The house was in a name we haven't been able to identify but if he's the man you told us about, the name is probably phony. We're having the whole contents of the safe brought to the Yard by the early train tomorrow. Mr. Holmes, do you think there is some connection to the gang in the papers you gave me?"

"Oh, yes, Inspector; I'm sure there will be a connection." Holmes had a mischievous grin on his face when he answered Gregson's question. The inspector thought for a moment and then, with an ironic grin, asked a rhetorical question, "You know more about this than you're telling, don't you, Mr. Holmes?"

"Have another biscuit and jam, inspector." Gregson, still with that little grin, put down his empty coffee cup, wiped his mouth with a napkin, and got up to leave. "Thank you, Mr. Sherlock Holmes. We all know who really did the job. We appreciate it - London will be a lot safer with this bunch in the lockup. And I will keep you informed as we round 'em up."

We both got up from the table and shook Gregson's hand. Holmes reminded the inspector as he held our door open, "I'm vitally concerned with Colonel Moran. He is as clever as he is vicious. I know he killed the man who tried to torture Doctor Watson but he's a will-o'-the-wisp. I hope the documents you said were coming from Dover will finally put him in the darbies. Inspector Gregson, you have done a yeoman's job."

Several days went by with nothing but a short note from Gregson telling Holmes that ten more gang members had been caught and charged, but no mention of Moran. During that time, Holmes was consulted by a young noble brought to 221B by Mycroft Holmes. The young man was smitten by an "exciting and beautiful" woman and wanted to pursue her, but his royal family had their doubts about her motives. Holmes obtained a picture of her from Wilson Hargreave, an American detective who had aided Holmes with information on a previous case, and from Francois de Villard, of the French detective service. He received clinching evidence that the lady in question was indeed, a *femme fatale,* and had left two rich husbands much less rich after her departure. Confronted with pictures of her with her ex-husbands, the young man reluctantly abandoned his passionate pursuit. I don't plan on relating this story in detail because of the family's royal position.

Brother Mycroft stopped by a few days later and gave Holmes an envelope from, as Mycroft put it, "A very relieved family". When Holmes opened it, he pulled out a check, whistled a jaunty little tune, and put it in his lockbox in our desk. A few days later, when I came home from billiards, a shiny, elegant dining table and six equally elegant chairs had replaced our rather bedraggled old set. Not only that, but in the far corner was a new, very modern, laboratory table. The old, stained, deal table had vanished. I was totally awed by the new additions; mostly because Holmes had never indulged in anything like this. I had only a few minutes to be startled by our new-found luxury however, when Holmes came in and, seeing my amazement, said merrily, "Yes Watson, I used the generous check given to me by a grateful family to give our somewhat drab quarters a bit of a re-do. I grimaced briefly and nodded at his old armchair, "I see you didn't re-do that."

Holmes shook his head, "Ah, my dear Doctor, I fear our sitting room will be forever burdened with that chair. After my monetary splurge, thanks to my last client's generosity, I even had some left over, with which I went to my bank and padded my account. I have a note here from Gregson. He will be here soon with what I fervently hope will be good news. Other good news is that Mrs. Hudson will be up shortly with tea and scones. We'll take the opportunity to christen our new table.

We didn't have long to wait for Gregson or the scones; both the inspector and Billy arrived at the same time. Billy had the tea pot and a plate of scones but Gregson did not look happy. As soon as Billy left, Gregson sat down, took a deep breath, and gave us the bad news. "Gentlemen, your Colonel Moran has, I fear, slipped the traces. The four of us divided up the documents found in Professor Moriarty's safe and even though what we uncovered dooms the gang, there is no direct evidence linking Moran to the gang that we can present in court. Even if we could use the papers and letters you gave us, he could always claim he was just collecting evidence he got from an informant. We know that's a lie, but we can't prove it. Without an eyewitness, I fear we're stuck tight."

Holmes and I both sank back in our chairs; our hopes to put Moran away fading fast. Suddenly Holmes straightened up abruptly in his chair, and almost shouted, "The letter, Watson! The letter from Moran to his brother in Budleigh-Salterton! It's quite a damning piece of evidence." I almost tipped my chair over jumping to my feet. "Of course, Holmes! I had forgotten about that. We should get in touch with Inspector Barrett immediately."

Gregson was looking back and forth between Holmes and myself with what I can describe only as anxious puzzlement. Holmes sat back in his chair and spoke to the inspector, "Sorry, my dear Gregson, for the enthusiastic outburst, but Watson and I just now remembered a critical piece of evidence that absolutely ties Moran into the criminal conspiracy of professor Moriarty."

After Holmes had explained what occurred in Budleigh-Salterton and the letter we found in Moran's brother's store, Gregson's face lit up with a big smile, "No need for you to bother, Holmes; I can probably contact this Inspector Barrett quicker than you can anyway. I'll get on it as soon as I check in at the Yard. I'll go there now . . . well, after I finish my tea and this last scone! And by the by, I tried to keep Moriarty's suicide quiet and succeeded here in London, but I heard from Dover police that a reporter got hold of it and put an announcement in the Dover Mercury. I hope none of Moriarty's boys live in Dover or Moran might be tipped off. The reporter may have given the notice to other south- England papers; we don't know that yet." Holmes shook his head slowly and got very serious.

"I think we can assume that Moran has indeed learned of Moriarty's death one way or another. He may well assume that his rash letter to his brother is in a case folder in Budleigh-Salterton. Inspector, how soon can you get that letter?" Gregson reacted with concern etched in his face. "I'll send a special messenger on the early train tomorrow. He can pick up the letter and be back on the afternoon train. I think that's as fast as it can be done." Holmes stood up from the table and turned to the inspector. "I agree, that's the best option we have. Please let me know as soon as you have it in hand." Gregson grabbed his jacket and said as he headed for the door, "I'll contact you at once. I'll be on my way now. Thank Mrs. Hudson for the scones, they were excellent. By the way, your new dining set is outstanding. Did you have a grateful client, perhaps?"

Holmes smiled as he opened the door for Gregson and replied, "Very grateful, Inspector, very grateful."

IX "Check"

If I had to describe that next day for Holmes and me, it would have to be "nervous expectation" or "on tenters". I kept trying to read, but after a few minutes I would put the book down, have a cup of coffee and a cigarette, pick up the book again, and realize I couldn't remember what I just read! Holmes kept himself busy setting up his new lab bench, arraying his test tubes, beakers, bottles of chemicals and his microscope to best advantage for his investigations. I didn't remark it, but I noticed that after he had arranged a section to his satisfaction, he would get up and pace up and down for several minutes before resuming. Once, he lit his old briar, sent wreaths of smoke swirling upward, paced a while, put the old pipe back on its stand on the mantle, stood at our window for several moments, then strode back to the lab bench. It was a helpless feeling knowing so much depended on a young man struggling with memory loss and a fragile piece of writing paper.

The tension was broken at four when Billy brought up the afternoon paper, tea and sweet rolls. Holmes reluctantly sat down at our fancy new table and we passed "tea time" in silence. Finally, Holmes picked up the paper but slapped it down again on the table.

"Watson, do you have our Bradshaw handy? Please see when the Exeter afternoon train is due. Apparently, Gregson's messenger didn't make the noon train; let's hope he made the later one."

I got the schedule book from our desk and thumbed through to the trains from Exeter to London. "The afternoon train should arrive about now, Holmes. The next one isn't due until seven-fifteen and it's the last of the day."

Holmes pushed his chair back abruptly and went to the window for a moment, and said, "Doctor, I fear something has gone terribly wrong. I know Gregson would have notified us by now if the messenger had been on an earlier train."

"But Holmes, how could Moran have known about the effort to bring the letter to Scotland Yard? And what could he do about it anyway?" Holmes grabbed his briar from the mantle and sank into his armchair with such force it moved back a couple of inches on the carpet. After re-lighting the pipe, and sending a thin stream of smoke straight out into the room he pointed the stem at me and asked, "Watson, if you recall, Gregson recounted the capture of most of Moriarty's gang - but not all. If Moran suspects we would go after the letter, which he must assume is at the Budleigh-Salterton police station, he would enlist the aid of one or more gang members to re-trieve it - by any means necessary! He may have sent a man to Exeter station to watch for the arrival of a messenger or a constable. We'll have to ask Gregson whom he sent for the letter. I hope he sent an armed constable. All we can do now is hope Gregson can bring us some good news after the current train arrives."

Five, six, seven o'clock came and went with no news. Holmes requested a light supper from Mrs. Hudson and we sat drinking coffee - waiting. At last, at close to eight, Holmes sprang out of his chair and went to the door. It was only then that my senses picked up the noise of a carriage stopping at our front door which Holmes, with his keen hearing, had heard. He hurried down the stairs to open the door since Billy was probably in bed for the night. I heard Holmes welcome Inspector Gregson and moments later they came into our sitting room. Gregson, much to my dismay, had a most downcast expression on his face. He removed his coat, hung it on our stand, and turned toward us slowly, shook his head sadly, and slumped into a chair at the table. He started speaking without preamble.

"Gentlemen, I have news so depressing, I hate to have to report it to you. The letter has been taken at gunpoint and burned. The messenger's cab was waylaid on the way to Exeter by a gunman who robbed the messenger, cut the horse loose and left in his own trap. It seems that the robber placed his trap crossways on the road a few miles from the station, then lay on the ground as if he was injured, concealing his gun. The messenger's cab stopped and the driver and the messenger got out to see if they could help. When they got close, the man stood up and confronted them with the gun, demanding the letter. The messenger had no choice but to comply, of course. Then he got into his trap, reached in his jacket pocket and pulled out the letter, lit it on fire, dropping it over the side of the trap when it was almost totally consumed. He then drove off toward the Exeter train station. It took the men almost half an hour to get help and by that time the noon train had left. Holmes, the description of the man tallies with the description we have of one of Moriarty's gang members, one with the most inappropriate name; Pleasant Pigot. We think, from reading the papers, that Moran nicknamed him 'Gunny'. Every time we came across his name, it was on a sheet that detailed an armed robbery, so we think, 'Gunny' was just that, a hired gunman. I couldn't be more sorry about this, Holmes."

Gregson took his coat off the stand and turned to leave, but as Holmes opened the door for the inspector he asked, "Just one question, inspector; was this messenger in uniform?" Gregson seemed startled by the question. "Yes, he was; why do you ask?"

"Because, Inspector, I think that's how Moran tracked the letter. In the first place, I'm sure he remembered the letter, and I feel he deduced from Watson's presence at The Rag that he was being investigated. The letter to his brother Silas became the one thing that tied him to Moriarty's crime ring. Remember, he thought Evan was dead - thanks to the quick thinking of Lucas McIvey; so the letter was the only evidence that would take him down if the Yard got it. He probably paid a handsome price for Pigot to stay in Exeter and check each train arrival for a constable or messenger; then follow him. If he went to the Budleigh-Salterton police station, I'm sure Moran was convinced the letter was the object of the visit. Pigot was then to get the letter whatever way he could. As soon he determined that the messenger went to the police station, he would go on ahead and set his trap." Gregson lowered his head and shook it sadly.

"My fault, Holmes. I should have sent an armed constable." Holmes put a hand on the inspector's shoulder and said grimly, "Then, Gregson, you would probably have gotten your p/c and the cab driver killed. Moran is clever and desperate and Pigot is obviously a cold-hearted killer."

"But Holmes, why didn't he shoot the messenger and the driver?"

"Ah, there we have to speculate. I think he didn't eliminate them because that would have mobilized every police force in the area and the Yard. This way, he could go back and report his success to Moran and probably collect enough money to disappear. The gang was falling apart, there wouldn't be any further need for his services."

"But wouldn't Moran get rid of him like you say he did Ambrose?"

"My dear Inspector, would you like to try to kill this deadly agent - without getting shot yourself?" Gregson let out a small smile.

"No sir, I wouldn't! And, you're right, we can't find him. He probably did just as you said - disappeared as soon as possible. I want you to know that we have a man watching out for Evan. If he recovers his memory, we will immediately remove him from danger."

"Inspector, I can't ask for more. Thank you. By the way, have none of the gang you've picked up so far told you how they got paid or got their instructions for their next job?"

"They all say they got their pay from this 'Gunny' and apparently, the ones chosen for a job would meet at the Rillington Place house. There they got the plan for their next job from a man in a big coat, with a hat pulled down over his face, and what they all said was obviously a fake beard. I'm sure none of them could identify Moran, even though we are sure it was him." Holmes nodded his agreement and said quietly to Gregson, "You must know that I will be away on a special job for an indeterminate time. If anything breaks in the case, please notify Doctor Watson. He will let me know through my brother Mycroft in the Foreign Office." Gregson looked surprised and puzzled but nodded his agreement.

After Gregson left, Holmes began packing for his secret journey to the Continent. "Mycroft will be here in the morning. He will pay to keep our rooms - you need pay nothing." I was so conflicted in my mind I could barely speak. I finally stammered out, "Holmes, I can't imagine staying here with all these memories. I . . . I think I should find lodging elsewhere." He put down the pipe and tobacco slipper he was packing and said gently, "My dear Doctor, why don't you open up a practice again? It would keep you too busy to reminisce much, and in any spare time, you could pull out your case notes and resume writing. It would also take your mind off the tragic loss of Mary Watson."

Tears came to my eyes then, but I knew Holmes was right. To dwell on my memories of Mary for any length of time was just too painful. Holmes, as usual, had hit on the right solution. "Holmes, I will do just that. It's been too long since I hung a shingle with 'Dr.

John H. Watson' on it anyway. I will go to my friend Doctor Bell at Barts and get the latest medical news. Thank you, you're right of course. Maybe my practice will also give me some ideas for a story not connected to crime!"

Mycroft came to pick Holmes up for his trip and suddenly it hit me - even though I thought I was prepared, the realization that Holmes was really gone and I was alone in our rooms with only the memories of the dozens of fascinating cases I had shared with the most incisive and intelligent detective in the world was almost overwhelming. I wandered around our rooms for a while but then I knew what I must do. I hailed a cab and set out for Barts and a new life.

Epilogue

I spent some weeks with my friend at Barts acquainting myself with the latest medical information and then rented a small office in Kensington with quarters in the rear. I hung out my shingle as I had promised Holmes, inwardly hoping I wouldn't be in business long. I located in Kensington partly for financial reasons - I found the office/living quarters at a good price, but also to be near McIvey's stables so I could monitor Evan's progress. Mycroft called me occasionally with bits of news but nothing very revealing.

My practice was minimal but at least kept me busy enough so I didn't dwell on the past much. Gregson kept me abreast of the efforts of the Yard to demolish Moriarty's criminal organization which were encouraging, but "Gunny" was still missing, the gang's dangerous killer. When time dragged - which it often did -I wrote up several cases of which I had made notes or that were fresh in my mind. They included "The Brighton Stalker" and "The Case of the Midlands Poisoner". I didn't have the motivation to publish, however. Maybe someday.

What I thought would be a short hiatus from my association with Sherlock Holmes turned out, much to my dismay, to last almost three years. I finally got fed up with my rather desultory life, sold my practice, and moved back to Baker Street. Finally, to my great relief, Holmes returned. The gist of his reappearance is recorded in my story "The Empty House". Many of the details of Holmes' activities in Europe were made up to cover the real reason for his presence there but the basic facts are accurate. The only remaining problem was that while Moran was in custody, the dangerous gunman, Pigot, was still missing and there was not enough evidence against Moran to indict him for the murder of Ambrose and the attempted murder of Evan Postlewaite.

END

A CASE OF JUSTICE
DELAYED

IT WAS THE morning after the capture of Colonel Sebastian Moran, who had fallen into a clever trap set up by Sherlock Holmes, which I chronicled as "The Adventure of the Empty House". There was much in the early part of that tale that was fictional, in order to conceal the real reason for Holmes's absence, which was a spy mission into Europe requested by Mycroft Holmes and two high ranking members of the government. It wouldn't be, as it turned out, the only time Sherlock aided England by his cunning, but that is a story which cannot be told for a long time.

I had sold my three-year practice and moved back to our rooms in Baker Street, and, as it happily occurred, just before Holmes returned from Europe. On that first morning after Holmes' return, I joined Holmes at our dining table for breakfast to find him making notes on a large sheet of paper. I could see a few sketches, and what looked like a map among the penciled lines. Billy and Mrs. Hudson came in with our meal and Holmes folded the paper up and set it aside. Smiling at the pair he said, "Ah, our superb breakfast delivered by our superb landlady and son." Mrs. Hudson giggled and blushed, as she usually did when praised by Holmes. "Oh, Mr. Holmes, you flatterer, you!" When breakfast had been laid on and Mrs. Hudson and Billy left, I asked Holmes what he had been working on.

"Doctor, I was trying to assemble a case against Colonel Moran that would get him put away for life or hanged. Preferably the latter. I'm not usually so vindictive but in the case of Moran, I think it's justified."

"But Holmes, he tried to kill you - and, there were witnesses. He also tried to kill Evan and he did kill my kidnapper." Holmes held up his hand and said, "Later, Watson; let us first dig into this delicious looking product of Mrs. Hudson's country cooking skills." I didn't have to be invited twice, and went at my eggs, ham, and biscuits with sausage gravy, with abandon. After biscuits and jam, and a cup of coffee, Holmes pushed back his chair and went to the mantle, picked out his calabash, stoked it, and settled into his armchair with the faded and somewhat worn padding. I poured a second cup of coffee and relaxed into my armchair. We must have presented quite a picture of contemplation and leisure. However, below the calm surface, Moran was still to be dealt with and a solid case, as Holmes mentioned, was needed. Not only that, but "Gunny", Pleasant Pigot, the last unaccounted for Moriarty gang member was still at large. Scotland Yard felt he escaped the country and they gave up any active searches for him.

"Watson, the case for attempted murder is unimpeachable, that I give you, but we know his crimes beg for a sterner fate. I fear that without Evan Postlewaite's eyewitness testimony, Colonel Moran will escape the gallows. I suggested to inspector Gregson that Scotland yard examine the slugs from Evan and Ambrose. If their characteristics match, and match to a bullet fired from Moran's pistol, it should be compelling evidence at trial."

"Holmes, it sounds like you have hit upon a new identification method!"

"I fear I'm too far ahead of the Yard on that, Doctor. Gregson's superiors told him the science was not advanced enough to present in court. I have heard of the work, particularly by Alexandre

Lacassagne, which shows that fired bullets acquire specific traces from the barrel. Watson, sometimes I despair of the level of intelligence of officialdom. How many murders remain unsolved for the lack of that kind of evidence, I wonder. It reminds me of the stupidity of not developing the resource of trained tracking dogs. Saucy Jack may well have been caught by a dog like Toby if only the hidebound dullards had listened when I suggested it, years before the Ripper horrors. Watson, you can't fix stupid; and you can quote me on that!"

We took a cab to Lucas McIvey's stables after breakfast that morning. Lucas greeted us and invited us in for tea and some of his wife's delicious biscuits. Lucas pulled up a chair and sat opposite us at his table/desk. A considerable time had elapsed since the killing of my kidnapper and the shooting of Evan, and Moran hadn't paid for those crimes.

Holmes related the capture of Moran, much to the delight of McIvey. Holmes then continued, "Unfortunately, Lucas, while he will certainly draw a long sentence, we can't prove he is also a murderer without Evan's account. That's why we called on you today. How is Evan doing? The last news Doctor Watson had was that he had not regained full memory of the frightening event yet, but was improving. Is that still true?"

"It is true, gentlemen. But poor Evan still has bad headaches and his memory is coming back only in bits at a time. He should be gettin' in soon. Would you like to talk to him, Mr. Holmes?" Holmes perked up noticeably at that and slapped a hand on the table, "You bet I would! And thank you Lucas, for asking. I won't delay him long."

After Holmes had talked to Evan, we headed back to Baker Street, disappointed that Evan was not yet ready to be cross-examined in court. He now remembered the shootings but his mind was still fuzzy about details upon which any defense council would be certain to fasten. We stopped for a quick lunch at Simpsons and then home. To our surprise, a police cab was parked at our door when we arrived and Inspector Lestrade was at our street door awaiting our return. Holmes clapped the wiry Scotland Yarder on the back and greeted him warmly; "Lestrade, to what do we owe the pleasure of your company today?" Lestrade had a large folder under one arm and his usual look of nagging puzzlement on his narrow, ferret-like face. Holmes gave him a friendly smile, winked at me over his shoulder, and opened the door for us. "Come on up, Inspector, and unburden yourself of whatever it is that bothers you about that sizable folder you have."

Lestrade was as familiar as I was with Holmes' mind reading and didn't remark on it anymore. We hung up our coats and invited the inspector to have a seat at our table and explain his visit. He opened the folder and produced several sheets filled with neat rows and columns of figures and notes. He spread them out and said, "These are records of Moran's financial doings for the past four years. We confiscated them after his arrest for trying to kill you, Holmes. As you can see, he was quite precise and, apparently, complete with the details. At first we couldn't understand why these entries didn't correspond to his bank records - which we also obtained of course. But since it was proved by the documents we found in Professor Moriarty's safe, that they were part of a criminal gang, we think these papers show the record of the cash received from the crimes they committed." Holmes was getting visibly bored and held up a hand to stop Lestrade's narrative.

"Yes, yes, inspector, I quite understand. But what is it that brings you to me with these records? Your own accountant must have gone over them."

"Yes, of course he did. It's not anything that probably means a lot, but still, it's unexplained, and we thought you would like a look-see." Lestrade then pulled out one particular sheet. "Holmes, this is the main record we thought was a bit odd, It apparently begins shortly after we were rounding up the gang when we received those papers from you." The inspector then separated out another sheet. "This is the form Inspector Gregson made up to get an idea of the structure of the gang. The initials of all the members are in this left-hand column and the different crimes they took part in are across the top, you see. This gave us several groups. Not all gang members were involved in all the crimes so this let us study how the gang functioned."

Holmes nodded his approval; "Quite so, Inspector. Let me examine this page for a minute." Holmes pulled the page over to his seat and slowly scanned the entries. "Now the chronological one, please." But Lestrade said, "Holmes, we can't tell the dates. All these sheets have are long numbers where the dates would normally be. But here they are; maybe you can do better than we did in trying to break Moran's code." Lestrade passed the first and second record sheets to Holmes who studied them for two or three minutes. He then leaned back in his chair and said to us, "Yes, I think I see what puzzled you, Inspector, and I am grateful you brought this to my attention."

I had looked over his shoulder as he read the pages Lestrade gave him but I hadn't a clue what Holmes meant. It seemed to be a simple recording of payouts to gang members. My face and Lestrade's must have shown the same puzzlement. Holmes smiled and turned Moran's ledger sheet so Lestrade and I could both read it and explained what he saw that Lestrade and I missed.

"First, remember the fourth page down; Lestrade, I assume these are in order. In other words, the bottom sheet is the oldest." Lestrade nodded. "Then it would be for the year 1891. As you see it is full of payout entries. Now we can't pin down the dates yet because Moran encoded them, but we can certainly work by assuming the oldest is 1891. Notice that we see a sudden decrease in payouts toward the end of that page - I'm assuming for now that each page is a particular year. Toward the end of that year - the four-year old one - we begin to see that decrease I mentioned. I believe that tells us the gang was being slowly rounded up. By the page that I think represents three years ago, 1892, we see an almost complete drying up of payments. I'm certain that was because of the efforts of the Yard, using the Moran papers Watson and I gave Gregson, in bagging the gang members."

Lestrade and I were almost comically looking back and forth at each other, nodding at each point Holmes was making! Lestrade spoke up when Holmes paused. "Yes, but what bothered the four of us was that one payout continues after all the others stop. You can see that 'G', the one we think is Pigot, the gunman, gets fifty pounds, regularly it seems, clear through the rest of the record sheets. If only we could solve what we think are date codes we would have a better idea of what it means."

Holmes got up from the table and paced up and down the room for a couple of minutes and then came back to the table. "Inspector, can you leave these ledger pages with me so I can study them? I would like to try my hand at decoding these notations, which, as you guessed, are almost certainly dates. They might tie the whole thing together." Lestrade leaned back in his chair with a very relieved look on his face and pushed all the pages across the table to Holmes' chair. "Holmes, I'm glad you offered. We would be very grateful if you could shed some light on this. I know we have Moran on an attempted murder charge but we feel, from what you told us, Moran should be up for the murder of Ambrose, Doctor Watson's kidnapper."

Lestrade retrieved his coat and hat and as he left he shook hands with us and said, "Good luck, if we find anything else we'll let you know right away."

After Lestrade had gone, Holmes went to our table and spread out the pages, went to our desk and sharpened a pencil, pulled out several sheets of writing paper and strode back to the table. I saw that well known look of intense concentration on his face so I knew he would be virtually unreachable while he worked to decode Moran's cipher. I got my jacket and hat and announced, "I'm going to do a little shopping, is there anything I can get for you?" He never looked up from the page he was studying, but muttered, "Order more Macnab #3, please. Oh, and buy a bottle of a good brandy."

It was a pleasant day and my leg wasn't bothering me so I walked instead of taking a cab. I knew also that it would give Holmes more time without any distractions to work on the code. I stopped at Bradley's for some cigarettes, the telegraph, to order more #3 from Angus Macnab's tobacco shop in Stirling, and meandered around the store in Cecil Court I had found that stocked a good selection of used books at very attractive prices. I also stopped at an import shop and bought a bottle of brandy. I was puzzled by Holmes' request as I knew we had brandy in our cabinet.

I arrived with my bag of goods at 221 close to supper time and sure enough, Holmes was clearing off the table and depositing the ledger pages on our desk. "Holmes, I got the brandy you wanted; did you forget we still have a good half bottle?"

"No Doctor, I remembered, but this bottle is for McIvey for all his help. I want to see him again soon about Evan." Answering my unspoken question, as he often did he said, "No, no answer yet, but I think I'm close. I've soaked up all I can from the total of the papers. Now I have to concentrate on the code itself. It's a purely number code, so I need to apply several arithmetic techniques. But right now I deduce from the savory odors I detected when you opened our door, that Mrs. Hudson is about to deliver a pork roast with herbs, and potatoes roasted with the pork. Concentrating on the roast will rest my brain, so I can tackle our mystery afresh. At least that's what I'm going to claim."

"That sounds like the best idea I've heard today. I had a long walk and I certainly worked up a good appetite."

After dinner, Holmes moved Moran's ledger pages back to the table as soon as Billy had collected our dishes and left a fresh pot of coffee. Holmes stoked his old briar, poured a cup of coffee and warned me; "Doctor, I'm afraid this may be a long night. I can't let this problem go so I'm going at it until I solve it." Holmes looked very determined so I took the book I picked up, *"Endymion"* by former Prime Minister Benjamin Disraeli, and tottered off to bed. I hadn't gotten very far when I must have drifted off because I awoke with the open book on my chest and heard the unmistakable sound of Holmes playing his violin. That may have been what woke me up. He was playing a jaunty tune from Gilbert and Sullivan's "Gondoliers", so I assumed he had solved the Moran code, but I was too tired to go and ask him and the tune was so pleasant that I soon put my book down and settled back to listen. The next thing I knew it was morning!

After I managed to get fully awake, I put my robe on and came out to our parlour. Holmes was already at our table reading the morning paper with the ledger sheets pushed to one side. "Ah, Doctor, I see you have joined the conscious. I assume you slept well. I hope my celebratory concert didn't disturb you too much."

Sitting down, I fixed Holmes with a direct stare, "You solved it didn't you? Your whole aura speaks it!" Holmes broke out in a big (for him) smile. "Yes, as you so correctly observed, I solved it. I'm not overly proud because it turned out to be fairly simple once I factored in our late, unlamented, professor Moriarty's obsession with Fermat."

"As usual Holmes, you're ahead of me. I remember your remark to Moriarty but I don't follow what it has to do with the code." Holmes pulled a ledger sheet and turned it toward me, "See here, at the top of the sheet is the number 3575881. Another sheet is headed 3579664 and yet another 3572100. I started by assuming they were coded dates, but they could be months or years. From the large number of entries on one of the sheets I thought was probably the oldest - that is, before the gang began to be nabbed by the Yard, and the one with the least payouts should be the last one before Moran was caught.

Then it all clicked; Fermat's last theorem was that the equation $x^n + y^n = z^n$ has no non-zero integer solutions for 'n' greater than 2. The simplest example is a 3,4,5 right triangle; $3^2 + 4^2 = 5^2$. Solving, it is, of course, 9+16=25, QED, as the texts have it. People, mathematicians and amateurs alike, have tried for two hundred years to come up with a rigorous proof. Prizes have been offered, as Moriarty mentioned, but no takers! One thing that motivates math buffs, aside from the prize money, is that Fermat scribbled a note in the margin that he had discovered, '...a truly marvelous demonstration of this proposition but that this margin is too narrow to contain.' No further mention of this 'marvelous demonstration' was made. I suspect it will be another hundred years or so before the thing is finally either proven or disproven."

I knew a lot more then, but I still didn't know how it related to the code. Noting the still puzzled look on my face, Holmes continued, "Then I examined the code numbers again, only this time I simply took the square root of each number, and behold, Doctor," at this, he pointed to the heading of each sheet and said, "1891, 1892, 1893, and 1894. I then assumed that the numbers down the left side were months. Trying an easy one on the 1891 page, 63001, the square root is 251, the next one, 49284, is 222. Going down the list, the final number increases by one each entry."

"Holmes, they're month dates, January 25th, February 22nd! Am I correct?" Holmes leaned back in his chair, smiled, and pointed his pencil at me. "Absolutely right, Watson. Now let's look at 1892, since that is right after Moriarty's death and shortly after Scotland Yard began locking up the gang. And, of course, your fanciful tale of mine and Moriarty's deaths." Holmes moved the 1892 ledger sheet so I could read it. "Now, looking at the month column, you will notice the payouts diminish steadily from January on until we come to a significant one, 100 pounds to 'G'. This is the first time a single individual is noted, so we can assume 'Gunny' got the total hundred pounds. For what service, Doctor? Think about it. The date is 6724, 8-2, February 8th."

I had to force my mind to return to that hectic few weeks. After mulling it over for a couple of minutes I couldn't fasten on any particular event at first; then a vague, fleeting thought. "Holmes, isn't that a few days before the Moran letter was stolen?" Holmes straightened up and circled the date. "Bravo, Doctor, you are correct. I think Moran panicked when he remembered that letter, knew he had to retrieve it before it got to the Yard, and paid Pigot, who was still on the loose, to destroy it. I think he sent the gunman to Exeter to watch for a messenger or a constable getting off the train from London and heading for Budleigh-Salterton. He was to follow, and if the messenger went to the police station, follow him until he was out of town, intercept and destroy the letter by whatever means necessary. It sounds a bit clumsy but Moran couldn't have the police station watched in such a small town, it would be noticed right away. The hundred pounds were for Gunny's 'fee' and expenses. At least that's my best guess."

I had been looking at the ledger sheet while Holmes was explaining his deductions and I noticed something strange. "Holmes, I see the 'Gunny' payouts all the way down the sheet. It shows fifty-pound payouts clear down the page. And no other payments."

"Ah, Watson, good for you again. That's why I think Lestrade, in addition to being unable to decode Moran's encrypted dates, was curious about the continued payments when virtually all the gang members were in custody." I looked blankly at Holmes for a moment and then said. "Do you think Moran hired Pigot as a bodyguard? He knows you had him in your sights." Holmes got up from the table, shoved the papers aside and said, "But why then, Doctor, would he travel around with a wanted man when he could hire a bodyguard for half the price? Does not another explanation occur to you? Well, never mind; I think I hear Billy approaching with our breakfast. I have a job for Billy that may reveal what I think is the real reason for the payouts. By the way, they are listed as being on the last Sunday of each month. Here is Billy. so let us pass the time with Mrs. Hudson's splendid idea of breakfast and delve into the mystery later."

I was in favor of that idea and helped Holmes clear the table. After Billy had brought up a pot of coffee on his second trip, Holmes handed him a note and two coins. "Billy, please take this and go the police station two blocks over; they have the new telephone service now. Have them call Scotland Yard and ask for Inspector Gregson and tell him Sherlock Holmes needs to see the Moran letter messenger as soon as possible. If Gregson is not in, try Lestrade." Billy tucked the coins away and with a salute, said, "Yes sir, Mr. Holmes, right away!" We could hear him take the stairs two at a time.

"Someday, Watson, the powers that be will be expanding the telephone service into our neighborhood. Billy won't like it though; he'll be losing a lot of errand commissions!"

We ate our breakfasts and, even though I was still wondering why Holmes wanted to see the messenger who was robbed, I felt lazily full and comfortable. Holmes got his calabash from the mantle and settled down in his armchair with a cup of coffee and I lit a Bradley's cigarette and settled into my chair. Holmes finished reading the paper and I thought he would relax, but he soon set his empty cup down and paced around our room for a few moments and then headed for his new laboratory table. I must have drifted off because I was suddenly startled by Billy's knocking on our door. I got up and opened it to a smartly dressed young man in a uniform. Billy announced, "A messenger for Mr. Holmes." I addressed the smartly dressed young man, "Please come in, Mr. Holmes will be with you momentarily."

I had heard Holmes put down a beaker he was heating over a spirit burner and push his chair back. He came quickly across the room and greeted the young man warmly. "Please have a chair; I am Sherlock Holmes and this gentleman who let you in is Doctor Watson. We just need a bit of your time. Thank you, Billy, that's all for now."

Billy nodded and closed the door behind him. Holmes moved a chair out, handed our visitor a large coin and bade him sit down. He then sat in the chair opposite the messenger and said, "I assume you are the man who picked up a letter from Budleigh-Salterton and was robbed of it on your way to the Exeter train station." The messenger looked from Holmes to me with a most disturbed, wide-eyed expression; "Yes sirs, and I'm still trying to get over it. The man had the most frightening look on his face I've ever seen. I thought sure the driver and I were going to die. He said, in the most menacing way, 'Hand over that letter. Now!' I almost fainted as he shook a gun in my face. Sir, there was no way I was not going to give him that letter. I'm sorry Mr. Holmes. By the way, my name is Eddie Johnston, but they call me 'Speedy'."

Holmes sat back in his chair and gave 'Speedy' a comforting smile. "Don't apologize, I know how terrified you must have been. I just want you to describe to me everything that happened after you left with the letter. Please don't leave anything out.

"Yes sir, I understand. I had the cab wait while I went into the police station and asked for Inspector Barrett. He came out and handed me an envelope. 'Take care', he said, 'there's a very important letter in there.' Well sir, I got in the cab again and the driver suggested we have a bite to eat. 'The next train to London isn't for two hours and a half.' As I hadn't eaten since breakfast, that sounded like a good idea so we went to a small cafe down the block. When we left for Exeter, there was practically no other traffic except way up ahead of us a trap-and-two was going at a great rate. Our horse trotted along nicely and I was sure we had plenty of time to make the train. But when we were about three miles from the station, we saw the trap crossways on the road. When we got up to it we noticed a man collapsed by the front wheel, laying on his stomach on the road and not moving. One arm was outstretched and the other under his body."

Holmes nodded. "And as you got close to help, he jumped up and pointed a gun at you. He had it in the hand that was hidden under his body."

"Yes sir, and he kept waving it back and forth at us. Scared out of our wits we was, Mr. Holmes, I tell you. That's when he yelled at me to hand him the letter. You bet I did. I opened the pouch I carry and gave him the envelope Inspector Barrett had entrusted to me. Honestly sir, I didn't really think about the importance of it, not with a gun in me face. All I could think of was what he might do to us. The cabbie was as scared as me. The man tore open the envelope, took out the letter, read it and then folded it, threw down the envelope and folded the letter twice more and stuck it into an inside pocket of his jacket."

Holmes nodded in sympathy. "I quite understand your fear. You had no choice but to hand over the letter. If you had resisted, I assure you, he would have removed it from your dead body. Now please continue; you're doing a fine job."

"Well sir, he pulled out a knife from a leather sleeve he had on his belt and cut several pieces of strap from the reins and harness and made me tie the cabbie to a wheel. Then he tied me to the other wheel, unhitched the horse and fired his pistol near the horse's head. Of course it reared up and galloped away. He then mounted his trap, pulled out the letter from his pocket, opened it, and lit it on fire. He let it burn until I thought it would burn his fingers and then he dropped the last scrap on the ground. He turned the trap around and whipped up the horses. He headed toward Exeter, sir, and that was the last we saw of him. Thank God! We tried to get loose but couldn't. About fifteen or twenty minutes later, a farmer taking a load to sell in Exeter came up the road and rescued us. Our horse had wandered back by that time, but it took us a long time to hitch because of the damage the robber had done. The reins were useless so the cabbie actually mounted the horse and we went off to Exeter. We did that, Mr. Holmes, because the farmer's trap was loaded with goods and was going very slow-like."

The young man paused for breath but Holmes waved for him to stop his narrative, "Well told, Eddie. I think I have the whole episode in my mind now. Let me have you focus on the action involving the letter. You said he took the letter, opened it, and refolded it twice more?"

"Yes sir, that's just what he did. It was folded the long way to fit in the envelope and he folded it that way but then folded it the other way twice." Holmes nodded again, "Then it would have been about three by four inches when he stuck it in his jacket - is that right?"

"Yes sir, that's about the size it was." Holmes paused, linked his fingers behind his head and leaned back in his chair. "Then, Eddie, you say he got the letter out and unfolded it, then burned it, correct?" Nodding his head vigorously, Eddie said, "Yes sir, that's exactly what he did Mr. Holmes."

"Two things Eddie; one, you're probably very lucky to be alive; and two, you have done a yeoman's job describing your ordeal. Thank you for your time." Holmes then got up and handed Eddie's cap back to him, went to our desk where his wallet was and pulled out a banknote. When he handed it to Eddie, I thought the young man was going to faint, He stammered, "Uh . . . I . . . uh . . . thank you Mr. Holmes. My heavens, a whole quid!" He clapped his cap on his head and almost stumbled out the door. Holmes closed the door and with a satisfied smile settled once again into his armchair, his lags out-stretched. "Well, Doctor, I think that solves the many payouts to Mr. Pigot, doesn't it?" I was a bit nettled by that, "Sometimes, Holmes, I despair of your mental leaps. I too often can't keep up! How does a folded letter solve the mysterious payouts to this 'Gunny'. What's the connection?"

"My dear fellow, I apologize. I believe there's a very logical connection. Blackmail, Watson, blackmail!" I could see the reasoning behind Holmes' conclusion but I saw what I thought was a flaw. "But Holmes, with the letter gone, if Pigot were to go to the authorities with the story, the documents uncovered clearly show he's a gang member. His story, against that of Moran, would be dismissed immediately." Holmes leaned back in his chair, relit the briar, and sent a smoke ring wobbling into the air. Then he turned toward me and cheerfully said, "Ah yes, Doctor, you are correct - that is if the letter was actually burned!" He smiled at my incredulous reaction. "But Eddie just described watching Pigot burn the letter, Holmes!"

"He described a piece of paper burning, Watson; but was it the actual letter?" Holmes got out of his chair and replaced his pipe onto the mantle and stood by the window for a minute. Turning to me again he said, "If my deduction is correct, Pigot was cleverer than Moran gave him credit for. I think 'Gunny', knowing by then that the Moriarty crime spree was over, knew his paydays were also over, and greeted the task of retrieving and destroying the letter as a golden opportunity to continue his lucrative payoffs. I believe he previously took an ordinary sheet of writing paper, folded it so it fit into a shirt or jacket pocket and then, for the benefit of 'Speedy', switched it for the incriminating letter. I wondered at the time, when Eddie described Pigot's folding of the letter and then, only a few minutes after that action, ostentatiously unfolding and burning it. I asked myself, why would he go to the trouble of folding it in the first place if he was simply going to burn it?"

As usual, Holmes' deduction seemed to light up my brain. "Good grief Holmes, I see now what you mean. Pigot could show Moran the letter and demand money - Moran wouldn't dare try to have a 'shoot-out' with the dangerous 'Gunny'. But Holmes, why not one large payoff? Why the monthly pay schedule?"

"There we can only guess. If you recall, there were a couple of stacks of notes in Moran's safe, but not a great fortune. Perhaps Moran talked Gunny into taking payments. After all, Moran was not going to be receiving a 'cut' of Moriarty's crime business any longer. He probably had no other fresh income outside of his card cheating. We don't know how much he was raking in but the Park Lane affair showed Moran and his unwitting partner, Ronald Adair, took eight hundred forty pounds from Lord Balmoral and Godfrey Milner; half that being Adair's cut. If my assumption is correct, Adair caught Moran cheating and was going to give back the ill-gotten gains to the other players. Moran couldn't have this, of course, so he shot Adair before the coming scandal ruined him and thus cut off his only remaining income."

"Absolutely tight reasoning, Holmes. I think you have hit on the answer. What else has your study of the ledger pages brought to light?" Holmes went to our desk and shuffled through the sheets, pulling one out and bringing it to the table. "Look at this one, Doctor, it's for the year 1892. All other payments stopped after March and from then on clear through 1894, until Moran's capture, the payoffs of 50 pounds per month were the only entries. Look at the dates, Doctor. I won't burden you with the math; I put the decoded dates next to Moran's coded ones."

I scanned down the 1892 page and saw, 24/4, 29/5, 26/6 and so on. "These are for April through December 1892 Holmes?"

"Quite so. Here's an 1892 calendar; look at the dates." I compared the dates Holmes had decoded to the calendar. "Holmes, these are, as you said, all the last Sundays of the month."

"Exactly, my friend, a fine choice for Moran. No worker traffic, most people in Church, less police presence, perfect. At first I thought Moran and Gunny wouldn't actually meet but that meant a possibility that mail could be compromised. Of course the Rillington Place house was out because the Yard raided it, and while they didn't find much - outside of some blood on the small table, Doctor, and a broken door! - they notified the owner and he rented it out. That leaves the possibility that Moran and Pigot arranged to meet somewhere."

"How could they do that without using the post? Arrange a spot and a time in advance perhaps?"

Holmes looked doubtful; "I think not; meeting at a prearranged spot time after time could attract unwanted attention." I thought for a while, but couldn't come up with an alternative. Holmes suddenly brightened and said, "I may have the answer, Doctor. I must change and be off to check my idea." He hurried to his room and I decided to change into my 'billiard day' clothes. I did so since it was a Thursday. When I finished shaving and dressing and came out of my room, Holmes was already gone. Where, I had no idea. I went on to meet Thurston for our regular game. My spirits were high and I won our encounter this time.

"A cucumber sandwich at his time of year, Mrs. Hudson? How do you do it?" I was back from billiards and Mrs. Hudson had just brought up the 'tea time' tray; scones with jam, tea, and this time, cucumber sandwiches.

"Oh, it's easy Doctor Watson; my dear sister grows winter vegetables in a greenhouse in her backyard. You and Mr. Holmes will be having roast squash with onions and cheese tonight. Will Mr. Holmes be here soon? I shouldn't want him to miss tea."

I was about to answer that I had no idea when he'd be returning when we heard the front door open and steps on the stairs. Our door opened and Holmes tossed a large envelope on the table and said cheerfully, "Ah, then, I'm not too late for tea. Thank you, Mrs. Hudson. And do I detect cucumber sandwiches? Hothouse grown, I presume."

Mrs. Hudson nodded; "You both have a nice tea time. Oxtail soup and lamb shanks tonight."

Holmes hung his jacket on our stand, sat down and said, "Yes, Watson, the day was well spent. I think I discovered how Moran and Pigot communicate." Saying that, he opened the envelope and dumped out a thick wad of notepaper. "Let's take care of this delicious looking snack and then I'll fill you in on my day."

It was a delicious meal but I was so curious about Holmes' findings that when I was finished, Holmes was only halfway through his tea time. He shook his head and between bites of his cucumber sandwich, admonished me that, "You're not being kind to your stomach, Watson, by stuffing it so fast. Have a coffee and a smoke and I'll finish up here and tell you what I found today."

I couldn't argue with that, so I poured another cup of coffee, got a cigarette, and tried to relax in my armchair. It was only partially successful. Holmes finished his snack, poured himself another cup of tea, got his calabash from the mantle and settled into his chair. After a few puffs he turned to me and began to relate his activities. "Watson, after considering several ways Moran and Pigot could arrange to meet safely, I hit on the dailies. Consequently, my day was spent in the archives of the newspapers - specifically, the personal, or so-called 'agony' columns. Come to the table and I'll show you what I found in the morass of bleatings, lost pets, lost loves, and the lovelorn." We moved to the table and Holmes spread a few of his notes out on the cloth.

"How's this, Doctor? 'To G. Party is on. Same place, ten a.m. M'. This was in the Saturday edition. I found this kind of message every Saturday before the last Sunday of the month in the Times. The only change was that every few months, 'same place' changed to 'new place'. Twice during the 1892 papers, this appeared; 'G. party off. no worry. two parties next month. M.' Watson, I checked back to the 1892 ledger sheet and two months were skipped but the next month's payout was 100 pounds. I know now how Moran and Pigot arrange the blackmail payoffs, and the language suggests to me that Moran was afraid of Pigot. Note the 'no worry'. I imagine they pick a spot where neither can waylay the other."

"Holmes; it's like a mongoose circling a cobra, waiting for a chance to kill the serpent but leery of the cobra's strike."

"Well put, Doctor. That's a perfect simile. Moran would like to kill Gunny but he knows how deadly his ex-gunman can be."

"But Holmes, where does your discovery leave us? We know the 'how' but not the 'where'. It would be very difficult if not impossible to follow Moran. It would be way too obvious on those country roads." Holmes nodded. "I agree it's a last resort, but it may be all we have except Evan. Maybe there's another way, but it'll take some work and there's no guarantee that the result, even if convincing, would be presentable in court. I'll get started on it tomorrow."

The next several days were highlighted by Mrs. Hudson's earnest enquiry, "Doctor Watson, do you know why Mr. Holmes brought two big washtubs into our back yard?"

My surprise changed into laughter, "Mrs. Hudson, I haven't the slightest idea what Sherlock is up to now. He must have brought them in while I was out."

"Well, I don't know if he knows, but there's a hole in one of 'em. He's got one right side up and the one with the hole upside down on top of it. Now I don't mind, but I swear I'd be pleased to know what he's doin' out there."

That Thursday, I returned to 221B after my billiard afternoon and saw Holmes at his new lab table bending over his microscope. I hung up my coat and went to see what he was doing. I looked over his shoulder and saw a strange metal rack-like device that seemed to replace the slide holder. Thin posts rested on the lab table and apparently supported whatever the thing was. Holmes was mounting two small metal pieces to one side of the rack and several other pieces were scattered about on the table. He saw me watching and straightened up and with a satisfied smile said, "Well Watson, it seems to be coming together as I had hoped. The machinist did a perfect job following my somewhat amateurish drawing. I have just one more small assembly to add."

I couldn't imagine what the contraption was, so I asked, "Holmes, add to what?" Holmes picked up one of the small assemblies from the table; "My comparator, Doctor. Please hand me the small package by that beaker while I install this last holder. Billy will be up shortly with our tea and I'll explain this endeavor."

A minute later I heard footsteps on the stairs so I opened the door for Billy with our tea time snack, a pot of fresh tea and scones with elderberry jam. Holmes glanced over and announced, "Finished! The beeswax works perfectly. I'll be there in a moment."

Before I could ask, Holmes explained, "I'm making a fixture with which I can compare fired bullets. I'll show you how it works after we enjoy Mrs. Hudson's baking acumen and her sister's elderberry jam."

When we finished our tea time, Holmes waved me to follow him for a demonstration of his invention. He sat down at the microscope and I saw where he had added the beeswax. It was on the right side of the rack, a small piece of it wedged into a round, apparently hollowed out container mounted to one arm of the thing. Holmes picked up a bullet that had been pulled from its cartridge and pushed the nose into the wax. "Now Watson, look through the scope, I put a three-power lens in. It's plenty with which to see the markings. I know this bullet will be fairly smooth because it hasn't been fired yet. It's just to demonstrate that you can examine the base quite closely."

I peered through the scope and saw some marks. "Those marks you see Doctor, were made when I pulled the bullet out. I wanted you to see what an unfired Webley 45's slug looks like - your Webley, by the way. If you would please load a round into your pistol I will show you what a bullet looks like after it's been fired."

After I loaded the Webley, we went to the backyard and I started laughing at the washtubs Holmes had placed there. "Watson, I know it looks a bit primitive but let's see if it works as I hope. The lower tub is filled with water - I did that early this morning and the upper tub has a hole through which you fire a shot into the water. On the bottom of the water tub I folded a large towel so, at least I hope so, the bullet won't deform by hitting the metal bottom. I'm actually hoping the water alone will stop the bullet. Then we will take it back to the scope, mount it in the other holder, which is turnable in a complete circle, and see what we can see. Point the gun along the line I have drawn on the side of the tub. It is, I hope, not shallow enough to skip along the water but not straight down. I drew the guide to be about 45 degrees from straight out to straight down. Stand to one side and fire away, Doctor!"

After some slightly nervous thoughts, I approached the tub. I saw that Holmes had cut a hole about an inch and a half in diameter in the end of the upper tub and glued a strip of leather around the cut edge so it wouldn't damage the gun when it recoiled. I cocked the gun and gingerly poked it through the hole, aligned it with Holmes guide marks and after some hesitation, pulled the trigger. The gun jerked in my hand and I quickly withdrew the Webley and took a large step back! Holmes was already lifting the upper tub off and looking for the bullet. He found it embedded in the blanket and held it up triumphantly, "Hardly deformed at all. Science wins again!"

Mrs. Hudson came to the back door and peeked out. Holmes had warned her about his experiment and not to be startled, but the tubs absorbed so much of the sound that I doubt she heard enough to really frighten her. She slowly poked her head out around the door and asked, "Is it safe now, Mr. Holmes?"

We looked at each other and chuckled. As we went inside,

Holmes patted Mrs. Hudson on the shoulder and said comfortingly, "Everything is fine, dear lady. Thank you for the use of your yard. If it's no trouble, can I leave the tubs in place?" She nodded, peered around the door again and shut it firmly behind us!

"You see, Watson? Holmes had mounted the fired bullet in his device and beckoned me to look through the microscope. You don't even have to rotate the fired slug to see the marks it picked up going through the barrel." I was completely surprised by what I saw.

"Amazing, I see what you are saying. Those striations must have been from the rifling but there are several other marks also. What's next?" Holmes turned off the lamp he had placed so that the bullets were easily seen and looked at our mantle clock. "While you were out I sent a message to Gregson to bring several guns of identical caliber - including Moran's. I want him to see the results you have just seen."

"But Holmes, you mentioned that before and Gregson said his superiors turned down the idea, saying it wouldn't be acceptable in court."

"I know, but maybe my little demonstration will convince them otherwise. At least I can try. At the least I will add another monograph to my small scientific output."

We didn't have long to wait. A few minutes later we heard voices downstairs and then footsteps on the stairs. Holmes opened the door and Inspectors Gregson and Lestrade came in. Gregson was carrying a small box and they both had very quizzical looks on their faces. Gregson handed Holmes the box. "Well Holmes, here they are, three pistols - including Moran's, two cartridges for each gun, and we have no idea what the blazes you want them for!"

"Thank you, inspector. Let's go downstairs and I'll show you what this is all about. Doctor, please get three envelopes and a pencil."

As we trooped through the kitchen, Mrs. Hudson looked up from kneading a ball of dough, gave a little shake of her head and went back to her work. When we entered the backyard and the inspectors saw Holmes' washtub apparatus, they glanced at each other and you could see they were trying not to laugh, but not doing too well at it.

"As you can see, gentlemen, my arrangement is somewhat primitive, but as Doctor Watson can attest, it works quite well. I'm going to take one of these pistols, load two cartridges, and fire into my 'bullet catcher'. When I retrieve the slugs, Watson, who has the envelopes, will put the fired slugs in one and mark it one, two, or 'M'. Inspector Gregson, will you please pick out Moran's gun and hand it to me."

Gregson gave one of the pistols to Holmes, who loaded two shells in and aimed the gun through the hole in the top tub. Lestrade and Gregson backed away so fast they almost tripped over each other's feet! I also noticed Billy was peeking around the backdoor.

Holmes fired twice and then removed the upper tub, rolled up his sleeves, and pulled out the slugs. They looked quite undistorted and I put them in an envelope and marked it 'M'. Holmes then replaced the upper tub and repeated the action with the other two pistols. I put them in the envelopes and marked them 'one' and 'two'. During this demonstration by Holmes of his "bullet catcher", both Gregson and Lestrade had carefully moved toward the contraption, exchanging looks that bespoke serious surprise and continued puzzlement.

"Well gentlemen, shall we return upstairs and continue this to its conclusion?"

I had replaced the guns in the box Gregson brought and we proceeded back to our rooms with the two inspectors who obviously were still clueless. We went to Holmes' lab bench where he pointed out the features of his bullet holder and invited the inspectors to have a look. The two slugs from my Webley were still stuck in the beeswax and after peering through the scope, Gregson said, "Holmes, they look entirely different. What's going on?"

"They are both from Watson's trusty Webley, one fired and one simply pried out of its shell. You can obviously see what the inside of the barrel did to the fired one. Its passage left quite distinctive marks. We are now going to play a little enlightening game with the bullets I just fired. Watson will hand me two bullets randomly picked from the envelopes. He will not tell us from which envelopes, or envelope, he got them, but he will note down where I place each bullet in the holder. We'll call the part near the viewer 'south' and the one farther away 'north'. Watson will then know from which gun the bullets being compared were fired. I'll remove the slugs from the Webley." He did so and I stood on the side of the bench away from where the inspectors were. I gave Holmes a bullet from envelope number one and one from number two. He mounted them and asked the inspectors to look at them through the microscope, explaining that they could turn the bullet mountings with a screwdriver which he provided. After taking turns inspecting the slugs they both agreed that the two bullets were different - the markings did not match. After about an hour of switching the bullets back and forth, Holmes asked, "Well gentlemen, what do you conclude from my little game?"

"Amazing, Holmes," Gregson said, "the only bullets that match are ones from the same gun! It seems that each gun barrel gives a bullet distinctive marks."

"Yes, neither of you could match any other bullet to Moran's gun except another bullet from that gun. That is true of all three firearms; and, I suspect of any gun. The unavoidable conclusion is that a fired bullet can be matched to the gun that fired it and to no other. Alexander Lacassagne was right, but unfortunately, Scotland Yard doesn't have an appreciation of the Frenchman's genius. I'm going to visit a barrister friend of mine and get his opinion, but in the meantime, Inspectors, if you wish to bring more guns to be tested, especially Moran's air rifle, I'll be happy to oblige."

After Gregson and Lestrade left, taking the guns and the slugs with them, Holmes, with a satisfied smile, poured us a whisky with a dash from the gasogene. Holmes stoked his calabash and I lit a cigarette and we both relaxed in our armchairs. I was curious about Holmes's reference to a barrister; "Do I know this barrister Holmes? I can't recall you mentioning one before." After a sip and a puff, Holmes turned to me, "That was before we joined forces, Doctor. I was consulted on a court matter that involved a questionable crime, so I poked around a bit and pointed out a few discrepancies in the Crown's case to Francis Rumpole of the Old Bailey. He won the case for the defense and we have not seen one another since. I think he retired shortly after the trial. I shall visit the Central Criminal Court tomorrow and ask about him. Watson, I've never met a man so steeped in the law. I would value highly his opinion on the efficacy of this bullet evidence in a court of law.

Holmes left right after breakfast but as the day loomed overcast and chilly, I decided to remain indoors and catch up on my reading. Damp and cold days usually meant my injured leg would give me a bad time if I tried to do too much so I didn't press Holmes to include me in his plans. He said he'd probably be back by lunch so I got a fire going and settled down in my armchair with a very interesting book, *"The Influence of Sea Power Upon History, 1660 to 1783"*, by Alfred Mahan; ordered for me by Hatchards. I got engrossed in my book so time passed quickly. Just before noon, Holmes came back, but not in a happy mood. I could tell his research did not go well when he quite threw his coat and hat on our rack.

"Bad luck, Holmes? He didn't answer at first but strode over to the mantle, grabbed his old briar and stuffed it with some scraps left from a previous smoke. That always presaged a diatribe about some particularly annoying turn of events. He plopped himself in his armchair, waved his pipe at me and said, "Watson, I despair of officialdom! I have, thanks in part to M. Lacassagne, a revolutionary test that could potentially solve many, if not most, murder cases, and what does my friend Francis Rumpole, whose legal expertise I rate highly, say about it? 'Sorry Sherlock, but it'll take much more documented experimental work before a court will accept it at trial. Believe me, I know how slowly new forensic methods become part of admissible law.' So there we are Doctor, slogging through a deep bog of outmoded jurisprudence while murders are being noted as 'unsolved' when a simple test could resolve the issue. I feel Francis is correct in his opinion. That, along with what Gregson told us, I fear dooms the project - at least for now. Mark my words, Doctor, someday the test will be part of every gun-involved crime. We must try some other way to prove Moran is a killer. If I see Francis again, I think you would like to accompany me. He is a most knowledge-able and enthusiastic student of the law. His family's involvement in jurisprudence goes back three generations and he is quite proud of his son, Gaius (from the Roman juror, Gaius Gracchus) - who now teaches law, and Gaius's son, Justin, who hopes to have a post teach-ing law after he earns his Honors. Justin plans to marry when he has secured a post and, since he also studies poetry, has decided on a name for Francis' great-grandson - Horace; and hopes he will also fall in love with the law, and if a girl, Calliope."

"Holmes, it's too bad we can't nab 'Gunny'; I'll bet, with all those crimes he was involved in under Moran's direction, he might have enough to tell so that at least, Moran never gets out of pris-on." Holmes looked pensive for a moment, got up and returned his pipe to the mantle and sat at our table. "Watson, possibly we can do something about Pigot after all. I have an idea, but I hear the distinctive footfalls of Mrs. Hudson coming up the stairs - with our lunch I imagine. Let's do justice to that and then see what we can do about justice for Gunny and Moran."

Holmes was right about our lunch - cold cuts, fresh bread and butter, cucumber slices in Mrs. Hudson's "secret sauce" and fresh cof-fee deserved our undivided attention.

After we made the dishes appear as if they had already been washed, I poured us a second cup of coffee and relaxed in my chair. Holmes, however, took his cup and paced back and forth for several minutes before settling down in his armchair. He didn't sit for long. After finishing his coffee, he sprang out of his chair, grabbed his coat and hat off the rack and said, "Watson, your little 'Gunny' speech got me thinking about how we could go about, as you say, 'nabbing' him. I'll be back shortly." And with that, he was out the door.

After Billy removed our dishes, I returned to my book. The fire had warmed the room nicely, and Mrs. Hudson's lunch took its toll; I soon napped off. I'm not sure how long I slept but I awoke with a start when our door opened and Holmes breezed in. "Well Doctor, I see you passed your postprandial period quite peacefully! You had better mark your place in that book which is open on your lap before it falls on the carpet."

"You're right Holmes, I'm afraid the warmth, the food and this excellent book conspired to waft me into dreamland. But Holmes, what have you been up to this afternoon? He hung up his coat and hat, and, glancing at the mantle clock, turned to me and said, "Oh, I've been quite busy. I called on the Yard and spoke to Gregson and Hopkins - Jones and Lestrade were out on cases -- visited the *Times*, and finally, called on our horsey friend, Lucas McIvey, and delivered that fine bottle of brandy you picked up. He was so appreciative he opened it at once and offered a couple of fingers to me." Holmes smiled; "Of course, I didn't want to be impolite so I joined him in a toast to the capture of Colonel Moran. By the way, Lucas tells me Evan is continuing to regain his memory. I'm not hungry so I think I'll resume my latest experiment to develop a quick test for human-only blood."

"Very well, Holmes. I'll return to my book then. By the way, if you're going to mix some potions that will be highly odorous please warn me so I can beat a hasty retreat to my room and close the door!" Holmes chuckled and sat down at his new bench. I heard the distinctive clink of glassware so I somewhat warily picked up my book and tried to concentrate on the history of sea power while hoping Holmes didn't fill the room with noxious fumes. I was curious about his remark of visiting the *Times* but I knew he would tell me later. He glanced back at me as he must have guessed my thought; "Nothing to do until Sunday, Doctor." Holmes then turned back to his bench and the clinking of glass resumed, so I took up my book. I was up to 1690 and the battle of Beachy Head when Mrs. Hudson and Billy brought our supper. Holmes ate quickly and returned to his lab bench. Knowing that it would be useless to interrupt him, I read for a while, getting to the Battle of the Boyne and a bit beyond when my eyes grew very tired and I retired.

When I came out to our sitting room for breakfast Saturday morning, Holmes was already up and sitting at our table reading the early *London Times*. As I sat down, there was a folded section of the paper in front of my place with a circle marked around a small entry. I picked up the paper and noticed what was marked; a small placement in the Personal column:

> *G. Must leave at once. Last party Sunday, 10AM my place. Prize is 500 quid. Bring letter or party is off for good. M.*

I stared at it for a moment and then it managed to penetrate my slightly puzzled brain; "Holmes, you placed it! But do you think Pigot will fall for it? I mean, Moran was caught almost two weeks ago."

"Watson, I don't know if Moran's capture has reached our gunman's ears or not, but it cost only a small price to put this 'invitation' in the place Gunny is used to checking - the Saturday *Times* on the day before the last Sunday of the month. I decided it was worth a try as we have absolutely no leads to Pigot's location. If he does take the bait, we will be there to meet him. I think you had better make sure your Webley is clean and loaded; Pigot is a slippery customer and we may have to confront him. We must be ready."

I spent what must have been the most nervous, anxiety-filled day of my life with Sherlock Holmes that Saturday. I cleaned my revolver and loaded it as Holmes had asked, tried to read about key sea battles, drank too much coffee and smoked too many cigarettes. Meanwhile, Holmes kept busy at his lab bench most of the time; but I noticed he did more pacing and staring out our front window than usual! Mrs. Hudson brought lunch but neither of us ate much. About tea time, Gregson called on us. Holmes ushered him to our table and said, "Inspector, please join us for tea; Mrs. Hudson will be here shortly. What news have you for two nervous amateurs?"

"Holmes, I didn't tell you this before, but when I brought up your plan, we were told by our superiors that they didn't believe anything would come of it and no one would be paid even if they volunteered. In fact one of them called it 'a fool's errand.' But then, p/c Rance stepped forward and said he'd help, 'if Mr. Holmes needs me'. After he declared his intention to help, a good friend of his, p/c Adams, offered to go with him. Holmes, I have to admit, we all think Pigot won't show.' I know you have pulled off things that seemed impossible, so if you want Rance and Adams to help, I will give them the key to Moran's house. We searched it thoroughly of course after his arrest. Not even the dog is there - a neighbor volunteered to take him."

"Inspector, I'm touched by John Rance's offer. As you know, he has been involved in two of my cases, the last one, in the capture of John Clay. Please tell him I will pay his and Adam's wages for Sunday. They will have to be armed and they should arrive at nine AM. Watson and I will meet them. By the way, Inspector, what will they do with the police carriage? Obviously, it can't be on the road where Pigot could spot it."

Gregson nodded. "There is a small barn in back of the house next to Moran's. I'm sure the owners wouldn't mind if the police parked a cab in there for a while." Holmes took this in, thought for a moment and posed a possible problem, "Pigot has proved to be clever as well as being a gunman. Suppose he spots something, assuming he shows up, that alarms him so much that he runs back to his cab - I imagine he will be driving it himself - and departs at speed. Rance and Adams would have no chance to catch him with their transport being in the neighbor's barn."

Gregson seemed stopped by this. He rubbed his chin, leaned back in his chair, and admitted, "Holmes, you're right. I didn't think of that."

Further discussion was halted because Billy came up bearing our tea-time snack. Holmes was about to ask Billy to bring an extra cup and plate for Gregson but Billy had already done that. "I let the gentleman in and didn't hear him leave so I thought he would stay for tea. Fresh crumpets and jam and cucumber sandwiches, gentle-men." Holmes gave Billy a big smile; "You take after your mother, Billy; and that's a very good thing."

After finishing off our food, which didn't take long, Holmes outlined his plan, which now had the benefit of two stalwart p/c's. "Gregson, I think I have a solution to the escape problem. Watson and I will be arriving at Moran's in a Hansom from McIvey's sta-bles. Suppose we park up the road from where Pigot stops and keep watch in case he bolts before Rance and Adams can nab him. They may not know he's escaping so I will arrange a signal to alert them as Watson and I go after him. A police whistle would work quite well, I think. How does that all sound, Inspector? I was hoping to confront him myself but perhaps this is best to assure his capture." Gregson sat back in thought, idly tapping his fingers lightly on the cloth.

"Holmes, I think it's quite a risk you're taking; from Moran's records we got from you, Pigot is an extremely dangerous criminal.

However, without the full cooperation of the Yard, I think it's the best chance we have. Let's just pray that Rance and Adams grab him before he can do any serious damage. When he knocks at Moran's door it will open quickly and Mr. Pleasant Pigot will be staring at two revolvers pointed right at him." Gregson chuckled, "I know I wouldn't want to argue with big John Rance!"

After Inspector Gregson left, Holmes asked Mrs. Hudson to pack us a couple of sandwiches for the morning as we would be leaving by 6:30. "Lucas will be sending a cab for us, Doctor. We can have some tea there, eat our abbreviated breakfast, and be on our way.

The morning air was heavy with a damp, clinging fog that blanketed everything in a thick, grey haze. We donned our greatcoats, thanked Mrs. Hudson for the newspaper-wrapped breakfast she handed me and went outside. Holmes was carrying a small sack and a black bowler hat so naturally I was curious about it. Holmes answered, before I could ask, "I will need to look like a cabbie, Doctor, so I brought a few things."

It was just on 6:30 and though we couldn't see very far through the mist, we heard the clip-clop of hooves and in a moment a closed carriage pulled up. At first I thought the driver had become confused in the fog and stopped at the wrong door. I was about to shout to him when the booming voice of Alroy Riley cut through the wet air. "You blokes like a ride?" Holmes smiled and shook his head, "How in the world did you manage this carriage? Thanks to you, Alroy, however you did it!"

"Well gentlemen, weddings and Church doin's don't hardly start this early so I thought I'd keep ya' dry whilst I could use this here royal-like coach afor the toffs get it."

Laughing, we gratefully climbed in out of the fog and settled down. Riley gave out his usual Irish Gaelic form of 'giddup' and we were off to McIvey's mews in considerably more comfort than in the usual London cabs.

When we arrived at McIvey's stables, Holmes tried to give Riley a pound note but Alroy said McIvey told him the trip was free. Holmes held a finger to his lips and slipped the note into Riley's coat pocket. Riley broke out a big grin and bowed to us; "My pleasure gentlemen."

Lucas ushered us into his office; "Your cab will be ready in a mo'. Tommy's hitchin' up me best horse. Have a spot of tea; 'tis a cold, wet'un this day. I think a bit of that fine brandy put into the tea wouldn't be amiss, hey?" I smiled and told Lucas it would be most welcome. We ate the sandwiches Mrs. Hudson sent along and shared several scones with Lucas while we drank our tea. Just as we finished, Tommy came in to tell us the cab was ready. "The 'Duke' is rarin' to go sirs. 'E's a big, fast, strong one, 'e is. Can outrun most any cab in London, 'e can. You won't have no cause to spur 'im; a runner 'e is gentlemen." I went outside with Tommy and he was right, the 'Duke' was rightfully named after Wellington. The fog was lifting, so our trip to Middlesex to meet P/C Rance at Moran's should go without a hitch. Tommy was holding the reins for us but Holmes hadn't appeared yet. Then I saw Tommy get a startled look on his face. I turned around and Holmes and Lucas were coming out of McIvey's office toward the cab. I couldn't help laughing; Holmes was wearing a black jacket, the bowler hat, and sporting a long, thin moustache! Lucas, with a big grin, wished us well. I climbed into the cab, Holmes took the reins from Tommy, mounted the driver's platform, and was about to give the reins a flip to get us going when Riley came out of the stable and hollered, "Allow me, Mr. Holmes." And bellowed, "dean deifir!". Duke seemed to be at full gallop instantly and I heard a loud, "Hey! Whoa!" from Holmes and I saw the reins tighten and Duke slowed in time to make the turn from McIvey's entry into the road. I peered out of the cab then and saw Lucas bent over with his hands on his knees laughing like crazy and Riley with his hands on his hips doing the same. Holmes opened the door in the roof and yelled down to me, "Are you laughing?" I said I was and Holmes answered. "I don't blame you!"

We made the trip to Moran's house in excellent time; 'Duke' trotted along at a rate I never experienced in the usual London hack. We came from the west of town and Moran's was on the south side of the road. We couldn't know from which direction Pigot would come, if he did come at all, so Holmes pulled us as far to the side of the road as possible. There was a rail in front of a dry goods store almost directly opposite Moran's so Holmes got down from his perch and tied Duke to the rail. It was very quiet; probably between services at the local church. We hadn't passed a church so chances were it was at the far end of the village. I joined Holmes and we crossed the road and walked up the cobblestone path to Moran's door. Holmes said, "I think Rance will be here by now, it's just about the time I told Gregson we'd meet the P/C's." Knocking lightly on the door he said in a firm voice, "It's Holmes and Watson; kindly don't shoot us!" The door opened and big John Rance greeted us with a grin, "Come in gentlemen, meet my friend and fellow constable, Edward Adams. Ed, I think this gent with the moustache and bowler is

Sherlock Holmes!" We laughed and shook hands all around. "Yes, John, I really am Holmes. I donned this simple get-up so our quarry will see me as a cabbie waiting for a customer to show up. I intend to look very bored about the whole thing while keeping an eye on his actions. Understand that if he suspects something is wrong and bolts, Watson and I will pursue him and I'll give one blast on my police whistle if he heads west and two if he escapes to the east. That way, when you retrieve your police wagon from next door you'll know which way we went. While Watson has his trusty Webley and I have my Penang Lawyer, Pigot is a formidable opponent and has no compunction to fire on anyone he sees as a threat. According to the records we gave Gregson, Pigot, known as 'Gunny' in Moran's papers, is probably responsible for as many as six murders. He's not to be taken lightly. I'd prefer to take him alive and question him about Moran's activities but if he makes any moves, don't hesitate to shoot." Rance and Adams nodded their understanding. Holmes check the time and said, "Watson and I will go across to our cab and try to be as inconspicuous as possible. It's about twenty minutes to ten so if he's coming, he should be here soon."

Back in the Hansom, Holmes reached into the sack he had put his moustache and spirit gum in and pulled out the last item, a part of yesterday's paper. "Here Doctor, since this cab offers little concealment, lean back and act like you're engrossed in the latest scandal when I give you the word. If Gunny comes from the east, he'll be looking right at you so I'll warn you. I'm leaving the top flap open so we can communicate. I'm going to rest my head on the top facing Moran's house and look half asleep."

I practiced reading the paper but I was so on edge that I wouldn't have been able to tell anyone what I just read. I kept checking my watch, which seemed to have stopped when I wasn't looking. It was very close on to ten when Holmes, in a loud whisper, said, "Watson, here comes a trap from the east. I can't see yet who's driving."

I tried to look relaxed but it was a struggle. In a moment I heard the clatter of the horses' hooves and when they were past, Holmes said softly, "I think it's him. He's pulling up in front of Moran's. He's not getting down, he's just sitting there. I hope he doesn't expect Moran to open the door and wave him in." Tension was thick in the air. I put down the paper and put my hand on my revolver; and waited. At last I heard Holmes whisper, "Watson, he's finally getting out of the trap, but he didn't hitch the horse to anything. You may have to untie Duke from the rail as quickly as you can."

Holmes kept me informed, but for a while there was nothing to report. I couldn't stand the silence so I asked in a very low voice,

"What's he doing now? Has he moved toward the house?" Holmes whispered again. "He's just standing by the trap. He has his hand inside his jacket, I assume on his pistol. Oh, now he's moving, but not toward the door, he's walking to the side of the house." After a long pause, Holmes said, "He's walking down the path that leads to the gate which we used to get to the back door. I hope Rance and Adams are on their toes. I imagine the door is locked and Pigot would have to make enough noise that the men would be alerted. If he gets the slightest advantage over them it could be a disaster. I'd never forgive myself for setting this up."

I couldn't stand it any longer and lowered my newspaper just enough so I could see.

Just as Holmes observed, Pigot was walking slowly down the path to the gate. When he got there he opened it just a little and pounded on it! "Holmes, what in blazes is he up to?" Holmes answered immediately, "The dog, Watson! I think he suspects a trap and he wants to see if the dog is still here. If not, he'll know something is wrong. If the dog is here, he'll be more assured that Moran is also. I told you he was cleverer than Moran gave him credit for." I remembered then what Gregson had said; the dog was taken in by a neighbor. Holmes broke into my thoughts, "I think he just realized that the dog is gone. He's walking quickly back up the path. Get ready to untie Duke."

A past case rushed into my mind; "Holmes, it's like King's Pyland!" I heard a soft chuckle; "Quite so Doctor, except this time the dog did nothing because there is no dog! Here he comes. I don't know if he'll bolt. I don't think the p/c's have any idea what's happening. In fact, they may have heard the noise at the gate and went to the back of the house. If they did, that will give Pigot a few extra seconds to escape."

I put down the paper and moved to the side of the cab so I could jump out quickly. I could no longer see what Pigot was doing but

Holmes said he paused by the trap. Suddenly, "Watson!, loose Duke - Pigot leaped up into his trap and grabbed the reins."

Just then I heard the crack of a whip. I got out of our Hansom, untied Duke as quickly as I could and climbed back in. "I'm in, Holmes."

I hardly had time to sit down when Holmes gave a single blast on his police whistle - Pigot was heading west. Holmes then yelled "dean deifir" as Riley had done. The result was the same and I was thrown back in my seat as big Duke lunged forward. Holmes had to haul hard on the reins because we were facing east and he had to get Duke to make a sharp turn to follow Pigot. As Duke spun our cab around I could see Pigot look back; I'm sure he heard Holmes whistle and now that we were behind him, he certainly knew the game was up. As we passed in front of Moran's, I saw Rance and Adams rush out of the house, look at us, and sprint toward next door's barn where their police cab was.

The roof trap was still open and Holmes leaned over and yelled, "Get ready Watson, we'll be on Pigot's tail soon - Duke is a faster horse but Pigot has a good lead on us. We may have to take him on alone; the reinforcements will be far behind." I had never gone so fast in a Hansom before; Duke's big hooves were pounding loudly on the road, the Hansom was rattling in every joint but we were gradually gaining ground on Pigot. Holmes shouted down again. "Watson, can you crouch behind the mud board? Pigot will undoubtedly start to shoot as soon as we get closer."

I started to do as Holmes asked when I saw Pigot turn, hold the reins with one hand and reach inside his jacket with his free hand. I hit the floor of the cab just as I heard the crack of a gun; a bullet slammed into the partition right where I had been only a split second before. Holmes again shouted; "Are you all right Watson?" I answered that I was but it was a close thing and asked if I should fire back.

"No, no, don't shoot yet. He doesn't know we're armed. Let him waste his bullets for now." I felt like telling him it was a wasted shot by only about two inches! I peeked over the mud board and Pigot had turned around again and was whipping up his horse so I took a quick glance behind and I could see a black dot in the distance. If it was the constables, they were pretty far astern. We soon crossed the Kensington road and were speeding west. In a few minutes we would be where Moran shot Ambrose and Evan.

"Watson, it looks like Pigot is going to turn off this road and into a narrow lane I see coming up. Here; take my hat and throw it in the road if we have to follow." I wondered for a moment why Holmes wanted me to pitch his hat but I quickly realized it was to guide the constables.

"Yes, Watson, he's turning and we are closing the gap. Lean to the right as far as you can, I don't want to tip this over. Drop my hat as we turn." I leaned as far as I could as we made a sharp left turn. The cab tilted but Holmes leaned as I did and after a brief, heart-stopping moment, we straightened up and continued the chase. I resumed my position behind the mud board. Pigot reached in his jacket again, pulled out his pistol and immediately, a bullet slammed into the mudboard, shattering a corner and sending splinters flying. At the same instant I heard another muzzle blast and a bullet hit the back wall of the cab. I could see a hole; the bullet must have gone clear through. I screamed at the top of my voice, "Holmes, are you hit?" Holmes shouted back, "No but not by much, Doctor!" I pulled the Webley out of my jacket but I couldn't get a decent shot from my position behind the mud board. Duke was in my line of sight also and I dared not to stand up. Pigot was too good a marksman to give him a target like that.

The lane we were on was so full of ruts and potholes our cab bounced around like a billiard ball on cobblestones. It was impossible to hold aim on Pigot or even his trap. We were coming to a heavily forested growth of trees and old hedgerows. Pigot turned again and took a shot at us but it must have hit a wheel because there was a loud clang and no sound of it hitting us anywhere else.

The lane now began to climb up a gentle hill and the land sloped away to our right with a meadow stretching away to farmland. Holmes yelled down through the trap door, "Watson, I'm going to back off a little, he knows now he can't outrun us and I don't want to give him a better shot at us. But keep your pistol handy." Holmes had barely finished when I felt our cab slow and we were gradually falling back a little, making us a more difficult target. Suddenly, Pigot yanked the trap to the right and off the lane. Down the slope it went, tilting hard to the left. I saw our reins tighten as Holmes pulled back to slow Duke even more. By then, Pigot's trap was halfway down the slope, and as we came to the place he left the lane and I could see he had taken the turn too fast and must have hit a stone or a mound of dirt because the trap was now on one wheel and could not recover. It tipped over on its side and trap and horse went sliding down the slope. I couldn't see Pigot, so he hadn't been thrown off the trap. Holmes jumped down from his driver's platform and I climbed out on the far side of our cab. We stood there watching as the trap came to a stop. Nothing happened for two or three minutes. Then Holmes grabbed my arm and pulled me behind our cab.

"Blast it all, Watson, Pigot must have hung on; I just saw his head peek out from behind the rear of the trap. He's using it as a shield and he still has two bullets left. Go to the back of our cab. You can keep him in your sights from there and have the protection of the cab body. Duke must be tired by now so I don't think he'll wander." I started toward the back and stopped; "But Holmes, what do you intend to do?"

"Doctor, I'm going to use the hedge and those trees for cover and try to sneak up on our friend from the rear. Just keep him pinned down. You have more ammunition than he has but use it wisely!"

I was horrified. "Holmes, why not wait for the constables?" Holmes shook his head; "We don't know if they saw my hat - the sign of our turn onto this lane.If Pigot can make it to that meadow we can't follow him in the cab, the ground will be too soft. That's why you need to keep him where he is. Look out Watson!" Then I saw why he warned me; Pigot had his pistol out and was resting it on the side of the trap. Just as I moved, a shot rang out and a bullet tore into the edge of the cab and ricocheted across my left arm. Holmes saw the rip in my jacket. "Watson, quick, give me the gun." He took it and fired toward Pigot to drive him back behind the trap. I tore off my jacket and saw that the bullet grazed my arm as it ricocheted but didn't penetrate. I pulled out my handkerchief and pressed it on the wound. "I'm all right Holmes, it isn't deep. If you'll tie my handkerchief around my arm I can still shoot enough to keep him pinned down."

After tying my makeshift bandage, Holmes handed the Webley back to me, looked at the trap and as Pigot had retreated behind it after Holmes' shot, he sprinted behind the hedge and disappeared into the copse. I knew he would run parallel to the road until he got past where Pigot was and then try to take him down. I have to admit I was petrified by the thought of Holmes taking on a gunman who still had a bullet in his gun. I knew one thing clearly; I must keep Pigot occupied and concentrating on me. I steadied the pistol against the side of the cab, ready to fire if he showed his face. My arm was beginning to throb but I had to do my best to ignore the pain until this standoff was over - one way or another!

After what seemed forever but was probably only four or five minutes, I saw Holmes come out of the covering copse and cross the road about twenty five or thirty yards past Pigot's position. I hadn't seen any move on his part so I took a shot close to the edge of the trap where Pigot had been appearing, just to get his attention. At the moment just before I fired, Pigot stepped out a few inches past the end of the trap but jerked back behind it again. My shot again splintered against the trap. I knew if he made a dash for the meadow and was successful, I could never hit him.

I could see Holmes working his way down the slope and approaching Pigot's position. I had to really bear down to keep my hand from trembling. Holmes would be so close in a moment that Pigot couldn't miss if he saw him. I held as steady as I could and fired again, hitting the edge of the trap as before.

There was a loud scream from behind the trap. My heart froze!

I stood for a moment in shock, but my instincts and concern for my best friend took over and I ran out from behind the cab and, with my gun in hand, started to run down the slope toward the trap, determined to help, or in the worst case, avenge Holmes' death. To my unbounded relief, Holmes and Pigot emerged from behind the trap. I saw that Pigot still had his pistol in his hand but Holmes had gripped Pigot's hand and was holding it skyward, his arm extended fully. They were pivoting around, Pigot trying to get his hand free. I couldn't risk a shot so I tucked the Webley in my belt and ran to grab Pigot's free arm so he couldn't hit Holmes. Suddenly, Holmes pushed Pigot back a step with his free arm and hit him with a powerful uppercut which grassed him. Holmes then firmly planted one foot on Pigot's gun hand. I rushed over and pressed my pistol against Pigot's chest and warned him not to move. Holmes removed Pigot's gun from his pinned hand. "Gunny" was no longer the dangerous murderer. In fact he was pleading with us; "I can't breathe, help me, I'm hurt." Holmes explained what Pigot's problem was; "He turned his head and saw me just as I was almost close enough to grab him. He was swinging his arm around to shoot so I threw my stick at him. The heavy end hit him in the ribs and stunned him enough so I could get close enough to grab his gun hand. Thanks for your prompt reaction, Doctor, and for keeping him behind his trap. If he made it to the meadow we may have lost him.

"Holmes, do you want my belt to tie him up?"

"I think that will be unnecessary; unless I'm mistaken, our constables are coming fast up the lane. They will, I'm sure, be happy to provide a sturdy set of darbies for our friend." I now heard what Holmes' sharper hearing had detected. The police carriage was just pulling to a stop behind our Hansom. Rance and Adams jumped out and hurried down the slope. Adams had a very disreputable looking hat in his hand which he handed to Holmes. "Sorry sir, we missed it the first time and went too far. Then we ran over it!"

We got a chuckle out of that. Holmes punched the crown out and stuck it on his head but it still looked a lot like it had, indeed, been run over.

"This gentleman on the ground is one Pleasant Pigot, ex of Moriarty's criminal enterprise; and the last of it I'm glad to say. He may have a broken rib or two so don't be too rough with him or you might cheat the hangman! When you get him cuffed, I need to search him for a very important letter I hope he brought along."

Rance and Adams went about securing Pigot quite handily. Holmes lifted his foot off Pigot's hand and gave Adams the gun. They lifted Pigot to his feet and slipped the darbies on. Holmes then began searching. With a cry of success, Holmes pulled an envelope out of the inside pocket of Pigot's jacket. He opened it and showed it to us. I recognized it immediately as the one I found on Silas Moran's lamp table in Budleigh-Salterton.

"That's it, Holmes. So Pigot actually did bring it. I thought he might fake bringing it, shoot Moran, and escape with the five hundred pounds he thought Moran was offering for the letter." Holmes looked doubtful; "I think Gunny knew Moran would be very, very careful about the transaction. It would be interesting to watch the maneuvering of the two villains; both trying to obtain what they wanted without getting shot! John, thank you for the effort today. Watson and I will now find a nearby farm and let our gallant but

probably thirsty horse have a drink before we head back to McIvey's."
Holmes then handed the incriminating letter to Rance. "Please be
certain Gregson gets this. It may help to have Moran join Mr. Pigot
up those last steps. Just two more things John, may I have what I
think is the last bullet in Pigot's revolver?"

Rance opened the breech and sure enough, there was one bullet left. He extracted it and handed it to Holmes. "Thank you John.
Now since Pigot is in the capable hands of Constable Adams, would
you mind giving Watson and me a hand righting Pigot's trap? I
think the poor horse would feel much better standing up as he has
not been able to do so since Pigot dumped the trap over. He isn't
hurt. I have noticed his efforts and he can't quite make it all the way.
He's been squatting there for some time now."

We pushed the trap upright and the horse immediately struggled to its feet. We shook hands and Rance asked, "What about the
trap and horse, Mr. Holmes? I would volunteer but I think Pigot
should be guarded and neither of us can drive and adequately guard
him alone." Holmes nodded his head, "I agree John. Doctor, can
you manage the trap? You can follow me. John, why don't you follow us also. Possibly we can leave the trap and horse at a local farm.
Since you represent the Yard, we should be able to work out an arrangement." That was an acceptable solution so we started our little
parade with a nervous doctor trying to remember what he learned
thirty years ago about horses on a small place in Scotland! I do remember shouting to Holmes, "Not too fast, not too fast!"

Back on the east-west road we proceeded; a tall, rumpled Hansom
driver with a crushed bowler and a stage moustache that was beginning to fall off, Pigot's trap, weaving a bit side to side, and an official
police carriage with a prisoner loudly complaining about his injured
ribs. All we needed now was Gilbert to write a patter song about us
and Sullivan to put music to it!

Fortunately, we didn't have far to go; about a quarter-mile past the Kensington road Holmes held up his arm for us to slow. We had come to a small farm or croft just left off the road. Holmes led us up a gravel drive to the house. We must have been quite a sight for the farmer as he came around the back of the house. He just stood there saying over and over, "What's this then, what's this then...?"

Holmes jumped down and calmed the startled man; "Don't worry, sir. My name is Holmes, the novice trap driver is my friend, Doctor John Watson and the big constable is John Rance of the Yard. We would like to ask a couple of favors - first, we need water for the horses and second we would like to compensate you if you would keep the trap for a day or two." The farmer looked at us, thought a bit, and finally said, "You mean you'll pay me for tendin' the trap?" Holmes pulled out his wallet and handed the man a bank note. His doubtful expression changed completely. "My name is Fred Tolliver sir, and I'll be happy to look after the trap, sir. I think I'd better drive it to me barn, though; your doctor looks a mite shaky. Methinks he might be a better doctor than a horseman, beggin' your pardon sir." With great relief, I threw the reins to Mr. Tolliver and exited the trap with alacrity.

Before regaining my seat in the Hansom I called up to Holmes, "Please take that bedraggled looking thing off your upper lip; you look like a cartoon!" Holmes laughed and gave the drooping moustache a yank. It came off easily and, other than the crumpled bowler, he looked a bit more respectable. We then followed Tolliver to the horse trough and gave Duke and the police carriage horse a good drink. They certainly had earned it.

We turned around and went back to the Kensington Road and south toward London. We waved goodbye to Rance and Adams at the turnoff to McIvey's. They would be taking their whiny prisoner to the Yard. The trapdoor was still open so I yelled up to Holmes, "Congratulations! That's the last of Moriarty's criminals." I couldn't see his face but his tone bespoke good cheer; "Yes, thanks. Now I hope I can resume, what Mycroft refers to as '...running here and there; lying on my face with a lens to my eye...' and indulging in the 'petty puzzles of the police court'. Mycroft has more powers of deduction than I do, but I have better observational skills. We would make a good detecting pair, but Mycroft is totally devoted to his work at the Foreign Office."

When we arrived at McIvey's, he insisted on hearing all about our adventure and was delighted to hear we recovered solid evidence of Moran's involvement in Moriarty's gang. As we waited for a cab to take us home, Holmes told Lucas of the splendid performance of Duke. "He's without question the best horse I've ever seen. You are lucky to have him in your stable." Lucas broke into an ear-to-ear grin. "I know, gents; I rode his sire, Earl's Choice, and he was a great horse too. Duke has always been strong but never quite fast enough to race. If he was, you can bet I'd try to ride him even with me gamy leg! But here's Alroy and I know he'd want to take you home."

Lucas was right, of course, Alroy wouldn't hear of anyone else driving us, so we said 'goodbye' to McIvey and climbed into Riley's cab. Holmes leaned over and said, "Now listen carefully." Then Holmes boomed out; "dean deifir!" and off we went. Holmes gave me a nudge in the ribs; "Hear that? I think I got it right!"

"Holmes, even though it was often a close thing, it was a good day; and your Gaelic is perfect. Duke wouldn't have moved other-wise; and I heard Alroy laugh."

"Yes Doctor, it was indeed a good day - for Justice.

END

EPILOGUE: Evan Postlewaite did finally recover his memory of the terrible event he witnessed, but as Holmes was preparing him for testimony against Moran, the Sword of Justice struck unerringly, and Moran died in prison of a heart attack. Pigot, alias "Gunny," pulled a life sentence. Sherlock Holmes had taken down one of the most dangerous criminal enterprises in English history. So clever had been their leader that no one, including Scotland Yard, was aware of the links in the chain until Holmes exposed them.

The Yard took the credit, of course; that's why I've written the true story of how Holmes destroyed the criminal organization of Professor Moriarty.

A CASE OF
INTIMIDATION

AN APPLE, ROLLING and bouncing down the pavement, is not a normal happening, especially when a good sized one connects with your ankle. When the apple is followed closely by an orange, the result is quite startling indeed.

I had been idly shopping on a pleasant early summer day when I reached a corner of the street I was on and the end of a lane that slanted upward at a gentle angle to my right. The fruit in question had come down that lane, so naturally my attention was drawn to its origin. To my surprise, I was facing an increasing onslaught of the greengrocer's wares and had to jump out of the way lest a large cabbage smash into my already bruised ankle. After dodging the cabbage and another apple, I saw a small, agitated group of people about halfway up the slope, maybe twenty yards or so from me, gathered around a man in an apron holding a cloth to his face; obviously the greengrocer himself.

Everyone was shouting and shaking their fists at a Hansom disappearing over the top of the sloping lane.

I was curious of course, so I went up to where the crowd was and announced I was a doctor and offered to check any injury the greengrocer may have sustained. The crowd backed off to let me examine the man. I pulled the cloth away from his face and I could see some blood coming from his nose and a gash in his left cheek. I told him I needed some clean water and another cloth. He led me into his shop and to a sink with water and handed me a clean cloth. I wiped the blood away and dried his face. I doubled the cloth and tied it around his head, covering both injuries.

"Leave the cloth on until the bleeding stops. Do you have any ointment or salve? I don't have my medical bag but you can do well just by keeping your injuries covered and clean. I don't think either one is serious; just painful."

He was a man of average stature with light brown hair and a small moustache, curled at the tips. His apron was typical of the common London tradesman, but now it was spattered with blood. He removed it and turned to me; "I thank thee much sir, me name is Cyrus Appleton and I gets some razzin' about me bein' a greengrocer with a tag like that. I ain't never in me life faced that what happened to me today, sir. See, t'other day, two bad lookin' men came in to the shop and told me I had to pony up some money every week for what they said was 'protection from people meanin' to hurt me and me business'. Sir, I ain't never had no trouble from a soul long as I been here. I told 'em I didn't have no need for 'protection' but they got real nasty and said bad things could happen if I didn't pay 'em.. Certain, sir, I didn't pay 'em. Now today, two big fellas jumps out of a Hansom and hits me and turns over some of me outside crates and then takes off. I can't think what to do, sir." Cyrus waved his arms in a gesture of helpless frustration. "And that ain't all, sir, I knows some more people around here been threatened by these devils."

Trying to comfort him some, I said, "Mr. Appleton, I see your customers have righted your crates and collected what items they could. Clearly they value you and your business. I'm going now to fetch my medical bag. I'll return with some help for your wounds. Don't despair. In the meantime, report this outrage to your constable as soon as you can."

I hurried down the lane to the main road and after a few minutes was able to wave down a cab to take me to Baker Street. When we pulled up at 221 I noticed a Yard Hansom parked in front of our door. Asking the cabbie to wait, I climbed the stairs and fairly burst into the room. Holmes and Inspector Stanley Hopkins were sitting at our table but I didn't have time to explain my hurry. "Sorry, medical problem, be back soon." I grabbed my bag from my room and went downstairs and out to the waiting cab. When I arrived at Appleton's shop I removed the makeshift bandages. Seeing that his nose had stopped bleeding, I left that bandage off and treated the gash in his cheek.

His displays had been cleaned up and the shop returned almost to normal. Several customers had stayed to help and commiserate with Appleton and one lady told me a customer had found a constable and described the incident to him. I climbed into the waiting cab and the driver, happy to have been paid for three consecutive trips, deposited me back at home.

On the ride back to 221, we passed many small shops and I couldn't help but think what a vicious thing it was to prey on those hardworking people, many with little education except in their jobs; truly the backbone of the Nation. I mused about my own service in the army, shoulder to shoulder with men doing their duty for England; some speaking in accents that were almost impossible to understand: Geordie, Gaelic, Cockney, Pitmatic, Cumbrian, Scouse, Mackem, and more. But they stood together in the face of the enemy, shouting their defiance in a dozen different accents.

I was surprised to see that the Yard Hansom was still in front of 221. Usually, visits from Scotland Yard were brief; Lestrade in his normal, puzzled state, Gregson, quite respectful of Holmes' talents, and Peter Jones, bulling his way through a case. Hopkins must have a serious matter to have taken so long consulting with Holmes. When I entered our rooms, this time not in such a hurry, Stanley

Hopkins and Holmes were still seated at our table. Holmes was inspecting several sheets with drawings or pictures of some sinister appearing men. Holmes looked up from the sheet he was studying and queried, "Well, Doctor, how did the medical mission go? The patient survived, I trust. Have a seat; Inspector Hopkins has just presented a pretty little problem you would probably title, 'The Disappearing Miscreants'. It seems several very nasty gentlemen of the underworld have been dropping out of sight as soon as the law closes in. Inspector Hopkins here went after the wrong man as the 'escape route' of these crooks and his bosses are less than happy about it." Hopkins gave me a somewhat sheepish look.

"It's true, Doctor Watson; I was overanxious and got in hot water for it. I'm here to ask Mr. Holmes if he can help find the real method these dangerous men use to escape."

As it was about four, I thought we would soon have tea so I pulled out a chair and joined the little conference. After my medical adventure I could use a snack. I also wanted to share my findings about the intimidation of Mr. Appleton. Since Hopkins was here, it seemed a perfect time to relate my experience. Holmes and Hopkins seemed to be finished with their meeting, so while we waited for tea, I explained my precipitous entry and exit and told of my finding criminal acts and threats on shopkeepers during my shopping trip. Hopkins spoke up; "Doctor; this is bad news indeed; obviously the work of a new gang we hadn't heard about. I'll report this to my superiors. We must stamp out this extortion before it gets out of hand! Please write down all the details you have so I can file a complete report."

I noticed Holmes raise his eyebrows a bit but he didn't say anything. Billy arrived with our tea and crumpets so we dug in. After I finished, I got a notepad out of our desk and wrote down everything I could remember for the inspector. Hopkins retrieved his coat and hat from our stand, folded the note and tucked it away. "Thank you Doctor Watson, I will pass this on immediately."

We shook hands with the inspector as he left and Holmes and I returned to our table for a second cup of tea. Holmes's small gesture puzzled me so I asked him about it.

"My dear Doctor, Hopkins is often enthusiastic to a fault. He is one of the most avid conclusion jumpers in the Yard! I hope he gets the co-operation of the force to go after this serious threat you have discovered, but in the meantime, I promised him I would look into these strange disappearances of wanted criminals." He got up from the table then, picked up his old briar pipe from the mantle pipe rack, packed and lit it, and settled down in his armchair. I was finishing my tea when I noticed Holmes leaning back and blowing wisps of smoke toward the ceiling. That meant to me that his agile mind was examining the evidence he had just heard from all angles and determining what action to take. As if following my thoughts, Holmes sprang out of his chair, put his pipe back in the rack and headed for the door.

"Doctor, please tell Billy that I'm going to invite Wiggins; have Billy take him upstairs and ask him to wait for my return. Also please give him some tea and a biscuit. I'm going to put out the word now and also call on a couple of old acquaintances whose ears are always open to bits of news from the underside of London."

"Don't you mean old adversaries, Holmes? He smiled, put a forefinger to his lips, and left. I rang for Billy and passed Holmes' instructions to him. I figured Holmes contacting some slightly shady characters was for the purpose of getting a line on the disappearance problem Hopkins had brought, but what he wanted Wiggins for (and presumably the Baker Street Irregulars) was a mystery.

As I sat mulling over the events of the day, smoking a cigarette, I became as frustrated as usual when trying to put everything together. Holmes as much as told me he was going to look up a few former opponents who knew better than to cross him again - that is, unless they wanted to go back to prison. Several, although more or less reformed, still kept an ear on the London crime scene and for a few bob, would pass the information to Holmes. I didn't have much time to speculate as I heard Billy answer the door, followed by footsteps on the stairs. I opened the door and the somewhat shabbily clad Wiggins, taller than I remembered, popped in, doffed his cap, and greeted me; " Doctaah, d'ja recalls me? Mr. 'olmes sent for me, ya?"

"Yes, Wiggins, Mr. Holmes will be here shortly. Billy will be bringing up some tea and a biscuit and jam. Have a seat at the table." Wiggins sat down, flipped his cap on the table beside him and asked; "Wot's it anyway? 'e didn't tell me nuffin' wots 'e wants me for, but me and me boys is like brovaahs an' we gonna do wha'eva Mr. 'olmes needs doin'." I removed his rather crumpled and stained cap and hung it on the rack, sat down across from him and confessed that I didn't know what Holmes wanted. Billy came up with a tea tray and Wiggins dug in as though he hadn't eaten anything all day. And sadly, he probably had not.

We didn't have long to wait. Holmes returned, thank goodness, about an hour after Wiggins finished his tea and biscuit. Conversing with Wiggins is for me, not being fluent in Cockney, a surreal experience. When he said "I 'ears 'olmes on tha apples," it stumped me until I figured out it meant, "I hear Holmes on the stairs" and by that time Holmes had just come in the door! He gave Wiggins a firm pat on the shoulder, hung his cap on the rack, pulled a sheaf of papers from his inside jacket pocket, tossed it on the table and hung up his light jacket. "Well Wiggins, I see you got my message. By the empty cup and crumbs on the tea tray I see you've had a snack and by the debris around your mouth I assume you had a biscuit with strawberry jam." Wiggins quickly grabbed the napkin from the tray and wiped off the evidence. "I have a job for you and your gan..... crew, that will get you plenty of bees." I didn't follow, but Wiggins broke out a big smile; "I loves to 'ear it, Mr. 'olmes. Wot's the job then?"

Holmes sat down, unfolded the papers and spread them out on the table. "These are maps I picked up from Mr. Thomas Cook & Company. I need the Baker Street Irregulars to do some spying for me on criminals who are picking on shop owners and extorting money from them in the guise of 'protection'. What I want you to do is track them. I'll give you a small notepad and a pencil to write down the shops where these crooks stop and what you and your boys see them do. They travel in a cab, so it may take you a while to follow their trail. Keep moving your crew along their route when they leave their nasty work until you find their base. Here's a map of the area where Doctor Watson came across their reaction to Mr. Appleton's refusal to pay their demand. They hit him and turned over his crates. They will probably be back to give him a chance to pay for his 'protection' or do more damage to him and his shop."

"Yes, sir; I knows where tha shop be. We sometimes 'elp ourselves to a apple or som'pin' when 'e ain't lookin'. I'se sorry to 'ear 'e's got 'urt." Holmes then pulled out a leather pouch from his back pocket and handed it to Wiggins. "I also stopped by my bank and got a bunch of coins for you and the Irregulars. Keep them in the pouch until you pass them out so they won't jingle in your pocket. Some unsavory character might mistake you for a rich toff!" Holmes smiled and Wiggins laughed out loud at that. "Me a toff! Could y'a Adam and Eve it? Fanks, Mr. 'olmes, me and tha boys won't let ya down."

"Fine, Wiggins. Two things; I want a report from you every day, and two, I want you to buy an apple for each of your boys tomorrow. Note I said buy - not nick!" Wiggins smiled, stowed away the map, notebook and pencil, and pouch. "I gits it, Mr. 'olmes. We'll track tha mingers down!" Holmes handed Wiggins his cap, opened the door and said, "I also want you to be careful - these mingers are bad Khybers, and don't forget it!"

After Wiggins left, Holmes sat down, folded the rest of the maps, and gave me the most phony innocent look I ever received. "Any questions, Doctor?"

"bees?"

"Money, Doctor."

"Mingers?"

"'Bad people', or 'minger'; person."

"Khybers?"

"Delicacy prevents me from translating that." With that, Holmes took his calabash off the pipe rack, stoked it, and relaxed in his semi-disreputable armchair with a box of matches. I knew I wouldn't get anything more out of him for a while.

A week passed and Wiggins faithfully reported his progress each day. Holmes would then mark it down on his master map. After Wiggins' last visit, Holmes marked the map and leaned back in his chair with a pleased expression; "Doctor, the Irregulars are doing a fine job tracking the crooks. It looks like they have their base near the East End. We should know by next week. By the way; I got a note from Hopkins - he will be stopping in today to tell us if he found anything helpful concerning the disappearing crooks. So far, my nosing around among my miscreant informants has produced nothing of value. They are aware that something unusual is going on but nothing beyond that. I hope Hopkins has had better luck."

We were just sitting down for our elevenses when inspector Hopkins knocked. Holmes got up and let him in, greeting him with, "Ah, is your timing that good or is it a coincidence that you arrive at morning tea, Inspector?" Hopkins looked embarrassed and began to stammer; "Uh...no, no...I..." but Holmes laughed and said, "Please, Inspector, have a seat, tea and a scone; I was just having you on a bit. You're welcome any time. Any news on the vanishing mingers? Oh, and excuse the Cockney - Watson and I have just been engulfed in the somewhat dense dialect of Cheapside."

Hopkins smiled and sat down; Holmes rang for Billy and had him add another plate of scones to our midmorning snack.

"Mr. Holmes," Hopkins began slowly, "I fear I don't have good news about the disappearances. I fact, I must admit, I have no news at all, except that if my informants aren't lying, they know as little as we do." Holmes nodded his agreement, "As do my contacts also, Inspector. It seems we are both without straw to make bricks. The only thing I can suggest is to keep the pressure on. We need something, no matter how small, to work with. Grill any known associate of the missing, inspector; perhaps one of them will let slip a clue we can use as a starting point. Let's get together whenever either of us has any new information."

Several days passed and we heard nothing from Hopkins except that he had enlisted the help of inspectors Lestrade, Jones (Altheny and Peter), Gregson, and Bradstreet in grilling the known associates of vanished criminals, plus any informants those Yarders regularly used. Wiggins made his nightly reports and Holmes gave him some more coins for the Irregulars. Holmes was encouraged by the progress Wiggins and crew were making, but still he had been growing tenser by the day from all the inactivity, pacing the room and peering out the window. His prediction of the finding of the extortionists' base "by next week" proved accurate, however. That Thursday, after my billiards with Thurston, I was relaxing in my armchair when there was a loud knock at our door. Holmes fairly raced to open it and, sure enough, Wiggins, with a triumphant look on his grubby face, announced, "We done it, Mr. 'Olmes; we found tha mingers' 'ome!" Holmes clapped Wiggins on the shoulder and pulled out a chair; "Please, sit and tell us all about it. Doctor, ring Billy and ask him if he can bring up a quick supper for our Mr. Wiggins." Wiggins smiled broadly at "Mr."

"Well sirs, we kep on movin', a block or two at a time 'til we found where they's got the Hansom. Simon Greedge mews it is Mr. 'olmes. I'se wrote down 'is place on tha noter ya gived me. Then, I spots tha mingers going inta tha office so's I took a butchers at 'em through the winda and saw they was two more toughs already in there, standin' at a table with tha ones we followed. Sittin' at the table, was, I guesses, Greedge, with a stack o' bees, divvyin' it up like 'e's tha awright geeezzaa!"

I sat there in my chair, not knowing exactly what Wiggins was saying but getting the idea that he and the Irregulars had accomplished the job Holmes had set for them. I was going to ask for a translation when Billy brought in a plate with some fish, boiled potatoes and peas for Wiggins. While he was eating, Holmes got out his wallet and put a pound note beside the plate. Wiggins grinned the widest grin I think I ever saw, scooped up the note, stuck it in his pocket, and finished his meal like a magician performing a disappearing trick! Wiggins got up from the table and Holmes handed him a pocket watch and his cap. "Now Wiggins, I expect you to treat your army with some of that quid. Just one more task; please check on them again and note what time they meet. If there's another job I need done I'll send for you. We will possibly have to find out where the other two men are causing trouble, but for now, good job fer ya', laddy; and good night!"

"Yes Mr. 'olmes, wha'evah you want. Lawd above! Goodnight, innit?"

Holmes fetched his calabash, tapped out some ashes, re-stoked it and sat down in his armchair with a satisfied smile. "Well, Doctor, we have a target and a place to start at last! Are you game for a visit to our friend McIvey? I don't want to spook this Greedge right away. Maybe Lucas can give us some scuttlebutt on him. Besides, we haven't said hello to Evan since we gave him the good news about Moran's demise."

"Good idea, Holmes. I always enjoy talking turf with Lucas. Tea and Mrs. McIvey's biscuits sound like a good elevenses. And perhaps a spot of that excellent brandy would do fine too; that is, if he has any left!"

The next morning after breakfast, while Holmes pored over a few of his reference books, I shaved and dressed. Holmes was already dressed, had Billy get us a cab, and soon we were off to McIvey's stables.

We had just pulled up in front and dismissed our cab when Lucas emerged from the stalls and, with a big grin, came out to meet us. He invited us into his office and gestured for us to sit down; "It's a fine thing to see you both again. Some tea?" Holmes smiled and thanked Lucas for his hospitality. We sat down and Lucas brought us a plate of biscuits and two cups; then he put a pot of water over his small burner. "Tea in a jiff, gentlemen. Now what is it I can do fer you? I reckon you didn't come out here just to see Duke, eh?"

Holmes and I laughed and Holmes answered Lucas; "My dear Mr. McIvey; we came for two reasons; one, how is Evan?, and two, do you know of a fellow mews owner named Simon Greedge?" Lucas was checking the tea pot and stopped dead when Holmes mentioned Greedge.

"Mr. Holmes; I knows plenty 'bout that skunk! He was once in racin' when I was a jock. Got throwed out for cheatin'; got caught usin' dye and stuff to switch horses when he could get big odds. Run a slow one and then fix a good one up when the odds went high. I hear he did some Queen's time too, he did. Brought in some toughs from Dublin and had a little robbery ring goin' afore he was nabbed. Used 'em cuz they wasn't known by the police. What's he up to now?"

Lucas turned back to his burner, checked the tea, and filled our cups. It was just in time to wash down a couple of Mrs. McIvey's delicious biscuits! Holmes nodded his head. "We suspect he may be running an extortion scheme now, using again, some toughs for muscle. We aren't sure yet, but your information makes it highly possible that he is indeed, at it again. I'm going tomorrow to find out if the Yard has a record on him. Back to Evan; how is he doing? The last we heard from you was that he had recovered all his memory of the terrible event he suffered."

Lucas smiled and answered Holmes. "He's doin' just fine; and happy as a slopped pig that he don't have to testify. He was scared shaky he was. He's workin' right now but I'll tell him you called after him. Some more tea? This time maybe a bit o' that brandy? I keeps it for special guests only." We accepted Lucas's offer and I spent the next fifteen or twenty minutes talking racing with Lucas. When we finished our spiked tea, we waited a bit until one of Lucas's cabbies returned, bid Lucas goodbye, and headed off for Baker Street; but after checking his watch, Holmes called to our driver to drop us at Scotland Yard instead.

"It's still early, Doctor, let's see if anyone we know at the Yard can help us with our investigation of the extortion gang and Mr. Greedge in particular. If so, there's no need to wait until tomorrow. The sooner we can stop this vicious racket the better."

We were in luck, Inspector Gregson was at Scotland Yard. He signed us in and escorted us to his desk. "Sit down, sit down please. What brings you gentlemen here today. I doubt it's about our weather, eh." Holmes chuckled and admitted that was not our intention. He then detailed what happened to the greengrocer Cyrus Appleton, the use of Wiggins and the Irregulars, and his concern that a serious extortion racket was taking place. Gregson nodded after hearing Holmes report and said, "Holmes, I have heard from three constables about this so I'm very pleased that you have gotten involved. It would have taken us much longer I'm sure to locate this Greedge fellow. That name rings a bell with me." Getting up from his chair, Gregson said, "Wait right here, I'm going to pull a file I'm sure we have on your Simon Greedge. As I recall, he's quite a bad apple." I remarked to Holmes, "I'm glad I got hit with that apple!"

"Yes indeed, doctor, I think we can hand the Yard some solid leads to put a stop to this scheme before it gets out of hand."

Gregson returned with a rather thick folder under his arm, sat down, and slid the file over to Holmes. "Take a peek at that, Holmes.

A record going back some twenty-five years." Holmes read each page then handed it to me. A long unsavory career unfolded as I read the rather dry police reports. Reading between the lines illuminated almost unrelenting criminal activity. "Holmes, Greedge was once a stage actor when he was in his early twenties." Holmes gave me a wry grin, "Read this next page, he was nabbed for embezzlement of repertory funds, but as the amount was not great, got a light sentence and was ordered to reimburse the company. Interesting note here by the investigating officer; seems there were soon, several very clever robberies. Greedge repaid the company! He was suspected but couldn't be charged, as each robbery was seemingly done by different individuals. The officer's statement reads, 'I suspect Greedge used his makeup skills as an actor to look different at each robbery, but I have no positive proof. I personally think he got away with them.' I think the officer was right, Watson; Greedge is a slippery one, without doubt. Reminds me of John Clay a bit."

We finished the dossier and Holmes handed it back to Gregson. The inspector looked intently at Holmes and asked, "We'll need plenty of solid evidence to nail him and you look thoughtful; do you have a plan, Holmes?" Holmes linked his fingers behind his head, leaned back in his chair, and detailed his plan: "Inspector, let me offer this; I'll continue to use the Irregulars to find out where the other two crooks Wiggins spotted are working their racket; I'll also keep at the task of attempting to find out how the wanted criminals on your list are escaping detection. Meantime, since you would be an 'official' presence, interview all the shopkeepers on Wiggins' list and convince them that if they all testify against these men, the crooks will be put away and the shopkeepers will have no fears of retaliation. The Irregulars will also keep an eye on Greedge's stable - Wiggins couldn't see the name of the lane where Greedge has his place because of darkness, but we know it's near where Cambridge Road and Mile End come together. I'll have him find it again, this time in daylight. How does that sound to you, Inspector?"

Gregson stood up from his desk chair, smiled broadly and declared loudly, "Spot on, Holmes. I'll get my part going first thing tomorrow. Give me what your boys find out about where these other two are working. Holmes, I just wish we had the manpower to cover tightly the blocks being attacked but since the horrible Ripper murders, the press has been on us to increase our presence in Whitechapel and we've had to drain other beats to do that."

Holmes nodded ruefully. "Understood, Inspector. Besides, these hit-and-run tactics are very difficult to stop. We will have to nab them all together at their base; which seems to be Greedge's stable. Watson and I shall return to Baker Street now. I must muster the troops and give them their new marching orders! Thanks for your help, Inspector. Finally, could you give me some pictures or official sketches of your missing criminals?"

"Certainly, Holmes; I have a stack here in my desk. We are about to spread them around and ask anyone who spots one of 'em to report it to the Yard." Holmes groaned and shook his head; "And almost, or more probably, all, 'sightings', will lead nowhere and tie up men who could be doing useful detective work on their regular jobs." Gregson nodded; "I know it, but the orders came from the top."

"Quite so."

On our ride back to Baker Street, Holmes made a brief stop at his bank so he would have small coins for Wiggins to pay his Irregulars and I bought a pack of cigarettes at Bradley's. I decided not to accompany Holmes on his search for Wiggins so I had our cabbie drop me off at 221. Holmes waved the driver on and called back, "I'll try to be back at tea, but don't wait up."

Before going up to our rooms, I informed Mrs. Hudson that Holmes would try to return for tea, but, "absolutely", I would be ready, having skipped lunch - except for a couple of Mrs. McIvey's biscuits and a cup of brandied tea! I washed up and settled into my chair with a Lew Wallace book, "The Prince of India; or, Why

Constantinople Fell" and a fresh Bradley's cigarette. I had heard that Wallace considered that novel his best, but I thought it would have to go some to beat "Ben Hur"!

I soon became engrossed in the story; time passed unnoticed, but I was brought back from Turkey to London by voices downstairs followed by footsteps on the stairs. The door opened and Holmes ushered in the somewhat unkempt Wiggins who greeted me with, "Robin day Doctor, 'a 're ya?", doffed his cap, bowed as if he just met the King, and placed it with exaggerated care on our coat rack. "Mr. 'olmes says 'e 'as anovver corn for me and me boys. Put bangers in me 'and; we's ready!

I was in my usual state of partial understanding, but I assumed that Wiggins was ready for another job. Holmes was watching me with a most amused look on his face. He waved Wiggins to a seat and rang for Billy. I hadn't realized it was tea time.

After we finished our little smoked salmon sandwiches, tea and scones, Holmes pushed aside our empty plates, handed Wiggins a handful of coins, and explained that he wanted the Irregulars to track the two other thugs so we could know where they were working their extortion racket. Wiggins, putting the coins in the pouch Holmes had given him, said, "They'll start in the bloody day's dawnin', I'll house to let. Taters out there then innit? I'll need me weasel. Thank ya for the tea, Mr. 'olmes. I'll be comin' hammer wif the news." With that, he retrieved his cap, bowed again, sweeping the cap onto his tousled head, and left.

I started to say, "Holmes, I don't....", but he held up his hand and said, "Wiggins just wanted cash-in-hand to do the next job. He'll need his coat because it'll be cold in the morning when the crooks start out from Greedge's stable. He'll be coming back to report as before." I shook my head, "I think I'll go back to reading about the Wandering Jew. At least that's in an English I can understand!" Holmes laughed and got out the 'Wanted' notices Gregson had given us, studied them for a while, lit his old briar, and settled back in his armchair with a thoughtful look on his face.

A week went by after Wiggins got his new assignment. I could tell Holmes was getting more and more frustrated from the way he paced around our sitting room. He was eating less and smoking heavily. No word came from Gregson or Hopkins, which made the waiting worse. At last, Wiggins, in his report on Saturday night, had some positive news.

"They's workin' around Folgate Street in Spitalfields, Mr. 'olmes. Me boys tracked 'em an' keeps their minces on 'em. More'n that, I peeped in at 'em this very night an' owd Greedge was doin' sum'pin' funny weird 'e was." Holmes's attention was now fastened on Wiggins. "What was it that causes you to call it 'weird'?" Wiggins arched his eyebrows and seemed almost embarrassed to describe what he saw. "E reaches over an', I swears it's true, takes off this bloke's Irish, fusses wif it, an' claps it back on 'is 'ead."

I started to laugh but I saw Holmes knit his brows, sit back in his chair, and remain silent for a minute or so. Finally, he said, "Wiggins, I want you to show us Greedge's stables tomorrow morning. Come over after breakfast and we'll take a ride. We'll need to stop at Scotland Yard and then come back here. At first, Wiggins nodded his head, but when Holmes said "Scotland Yard", Wiggins looked like he had stuck his finger in an electric socket! He gripped the table with both hands, leaned over toward Holmes and said, in a startled tone, "Lawdy me Mr. 'olmes! Scotland Yard? Crikey, ya wants me ter scapa wif ya? Does I 'ave ta?" Holmes smiled broadly, shook his head and assured Wiggins; "No, no Wiggins, you can stay in the cab if it bothers you that much."

"Bovvers me?! It scares ter fin' abaht it!" Holmes walked over to Wiggins, patted him on the shoulder and laughed. "You just be here after breakfast tomorrow. You can show us Greedge's place and you don't have to go into the Yard." Wiggins looked as if he had just received a stay of execution! Holmes handed Wiggins his cap and he bolted out the door and down the stairs. Holmes got some writing paper out of our desk and sat down and began to write up our findings thus far. I returned to my book - about which I found, ran a thousand pages in two volumes! I seriously considered abandoning The Wandering Jew to his roaming and pick up a less daunting work.

The next morning promised warm weather for our mission to take a look at Greedge's stables. When I came out to our sitting room, Holmes was, as usual, already at the table, reading the early paper. He handed me the sporting section and after a few minutes, Billy and Mrs. Hudson brought us breakfast. We thanked them as always and sat for a few moments just breathing the delicious smells of fried ham, eggs, country potatoes, and fresh biscuits and coffee. As I put down the paper and tucked in my napkin, I noticed a third plate and cup. Holmes saw my puzzled look; "I thought Wiggins might welcome some of Mrs. Hudson's sturdy fare. I doubt he gets much at home except the bare necessities. I imagine he knows when we eat so I expect him any time now."

Holmes had barely spoken when we heard voices downstairs and the front door close. We immediately heard someone obviously bounding up the stairs two at a time. Smiling, Holmes got up and opened our door to an animated Wiggins.

"Robin day's dawnin', 'a 're ya's." he paused, took a deep breath and said, "It smells so Robin in 'ere I'm droolin'!" Both Holmes and I stifled a laugh and Holmes waved Wiggins to a chair. "That plate, cup and those utensils are for you; help yourself if you're hungry." Wiggins wasted no time applying himself to breakfast. "Old poppy and sum beans, 'at's what I 'ad. They feeds ya better in bucket."

As usual, I had only a vague idea what Wiggins said but Holmes sat back in his chair and translated.

"Our Mr. Wiggins had only some old bread and beans and re-marked that they feed you better in jail! When Wiggins finishes, I'll tell Billy to get us a cab and we'll put Simon Greedge's mews on our map. Then we'll make a brief stop at the Yard - Wiggins. you can stay in the cab as I promised - then back to 221. I'd like you to look at something I thought of last night." Wiggins was just wiping his mouth after doing a yeoman's job on the food.

"It's O.K. wif me, Mr. 'olmes - long as I daan't 'ave ter rabbit ter nah inspector." Holmes smiled, "I promise; no talking to an inspec-tor." Wiggins donned his cap, Holmes and I our hats, Billy was de-tailed to get us a cab and we all trooped downstairs.

A Hansom cab is not made for three passengers but with Wiggins' thin body, Holmes being tall and lean and my somewhat stocky self, we fit without undue discomfort. Holmes paid the driver and directed him to the area of Cambridge Road and Mile End. "Our friend here will guide you from there." The cabbie nodded and yelled "Gang!" and off we went. I knew, being of Scottish blood, that "gang" meant "Go!"

Even though the day was sunny and dry, we put up the mud board - sometimes, the horses kick up more than mud! It was a pleasant ride and when we neared Mile End Road, our driver pulled over to the side and stopped, opened the trap, and asked, "Where to now gentlemen?" Holmes turned to Wiggins; "Take over, navigator!" Wiggins got a great kick out of "navigator". He stood up, looked all around, and pointed to an area of buildings with lanes ending at our road. "It's third from 'ere. Turn in and stop, me pitch n' toss wants ter clock the bleedin' name." Our driver, as every cabbie, knew Cockney, so he drove to the third lane, turned in and stopped. The brick wall, which one long ago day, had a legible name in white paint now showed just a few streaks of faded paint. You couldn't begin to tell what its name was. Holmes instructed our driver to go slowly up the lane. In about fifty yards or so, we saw a stables on our right that looked like it had seen better days. A board above the stable entrance said "Greedge Cabs". A small office was attached to one side of the building. The rear of the property abutted a commercial building so there was no exit that way. Holmes had our cabbie stop, and to my surprise, climbed down, pulled a folded paper out of his jacket pocket and walked toward the office. Our presence must have drawn attention because a man of middle size came out of the office sporting an elegant handlebar moustache and curly brown hair down to his shoulders. He had a scarf wrapped around his neck with one end thrown over a shoulder in a very theatrical way. His complexion was an unhealthy looking pale, washed out white.

Wiggins whispered, "'at's 'im aw wite! The one I seen dividin' up the chuffin' bread 'n honey." I might have been catching on a bit; I assumed he meant dividing up the money.

I saw Holmes had completely unfolded the map and was holding it up in front of the man's face. I could see that Holmes, being taller, was actually inspecting the stables while he kept the attention of Greedge on the large map. The door to the office was open as Greedge didn't close it when he came out to see what Holmes wanted, so Holmes could see into it easily also. Apparently, Holmes' inspection was over because he refolded the map and joined us in the cab.

"Oily and slick, Watson. Acting every moment as I talked to him. Fake as a homemade bank note!" He then said loudly, "All right driver, back to the road." Our cabbie turned the Hansom around and headed back down the lane. When we got to the main road again, Holmes called through the roof trap. "Scotland Yard please." I saw Wiggins cringe, but he didn't say anything. I probably wouldn't have understood it anyway.

As we pulled up in front of Scotland Yard I had to chuckle as Wiggins slumped down in the seat and yanked his cap over his face.

Holmes tossed another coin up to our driver and asked him to wait. Inspectors Gregson and Hopkins were in but Lestrade and Bradstreet were out on cases. Holmes briefed both on what he had discovered about the extortion racket and added, "My Baker Street Irregulars were invaluable; without them the case would have taken much longer and more shopkeepers would have suffered." He spread out the map he had been working with and pointed out Greedge's stables and told the inspectors of Wiggins' finding that they gathered at the stable every night, "According to Wiggins at about seven o'clock - that is if the old watch I gave him is still accurate- to get their 'cut' from Greedge."

Holmes asked Gregson how the effort to get the shopkeepers to testify was going. Gregson shook his head but not emphatically. "Some are willing, Holmes, but many have been so intimidated that they are still reluctant about appearing in court against these thugs." Holmes nodded, "I understand. We may not need many, however. How about the new area the Irregulars found that was being worked?" Hopkins answered that question; "They seem to be closer knit than the first group. I think we can count on five or six brave enough to testify."

Holmes gestured to me and as we got up from our chairs, he addressed the inspectors. "Well done, gentlemen. We simply need to set a date, line up three or four armed constables and remove this scourge from London. I suggest you recruit John Rance and Edward Adams. They were the two that aided Watson and myself to capture Pigot. By the way, how are his ribs? Still whining about taking a Penang Lawyer in the chest?" Gregson laughed and got up to escort us out. "He never stops complaining." Hopkins added, "About everything! He acts like a spoiled little child - but we know bloody well that if he got the chance, he'd murder us all with no compunction. We'll round up the men we need and let you know. It shouldn't take but a couple of days to get the go-ahead. We are in your debt for tracking these vicious crooks down."

As we left, Holmes called over his shoulder, "If I'm right, you may have even more to celebrate, gentlemen." And with that enigmatic comment, we regained the cab and headed for 221 Baker Street.

Wiggins was unusually quiet during our ride home, but he did at least push his cap back sit up straight. Apparently, his proximity to a whole building full of police temporarily overwhelmed his system. When we arrived, Holmes waved Wiggins in. We hung up our jackets; Wiggins' was not as shabby as you might expect. He probably picked it up from a second-hand clothes shop after Holmes' last payment for the services of the Irregulars. Why he didn't replace his bedraggled cap I don't know. Holmes pulled out a chair for him at our table, went to our desk and returned with a sheaf of papers. Laying them out on the table, he asked Wiggins to study them. He got a pipe from the mantle and stuffed it with fresh Macnab #3. I rang for our tea and sat next to Wiggins and inspected them along with him. They were pictures taken by Carl Durheim of four criminals, arrested at one time or another. We stared at them for a couple of minutes, shrugged our shoulders and waited for Holmes, who had lit his calabash, pulled out a chair opposite us and was leaning back, casually puffing rings into the air. Finally, I asked, "Holmes, what should we be seeing other than these rather scary looking faces?"

"Ears, Doctor, ears. Study them, compare them, and tell me your findings. You too Wiggins, what do you notice about them?" We glanced at each other blankly and resumed our assignment. I finally thought I had an idea of what Holmes was getting at - "There are small differences between these ears. Is that what....", but I was interrupted by a sudden loud outburst from Wiggins: "Mr. 'olmes, I pearly that ear wif the nick aahht o' it before. I swears it!" Holmes smiled, went to the mantle and put the calabash in its holder, turned and said, "At Greedge's?" Wiggins nodded; "Just as I thought; Good job Captain Wiggins! I think you deserve an extra bonus and a promotion. If I have another job for the Irregulars, I'll let you know."

Holmes went to our desk and pulled out the cash box, extracted a note and handed it to a startled Wiggins. "Crikey, a Godiva!" He stuffed it quickly in a pocket, saluted Holmes, and grabbed his cap. Holmes opened the door and an ecstatic Wiggins rushed out. Holmes called after him; "Two things Captain; spread the fiver around your troops and, two, get a new cap!"

As soon as tea was over, Holmes headed for his room, called over his shoulder, "Need to get some supplies ready, Doctor. With luck, Gregson will have a crew ready for tomorrow night's 'roundup', as the cowboys would call it." I heard Holmes rummaging around in his room so I studied the pictures he had laid out for Wiggins and me to look at.

Four sinister visages stared out at me. Looking carefully, I spotted the nicked ear Wiggins had noticed. I suppose if there's a "typical" London criminal, these men certainly fill the bill! Their names spoke of a variety of ancestry, Aiden Quinn, Angus McCracken, Sean Duffy, and James Wellington Godwin.

That evening at dinner Holmes seemed a bit on edge. I knew why of course; the wait for news that Gregson and the Yarders were ready to grab the gang. Holmes was at times very meticulous and patient but when he must wait on others to conclude a case he has already solved, he can be sharp and impatient. I tried to engage him in conversation but he was too distracted for much talk. I have to admit, I got a little testy myself. Finally, I came straight out; "Holmes, you can be quite frustrating at times. Please just tell me the whole story now. It's obvious you connect this man with the nicked ear to Greedge and his gang. I understand that, but why the elation and the unusually large payment to Wiggins for the help of the Irregulars?"

Holmes looked genuinely contrite. "My dear Doctor; I'm so sorry. I got so wrapped up in the discovery that the man Wiggins saw at Greedge's was in one of the photos that I forgot that my friend and biographer was not in on the excitement. Watson; those photos are of four of the wanted criminals who have mysteriously disappeared!"

I think my jaw actually dropped like the old expression says. "Holmes! That's a great find. But how has he escaped detection all this time? He relaxed some at last, got up from the table and busied himself with his old briar pipe. After he got it going he turned to me and with a sly grin, said, "That question, Doctor, I hope to answer as soon as the armored division takes us on a surprise visit to oily Mr. Greedge and his nasty worker bees."

The next hour was spent drinking coffee and watching Holmes pace, sit down, get up and pace again, stand by our front window, and sit down again for a few minutes before resuming pacing. I was just about to burst out again when he cocked his head toward our door and said, "Watson; did you hear it? I think a cab stopped out front." He went quickly to our door and opened it just as the bell rang. Billy must have come out to answer the bell because Holmes called to him, "If it's an inspector, send him right up, Billy."

Sure enough, our visitor was inspector Gregson. I fervently hoped he had some good news about the impending capture of the extortion ring. Holmes ushered him in but even before he could ask Gregson anything, the inspector said, with a big smile, "It's on! We go tomorrow night. Lestrade, myself, and three armed constables; Rance, Adams, and Harry Murcher - he says he was with Rance on a Holmes case. Hopkins can't go, he's off to Sussex to talk to the local police about a bank robbery."

"Glad to have some people I've worked with before. Rance and Murcher were constables during the Lauriston Garden affair and Adams was in on the capture of Mr. Pleasant Pigot, that most dangerous character. Watson and I will be ready, Inspector, whenever you wish us to be. Hang up your coat and hat, we need to make a plan for tomorrow night's foray." Gregson did so and turned to us with his news.

"We'll pick you up at six o'clock sharp, tomorrow evening. We'll have two cabs for us and a wagon for the prisoners. Since you know the ground, you will be in the lead van. How should we approach Greedge's place?" Holmes got the big map from our desk and spread it out on our table. Gregson and I leaned over the table as Holmes outlined his plan. "First, we must park the vehicles on the main road. The lane is a narrow one with almost no traffic except for Greedge's cabs and three police vans would alert the gang before we could surprise them. I will lead you, Lestrade and the constables, up the lane to a spot just out of sight of the office. I'll go have a quick butchers, as Wiggins would say, through the window to be sure they're all there. The best time will be when Greedge is dividing the day's take among the thugs because their attention will be fastened on the money. I suggest we have big John Rance blast through the door followed by Adams and Murcher - with guns drawn, of course. The door is an ordinary one. When Rance hits it, it will probably come clear off its hinges! There is a back door into the stables proper so I think you or Lestrade should cover it just in case someone tries to run." Gregson rubbed him chin in thought for a minute and then asked, "Wouldn't it be better to come in through that back door in the first place. Holmes?"

"Remember inspector, there will be several horses in the stable. If we come traipsing through, the chance we might cause them to react is too great. That would alert the crooks, and although I feel they probably won't be armed, there is no use taking any unnecessary chances. I don't wish to add "Gunfight at Greedge's Stable" to London's criminal lore!"

We got a big chuckle out of that. Gregson nodded his head; "Right you are, Holmes. We'll do it your way. I'd better go now, tomorrow I'll make sure everyone knows the plan. We'll see you then, at six tomorrow evening." After showing inspector Gregson out, Holmes' mood changed from impatient pacing to exuberance, smiling happily as he folded the map he had shown to Gregson, pacing the room again, but this time, rubbing his hands together in anticipation of the capture of Simon Greedge and his gang.

"This calls for a celebration, Doctor. I was thinking a large whiskey and soda might fit the bill; what do you think?" I put down the book I was about to return to and answered, "I'll fetch the glasses and the gasogene if you'll bring the whiskey! We'll drink to ridding London of these brutal thugs." He went to our liquor cabinet and picked out a bottle and then said, enigmatically, "Yes, and maybe more than that, my dear Doctor."

The following morning we ate a leisurely breakfast in pleasant anticipation of the night's activities. When Billy brought up our food, Holmes made what I thought was a strange request. He was reading the early paper and after Billy had placed the platter on our table, Holmes asked, "Billy, would you please ask your mother if she can spare a couple of cleaning rags? Just old ones, because they won't be usable in the future." I was filling my plate from the breakfast platter and didn't pay much attention to Holmes' request until later. I picked up a book and a cigarette after eating and retired to my armchair but Holmes headed for his room, calling over his shoulder, "I have some shopping to do. Should be back by elevenses. I know we'll have five armed men with us tonight, but I'd slip your faithful Webley in your coat anyway. You never know how these things 'aft gang agley' as the poem wisely says. You might want to clean and load it for tonight's foray into enemy territory!"

After Holmes left, I got my Webley out and cleaned and loaded it as Holmes had asked, then I poured a fresh cup of coffee and picked up my latest book, "In Darkest London" by 'John Law', which is, I understand, a *nom de plume* of Margaret Harkness. After the horrible Ripper murders, the book, although classified as fiction, really exposes the degradation and hopelessness of Whitechapel.

At eleven, Billy brought up a tray with fresh scones and jam and a pot of tea. Under his arm was a bundle of cloths, old looking but clean. "I brought three Mom says she won't miss. She was about to throw them out anyway. I hope these are what Mr. Holmes wanted." He put the small bundle on the table and turned to go when we heard the outer door and footsteps on the stairs. "Billy, I think you can ask Mr. Holmes yourself."

Billy opened the door and Holmes came in carrying a medium size bag, folded over, put it in a chair and picked up the rag bundle. "Billy, thank your mother please, these will do admirably. Ah, fresh scones I see; they will do admirably also!" Billy left and we turned our attention to the tea and scones. I glanced at the bag Holmes brought in, but as it was folded, all I could read was *"Theatrical Supplies"*. I was curious, naturally, and asked Holmes, "Are you working on a new disguise?" We were through eating our snack, and Holmes got up, took the bag and strode off toward his room. He called back as he went through the door to his room, "No, Doctor, quite the opposite."

Since it was Thursday, I had a surprise for my billiards opponent, Thurston. His birthday was Friday, so I decided to take us both to lunch at the Rag. My membership was still in force (thanks to Holmes) so I thought it would be nice to lunch there and then have our usual game. I informed Billy that I would not be in for lunch. I had wanted to quiz Holmes about the theatrical supplies but he busied himself at his lab bench immediately after our elevenses. He was engrossed in his blood experiment with all the clinking, stirring, heating and odors that entailed. When I told him my plans, he simply nodded.

Thurston was quite surprised by his birthday present. I gave him a tour of the club, including showing him Coronel Moran's favorite poker table. I had already related my near fatal adventure and Moran's downfall at the hands of Sherlock Holmes. He was as awed as I was in looking at the portraits and photos of the famous members. We enjoyed a very leisurely lunch and then proceeded to our favorite billiards parlor. We had a very good game but I needed to get back to 221 before Gregson and crew picked us up for our Greedge 'raid' so I wished him 'Happy Birthday' and caught a Hansom home.

When I opened our door, Holmes was seated at our table reading the late paper. He looked up and said, "Ring for dinner will you please, Doctor; we need to eat and get ready for our attack-in-force on some unsuspecting miscreants. How did your celebration at the Rag go?" I rang for Billy, hung my hat and coat on the rack and sat down at the table. "Our lunch went very well but Thurston beat me with a losing hazard on his last shot, winning our game by two points." Holmes put his paper down and cleared an area for our dinner tray. "Oh well, it was his birthday. It'll give you an incentive to even the score next time."

By the time we finished supper it was near six so I got my Webley out, Holmes went to his bedroom, retrieved his theatrical supply bag and a jacket and we waited for the troops. Soon, we heard the sounds of horses and carriages pulling up. Holmes went downstairs to greet them. To my surprise, I heard talking and heavy footsteps on our stairs. Holmes came in followed by Gregson, Lestrade, and three constables. Holmes waved them to our table. "Pull up a chair gentlemen, I think we had better review our plans. The people we are after are tough and won't hesitate to fight if they're given a chance. We need complete surprise, which means a quiet approach and a quick, overwhelming attack. The lane we will be using to sneak up on Greedge's stable has virtually no traffic so we will park the wagons on the side of the main road so we don't alarm the crooks. The office is on the right side of the lane and the window faces the lane. The back of a building lines the lane so we will be able to get very close. I will sneak around the corner of the building and along the side of Greedge's office and have a quick peep through the window to be sure they are all there and engrossed in dividing up the money. I'll come back and we'll use the same route. Be sure to duck below the window when we go by the office. As soon as we all make it, Lestrade will cover the back door into the stable and John will blast through the front door followed by Adams, Murcher and Gregson - all with guns drawn. When you have subdued the bunch, I have a surprise for the inspectors. Any questions?"

Gregson smiled and said, "None at all; it's your show, Holmes. Let's go men!" We all clumped down the stairs, making quite a racket. As we exited, I noticed Mrs. Hudson and Billy peering around the door at the end of the hall. It must have felt like an earthquake!

There were two police cabs and a 'cell' wagon, Murcher driving it, Rance and Adams the two cabs. Holmes had given Rance, driving the lead cab, instructions how to approach and park along the main road. When Holmes and I got into the lead cab there was another p/c sitting inside, a very young one. Before we could comment, he said. "I'm just along to watch the horses while you all grab the crooks. My name is Charlie Crosse. I was made a constable just this week." Holmes congratulated him as the cab started off.

We didn't want to arrive when there was still a lot of light so our pace was quite stately. We also needed to let the nightly money meeting get under way so we could nab all five men. John Rance was a good horseman and he paced our trip perfectly. The cabs and cell wagon parked along the main road at ten minutes to seven. P/C Crosse jumped out to watch the horses and we gathered around Holmes for a quick review. Holmes then lead us up the lane, staying close to the building lining the narrow passage - Holmes, then Lestrade, Rance, Adams, Murcher and Gregson; I brought up the rear.

When our little procession reached the end of the building, Holmes motioned for everyone to stop. He then disappeared around the corner. Everything was still except for some snorts and soft whinnies from the stable's horses. We all craned our necks to catch site of Holmes and a minute later we saw him at the edge of the office. He very slowly crept toward the side of the window, which gave off a soft yellow glow, had a quick peek, motioned to us to follow, and then retreated to the side of the office again. We couldn't see him anymore but his gesture was enough. Lestrade, then the rest of us, proceeded as quietly as possible around the corner, down the side of the building and then across to the side of the office where Holmes was waiting. He crouched down and crept past the window and we did the same; keeping flat against the office wall as we turned the corner, meeting just past the office door. Holmes waved Lestrade toward the back door, the constables and Gregson pulled their guns and Holmes said softly to Rance, "Now!" Rance backed up a few feet and then, like a lorry sailing downhill, hit the door. As Holmes had noted, the door was an ordinary frame door and Rance's charge knocked it not only open, but almost off its hinges. Adams and Murcher were right behind him, their pistols pointed at the startled men. Lestrade then came through the back door with his gun. It was so well done there was no hint of resistance from the four thugs - eight arms stretched up toward the ceiling. Greedge however, spun around in his chair and looked like he might make a break for it but when he turned, he was staring into Lestrade's pistol. Then there were ten upraised arms!

Holmes had been right behind Gregson, smiled broadly, thanked the 'raiders', then asked Gregson to pull the men's arms behind their chairs, clap the darbies on, and search the crooks while he took a minute or two to retrieve his theatrical bag from the cab, announcing, "This little *soiree* isn't over gentlemen. I may have a bit of a surprise for you." Saying that, he headed out of the office and down the lane where our cabs were parked, leaving everyone with puzzled looks.

The constables went about their job with professional efficiency and soon the five prisoners were securely fastened and searched. As Holmes had guessed, they were not armed. Even had they been, they would have had no chance to resist the sudden onslaught. Holmes was right, though, there was no need to take any unnecessary chances. Gregson turned to me with a curious glance and asked what Holmes was up to now. I shrugged my shoulders; "I think it has to do with one of these men. Wiggins and Homes seemed to be very excited about one of the photos you gave us of the wanted men. But I believe I hear him returning, so we'll soon see."

Indeed, Holmes came in with the bag, set it on the table, pushed the five piles of money aside, and pulled the photos out of the bag. "Gentlemen, these are the arrest photos of the wanted men who seem to have disappeared. Inspector, please examine this one of Sean Duffy, particularly his left ear." Everyone in the room was suddenly staring at Holmes but he just grinned. "Well, Gregson, what do you see?"

"Holmes, the only thing I notice is that there is a little piece of that ear missing. Of what importance is that?" Holmes pointed at one of the men; "Check his left ear, please." Gregson did so, straightened up instantly, and exclaimed, "It's identical - but Holmes, Sean is Irish and this man has a dark complexion and dark hair." Holmes reached into his bag again, extracted one of Mrs. Hudson's cast-off rags and a bottle of some fluid. Wetting the rag he swiped a path down the middle of the man's hair, revealing to our amazement, light reddish hair. Next Holmes got out a bottle of some lotion, wet another rag and tried to wipe the man's face but he squirmed and shook his head violently.

"Mr. Rance", Holmes asked, "would you please hold this bobbing and weaving head still?" Rance grinned widely and gripped the man's head in his large hands. No movement was possible with those big paws clamped on. Holmes now wiped the rag across the man's face and the dark complexion became white with freckles. Holmes stood back and, addressing us, announced, "I'd like you all to meet

Mr. Sean Duffy, no longer among the missing." We stood there for a minute, stunned; then we simultaneously broke into applause! Holmes bowed, acknowledging our enthusiasm, but then said; "Oh, that's not all." He went over to one of the remaining men, a rather meek, clerk type with glasses, a trim beard and small moustache. Holmes removed the glasses and handed them to Gregson. "Note, Inspector, that they are not real glasses; the lenses are just flat glass. They are just for appearance. He tugged on the moustache, then the beard, and said, "The moustache is real but the beard is fake, held on with a bit of spirit gum. Also, I think a wipe of the lotioned cloth will show a much more London pallor, similar to Mr. Duffy's. This man is the elegantly named James Wellington Godwin, wanted for fraud, embezzlement, and attempted murder." Lestrade was shaking his head slowly back and forth, speechless - unusual for him.

"Now, let us turn our attention to this third miscreant. I think this is the one Wiggins saw Greedge briefly relieve of his 'Irish'. Let's see, shall we?" Holmes reached over and grabbed the man's hair and gave it a yank. It came off - it was a wig. "Irish jig: wig, Doctor." Using the rag he had soaked with the clear liquid, he dabbed it on the man's moustache and beard and removed both of them. "It seems we have a Scotsman gone bad here. Lestrade, I think you a special interest in Mr. Quinn. He's all yours." Lestrade leaned over the table, fixing Quinn with a baleful stare; "You'll not escape me this time, you scoundrel! Thanks to Mr. Holmes, you'll spend the rest of your life behind bars!"

Holmes backed away from the table and handed the last photo to Gregson. "It's your turn Inspector. Unmask this rather sullen looking individual for us." Gregson took the photo and looked from it to the thug, to Holmes, back to the photo, and finally back to the man; cleared his throat and began. "Well, his ears look damaged and his nose seems a might crooked." Holmes clapped him on the back. "Good, Inspector. Right you are. He has what are referred to as 'cauliflower ears'. Gregson broke into a big smile; "It's Angus McCracken, by God. The former boxer and strong-arm robber!"

"Yes, inspector; and I think if you examine his hands you'll find scarred knuckles and possibly signs of broken fingers."

As the crooks were being led away, Gregson and Lestrade came over to Holmes, who was packing his rags and bottles away in the bag. Both inspectors then shook Holmes' hand in turn. Gregson said, "Holmes, this is something I'll never forget. I've seen you do some amazing things but this is one of the best. Two serious cases solved at the same time - incredible!"

"Thank you both. I appreciate your indulgence with my sometimes odd methods. By the way, I think Greedge and the boys had their eyes on a bigger score than this extortion scheme. I think this racket was just to raise money for something much more profitable. I think they were planning a job that required tools and supplies they didn't have the money for and were saving towards whatever was needed. A bank, possibly, or a train carrying bullion, or something like that. I would examine Greedge's papers for that sort of thing. If you find Greedge's 'stash' I think it would be a good thing to return as much as you can to the shopkeepers who were victimized by this bunch. By the way, Gregson, the credit for uncovering this scheme and the vanished crooks goes a lot to Doctor Watson's ankle and the Baker Street Irregulars! It's true, I had my first clue when reviewing the sordid history of Simon Greedge. I briefly thought it would be possible for an actor, skilled at makeup, to disguise a crook, and then, the report by the inspector who posited that Greedge had pulled robberies in disguise got me more interested. But the real light went on when Wiggins remembered seeing the nicked ear on one of the men in Greedge's office. Also, Inspector, I recommend you post a constable here in the morning and interview the cabbies. At least two must know what was going on here. They drove the Hansoms the thugs used. I think, with the proper persuasion, they'll be happy to testify - especially if it means lessening the charges about their involvement in the crimes."

Gregson nodded his approval. "A night to remember Holmes! Now, I think we should waste no time in depositing these thugs at what will be an astounded Scotland Yard."

Except for the five passengers in the cell wagon, it was a thoroughly happy group in our miniature parade. Holmes and I were dropped off at 221, the constables and inspectors all shaking our hands again. Since we were so much later than our usual supper time, Holmes apologized to Mrs. Hudson and asked if she might have some leftovers for us. She answered, "Oh, Mr. Holmes, I can see you've had a busy evening but don't you worry, I'll put something together for your supper in a few minutes. You just go on now."

We did just that. Holmes put away his lotion and spirit bottles and I washed up and changed into some comfortable clothes. As we met at the dinner table, I saw that Holmes had done the same. We didn't have long to wait as Billy and Mrs. Hudson brought a platter of sliced beef, bread and butter, sliced tomatoes from Mrs. Hudson's sister's hothouse, tiny potatoes sauteed in butter and garlic, and a pot of fresh coffee with a plate of crumpets and a jar of orange marmalade. Needless to say, we made short work of it.

After Billy had cleared the dishes, Holmes poured us a second cup of coffee, went to our liquor cabinet and brought a dusty bottle of very old brandy to the table, added a good fat "thumb" to our coffee, and proposed a toast. "To your ankle, my dear Doctor. Without it having been battered by speeding fruit, we never would have netted such a double catch of scoundrels."

"A Robin day 'olmes, innit," I replied. "Holmes! I think I might just be catching on to it!"

END

EPILOGUE: The five crooks all got long sentences. Greedge's "savings" were found and divided up among the shopkeepers who were victims of the gang's racket.

Things were quiet for several weeks; interrupted by occasional visits from Lestrade and Hopkins, asking for help with cases they were on. Holmes was able to set them on the right path without getting out of his armchair. I started to write up several cases I had been too busy to tackle, while Holmes wrote two new monographs, "The Forensic Importance of Matching Expended Bullets to Firearms" and "Identification Through Ear Shapes, with Examples and Descriptive Classification".

ADDENDUM: The first acceptance of bullet-to-gun evidence in court was not until 1902

Notes:

The Shakespeare Affair: A stolen quarto, a slick crook and some friends from the Yard on the chase. Twelve of the Bard's comedies are mentioned in the story - did you spot them?

The Scottish Heir: One of the lingering mysteries regarding Holmes and the Ripper murders answered. The best reference book is "The Complete Jack The Ripper"; Donald Rumbelow, New York Graphic Society. Examines each murder and the investigations. Describes the turmoil at Scotland Yard and the fiasco surrounding the failure to use bloodhounds in the search.

Seaside Murders: References to literature and movies amongst the homicides. Example; Nick Smith, one of the victims, appears in a 1946 movie starring John Garfield and Lana Turner. Question; what was the movie? The owner of the curio shop owes her name to Charles Dickens and other characters to movies and literature. Henry Smart was an author of the time who lived in Budleigh-Salterton and was once in the India Army, as was Watson.

The Abduction of Lady X: We meet Sherlock's imposing brother Mycroft again - and a deadly crossbow.

The Hunt for Professor Moriarty: In which we learn the true story of why Dr. Watson wrote "The Final Problem" and why part of "The Empty House" was also a cover for a Holmes mission. Watson falls into a trap and the real 'final battle' between Holmes and Moriarty takes place.

Justice Delayed: Holmes and Watson pursue the last Moriarty gangster; gunman Pleasance Pigot. A fire fight ensues when the murderous Pigot is cornered.

A Case of Intimidation: Wiggins and the Baker Street Irregulars are invaluable - despite the good doctor's lack of familiarity with Cockney rhyming slang.

Note: Cockney rhyming slang is constantly changing. New stars in music, movies, sports, politics, etc. bring about new expressions. Some of the old rhymes have survived pretty well: "apples and pears" (stairs), "bees and honey" (money), "butchers hook" (look) - "I took a butchers in 'er window." and some of the single words; "mingers", have hung on fairly well. "It's a Robin day innit?" (Robinhood - good). 'Ardly no aitches are allowed and 'th' can become 'f' in some cases. Benny Hill could do good Cockney and Michael Caine is a real Cockney.

Fanks fer yer attention; I 'opes ya enjoys me jackdaw. (Jackdaw and rook - 'book')

Robert Douglass Armistead, copyright 2016.

BACK PAGE TEXT

"Doctor Watson's Trunk" provides the answer to one of the main concerns of Holmesians - "Why is there no mention anywhere of any involvement of Sherlock Holmes in the Ripper murders?" Watson explains in "The Scottish Heir", why that situation arose.

The good doctor also tells us the "Final Problem" was a cover for a secret mission to Europe by Holmes. Actually, both Holmes and Professor Moriarty were alive to continue their battles.

The kidnapping of a Lady endangers an English/European alliance in "The Abduction of Lady X", and Holmes gets a hint of a criminal mind behind the plot.

"Seaside Murders" confronts Holmes and Watson with a deadly method of murder and a further clue to the clever criminal schemes of "The Professor"

As Holmes goes after this mastermind, Watson falls into a trap, Colonel Sebastian Moran is exposed as the accountant in the criminal gang, and Holmes meets Moriarty in the final, deadly confrontation.

As the Moriarty criminal conspiracy comes apart due to Holmes pursuit and Colonel Moran is the victim of a Holmes trap, only one gang member has escaped; the gunman, Pigot. Holmes and Watson pursue the dangerous crook, ending in a gun battle.

Learn some Cockney rhyming slang as Wiggins and the Baker Street Irregulars make an appearance to help Holmes and Watson stop a vicious extortion scheme preying on innocent shopkeepers in "A Case of Intimidation".

Holmes writes two new monographs which are key to the cases he takes on and continues his research into a more reliable blood test as he awaits more cases.

CPSIA information can be obtained
at www.ICGtesting.com
Printed in the USA
FSOW02n2114011216
28070FS

9 781478 779346